A BOATFUL OF LEMONS

AN UNFORGETTABLE SUMMER ON THE AMALFI COAST

By Nicki Storey

Dedicated to my mum:

We both talked about writing a book one day. I thought it would be you that did it but it turned out it was me. I hope you can read it from all the way up there.

Contents

How on earth do you even start to tell your adult daughter about her birth father, who knows nothing of her existence? Where do you begin? How will she take it? Will she be angry or excited, let down or indifferent? Will she want to contact him? Probably, Wendy realised. She sighed and folding the letter in half, stuffed it into the back pocket of her jeans. *Bloody Amanda*, she thought

It was one of those Indian summer days when the weather was so perfect that you could almost forget you were in England and pretend you were somewhere in the Med, which is exactly where Mia's biological father was. Tucked away safely in South Italy, completely unaware that he had a fully grown daughter in Cornwall. And now Amanda had brought it all up again.

The sky was periwinkle blue, and the sun blazed down, making the sea sparkle and the tarmac go soft on the roads. Wendy had opened all the doors and windows of the guesthouse and a gentle breeze was blowing in from the sea, bringing with it the sounds of children having the time of their lives on the beach below, before school started in a few days' time.

She had just wanted a few moments to sit outside in the front garden, on the little wrought iron bench that had been there when they moved in, to enjoy the warmth and the sea view. The fabulous climbing rose was in bloom, weaving itself around the window to the side of her and she could smell the perfume on the breeze. Over the rooftops on the hillside below, the estuary was dotted with sailboats. Through a gap in the trees and houses she could just see a corner of the harbour, bustling with life as the tourists made the most of the weather.

Everything was perfect, she was basically living the dream, and then the letter had arrived.

"Mum! Here, I saved the postman a trip!" Josh had come rushing through the gate, thrusting a pile of letters at her. Her son was twenty-two and had been taller than her since he was twelve. He was a photocopy of his father, vivacious and funny with a light dusting of freckles across his nose. His wavy chestnut hair was in need of a cut; he was constantly pushing it out of his eyes, as he did now. He was panting after climbing back up the steep steps from the harbour where he had picked up some fresh pastries and bread for the breakfast guests.

"Gotta take these into the kitchen!" He rushed off to the back of the house where his girlfriend Rebecca was holding down the fort in the dining room.

She had tucked the letters under her bum to look at later and tilted her face back up to the sun. *Another five minutes*, she thought to herself.

Her quiet time was soon interrupted again by a couple of young guests on their way out to the beach, and the scent of their sunscreen drifted past her nose as they smiled and wished her good morning. She waved to them and stood up, forgetting the letters that she had been sitting on which tumbled to the floor. She bent down to pick them up, mentally stopping herself from groaning as she bent over, and straightening back up flicked through them, brightening as she saw that one was handwritten with an Italian stamp on it.

Oh good, a letter from Amanda, she thought and sat straight back down to read it.

Positano
August 14th 2016

Dear Wendy,

I'm sorry I haven't written in a while. It's the thought of having to go to the post office and queue up for half an hour to get a bloody stamp that puts me off! I know snail mail is much nicer and I do enjoy choosing the writing paper and choosing which pen to use, and of course I love receiving your beautiful letters, but email is sometimes just so convenient! But we made a promise to communicate by snail mail, so I hope the never-ending post office queue (listening to the dreadful gossip from the Signora Alba who was in front of me) is appreciated!

I hope Rebecca is pulling her weight. Isn't it funny that she and Josh have fallen in love? We couldn't have planned that better, could we? But do feel free to send her back to me if she is not behaving, I do miss her!

All is well here; it seems to get busier and busier every season. The road through town has been in gridlock all summer, and the beach is crammed with hordes of tourists. I am grateful that our house and garden are tucked away from all that chaos down in town. Enzo seems to work all hours since they redeveloped the beach bar last year. Now it looks so swanky, with swaying palm trees, double sun loungers, waiter service, and trendy music blasting out night and day—you would hardly recognise it, I'm sure.

I'm writing this letter because something has happened that I think you need to know about. With this information, everything could change ... or it could stay the same, that's for you to decide.

I'm sure you remember Elena? Of course you do. Well, she passed away a few weeks ago, at the beginning of June. She had cancer, poor thing. I didn't know anything about it until I saw the funeral notice outside the bar. Then I bumped into her husband yesterday and of course had to stop to give him my condolences. He thanked me and we talked for a few minutes. He's okay about it; I get the idea that theirs was a relationship of comfortable companionship rather than never-ending love, if you know what I mean. He also mentioned that it was almost 30 years ago to the day since Antonio's famous party at the Marinella Beach. 30 years, Wendy! Can you believe it? Well, of course you can, you have the proof walking around in front of you—but where did the time go?

I know you don't like to think about the events of that summer, but time has passed and maybe now is the moment to think about putting things right and maybe introducing two people who should be in each other's lives before it is too late?

Think about it and don't be angry with me for bringing this up, you know I have your best intentions at heart.

All my love,

Amanda

Wendy sat there for a moment, stunned at the news of Elena's passing. A woman that she had never spoken to but had thought about many times over the years.

A woman whose passing now changed everything.

Amanda was right, there were two people that needed to meet and know each other, father and daughter, and now that Elena was gone there was no reason to hide the truth anymore. Where on earth did one start, though?

Chapter 1

Positano, Italy, May 1986

The bus lurched around the hairpin bends of the coast road as the sea glittered temptingly below. A couple of tourists laughed and exclaimed uneasily at the sight of the steep drop down from the side of the road. Wendy gripped the armrest of her seat with white knuckles too, but it was with excitement at what lay ahead, not the fear of falling into the ocean.

They stepped off the bus into the heat of the day, both looking decidedly less glamorous than they had hoped for their arrival in Positano. The humidity was extreme, and Wendy could feel her clothes sticking to her body. She peeled her t-shirt away from her skin and fanned it back and forth as she watched Amanda run around to the side of the bus to pull out their luggage from the storage area.

Amanda was her best friend. They had met at summer camp when they were about nine years old and had hit it off straight away. Too young to think about swapping addresses or phone numbers, they had lost contact until two years later when Wendy had been delighted to recognise Amanda as one of the new kids at the start of the new school year. Amanda had the sort of pale blonde hair that turned green in the summer from chlorinated swimming pools. She was petite and tidy, confident in chatting to complete strangers and a fantastic dancer. Wendy thought of herself as more introverted, although those who knew her would probably disagree. She had thick, unmanageable chestnut hair, preferred books to people and was a terrible dancer. Both girls openly coveted each other's hair, Wendy loving the smooth, sleek locks that Amanda could effortlessly style and Amanda secretly envious of the luxurious thick tresses of her friend. They were the same dress size, which came in very handy as they could freely swap clothes and borrow from each other.

A couple of boys dressed in military uniform stepped down from the bus, hugged each other with much back slapping and went their separate ways. Wendy took a queasy gulp of warm air and looked around. The bus had pulled up opposite a bar with a couple of deserted tables outside. At this time of day, it was far too hot to sit there. *Bar Internazionale* was emblazoned across the front of the building in spindly metal letters. The long bottle green door was open, and through it she could see a couple of old men sitting inside the dim interior, and a big shaggy dog stretched out on the floor, knowing it was the coolest place to be.

The road ran between the bar and a low wall, just the right height to sit on, and behind the wall was the most incredible view. A wide expanse of baby blue sky above a cobalt sea stretched all the way along the coast to the next village, and Wendy could quite clearly see over to the other side of town where the road wound round like a ribbon, dotted with cars that glinted like sequins.

A sultry teenage boy drove by on a noisy scooter. He was barefoot, wearing only swimming trunks and stared at her curiously as he passed by. The scooter was strange, not like the classic Italian Vespas she had expected to see; it was much smaller and had pedals like a small chunky bicycle.

"Wendy! Give me a hand here, will you?" Amanda stepped back from the departing bus, dragging the two bulging rucksacks out of the road.

Wendy grabbed a bag and hauled it onto the tiny pavement in front of the bar. She looked at her friend, a smile starting to appear on her face as the queasiness of the bus journey faded.

"We've made it! I can't believe we're back!" She pushed back a damp strand of hair that had escaped from her high ponytail.

"Come on, let's go and tell Rob and Ted that we've arrived!" Amanda hauled her rucksack onto her back, pulling her pale blonde hair out from where it had got trapped under the straps.

"Bloody hell, it's heavy," Wendy complained as she hauled her bag onto her shoulders. "I'll be glad to not have to lug this around anymore."

They crossed the road and started walking down towards the house with Amanda leading the way.

"Remember this is a one-way road? It leads

from the main coast road all the way through town and then joins up with it again the other side, but you can't really get lost because it's the only road in town."

"I remember the road near the hotel we used to stay in, but not this bit."

Amanda's family had been holidaying in Positano since her grandparents discovered it when it was still a sleepy fishing village in the '50s. Wendy had been invited along on the family holidays a couple of times when they were in their teens so that Amanda's parents could relax and sunbathe in peace, leaving their daughter and her friend to play and swim and roam the beach, making friends with the local kids. The first summer together, they had brought with them a small Italian phrase book that they had carried around and used to communicate with the local kids. Over the next few years, the two girls had been determined to learn the language better and had eventually enrolled in Italian classes in college and practised by writing letters in Italian to the kids that they had met on the beach. Wendy hadn't been back since they were sixteen as real life had kicked in with A levels then university, jobs and boyfriends and now, 10 years later, they were both in a high state of excitement about coming back to Positano together for a whole summer.

They came to a hairpin bend with another breathtaking view. Wendy would have liked to stop and look for a while, but Amanda pulled on her arm, eager to show her more.

"This part of the road zigzags back and forth, all the way down to there, and the tourists always walk

14

all the way around it because they don't know that just here, there are steps that are a short cut to the next level." She waved her hand towards a set of steep steps off to the left that weaved under the entranceway of a yellow house and off down the hillside.

"But to get to Rob and Ted's house, we take these steps that go straight ahead."

Rob and Ted, friends of Amanda's parents, were a couple from New York with a second house in Positano which they didn't like to leave empty, especially because their beloved dog was getting too old to travel to New York with them. Ted was a set designer and had worked on two of Wendy's favourite films, *Endless Love* and *Fame*. When Amanda had been asked if she was interested in housesitting for the summer, she had jumped at the chance and immediately asked if she could bring a friend. Amanda had been temping as a secretary since she had left Uni so was the perfect candidate for the job.

Wendy had been looking for an excuse to quit her job in the little beauty parlour that she had worked in for the last few years. It was definitely time to move on, maybe set up her own beauty business. She was thrilled when Amanda had called her and asked her to come, too. She had always dreamed about coming back to Positano and reliving those idyllic childhood summers and hopefully she would remember enough Italian to be able to add it as a second language to her CV when she returned home.

The steps took them down through a narrow alleyway, past arched doorways with flowerpots outside, windows with shutters pulled closed against the afternoon heat and strings of washing hanging under the sills, past a house with a tiny garden and an even tinier goldfish pond and suddenly out onto the road again. In front of them was a hotel, the Villa Franca. An unpainted, slightly crumbly looking building stood next to the hotel and the steps carried on down between the two.

"That's it!" Amanda darted across the silent road and over to the doorway, tucked around the side of the stone building. Wendy looked doubtfully at the house in front of her. It didn't look like a house, more like an unkempt windowless garage with a door. There wasn't a doorbell, so Amanda banged on the door with her fist and waited. They heard footsteps and the door was opened by a tall, rotund, cheerful looking man with thinning grey hair and round spectacles. A big shaggy black dog trailed behind him and watched placidly as the man enveloped Amanda in a big hug.

"Amanda! It's lovely to see you again, my dear! Did you have a good trip down?"

"Lovely to see you too, Ted! Dad sends his regards. The train journey was fine, we stopped overnight in Paris but then came straight down, we couldn't wait to get here! This is my friend Wendy, by the way. Where's Rob?"

"Oh, you know Rob, he's here somewhere, I'm sure he'll be out as soon as he realises you've arrived."

Ted turned to Wendy and bent towards her, giving her her first proper Italian greeting, the double

16

cheek kiss. She could never remember which way to turn first but he lightly guided her, left cheek first, then right cheek.

"Welcome back to Positano, my dear! I'm sure you're going to get up to all sorts of trouble, two pretty girls like you! Now, let's go and find Rob and get you settled. Leave your bags here for now," he gestured to the bedroom on the right. "You'll have to share until we leave but when we've gone you can fight over who gets the main bedroom downstairs!"

The dog plodded over to Wendy and wagged its tail cautiously.

"Nerone, be a good boy, these girls will be looking after you for the summer." He patted the dog affectionately as he passed by.

Wendy stroked Nerone's soft head and had a sneaky look over his shoulder. There was a staircase to the left, winding down towards another floor and she could see through a door on the right into a bedroom, a double bed draped with a colourful Indian throw.

Ted led them down the white stuccoed staircase, past a small room on the left that must be an artist's studio. Wendy got a glimpse of stacks of canvases piled haphazardly as she passed by. The next room was a big kitchen with the most enormous old fashioned bread oven that took up about a quarter of the room. She stopped and stared at it.

"It's big enough to sleep two people in!"

Ted smiled at her, "You can sleep there if you want!" He winked at her and turned to the fridge.

"The house is around three hundred years old so that oven was probably once the most important part of the building." He pulled out a jug and poured two glasses for them. "In Positano, we always drink our water with lemons in it." The lemons had been squeezed into the water before being chopped up and thrown in with a handful of fresh mint leaves, creating an icy cold lemon water that was lovely and refreshing.

"Ah! There you are, look who's here, Rob, it's Amanda and her friend Wendy! Wendy, this is Rob."

Rob had just walked in from a leafy terrace that Wendy hadn't quite managed to look out at yet and came over to greet them. He was shorter than Ted with a round, friendly face and was a little thinner but quite similar looking.

"Hi girls, so you're going to take good care of our pup while we're away? Or is he going to be taking care of you?"

"We will spoil him rotten and teach him all our tricks!" Wendy laughed, bending down to the dog's height and looking into his big brown eyes. "Can I go out onto the terrace and have a look, please?"

"Of course you can, my dear, come, let me show you!" Ted took her by the arm and guided her past the huge oven and out of the door.

The terrace was dominated by a big tree that

cast a welcome shade over them and a wooden table that was set up in a corner. Fairy lights were strung up, criss-crossing above them, and a variety of terracotta vases and pots were pushed up against the ochre wall of the house. Wendy walked over to the railings and breathed a big sigh of contentment. The view was spectacular! A jumble of pastel-coloured houses perched on the mountainside in front of her, all crammed on top of each other with the colourfully tiled church dome nested in the middle of it all. Below them was the beach, half of it dotted with pristine rows of orange umbrellas and matching sun loungers, the other half scattered with small wooden boats and a few people that lay sunbathing on towels. She could see a little promenade with restaurants and beach bars and a pathway that ran right along to the end of the beach, lined with a row of changing huts, which finished with a big rock that seemed to have a gate in it.

"What's that?" She pointed to the big rock as Rob came to stand next to her.

"That, my dear, is a discotheque in a cave. It's called Music on the Rocks and can be quite magical."

"Wow, it sounds amazing! Are there other discos here or is it just that one?" As a child on holiday, discos weren't something that had been on Wendy's radar, but now they sounded like great fun.

"Well, let's see now, there is one in a basement near the fish market. It's called La Fregata. Up at Fornillo, near the Grotto, there's a small one called Mille Luci, and of course everybody is talking about the new one that's supposed to open this summer at the top of the town. I'm not sure if it has a name yet. Ted? Has the new disco got a name yet?"

Ted and Amanda had wandered out onto the terrace, sipping their drinks.

"I heard they were going to call it the Paradiso, but don't take my word for it."

Amanda turned away from the view to look up the other way, but the top of the town wasn't visible from the terrace. The houses above were in the way and the tree blocked most of the view. She turned back to the others and asked, "When's it supposed to open? And where exactly is it?"

Ted pointed up high, "You can't see it from here but it's right at the beginning of the town up on the coast road near where the Garita viewpoint is. Supposedly, it will open in mid-June but they keep having setbacks and I doubt it will be ready in time. The bureaucracy in this country sure is something!" He shook his head and wandered back inside.

"Girls," he called back, "why don't you go get unpacked and showered and then we will take you out for dinner later."

"Good idea," said Rob, "you must be exhausted after that journey in this heat."

"Thanks so much, guys," Amanda said, making her way back in. Wendy took one last look at the view, still not quite believing that she would have all summer to enjoy it and followed her friend up to the bedroom.

A few hours later after a nap and a much-needed shower, the girls were preparing for their first night out in Positano. "The Glory of Love" by Peter Cetara blared out of their portable cassette player and the bed was piled with crumpled clothes from their rucksacks. Wendy was dressed in a short black ra-ra skirt and a bright pink sleeveless top. Chunky hoop earrings dangled from her ears and her hair was swept up into a high ponytail in a futile effort to combat the frizz caused by the humidity.

Amanda was pulling on a pair of white Bermuda shorts to match her white off the shoulder top. Her blonde hair was backcombed, sprayed and and adorned with a big floppy white bow. White bangles and white sandals finished the look. The scent of Flex shampoo wafted around the room, mixing with The Body Shop's White Musk body cream.

Rob and Ted had left earlier to meet friends for an *aperitivo* at the beach and had told the girls to meet them at the restaurant Le Tre Sorelle at 8 o'clock.

The sky was violet, not quite night but a while past sunset, and the temperature had dropped a few degrees since the afternoon. They took the steps down to the beach, a labyrinth of steep lanes between pastel-coloured walls. They passed a grand old villa with a beautiful entrance: cobbled flooring, stone balustrades wrapped in fuchsia bougainvillea, a big arched gateway and the sea behind it, reflecting the last of the purple tinges in the sky.

They passed a small church in a tiny piazza and then a little whitewashed tunnel and a few more steps and they were suddenly out on the road again. There was a bar on the corner, a group of elderly men sat outside playing cards with elaborate hand gestures and loud exclamations. Opposite the bar, there was another viewpoint, overlooking the main beach, similar to the view from the house but closer. Tables and chairs had been put out there for the clients of the bar and it was obviously a popular place as there didn't seem to be any empty tables. A group of boys sat on a stone bench to the side of the tables, one of them was playing a guitar. As they crossed the road Wendy turned back to see if the cafe had a name. Bar de Martino, it was called, and they had come down the steps to the side of it. She wanted to start getting her bearings; she didn't know this side of town so well as they had always stayed at Le Sirenuse hotel over on the other side.

"Down here," said Amanda, leading her between the boys and the tables where more steps snaked downwards. Down through an area where all the houses seemed to be painted in shades of salmon pink, a statue of the Virgin Mary in an alcove in the wall, left where the steps widened, and then they passed a hotel with burgundy walls. A grey cat sat by the doorway, uninterested in the two girls, but as they passed by a small alleyway at the side of the hotel a couple of boys in kitchen whites called out to them.

"Ciao bella! Dove vai?"

"Hi!" Wendy replied, waving back and smiling at her first *ciao bella*.

"Wendy!" Amanda laughed and linked arms with her friend and forced her to keep walking.

"Remember you have to ignore the boys unless you're actually interested in them, or they'll be pestering us all night! They're terrible here!"

In fact, she could hear the boys behind her, still calling out questions, trying to get their attention. Down more steps and suddenly they were nearly there. She could see the huge church in front of them and the sea behind it. They turned a corner and could see the last set of steps leading straight down to a piazza strewn with fishing nets, crates and barrels, and bordered with little clothes shops. The girls ran down this set of steps together, arm in arm, giggling and half terrified that they would trip and tumble the rest of the way. But they arrived safely at the bottom, panting with trembling legs.

A window opened above them, and a woman stuck her head out, calling for someone.

"Cicchetto! Vieni! Ciccio, vieni e pronto!"

Within seconds, a couple of small tow-headed boys dashed past and disappeared into the house.

"That must have been the mother calling the kids for dinner," Wendy said. "*Vieni, e pronto* is 'Come here, it's ready,' isn't it?"

"Yes. Don't they say that when they answer the telephone too? *Pronto?* Instead of hello? We have to try and remember as much Italian as we can – I want to know what everyone is saying to each other!"

Rob and Ted were waiting for them in another

23

little piazza that opened out onto the sea front, nestled between a row of shops and restaurants. A couple of bronze lion statues sat each side of a set of steps that led up to more shops. The two men were sitting on the steps, casually chatting with a group of barefoot Italians who had obviously not yet made it home from a day at the beach.

The boys all seemed to be wearing variations of the same brand of swimming trunks, in different colours but all with the same rainbow stripe running across the back and down the sides. They all clutched brown bottles of beer and Wendy could see the condensation dripping from the bottles onto the floor.

She stared in admiration at a girl sitting below Ted with dark curly hair and the most beautiful toffee-coloured tan that was enhanced by a gold crocheted beach dress. She had a feeling that they had met before.

"Didn't we used to know her? She looks familiar."

Amanda thought for a moment, "Yes, I think she had an older brother called Piero, do you remember him, with the spikey hair?"

"Yes, that's right," Wendy exclaimed. "She's so pretty! I wonder if she remembers us. I was always in awe of her tan. I'd never go that colour, no matter how long I tried to tan for," she sighed, looking down at her pale freckly arms.

"Me neither," shrugged Amanda, "but maybe they consider us exotic with our pale and interesting skin!"

Wendy rolled her eyes, "I wish!"

Rob got up and introduced the group to Wendy and Amanda. There was suddenly a lot of hand shaking and name swapping which mostly went in one ear and straight out the other, but the toffee tan girl introduced herself as Claudia, pronouncing it *Cloud-ee-ya*, which Wendy though was as lovely as her tan.

"Claudia, *si, mi ricordo,* yes, I remember! You have a brother Piero, right?"

"Yes! Wait, I remember you too! The two white foreign girls that swam always with their t-shirts on, no? You speak Italiano now?" Claudia asked, still holding Wendy's hand.

"Yes, *un poco, a* little? I want to learn more though, this summer." Wendy flushed in shame, feeling slightly inadequate.

"It is not problem, we help you, yes?' Claudia turned to one of the boys—was it Simone or Gianni? She couldn't remember.

"How long you stay here?" he asked. He had the most amazing green eyes, and was pretty tanned too, Wendy noticed. Claudia slipped an arm through Gianni's at that moment, claiming him without having to say anything.

"We're here all summer!" Amanda said, "We're dogsitting for Rob and Ted."

"Aah, you are the English girls Ted talk about. All summer is long time, no? We have many days to help remember you Italian, yes? Enzo is very good... how you say, to teach, *insegnante?*" Gianni turned to one of the other boys and pulled him into the conversation.

He turned to face them, and they both gasped in surprise. It was their Enzo, the one Amanda had been obsessed with when they were fifteen. He had been her first proper crush and her first proper kiss, and they had exchanged love letters all through the winter which Amanda would bring into school and share excitedly with Wendy at morning break time. One letter in particular had become famous in school when a cheeky boy called Chris had snatched it out of Amanda's hand and read it aloud to the class, causing everyone to shriek in amusement.

My Dear Amanda,

I miss you I love you. I come England my small motor,

Your wooer,

Enzo

He had never arrived in England with his small motor and the letters had gradually petered out. The next summer they had heard that Enzo had a girlfriend in Sorrento and spent most of his time there, and they hadn't seen him again, until now.

Enzo was taller than Gianni, his hair was dark and wavy, and he looked like a better version of Ralph

26

Macchio in *The Karate Kid*, a film that the girls had watched over and over again on a rented VHS tape from the video shop. He was wearing a peach-coloured Best Company t-shirt over his orange Sundek trunks.

"Amanda! Wendy! *Ma che piacere!* What a pleasure, you are here again and both so beautiful! It has been many years, no?"

Amanda blushed and Wendy could tell immediately that the attraction was still there for her. She decided to make the situation easier for her friend.

"Enzo, *ciao!* How have you been? We heard you were practically living in Sorrento? Are you back here now?"

He laughed and nodded, "Yes, I was with a girlfriend there for a few years but then we finish so now I'm home."

"And Roberto, your friend? How is he?" Amanda asked, still blushing and changing the subject.

"Aah, Robbie, you remember, eh! He is now the *farmacista*, you can find him in his shop on the road! He would be happy to see you both again!"

Enzo slapped Gianni on the back and picked up a canvas beach bag from a pile on the side of the lion statue.

"*Ragazzi, andiamo*?" He turned back to Wendy and Amanda and winked. "So nice to see you again, I will come find you and we all go out sometime, yes?"

The girls nodded in agreement and there was a flurry of cheek kisses and *ciaos* before the group walked up the steps.

"Yes, come on kids, let's go eat," Ted heaved himself up from the steps and dusted off the seat of his trousers.

Le Tre Sorelle restaurant was right next to the Lion Steps. Little square tables with red chequered tablecloths were lined up facing out towards the sea.

"*Buonasera* Michele!" Ted called to a short smiley man sitting with a much taller lady at a table in the corner. Michele, the owner got up and came over to greet them. Rob introduced the girls, reminding Michele that Amanda was the daughter of Carol and Peter from England and to treat them well this summer.

"Aha yes, I know your parents very well!" Michele said, pumping Amanda's hand up and down, "And you? Don't tell me you were that little blonde child that would sit under the table, just over there, no? I am right?"

Wendy laughed as Amanda went bright red and nodded that yes, that had been her.

"Maybe now you bigger, you stay sitting above the table, yes?" Michele led them to a front row table, chuckling and pulled out chairs for the girls to sit facing the sea. A waiter appeared with four glasses of sparkling prosecco.

"Enjoy!" Michele handed them a pile of menus

28

with a flourish and left them to it.

The meal was amazing, heart-shaped pizza bites oozing fresh basil and melted mozzarella, plates of fresh steaming seafood laced with garlic, hand-made pasta and the best tiramisu that Wendy had ever tasted. Glasses of wine were poured and refilled, and conversations were interrupted by people passing by and stopping to greet Rob and Ted. Finally, small icy glasses of limoncello were set down in front of them just when they thought that nothing else could pass their lips. Wendy had heard about this local liquor and was curious to try it. She took a sip, swallowed and immediately coughed, tears welling in her eyes. It was so strong! Quite thick, syrupy and lemony, but very, very strong.

"What do you think?" Ted asked Amanda, leaning forward. "If you don't like that one, they make plenty of different flavours."

"Er, no, this is fine, thank you, I think I've had enough to drink!"

"What do you mean, other flavours?" Wendy took another sip cautiously.

Rob picked up his tiny glass and downed it in one. "They make these liqueurs from anything: mandarin, fennel, wild strawberry, liquorice and even chocolate. They call them *digestivi*, as they're supposed to help you digest the enormous meal that you just ate, but in my opinion it's just an excuse for another drink!"

The restaurant was nearly empty. Waiters were

re-laying the tables for the next day and the kitchen staff were leaving, sliding past them quietly. Wendy watched as two of them walked over to the piazza and lit up cigarettes. They stood there for a while looking around before sitting down on a little stone bench facing the sea.

The bars were starting to close too, and most of the people who had been milling around earlier had vanished. A stray dog wandered over to the table, hopefully wagging his tail but there was nothing left to give him, and he left again, sniffing the ground as he went.

The four of them decided to take a stroll down to the end of the beach before walking back up. The last bus had long gone but Ted assured the girls it wouldn't take longer than 20 minutes to walk back up again.

The beach was dark and mostly deserted, umbrellas all closed and the sun loungers lined up in perfect rows. Here and there Wendy could see an orange glow of a cigarette or hear an occasional peal of laughter marking out where groups of people were sitting. Out at sea, a scattering of small boats bobbed, lit by silver moonlight which cast an ethereal glow across the ripples. The sky was inky black and a few stars glinted above.

"Let's put our feet in the sea!" Wendy kicked off her sandals and walked across the pebbles. Amanda hobbled after her, wincing and muttering as the uncomfortable stones dug into her feet. The sea was deliciously cool, and they stood there for a few minutes taking in the view around them. Rob and Ted sat down on a nearby sun lounger and also admired the view. There was nothing quite as magical as the view of Positano from the end of the beach on a moonlit night.

The whole beach lay before them, rows of closed umbrellas like soldiers in a line, and rising majestically at the end of the beach was the pyramid. From this angle, the town looked like a perfect triangle of pastel-coloured houses, all piled on top of each other with one white building perched high on the top, a row of flags waving on top triumphantly. Lights were on in most of the houses, creating a magical scene, the whole hillside twinkling with the silver shimmering below.

"That's the Villa Franca at the top," Ted pointed it out to the girls. "It's too dark now, but in the daytime, you can see the big tree and our house just below the hotel."

A small wooden rowboat suddenly appeared, arriving silently very close to the shoreline behind Wendy, causing her to yelp in surprise. The oarsman grinned and called out, "*Scusami, non ti volevo spaventare, stasera si pesca per i totani!*" He waved one hand out toward the sea where Wendy could see a small cluster of lights. She wasn't sure what it meant and turned to the men.

"When the moon is bright, the men like to go out fishing for squid. He didn't mean to frighten you. *Ciao Stefano, Buona serata!*" Bob waved at the fisherman and stood up, stretching. "Come on, let's start the dreaded climb home!"

It actually wasn't as bad as I thought it would be,

31

Wendy thought about half an hour later as she padded into the kitchen for a glass of water. They had all staggered home, a bit worse for wear but the narrow alleyways were quite handy for bouncing off the walls if you lost your balance due to too much wine. And the walk seemed to have cleared her head, maybe she had walked off all the alcohol? She turned off the light and padded back up to the bedroom. *More steps*, she thought, *I definitely won't need to do any aerobics classes while I'm here.*

Amanda was already fast asleep, on top of the covers and with the light still on. Within a few minutes, Wendy was fast asleep, too.

Chapter 2

Cornwall, September 2016

Conveniently, a few days after the letter from Amanda had arrived, the weather turned bad, as it tends to do quite often in England. Wendy awoke to find the sky was leaden and grey and the waves rolled relentlessly into the beach, causing a multitude of surfers to appear, swathed in full body wetsuits and eager for a day of bracing fun.

She had spent most of her life living and working just outside London, never quite satisfied with what she had achieved. Living in Cornwall was something that she had dreamed about for years. It was second best to living on the Amalfi Coast, like lucky old Amanda, which was something that she would probably never be able to do. She had secretly envied her friend who was living the life she wanted and vowed one day to chuck everything in and move away from the city.

Six years ago, she had hit fifty and with that big milestone she had decided to shake up her life and do what she had always dreamed of. An amicable split the year before with Ben, her husband of twenty-four years had prodded her into looking at her life and assessing how she wanted to live the rest of it. Up until then, she had run a successful beauty business with three salons and a team of talented makeup, hair and nail girls that were booked months in advance for weddings, hen nights and proms. It had been fun and hectic, and the freedom of having the girls to work for her while she was bringing up the kids had been very handy too, but Wendy had always had another dream.

She had always imagined herself in a house by the sea, running a bed and breakfast. She loved the idea of turning a home into a business, having people to stay and the idea of living by the sea had never left her head since a long summer in Italy when she was younger. So, she had invited Ben over to dinner one evening when the kids were both home and presented her plan to them all.

Ben was a Formula One photographer, always jetting off around the world with his camera bag. They had met in 1990 when he was still working as a wedding photographer. He had come into the salon where she was making up the bride and bridesmaids, to photograph the wedding preparations and they had become fast friends. They had ended up working together as a team; after all, every bride needed a makeup and hair artist and a photographer, so it made sense to pair up. Ben was easy going, easy on the eye and it had been easy to fall in love with him, too. It wasn't one of those passionate, explosive loves that rocked your world, but that was not what Wendy was looking for at the time. She had experienced that once and it hadn't worked out well at all and had hurt for a long time afterwards. She was happy with the easy going love she had with Ben. Most importantly, he was besotted with Mia, Wendy's young daughter, and once their son Josh had been born a few years later, he had officially adopted Mia as his own. (She had always told everyone that Mia's father was "someone she had met while in Italy, it hadn't worked out," and left it at that.)

Their marriage was an easy one; they rubbed along well but with Ben flying away increasingly more often as more and more racing fixtures were added to the calendar, they started to grow apart. Eventually, they realised it would be fairer on all of them if they separated and lived their lives independent of each other instead of being frustrated that the other wasn't there. After the divorce, there had been a couple of years of awkward resentment and bitterness towards each other, but eventually they had both come to terms with it and realised that they were better off as friends. Wendy was still surprised today how easy it had been to transition from being Ben's wife, to ex-wife and then back to being his friend.

She had sat Ben and the kids down to dinner and explained that she was thinking about selling the business and the house, and relocating to Cornwall. She had seen some fantastic properties online that would be perfect to renovate and turn into a small boutique hotel, and the prices were so low compared to London prices that she would have enough money for the renovations too if needed. Ben was enthusiastic for her from the start; they had talked many times over the years of their dreams and hopes, and he had no reason to think that it wouldn't work.

Mia, at twenty-three, greeted the idea with caution. She had already moved out of home after university and was happily living with her boyfriend in Clapham but wasn't sure if having her mother move a five-and-a-half-hour drive away was a good idea or not.

Josh, her 16-year-old facsimile of Ben who would be going with her had shrugged and asked if it meant he could learn to surf. Wendy was pretty sure it didn't cross his mind that he would be far away from all his school friends and everything he knew, but as he was about to start sixth form college in a few months, his life would have changed anyway.

At the end of the summer that year, Wendy and Josh had said goodbye to their London life and driven a packed self-drive van down to Falmouth. Mia and her boyfriend followed on behind in Wendy's car, curious to see the old rambling house that Mum had bought.

Rosemary House was a seven-bedroom Georgian former rectory with a two-and-a-half-bedroom annexe to the side. It had already been functioning as a guest house, but the owners had retired and sold up. The kids hooted at the terribly old fashioned '70s wallpapers and matted shag carpets, but Wendy could see the huge potential and couldn't wait to get stuck in. Six years later, the guest house was doing a roaring trade, she had repeat clients that came back every year and she had never regretted a moment of it. The rooms were airy and light with Egyptian cotton sheets and curtains that floated in the breeze. She had kept each bedroom white but then thrown in splashes of colour with bright cushions, throws and artwork, and there was always a vase of fresh flowers to greet the guests.

Mia had eventually split up with the London boyfriend and come to stay for a while to get over the breakup. That had been two years ago, and Mia was now sharing the running of Rosemary House with her although she had opted out of actually living there. She had found a darling little cottage in the next village and happily shared the rent with Ben who would drive down and crash for a week or two between jobs.

Mia, her darling Mia. Fiery and passionate, she came along unexpectedly just when Wendy needed her the most. Taking care of a newborn and then a young child had kept her busy and focused, and bringing Mia up as a single mother had been one of the hardest things she had ever done. But it had also been the most rewarding thing that had happened to her, a constant reminder of that summer in Italy, a most unexpected gift that made up for what could not be and something that she had never talked about since, except to Ben. And now it was time to tell Mia.

Josh headed out after breakfast with no intention of coming home anytime soon. He would be meeting friends and surfing all day, stopping for a pasty and probably sharing some hot chips from the cafe at the end of the beach by the car park.

The guesthouse was quiet, the clients out for the day, taking advantage of the bad weather to visit the Eden Project and do some shopping in Truro. Wendy had thought about it over the last few days and decided that the best thing to do was to sit Mia down and just tell her exactly what happened that summer in Italy. She had a small jewellery box of photos and a few keepsakes; a letter, a leather bracelet, a few old ticket stubs and a handful of coloured sea glass. It had been tucked away, locked, in the back of her wardrobe for years, the key hidden elsewhere. Mia had often dug the box out when she was younger, from behind a pile of sweaters and rattled it curiously. "Mummy! What is in here? Is it treasure? Why can't I see?" Wendy had always firmly taken it out of her daughter's hands and put it back in the wardrobe. "Not now, darling, but I will show you one day."

Mia knew that her father was Italian, but she didn't know much else. When she was a teenager, she had challenged her mother, demanding to know his name and Wendy had point blank refused to tell her. It had just been a passionate summer affair that had finished when Wendy returned to England and that was all that there was to know about it. Of course, Mia had pressed for more details, and they had bickered many times about it. Wendy had been adamant that there was nothing more that Mia needed to know and eventually Mia had realised that her father had probably wanted nothing to do with her and had therefore decided that she wanted nothing to do with him and had stopped asking.

Ben was the best Dad anyone could ask for anyway; he doted on her, had a really cool job that her male friends were in awe of, and she really didn't need another father in her life. Who cared about some sleazy old Italian that hadn't wanted to take responsibility?

But now, they sat together, mother and daughter in the small private living room at the top of the house, the jewellery box on the table between them. Outside the sea rolled and the surfers surfed, and finally Wendy started telling Mia all about the summer of '86 in Italy.

Chapter 3

Positano, May 1986

She awoke to find Amanda's elbow very close to her eye and the sound of church bells ringing melodiously around town. Carefully climbing out of bed, she stepped over Nerone, who was curled up on the floor like a big black bedside rug, and made her way downstairs to the kitchen. The sun was already streaming in through the windows, lighting up the whitewashed staircase. Nerone padded after her, his toenails clicking on the tiled floor as he walked.

"You want some breakfast, pooch?" She opened the door to the terrace, letting the morning light flood in. A fresh breeze wafted in, and Wendy stepped outside for a moment to admire the view. The sun had recently risen from over the mountain in front of her and a light haze hung over the town. The sea was dead calm, not a ripple to be seen. She could see a fishing boat way out, heading toward Praiano in the distance, a tiny trail behind it the only mark on the otherwise flat surface.

Rob and Ted had left for New York the day before. They had all spent the morning looking around the house, learning how everything worked.

The electricity box was behind the front door, and if there was a thunderstorm, the power would probably go out, so they had to know where to turn it back on again. Torches and candles were in every room and often needed. The oven was fuelled by gas, and they had to learn how to change the gas canister over to the spare for when it ran out. The town water was often cut off overnight in the summer due to shortages and there was a stash of jugs and bottles kept in a cupboard in the studio. If the water was turned off, there would be warning notices pasted to various lamp posts around town and you would have to go home, fill up all the bottles and jugs and place them in the shower so that you could wash at the end of the evening.

Nerone was to be fed twice a day and taken out for at least one walk a day. But he was an old dog and quite happy to stay home, dozing in the corner of the kitchen by the breakfast nook. If it was very hot, it was best to walk him first thing in the morning before the heat became overwhelming.

She turned back into the kitchen and found the scoop to measure out the dry dog food. Nerone sidled up to her and butted her arm with his head, tail wagging happily.

"Here you go, you soppy old thing. Eat it slowly!" She laughed as he wolfed down the food faster than she could put it into the bowl. Amanda walked in, still half asleep and winding her hair up into a ponytail, out of her face.

"Morning, or should I say, *Buongiorno?*"

Amanda grunted and stepped outside without answering. She had never been a morning person.

Having known Amanda for so long, she didn't really expect much else from her until she had some coffee in front of her, so she took the funny little mocha pot from a shelf, heaped some cafe Kimbo into one section of it, filled the other section with water as Rob had taught her the day before and balanced it on the gas ring, leaving it to boil.

Soon, the aroma of fresh coffee enticed Miss Grumpy Guts back inside and they sat down together for breakfast.

"We should decide who gets the main bedroom. There's no point sharing a bed anymore, we'll end up driving each other mad!" Wendy buttered a piece of toast, remembering the elbow close to her eye earlier. "You can have it if you want, I'm really not bothered where I sleep, I'm just grateful to be here."

"Are you sure? You can have it – it's got the view." Amanda reached for the apricot jam and stuck her knife into the jar.

The main bedroom was on another floor, below the kitchen and had a big window overlooking the beach, although a branch from the tree outside blocked some of the view. The house was built on three floors, carved out of the mountainside. The inner walls in the kitchen were roughly hewn, whitewashed but jagged and uneven, giving the room a cave like effect. There was a tiny sitting room next to the main bedroom, then a white stone staircase leading up to the kitchen floor which was the hub of the house. Another staircase led to the front door which separated the spare room which the girls were still sharing and the little artist studio.

"No, really, you should have it, it was you that got the housesitting job so you should get the room, I don't mind, really!"

The spare bedroom had a window that was set quite high in the wall and overlooked the alleyway and the hotel in front. But Wendy quite liked the idea of waking up in the morning, coming downstairs and stepping out onto that fabulous terrace to greet the day.

Amanda popped the last bit of toast into her mouth and pushed her chair back.

"OK, well if you're sure, I'll take it. You can always come and sleep over!" She grinned at Wendy, the coffee having done its trick, and collected the plates and cups to take to the sink.

It didn't take long to move Amanda's belongings down to the other bedroom and afterwards the girls decided to take Nerone for a walk before heading down to the beach for the afternoon. Nerone, who had been plodding round, following them from room to room like a big black shadow perked up once he saw the lead in Amanda's hand. She clipped it to his collar and they stepped outside, turning right on the road to head up towards the bus stop where they had arrived.

"I want to go visit that bar that we saw when we arrived. I remember that it's where all the locals hang out and we can start asking about jobs." Amanda was going to look for a job in a clothes shop or a bar. Wendy wasn't really sure what she wanted to do, but knew that she would have to find something to help finance her long summer in Italy.

As they walked around the curving road, they came across a small building that was plastered in handwritten signs. All different shapes and sizes, the signs were painted in red, blue and green paint on white backgrounds. Some were stuck to the walls, others propped up on the floor, leaning against the walls and on the domed roof and there was even one tied to a chimney. There were quite a number of Italian flags fluttering in the breeze too.

"What on earth is that all about?" Amanda squinted, trying to decipher the words.

"Is it a sign shop? How strange," Wendy said as they passed by. A few seconds later they turned another corner and came face to face with the sign painter. A short man with long frizzy grey hair and a big moustache was walking along, sandwiched between two handwritten boards, attached over his shoulders with rope. He was ringing a bell with one hand and was holding up another smaller sign on a stick. He looked rather angry, but when he saw the girls in front of him, he nodded his head and called *"Buongiorno!"*

"Buongiorno!" Chorused the girls together, walking slightly faster to escape this odd character.

"Bloody hell," Wendy laughed, "it was like coming face to face with Enid Blyton's Saucepan Man!"

A Vespa sped around the hairpin bend in front of them with and suddenly came to a halt just as it was about to pass them by.

"*Ciao* girls! *Come va?* How's it going?" It was Enzo, the Karate Kid lookalike they had met the other night at the beach.

"Hi Enzo!" Amanda smiled and self-consciously touched her hair. "Everything's great, thanks. Rob and Ted left yesterday so we're just settling in."

"Great! Well, if you need any help you know where to find me. Oh, wait, maybe not, eh?"

The girls shook their heads, they had no idea where he worked.

"You find me on the beach, there is a *stablimento* … how you say? A beach club, yes, just at the end of the big beach. You go past the *discoteca*, around the corner and I am there, every day. Is called La Scogliera, you come find me, okay?"

"We will, thank you Enzo," Amanda smiled at him.

"Oh, wait, I have to ask you something," Wendy said, laughing. "'We just saw the strangest man ringing a bell and covered in words, and there was a building too, just down there. Er, what…who is he?"

Enzo laughed and nodded, "Ah, yes, he is the VEP, a local personage. He is an *ambientalista*, er, you call it when one is worried for the environment, you

know he fights for it and wants everybody to know."
He let go of the brake and started wheeling down the
road, calling back, He is no danger to anyone. *Ciao
ciao!*"

"Hmmm," Wendy turned to Amanda, "I still
think he was the reincarnation of the Saucepan Man!"

The Bar Internazionale was buzzing. Groups of
locals stood out on the steps passing the time of day,
eating pastries and smoking. A crowd of scooters were
parked haphazardly by the wall opposite the bar and
four old men sat on the corner of the wall, watching
everyone else and commenting between themselves.
A pastry chef in kitchen whites appeared out of a
building next to the bar and passed by with a huge tray
of fresh croissants. Inside, the tables were full of people
chatting noisily and a huddle of men stood at the bar
ordering espresso. At least three dogs lurked under
tables and Nerone wagged his tail happily, hoovering
up any crumbs he could find. People came and went,
shouting *buongiorno* and *ciao*, stopping for a quick
word, and it seemed as if everyone knew each other.

The girls ordered pear juice and *cornetti*, fresh
warm croissants oozing with apricot jam, and squeezed
into the corner of a bench seat in front of a huge mirror
that had been painted with flowers and cherubs. Next
to them sat a group of local ladies, obviously having a
break from their shopping, judging by the many bags
at their feet. One of them said something funny with a
big hand gesture and the others creased up laughing.
A man at a nearby table called something to them and
they laughed even more, the men joining in. It looked
like a fun place to hang out and definitely the right

place to start asking about work.

Wendy was just wondering who they should try to talk to when an elegant older lady with long silvery hair swept up in a chignon and a billowy linen dress got up from a table near the bar and came over, bending down to talk in English to Nerone.

"Hello, old dog, what are you doing up here. Are these your new friends?" She looked at Wendy and held out her hand. "Hello, you must be Ted and Rob's house sitters? I'm Lily, a friend of theirs." Her voice was refined and soft, her accent was a bit like the Queen's, old-style English, and she had armfuls of jangly bangles.

"Hi, I'm Amanda and this is Wendy, nice to meet you!"

Wendy leaned across Amanda to shake Lily's hand, "Hi Lily, nice to meet you. Do you live here too?"

Lily sat down on a chair, which one of the laughing ladies had just left, and told them a bit about herself. She had been married to a local doctor, who had died a few years and had lived here for "decades, darlings, far too long!"

"Why did you stay then?" Amanda wanted to know.

"Well, I was so young when we moved out here, it was just before the war you see, and so much has changed. After the doctor died, I really didn't have anywhere to go back to, this is my home now. It's not too bad, rather dull in the winter though ..." She paused and looked thoughtfully at the two girls. "You be careful, girls, don't you go falling in love and get trapped here too!" She let out a laugh that sounded more like a cackle and started to get up from the table.

"Wait, please!" Wendy put an arm out to stop her. "You wouldn't have any idea where we could find jobs would you? Just something to get us through the summer."

Lily sat back down and thought for a few seconds.

"Do either of you speak Italian?"

The girls both shook their heads. "Not very well yet, but we can get by."

"Well, you're just going to have to ask around, my dears. You could probably give English lessons or babysit for tourists. Ask around on the beach, there might be something at a beach bar or on the boats. The new nightclub is going to need all sorts of staff, but heavens knows when it will actually open ..." She stood up again and brushed imaginary crumbs off her dress. "Lovely to meet you girls, I'm sure you'll find something!" She swept out of the bar with a whoosh of linen and was gone.

"Well, we're going to the beach later so we can ask around, maybe ask Enzo if he knows of anything," Amanda said, getting up to pay.

Wendy bent down to pick up the dog lead and

47

extracted herself and Nerone from around and under the table. As she walked out the door, a young man came in carrying a crate of big knobbly lemons and she had to jump sideways to make room for him to pass. He was wearing a yellow polo shirt that matched the lemons and had dark wavy hair and caramel-coloured skin. For a split second she thought she might already know him, but of course she didn't. She locked eyes with him for a moment, and he smiled at her. She just had time to think what a nice smile he had before she was out the door, he was in, and Amanda was coming out and they were off back down to the house.

Over the next few days, the girls worked their way around town asking if any jobs were available. They were turned away by many shops as they didn't speak enough Italian, they were laughed at by the restaurant owners on the beach who declared that women were not strong enough to wait tables.

"How you think you can manage? All these plates are too heavy for you small girls," one man guffawed. Wendy indignantly told him that women managed perfectly fine as waitresses in other countries, remembering one summer working in a large pub garden, carrying heavy trays full of plates and pints down to the riverside and back all day.

Enzo asked around for them, and so did Claudia and Gianni, who they had spent an afternoon sunbathing at the beach with. Claudia assured them that word would get around and something would come up soon.

Cornwall
September 2016

"That was the first time I saw him. We didn't even speak, but I swear, I have never experienced a connection like that with anybody ever since. Something passed between us, whether it was love at first sight or, I don't know, but whatever it was it was strong. The best way to describe it is that as soon as I saw him, I thought, 'Oh there he is' – I felt that I had found him, that I already knew him … Oh I don't know, you probably think I'm mad."

Mia twisted a tassel on a cushion and frowned. "What about Dad? When you first met him, wasn't it the same?"

Wendy sighed and shifted to a more comfortable position, folding a leg underneath her and stretching the other one out.

"No, love, it was different with your dad. We were colleagues and worked together for ages before anything actually happened. We just grew to love each other and were comfortable together. That's why we lasted so long together, we just rubbed along well, I suppose."

"Come on then, what happened next?" Mia leaned back and waited for her mum to continue. It was actually quite interesting; she hadn't really ever given any thought about what her mum had got up to when she was young.

"Well, next Amanda and I had to find ourselves jobs for the summer."

Chapter 4

Positano, May 1986

It was late afternoon, the sun was casting golden beams over the tops of the mountains and Wendy was at home, relaxing on the terrace with a Danielle Steele novel that she had brought with her. Amanda was out buying something for dinner, and it was nice just to sit in silence for a while. Her thoughts drifted from her book as she imagined her friends back home, at this time of the day either stuck in an office or battling their way home through rush hour traffic. It was six o'clock and the church bells started ringing, first from the church over in the old part of town and then joining in from the big church down in the centre. *Such an Italian sound*, she thought dreamily. Over the sound of the bells, she heard the front door slam and a few seconds later Amanda came rushing over, panting and red faced from the effort of carrying the shopping home.

"Guess what? I got a job offer!" She dumped the shopping bag on the outside table and pulled up a chair next to Wendy.

"I was standing at the bus stop and this guy came up to me and asked if I was one of the English girls looking for a job. He says he has an art gallery and needs someone to work there while he's in his other shop, and it doesn't matter if I don't speak Italian!"

"Why not?" Wendy sat up, interested in this proposition.

"Um, he said that he doesn't want to sell to Italians, he's only interested in rich foreigners, and anyway if I get a possible client, I'm to call him and he will come and look after them. So, the language isn't a problem."

"Who is this guy, how did he know about us?"

"His name is Matteo, he has an antiques shop and an art gallery, and he said he was friends with Gianni. He gave me his card, look, so we can check."

Gianni and Claudia were reassuring when Amanda questioned them about Matteo's job offer. She had come across Claudia on the road one morning, while walking Nerone, and together they had walked down to see Gianni who was at work. His parents owned a small *pensione*, a bed and breakfast over at Fornillo, and he usually worked the morning shift from 7am to 1pm.

Fornillo was a quieter part of town, with its own beach that was accessible from the main beach by a pretty cliffside pathway. The higher part of Fornillo, also connected to the beach by lots of steep steps and very narrow lanes, was mainly residential with a few hotels and cheaper B&Bs scattered throughout. Pensione Cinque was a whitewashed building off a tiny square with handpainted green tiles and a big cheeseplant in a vase by the entrance. A girl in a maid's uniform was dusting the big flat leaves of the plant with a yellow cloth as they walked in, and Gianni was sitting at a big wooden desk, busily filling out a pile of forms.

"Yes, Matteo is a good man," Gianni reassured her, "it should be okay for you with him, don't you worry, I tell him to be nice to you!" And just like that Amanda had a job, all very informal, no contracts or anything. Just a casual "come to the shop at 10am tomorrow and I will show you what you will have to do."

****

Wendy ended up with a much more interesting proposition, in her opinion. She was out walking with Nerone on the beach early one morning. It was a clear sparkly kind of day with cobalt blue skies and slightly choppy seas. The surf was breaking high on the beach and the deckchairs and little wooden boats had been pulled higher up, out of harm's way.

She wandered over to the wharf where the boats docked. It was at the side of the beach, where a little jetty jutted out from a jumble of big rocks that the local kids loved to climb on. Nerone followed behind her, off the lead, happily sniffing his way around. A couple of fishermen were wrestling with a big barrel of orange nets, pulling them out in armfuls and transferring them onto a trolley. They looked like the fisherman version of Laurel and Hardy; one was large and round and balding, the other was short and skinny with a shock of shaggy greying hair. Both shirtless and barefoot, the larger man was wearing what looked like home-made trousers held up with a piece of rope, and the other had an old, battered pair of cut-off jeans. They were bantering with a small round lady sitting on a stool, mending nets from another barrel. She had rosy cheeks, and a halo of wavy blonde hair surrounded her face; she was dressed in a long, loose denim skirt and a pink t-shirt and kept laughing at whatever the fishermen were saying to her. As Wendy drew closer, she was surprised to hear that they were speaking English.

"You like to go on the boat because you like to see the men all nekked, no? *E vero*, Gloria, it's true, tell me the truth!"

"Oh, just stop it Sandro! You know that's not true!" She chortled with mirth and he flicked a piece of seaweed at her. She brushed it off her skirt, laughing, "Honestly, you two are like giant children!"

"Hello," said Wendy, directing it more to the jolly lady than the two impish fishermen.

"Ello, darlin," drawled the fisherman with the homemade trousers, "you like big fish?"

"Mauro!" Gloria shot up onto her feet, horrified, and threw a fishing net float at him. "That is enough! Now, behave yourself or you can mend your own bloody nets!"

Much later on that summer, Wendy learned that the word "fish" in Italian also referred to a certain male appendage, and only then did she understand Gloria's shocked reaction to the fisherman's words that day.

Gloria turned back to Wendy, "Ignore them, my dear, they are ridiculous but mean no harm. Isn't that Ted's dog with you?"

There was a concrete bench right next to where Gloria was sitting, so Wendy sat down to chat. Nerone was perfectly happy chasing pigeons and sniffing piles of seaweed.

Gloria was originally from Ohio; she had moved to Positano a few years ago. A single mum, left with no reason to stay after her children had flown the nest, she had decided to retire to Italy and live the dream.

"And now I'm here mending nets for these two idiots," she said affectionately, waving her hand at the fishermen who were now concentrating on their job.

It turned out that the fishermen did a sideline of boat excursions along the coast and were also about to start doing night fishing trips, with whatever they caught cooked on board and served up to around 25 guests. They were looking for helpers, if Wendy was interested. Gloria would be on board and a local girl would be helping too. She was very interested and quite excited by the prospect of working on a boat for the summer. Much more fun than being stuck in a shop or an office back in dreary old London!

And that is how Wendy found herself sitting on the side of a fishing boat at nine o'clock in the evening, two days later, de-heading anchovies with her bare hands and flinging fish innards over her shoulders into the sea behind her.

There were four fishermen on board, Sandro and Mauro, who were brothers, and two other local guys that Wendy hadn't really spoken to yet. Gloria was in charge of the cooking and Wendy was on food prep and waitressing with a girl around her own age, called Maria. She had met Maria when she arrived for work and got the impression that she wasn't too happy to be sharing her job with an English girl. She had swept past Wendy with a tray of lemons, ignoring her and nodding briefly when introduced by Sandro. She had a curtain of silky dark hair that she wore swept back from her face with two combs, was dressed in baggy jeans belted over a black sleeveless leotard, and was engaged to the son of the fishmonger. Every time she passed by the shop, she would duck in for a stolen kiss, and every time he came down to the dock with his wellies and his wheelbarrow, she would forget what she was doing and sneak off to see him.

Together as the sun set, they had loaded the docked boat with fresh bread, boxes of local lemons and onions, condiments, paper plates and lots of wine and water. The food they had taken down to the galley and the bottles had been submerged in big coolers full of ice. The ice was made in ice cream cartons and left to freeze in a freezer in the fishmonger's store. The girls had enjoyed the job of smashing the blocks of ice with a hammer and had finally exchanged a shy word or two.

On board, they had welcomed the twenty or so guests and then ducked down into the galley to prepare the food. It was very simple. The loaves of bread were cut into big slices, the lemons and onions into quarters.

"Who eats raw onions?" Wendy asked doubtfully.

"Well, Mauro certainly does, you can smell it on him," Maria answered, wrinkling her nose in disgust before turning slightly further away from Wendy, tossing her dark hair in a curtain to one side.

Gloria popped her head down through the hatch and told them that once they were done, they should come up and start pouring drinks for the guests.

The fishing was the most interesting part of the evening. Another fisherman had gone out earlier in a small orange rowboat with a big round lantern hanging off the end. The light from the lantern would attract the fish toward the small boat, and by the time the fishing boat arrived, it would be time to cast the nets.

Sandro drove the big boat around the smaller boat in a large circle, letting out a very long net that was weighted at the bottom, which was then, once the ends met, pulled tighter and tighter, effectively trapping any fish that had been attracted to the light. The little rowboat made its exit, and the nets were then hauled up into the big boat by crane.

That first night they caught nearly 100 kilos of fish, mainly anchovies, or *alici* as they called them, but there were other fish including little squids and tiny octopuses – *polipetti* – that made Wendy squeal when Sandro placed one gently on her arm.

57

The whole crew pulled together to gut and clean some of the fish. THer rest would be taken to the fishmongers and sold in the morning. Wendy found a place sitting on the edge of the boat next to Gloria and was shown how to stick her thumb under the gills at the side of the little fish, snap the neck, run her thumbnail down the underbelly and scrape out the innards and throw them overboard. This definitely was not the highlight of the evening, and Wendy felt quite bad for the poor little fishes.

"*Fa schifo!* Disgusting!" Maria shuddered every time she picked up a fish and complained so much that she was eventually sent off to do something else.

Gloria cooked the fish in a giant frying pan balanced over a camping stove in the middle of the deck while Wendy and Maria stood by with plates, ready to be filled and passed around to the guests on board. Gloria scooped a ladleful of fried fish onto a plate, passed it to Maria who added a slice of lemon, onion, and bread. Maria passed it to Wendy who then circulated, making sure all the guests had platefuls of food. She kept cooking as the boat swayed gently in the moonlit sea until everybody, including the staff, had eaten their fill.

Wendy and Maria then had to circulate again with trays full of tiny, delicate almond biscuits from the pastry shop in town, topping up glasses and clearing up the plates from wherever they had been left.

As the boat made its way slowly back to the village, which from the sea looked as if it was made of fairy lights, Wendy and Maria climbed up onto the roof of the cabin with a half bottle of wine that had been left.

"It's so beautiful," murmured Wendy, sipping her wine and gazing along the twinkling coastline.

"Hmm," replied Maria. She took sip of wine and balanced the glass on the roof beside her, wiggling around for a moment before pulling a ready rolled joint out of her pocket and lighting it. She inhaled deeply and held it in for a moment before letting it out. She looked at Wendy and raised her eyebrows, "You want?"

"Won't they smell the smoke below?"

"I think not, it goes out to the sea, no? Don't worry, I do this many times."

Wendy smiled and took the joint.

"So, how long have you been with your boyfriend?" She asked, blowing out the smoke and passing the joint back to Maria.

"Oh, about five years now," she shrugged. "We get married this summer, you know? In August."

"No! I didn't know, that's lovely! Well, if you want help getting ready on the day, I'd be happy to help you." Maria looked at her, unsure what she meant.

"Oh, back in England I worked as a beauty therapist. I do lots of bridal makeup and manicures, stuff like that."

Maria brightened at this, "Yes, that is good, we could maybe try it one day so I can see? I already try my look at the hairdresser's here and I not like at all. She make me like a ... how you say ... circus man?" She mimed juggling.

"A clown!"

"Sì! I no like clown. We try, you and me, maybe next week, yes?"

"Yes, that would be great. I promise I don't do clown makeup!"

When the boat docked, they helped take the trash bags over to the skips and were dismissed.

"*Brave ragazze*! Well done, girls. We do it again *dopo domani*, okay?" Sandro smiled at Wendy as he trundled off with a wheelbarrow.

"*Dopo domani* ... that means after tomorrow, right?" Wendy recognised both of those words, but when after tomorrow?

"It means the day after tomorrow. We do this five evenings a week, are you joining the crew, Wendy?" Gloria came over and linked arms with her.

"Yes, I'd love to, thanks! I really enjoyed myself." Wendy was thrilled to have found a job for the summer, and on a boat, no less!

"I go, *ciao*!" Maria rushed off; her boyfriend was waiting.

Cornwall
September 2016

"I can't believe you worked on a boat and never told me! Deheading fishes and stuff! Mum, that's hilarious!"

"Well, I was lucky, really. They were a fab bunch, Gloria and those two brothers, just like an Italian Laurel and Hardy they were. I know that Gloria died a few years ago. Amanda told me – she visited her in hospital. Apparently there's a little memorial tile in her memory cemented into the stone bench that she always sat on by the jetty."

Wendy stood up and stretched her arms above her head. "Right, I want a cup of tea, do you want something? All this talking, I'm parched!"

They made their way down to the kitchen and Mia flipped the kettle on while Wendy pulled their favourite mugs out of the cupboard.

"Amanda had a terrible time with various jobs over the years. She always wrote and told me about them. It's shocking, some of the things employers over there get away with, really."

Mia dropped a teabag in each mug and reached for the biscuit tin for something to nibble on. "What do you mean?"

"Well, the pay is incredibly low there still and quite a lot of workers don't get a day off all summer.

They work up to 12 or 14-hour days seven days a week for six months, and the employees think it's okay because they get the winter off. And the bosses can be quite unreasonable and make things very hard for the staff. I remember her telling me when she was the hostess in a hotel restaurant in Sorrento for a couple of years. The owner of the hotel came up to her one evening and told her that there was a new rule. Men were not to be allowed into the restaurant if they had short sleeves. They could only enter if dressed in long-sleeved shirts, never mind that it was often over 26 degrees in the evenings.

So, one evening Giorgio Armani arrived for dinner, and of course he is famous for wearing short-sleeved black t-shirts. Poor Amanda had just started trying to explain to him that she wasn't allowed to let him in when the hotel owner swooped in and told her off, taking Mr Armani by the arm and leading him to the best table.

Amanda shrugged and thought the rules had been relaxed for the evening. A few minutes later she let another short-sleeved shirt in and led him to a table. Within minutes, the hotel owner was marching over and demanding that Amanda ask that man to leave. Poor thing, she was mortified! She had to go and tell the man she had just seated that he had to change his shirt or leave even though Mr Armani was sitting in short sleeves just nearby!"

"That's ridiculous! Poor Amanda!" They sat down together around the kitchen island, steaming cups of tea in hand and a plate of cookies between them.

"Right, where were we?" said Wendy

The pink valerian flowers were in full bloom, swaying gently in the breeze and completing the palette of primary colours around him in the lemon grove. Yellow and green from the lemon trees, bright blue from the sky and a deeper blue from the horizon. There were yellow dandelions and a few bursts of red from the delicate poppies that had grown and flowered seemingly overnight. He sang tunelessly as he hefted the plastic crate of lemons onto his shoulder and turned to traipse back through the grove and down to the tiny truck. Papá was there, shifting the other crates around in the truck bed, muttering to himself as he checked off the delivery list.

"How slow you are! Come on now, the Hotel Sirenuse are waiting for their delivery. And the Bar cannot do without its lemons. Quickly, boy!"

Francesco sighed and lowered the crate into the back of the battered green *ape* before climbing into the creaky driver's seat.

"*Calmati Papá*, calm down, Dad, I'm going now. Tell Elena I'll be late for lunch!"

And with that he started the engine and puttered off towards the village below.

Francesco worked in the family lemon groves, just like his father and his grandfather before him. Three acres of terraced mountainside had been painstakingly planted with hundreds of Amalfi Coast lemon trees by his enterprising grandfather many years ago and had been lovingly cared for by the whole family for years. They now supplied most of the restaurants and hotels in town with the big, fragrant, sweet lemons and the potent limoncello that they made.

It was backbreaking work though, out all day traipsing up and down the terraces, lugging crates of lemons back to the storeroom or the road. Then there was the pruning and the tidying, spraying each tree to protect against disease and insects and checking the branches and leaves for problems. In the winter they had to cover the trees with huge black nets, metres and metres long, that had to be sewn in place and would protect from any harsh winds or possible frosts that occasionally occurred.

But Francesco loved it. He had grown up playing in the groves with his brothers and loved the freedom and the sun on his face. He had hated being shut in a classroom at school and had shuddered in horror at the thought of having to grow up and work in an office or anywhere enclosed. He happily left school as soon as he could at 13 years old and had started helping his father and grandfather in the groves, only stopping for two years to complete his obligatory military service on a naval ship in La Spezia. His favourite part of the job was the deliveries. Francesco was a social person and just loved driving around town, waving to people he knew and stopping to deliver lemons all around town, catching up on gossip with his clients.

The road was steep and full of curves, but he knew it like the back of his hand. The *ape* puttered past the water fountain where the old folk filled up their glass bottles, swearing the water was good for their blood pressure, past the valley that at this time of year was full of *fiore di sambuca*, elderflower blossoms, and down towards the higher part of Positano.

He pulled up by the wall in front of the bar, greeting a couple of locals who were sat there as they did every day before lunch, with a cigarette in one hand and a glass in the other.

"*Ciao* Aldo, how's it going?" He grinned, cheerfully greeted a large man, passing by on a Vespa with a small dog balanced on the seat behind him, before pulling a crate of lemons out of the back of the van and crossing the road to the bar. As he walked through the open door, he nearly knocked down a tourist, a girl with dark red hair who was on her way out. A big black dog jumped out of his way and the girl flattened herself against the drinks fridge. As he squeezed past her, their eyes connected and he smiled, thinking for a moment that he already knew her. But she wasn't from around here – he knew that instantly. Then she was gone and by the time he had offloaded the crate around the back of the bar and stepped outside again, there was no sign of her.

He hoped to see her again as he drove around town with the rest of his deliveries, but she had vanished into thin air. The split-second image of her face seemed to have burned into his retinas and he couldn't dislodge the thought that something had passed between them in that tiny moment in the doorway of the bar.

What on earth was he thinking, though? As he drove back up to the lemon groves, he tried to put the image of the girl with the red hair out of his mind and replace it with loving thoughts about his wife.

Elena and Francesco had been together forever. They were childhood sweethearts, had been together since they were sixteen and had been married for seven years. Elena had a heart of gold and was the perfect wife in all ways apart from one niggling problem. She hated socialising. She was at her happiest at home, cooking huge meals for the family and the workers in the groves, helping out with the limoncello production and hand painting the glass bottles with lemons and leaves. She cooked and cleaned and looked after their adorable toddler, happy as could be, but if Francesco suggested they go out for a meal, or for an evening walk along the beach front, she would become flustered and jittery and invent all sorts of problems, so it wasn't worth pursuing.

Francesco longed for her to be more outgoing. He had always wanted a partner who would go to the gym with him or jump on the Vespa and drive along the coast at a moment's notice. Elena was trusting and generous and had no problem with him going out for the evening, a dinner with friends, a boat trip along the coast, but she hardly ever joined in, which made him unhappy and frustrated. He had tried to talk to her about it, but she just batted his worries away, telling him to go and enjoy himself. She just didn't get that he wanted to share the experience with his partner and be able to discuss the intricacies of the outing with her rather than just recount them to her.

He pulled up outside the gate and turned off the engine. Ignoring the lingering image of the girl with red hair, he walked into the house, calling out that he was home and scooped up his son, Leonardo who toddled over with glee at the sight of his father.

Chapter 5

Positano, May 1986

Wendy's arms were wrapped around Enzo's waist; she was perched on the back of his battered white Vespa. They were speeding around the village, cutting a breezy path through the warm muggy air. Every now and then, they passed through refreshing pockets of cool air for a few moments where the mountainside loomed and the sun never shone. As they reached a particularly dark corner, surrounded by high cliffs, Wendy thought she saw lights moving in the darkness.

"*Le Lucciole!*" Enzo shouted, "How you say? Light flies ... no, fireflies?"

Hundreds of tiny fireflies, glowing and twinkling like magic fairy dust appeared all around them. Enzo slowed down and pulled over, cutting the engine and laughing out loud. They were in the middle of a hairpin bend, right at the back of the village. It was cool and damp and there was the sound of water running nearby. Wendy looked up, surprised to see a tall waterfall cascading down the mountainside into a small pond. She climbed off the Vespa and Enzo kicked it up on its stand. They stood for a moment watching the magical twinkling lights and then they were dancing around amongst them, laughing like children, until the fireflies drifted off on an invisible current of air.

Laughing and out of breath, they climbed back onto the Vespa and drove up the hill, past the bar and back down the other side of town until they pulled up outside the house. Enzo parked the Vespa neatly in the alleyway next to the hotel. Amanda was out for the evening on a blind date set up by her boss. Wendy had opted out of a double date in favour of dying her hair at home, and Enzo had laughingly agreed to help her. In the kitchen, he opened a bottle of wine while she pulled bowls and spoons out of cupboards. She put a pan of water onto boil, took the glass of wine that Enzo was holding out to her and read the first few instructions on the packet of henna hair dye. She wanted to freshen her colour but wasn't earning enough to pay the rather expensive hairdressers in town. Luckily, she had suspected this might be the case and had slipped a couple of packets of natural dye from The Body Shop into her rucksack before leaving the UK. She opened the packet and Enzo came closer so that they could inspect the contents.

"Looks like old leaves and mud to me," said Enzo, shrugging. She ignored him and poured the contents into the boiling water. Enzo was brandishing a wooden spoon already, so she let him play chef and mix it together. He was right, it did look very much like mud and leaves. It reminded her of the "mud-soup" she used to make, playing in the back garden when she was small.

"You are really going to put this thing on your hairs?" Enzo asks her, amusement bubbling in his

70

voice.

"No, you are going to do it for me – I can't see if I leave gaps or not. It's easier for someone else to do … and we say hair, not hairs."

Enzo rolled his eyes at her, "You have more than one hair, no? So, it is plural, hairs!" Wendy decided to leave that conversation right there.

They left the mixture to cool for a while, and drank the wine, contemplating the task ahead.

"How exactly am I going to get this mud onto your hairs?"

Wendy hadn't thought of that. They discussed various options and the solution they came up with was messy, but it got the job done. Wendy turned her head upside down over the bowl and lowered her hair into it. Enzo, wearing plastic bag gloves sellotaped onto his wrists, scooped up handfuls of the mud mixture and rubbed it onto her hair until the bowl was empty. She tipped her head the right way up again, splattering flecks of henna onto everything in the vicinity.

Enzo roared with laughter, slapping his leg and pointing at her head. Embarrassed, Wendy got up and walked over to the nearest mirror to see what was so funny. Her hair was a mud-coated, dreadlocked lion's mane that was threatening to topple onto her face. She looked absolutely ridiculous, like a caveman, a Stig-in-the-dump wannabe. She now realised that she should have tipped her head backwards over the bowl, not forwards. She was also shedding dried pieces of sticks and leaves all over the place.

Enzo kindly fashioned her a turban out of an old plastic bag and more sellotape.

"Here, let's put this on your head. It will contain the neanderthal in you!"

They drank some more wine and Enzo rolled a spliff.

"So, how long has this got to stay on for?" He asked, unfolding a small square of folded newspaper which revealed a small stash of marijuana. Wendy hadn't actually finished reading the instructions on the pack. She picked it up now and squinted at it.

"Oh … oh dear," she said, "it says here 5-6 hours … damn…" It was 9.30pm.

"What! No!" exclaimed Enzo, "What are we going to do for six hours? You're can't go out with a plastic bag on your head … can you?"

"We could go for a walk in the mountain," Wendy suggested, deadpan. "We might find more fireflies."

They rolled a couple more joints and took the rest of the wine. Enzo drove the wrong way back up the one-way street to the Bar Internazionale and then took the road that headed out of town. After a few minutes he pulled over and parked in a large lay-by. "It's called La Garita, you have been here before, no?"

Wendy didn't think she had, and he led her over to a little set of steps that plunged down into darkness. She hesitated, embarrassed about being seen with a plastic bag on her head, but Enzo reassured her that there would be nobody around at this time of night. There was no moon that evening but the stars shone, and the air was perfumed with jasmine.

She walked down the steps and gasped. The whole town was laid out below her, lights twinkling like magic. She had never seen anything like it it almost felt like she was flying. When she was about eight, her parents had taken her to Disney World in Florida and she had fallen in love with the Peter Pan ride, the part where they flew over the streets of London, surrounded by stars. This felt similar, leaning over the railing with the whole of Positano laid out below her.

"This is amazing!"

"Come, let's go, I show you something even better!" Enzo tugged her arm and led her back up to the road.

They walked along the road for a bit until they came to a low white gate in the wall. "Come through here, it's okay, it's not dangerous." It was dark though, and she had to feel the steps, tapping her feet in front of her to find the edge as they made their way down a pathway surrounded by flowering bushes. It zigzagged back on itself, and then they were out in front of a building. It was dark, no lights were on, and the silence made Wendy whisper.

"Where are we? This isn't your house, is it?" She

could just make out a pile of bricks and a cement mixer to the side of the big arched door. There was a paved area in front of the door and a pathway led around the side of the building where she presumed the view over the town would be.

"No!" Enzo laughed, too loudly and immediately lowered his voice to a whisper.

"This is the new *discoteca* that is going to open soon, you have heard about it, no? The Paradise! It will be fantastic, come, look at the view!" He led her around the building and she tiptoed after him, half sure that a security guard was going to jump out at them at any moment.

The front of the building was nearly all glass; two huge arched glass windows looked out on a view almost as good as from the lookout point they had just come from. Enzo stepped up to the window and cupped his hands around his eyes to see inside. Wendy did the same and felt the plastic bag that she had forgotten was on her head. *Who does this,* she thought, *creeping around empty nightclubs with random Italian men wearing plastic bags on their heads? I must be mad.*

It was too dark to make out much inside, but she could see that there was a big room with a curving bar to the left and what looked like a lot of chairs and sofas that still needed to be put in their places.

"It must be nearly ready, when is it opening?" She pressed her face close to the glass, trying to see down the far end of the room.

Enzo shrugged and slid down to sit with his back to the window. He took a spliff from where he had lodged it behind his ear and tore the twisted end off.

"I think now they are saying it will be open in July. It was supposed to be opening next week but, you know, in Italy nothing is easy." He lit the joint and took a drag, tapping the embers into a gap in the paving.

Wendy slid down next to him and pulled the wine bottle out of the backpack she had brought with her. She slid the cork out, took a swig and waggled it at Enzo.

"Swap?"

He took another drag and passed the joint over, taking the bottle in exchange, and they sat there sharing the wine and the spliff, happily lost in their own thoughts for a while.

Enzo stubbed the joint out and squashed the roach into the gap in the paving stones that he had been using as an ashtray.

"Wendy," he said in a low serious voice. "It is now almost eleven o'clock. Are you really going to stay like that until 3am?" He gestured at her head, smiling.

Her hand flew to the plastic bag. Damn, she had forgotten about it again!

"No, I suppose not, we can go if you want." She stood up too fast and put a hand against the window to steady herself.

"I show you one more thing, then we go," Enzo decided, getting up with a groan. They made their way back up to the road. It was quiet; at this time of night, everyone was either at home or still down at the beach area. There was a very old, small crumbly building on the other side of the road with an equally old-looking set of steps wrapping itself around the side and up into the dark.

"You feel like climbing a bit? Or you too stoned?" Enzo smirked at her, which of course made her want to prove to him how well she could handle the weed.

"We climb," she replied, accidentally starting to speak like him.

The steps curved up into the mountain above, and after about a minute they became less steep and snaked around a steep crevice, starting to head inland. The moon had finally appeared from over the top of the mountain and shone a silvery light that made it easier to see. They could just make out the path in front of them, but the trees to the side were a sheet of blackness, as was the deep drop-off to the right.

"Where are we going?" Wendy asked, whispering again as she nearly stumbled on a tree root. She let out a little shriek and grabbed Enzo's arm to steady herself.

"Up in front, just a bit longer, there is a how you call it, *un laghetto*? A little pool with water?"

"A lake? A pond? How big is it?"

76

Enzo held a bramble out of the way as Wendy passed, "Not big, a pond I think."

It was a pond, possibly manmade as it seemed to be oblong in shape, siphoned off from a mountain stream. Stepping-stones passed through the middle of the still black water and reeds grew at the edges. There was a building over the other side, but Enzo reassured her it was just an old abandoned house and nobody came up there anymore. The pond was in the garden of the house and although it looked quite sinister in the moonlight, Wendy could imagine it being a thriving homestead a couple of hundred years ago.

They sat by the pond and smoked the last joint, listening to a couple of owls that hooted to each other in the woods and little rustling noises from whatever else lived there.

"It is good to know these places, I think," mused Enzo, blowing out a stream of smoke.

"Places that you can come and be alone, where nobody ever comes."

"Hmm," replied Wendy, "maybe I would come here in the day alone, but definitely not at night-time."

Enzo agreed with her, "Yes, only at night-time when you wear plastic bags on your head, no?"

Wendy whacked him playfully, glad that it was too dark to see her blushing. She had forgotten about the bag on her head again!

"Come on, let's go back. I'm going to wash it off, it was a silly idea anyway!"

Enzo stood up and reached out an arm to pull Wendy up too, "Hmph, now she decides it is a silly thing to do!" He teased her all the way back down to the road.

Chapter 6

Positano, June 1986

Amanda closed up the gallery and walked down to the local delicatessen to pick up a *panino* and an iced tea. The only good thing about this job was the three-hour lunch break which gave her time to catch up with Wendy and sit on the beach for a while. Nibbling on a piece of fresh *parmeggiano* that had been thrust into her hand by the shopkeeper, she headed over to the far end of the beach past the disco, near where Enzo worked, to a little inlet where they could sunbathe in private. Wendy was already there, stretched out on her back on the sand, trying to read a book while holding it up in the air above her.

"Hiya!" Amanda called. "Did you bring something to eat? I just got a *panino*, but it's huge so we can share if you want."

She sat down next to Wendy and showed her the sandwich, wrapped in paper inside a plastic bag.

"My God, it's basically a whole loaf of bread cut in half!" Wendy laughed. She leaned over to her bag behind her and pulled out a rather sad looking sandwich cut into two triangles that she had made at home earlier. "Looks much nicer than my effort though!"

Amanda sat down and started wiggling into her bikini, trying not to flash any hidden body parts while doing so. There were plenty of changing huts in rows all along the back of the beach, but they were either privately owned or for hire by the day, so it was easier to just wiggle in and out of their swimwear where they were sitting.

They had already been in Positano for three weeks and were both settled into their new routines. In the last week they had taken to meeting on the beach during Amanda's lunch break so that they could catch up and have a gossip. Wendy unwrapped Amanda's enormous panino and used the paper as a tablecloth, laying the sandwiches and a few tiny, crunchy pears out in front of them while Amanda covered herself in sunscreen.

As they ate, they swapped stories from work. Wendy, laughing as she told the story that Sandro the fisherman had entertained the clients with the night before: He had been to see friends in England and had visited a few fishmongers to see what they sold and how the prices compared with Italian fish. He had been surprised to discover that the lobsters were way cheaper in England and so had decided to bring some back with him. He could sell them on for four times the price when back in Italy, so he popped a few into his hand luggage.

"Can you imagine the faces of the men at airport customs when they checked his bags and found a bunch of live lobsters in them!"

Amanda laughed and got up, brushing off crumbs from her lap and went to rinse her hands in the sea. The sandwich had been so big she hadn't even managed a quarter of it.

"Sounds like you got the better deal, job-wise. Let me know if that Maria goes away and I'll come work with you."

"Why, what's happened now?" Wendy had heard all about the father of Amanda's boss, a stern, grey-faced man who seemed to disapprove of her and everything she did. He had told her that the people in the shops to either side of the gallery were "bad people" and that she would do her best not to talk to them. But as far as Amanda could see, they were all lovely people. The two girls in the ceramics shop were absolute sweethearts. They had gifted her a beautiful ceramic mug and had made it their personal mission to perfect Amanda's Italian, and the kind old man in the limoncello shop on the other side brought her coffee and a pastry every morning.

Amanda sighed, "He keeps driving past on his Vespa and checking up on me. He said this morning that he has seen me twice, talking to the people from the next shop, and that if he sees me with them again, he'll fire me."

"But that's ridiculous!" Wendy exclaimed. "He can't tell you who to talk to. What does he expect you to do, ignore them when they offer you coffee?"

"I know," Amanda said miserably, "it's boring enough as it is just sitting there all day with nothing to do. Now I'm not even allowed to talk to people." She combed her fingers through the little pebbles on the beach, making a pile of all the little pieces of sea glass that she found among them. Sometimes you could also find pieces of coloured tiles, the terracotta edges worn smooth and the top brightly patterned.

"It's ridiculous really, they're all related and apparently they argued about some building they all inherited together, and now they don't speak to each other. I don't get why I have to take sides, it's nothing to do with me."

Wendy had a handful of tiny black rocks and was looking for more. "Have you seen these? Claudia showed me the other day; she said they're semi-precious stones, called tourmalines. Look, if you hold them up to the sun, you can see they're actually dark green." She held a bigger one up to the sky and watched it glitter.

"Looks like black glass to me," Amanda said morosely.

Wendy turned to her friend, "Manda, you can always quit and find something else if you're not enjoying it. We came here to have fun. It's not worth ruining the summer for a shitty job."

"Yeah, I know," Amanda flipped onto her stomach and rested her head on her arms. "I think I'll start looking for something better."

Amanda had reluctantly gone back to work. It was four o'clock and the temperature was perfect. Wendy stretched lazily, brushing off a few pebbles that had stuck to her thigh. She could hear the far-off sounds of children shrieking and splashing in the water, small waves lapping gently against the shore, the hum of outboard motors, and then, the sound of oars paddling close by.

How annoying, she thought. In her mind, she had claimed this part of the beach as her own private area. Who was this person that dared to enter her zone? She opened her eyes to see what looked like a cross between an advert for a Brut aftershave and a re-enactment of the "wading out of the water" scene from that James Bond film. A well-built man was paddling towards her, on a white surfboard, as if it were a canoe. He had shoulder length, wavy black hair and almond-shaped eyes, caramel-coloured skin and actually looked more Polynesian than Italian. He slid off the surfboard and waded onto the beach, dragging the board onto the sand.

Suddenly, she realised it was that guy she had seen in the doorway of the Bar Internazionale a few days after she had arrived. They had locked eyes for a second and then he had gone. For some reason, Wendy wanted to hide, or at least cover herself, but there was nothing to hand. She suddenly felt vulnerable and very white and pasty in front of this guy. He looked as if he was a typical Italian playboy, probably had all the girls falling at his feet and most likely had a different girl every week. She looked at him critically, noticing that his stomach wasn't washboard flat. *Well, he's not perfect*, she thought. She was surprised that he wasn't wearing a gold medallion. He smiled vaguely in her direction, probably blinded by her whiteness, she thought, and walked on by.

****

It was hot and humid, even worse at the harbour where there was no shade. Wendy was making her way to the jetty from the middle of the beach, paddling along the shoreline, calf-deep in the salt water. Amanda had a day off and so did Enzo. Gianni could take off time whenever he pleased as he worked for the family business, and Claudia, who didn't work much at all in her mother's clothes shop, had suggested that they take out a *gozzo*, a small wooden boat, and go for a picnic lunch along the coast.

She noticed him from quite a way down the beach. The surfboard guy from the other day was standing on the shore with two other men, one of whom she suddenly recognised as the local traffic warden. *How weird to see a traffic warden in swimming trunks instead of a uniform,* she pondered for a moment. As she drew closer, a small boy darted out in front of her and belly-flopped into the water, splashing her. The surfboard guy lunged out and grabbed the wriggling child. There was a moment of eye contact between them. *"Scusa!"* He apologised, smiling and gesturing at the child. Wendy smiled back and couldn't think of anything to say. For some reason, her heart was pounding in her chest and her stomach was churning. This was ridiculous, she thought, he was short and tanned, not at all her usual type. She was used to tall, pale English men.

She was almost at the dock and was inclined to sit on the shore for a while so that she could surreptitiously watch him for a while to figure out the odd feelings she was having. But the others were waiting, calling and beckoning her to hurry.

A little blue and white wooden boat with a striped sunshade was bobbing next to the dock. The girls were already in bikinis, lying on the cushions on the front of the boat, Amanda looking startlingly pale next to the bronzed goddess that was Claudia. Gianni was at the back, sitting with a guy that Wendy had seen a few times with them. He was tall and skinny, with a shock of dirty blonde hair, and pale as if he didn't spend much time outside. They were fiddling with a portable cassette player that seemed to be trying to eat up a cassette. As they pulled the ribbon out from the machine and tried to wind it back into the cassette, the blonde guy let out a stream of expletives. Enzo was standing on the dock, rope in hand, waiting to help Wendy aboard.

"Sorry I kept you waiting!" She clambered aboard, dumping her bag on the floor with the others and climbing over to the front to sit with the girls. Enzo jumped on board, pulled up the fender and turned the engine on.

And they pulled away from the shore slowly, Wendy leaned over to Claudia and asked, "Claudia, you see that guy on the beach over there with the traffic warden?" Wendy pointed over to where the surfboard guy was still talking with his friends.

Claudia raised her sunglasses and squinted, "Hmm? Yeah?"

"Who is he? Do you know him?"

"*Sì, perche?* Why?"

"No reason, I was just wondering ..." Wendy shrugged, trying to seem uninterested. But Claudia understood immediately.

"Forget it, he's married." She dropped her sunglasses back onto the bridge of her nose and leaned back as if to finish the conversation right there.

"What! No, he can't be!" Wendy was so surprised by this that she forgot to act cool and uninterested.

"Yeah, he's been married for a long time; he has a *bambino*, too." Wendy felt her heart thud into the pit of her stomach. She felt more upset than she should have done, seeing as she didn't even know the guy's name, but resolved to put any further thoughts of him out of her head.

The sea was smooth and transparent, and as the town receded behind them, they could see all the way down to the rocky seabed below. Enzo introduced Wendy to his friend Simone who was now perfectly happy as his cassette player was working again. They drove the boat past a floating bathing platform, a big raft anchored in the middle of the bay. Two ladies in bikinis sat gossiping on the edge, legs dangling in the water. They waved as the boat passed by, and a cheeky boy launched himself off the platform as if trying to jump right into the passing boat. His friends jeered at him as he landed nowhere near and he bobbed back up again, sleek as an otter, comically shaking a dripping fist at the boat.

They passed a smaller beach that was almost deserted. Just a group of kids climbing the rocks to the side of the beach and flinging themselves off with whoops and screams.

Around a cliff, another beach appeared in front of them. The beach was longer here; a few rows of orange and white umbrellas were set out and there was a small, rickety, wooden beach bar on stilts. A stone wall with railings on top separated the beach from a tall, oddly shaped yellow villa surrounded by lush tropical gardens. Huge palm trees dotted a wide lawn and fuchsia bougainvillaea trailed up the side of the building. The rest was hidden from sight by flowering bushes and leafy trees.

"Wow," said Amanda, sitting up, "I've never seen this before, is that a house?"

"Is Arienzo Beach and that," Claudia pointed at the building, "is the old *Mulino* … Enzo? How you say *mulino* in *inglese?*"

Enzo had slowed down and was steering in towards a little dock carved out of the cliff at the side of the beach.

"Is an old mill where they made flour, it is

beautiful, no? We stop here for a few minutes. Simone has a little *servizio* to do, he has to take them something, but will be back very soon, yes Simo?"

"Yes, excuse me, girls, I will be no time at all."

He threw the fender over the side, talking rapidly in Italian to Gianni, jumped out of the boat and jogged over to a gate at the end of the jetty. They all watched as he rang the intercom. After a moment, the gate opened and he disappeared inside.

Claudia sighed and flipped onto her stomach as if it was all just too boring.

"So, is it a house or a hotel?" Amanda asked, looking over to Gianni for an answer.

"Is a private house, is owned by a rich family from Napoli. You must try to go one day, the garden is *bellissimo*. They have a pool like a small lake, is a natural pool with dark water, no blue like a hotel pool. And they have a lawn, very rare in this town!" He shifted from the rudder to the side of the boat to the cassette player and swapped Simone's tape for one of his own. Italian pop music blared out of the speakers, and he turned the volume down so they could hear each other.

"They have parties sometimes," Claudia turned to them, "really good parties. Maybe we go to one this summer."

"What's Simone doing there?" Amanda asked.

"Oh, he just had to deliver something to … *Ecco,*

he is back already!" Enzo stood up as Simone closed the gate behind him and jogged back to the boat.

Simone was from Torre del Greco, a run-down suburb of Naples reaching from the shoreline up onto the slopes of Vesuvius. The town was known for the cameo brooches and jewellery made from the bright red coral that used to be plentiful in the bay. Simone's father had a small coral jewellery business, and in the summer months he would shut up shop in the centre of town and move the whole family to Positano. He had a tiny shopfront on the Main Street that had once been a stable, with room for just one horse, and rented a small, battered apartment in Li Parlati, the older part of town. Simone slept with his brother and two sisters, all together in the one small bedroom and their parents slept on the fold-out bed in the kitchen/living room. This year was different, however; there were only him and his younger sister left, and the bedroom felt quite spacious all of a sudden. His elder brother and sister had both married in the last year and left the family home. His sister was in nearby Praiano with a baby on the way. His brother had stayed in Naples and had taken over the jewellery store there, permitting it to stay open all year round, and their father was very pleased with him.

Simone wasn't really interested in selling or making jewellery. He had always known that the business would be passed on to his elder brother and had resented him for it. He had stubbornly refused to follow in his brother's footsteps and learn how to make the world-famous cameos and coral beads. Instead, he had borrowed some money from his father to buy some cheap trinkets that he was now selling in

89

a small market stall on the street leading down to the beach. Fake coral necklaces, leather wristbands, and friendship bracelets were all the rage this year and he was selling quite well, when he could be bothered to open up the stall.

He only worked when there was nothing else to do. Any opportunity to go out on a boat, spend a day at the beach with friends or any excuse really was always accepted gladly by him. He would sometimes make up for it by opening the market stall in the evenings anyway if there were no social arrangements, which did just as well as the daytime.

Besides, he had recently started up a lucrative little sideline which was proving to be a great success and a much easier way to make money. After a few weeks in their summer home, he had realised that nobody was providing the young townsfolk with marijuana or hashish. This was a great shame as people were having to risk driving to Naples and back every week or so. He had borrowed some money from his parents, a little bit more from his older brother and had invested in a nine bar, that is, nine ounces of plastic-wrapped hashish that he had picked up at a major dealer's home in Torre del Greco. He had actually been terrified the first time he had gone there, not sure who he was about to meet. The guy he bought his personal supply from had taken him to meet the dealer, a short pale man with a shaved head and a huge slobbering Neapolitan Mastiff that eyed Simone dolefully throughout that first meeting. The dealer had wanted to know where he was planning on selling, whether anyone else already worked the area, and had then explained in great detail what would happen to him if he was caught selling on somebody else's patch or if he was caught by the authorities and talked.

Simone had left the meeting with trembling hands, an empty wallet and a nine-bar hidden in his rucksack. But within ten days in Positano, he had sold the lot, doubled what he had spent and gone back for more, buying in as much as he could afford.

He whistled cheerfully as he shut the gate to the Villa and strolled back to the boat where the others were waiting. *Easy money*, he thought happily, earnings made for the day and a boatful of girls in bikinis at his disposal.

They had a fantastic afternoon, anchoring in sapphire bays, jumping off the boat and swimming around rocks slippery with seaweed. They ate lunch on board, sharing slices of spaghetti cake that Claudia had made. Cooked spaghetti was mixed with pieces of salami and mozzarella and then cooked up in a big pan with eggs, like a big spaghetti-filled omelette. It was delicious. Enzo had brought a bag of fresh apricots, ripe and juicy from his uncle's garden. Wendy had never seen fresh apricots before – in England she had only had the dried ones that you could buy in the health food shops at Christmas time.

After lunch, they were sticky with apricot juice and oil and hot from the sun. Enzo anchored the boat near a rocky shoreline and made them all jump in.

"Come with me, I show you a secret cave!" He swam toward the shore and the others followed him in a line. Claudia hung off Gianni's back, laughing and complaining at the same time.

"No, I don't want to go there! Girls, don't follow him, it is cold in there!" Gianni suddenly ducked, taking Claudia under with him. They broke apart and came up splashing water at each other, swearing cheerfully.

The cave was invisible from the sea. They had to climb up onto the rocks and through a narrow crevice which then opened out into a small, dark sea cave with a pool of water at the centre.

"OK," said Enzo, panting slightly as he climbed across to the far side of the cave. "Come inside, but stay above the water. Nobody must touch the water!"

One by one they all squeezed through the crevice and into the grotto. There was just enough room for them to all stand around the edge, feet on rocks just above the water level.

"OK, now what?" Wendy laughed; they all looked so funny, clinging to the rocks with their arms in strange positions to keep them steady.

"Now, when I count to three everybody must put their feet in the water and splash! Really, really hard, okay? Ready…Uno…*due…tre!*"

He plunged his leg into the water and kicked it up towards Claudia who immediately copied him. The water hit them all at the same time and it was freezing! Claudia screamed, Wendy, and Amanda screamed louder, and the boys hooted and bellowed and roared. They kicked and splashed until their legs were numb and they were shivering and worn out from laughing. Finally, they emerged into the bright sunlight, warming up again in a flash as they sat on the rocks outside the cave, panting like a pack of dogs.

"That was hilarious," said Wendy, "Why was it so cold though?"

Gianni placed his still cold foot onto Claudia's stomach, making her jump. "It is a cold spring, water from the mountain stream comes out there. Fun, no?"

They swam back to the boat, using the tiny fold-up ladder to haul themselves back on board. Simone rolled a couple of joints and Enzo cracked open two giant bottles of beer. They smoked and passed around the beers while Bananarama sang about Venus and the sunlight softened into golden sparkles that hit the water like fairy dust.

Chapter 7

Positano, June 1986

"That's it, I've quit."

Amanda slung her bag onto the table and sat down. She then got straight up again, picking up a glass from by the sink and filling it with wine from the fridge before sitting back down.

"Oh dear," Wendy murmured, peeling cucumber for the salad she was making for dinner. "What's happened now?"

Amanda took a big sip of wine and sighed. "It's the bloody father. He summoned me to his antique shop this morning, made me lock up the gallery and walk over there. Then he had the cheek to tell me that I was hanging around with the wrong type of people. He basically said that Enzo and Simone are not good people and that I shouldn't spend time with them anymore. I asked him who he suggested I should be friends with, and he keeps harping on about his son and that creepy nephew of his with no personality, ugh!"

She took another sip of wine and carried on.

"Then, he told me he had 'caught me' talking to that lovely old man from the next shop and that I was behaving very badly. For fuck's sake Wendy, I'm not a child! I have the right to make my own judgements about who I can talk to. I told him that he's got no right to tell me what to do when I'm outside the gallery – it's none of his business. Can you believe he said that it was his business because anything I did would reflect on him?! I told him I would finish the month, which gives them a week to find someone else and then I'm done. Honestly, the people in the shops next door have been nothing but nice to me. There's nothing wrong with them! Or our friends." She downed the last of the wine and slammed the glass back onto the table.

"Sounds like a nightmare. What on earth has he got against everyone?" Wendy pulled the wine out of the fridge, topping up Amanda's glass and pouring one for herself.

"He's just a bitter old man who thinks he owns me. Well, sorry, that is not happening. I'd rather be penniless and sit on the beach for the rest of the summer than have to put up with him spying on me every day."

"OK, well you've done the right thing. I'm

sure we can find you something much better than that anyway. Here, take this," Wendy passed Amanda the salad bowl and a plate of sliced mozzarella and prosciutto, gesturing to the door. "Let's sit out on the terrace, eat and drink some wine and see if we can spot the marching band that's been playing around town all day."

It was the Feast Day of San Vito, the Patron Saint of Positano. The girls were fast learning that every day in Italy was a saint's day, and a lot of them were celebrated. Marching bands, market stalls full of sweets and nuts, and fireworks at midnight seemed to be the norm. Each suburb of the town had its own special Saint's Day to celebrate and many of the people did too, especially those with popular names like Giuseppe or Maria. It was almost like having a second birthday. Both the girls had been peeved to find that neither of their names qualified for a Saint's Day.

They ate at the table under the fairy lights, with citronella candles lit to ward off the mosquitos. The sky faded to peach and then darkened to plum and slowly the houses lit up around them. After dinner was cleared away, they pulled up chairs to the balcony railing and settled in to watch the show.

Down on the beach they could see the band marching past the restaurants and a religious procession from the church that snaked along the shore. An effigy of the saint was being carried along on a pedestal, led by the robed priest and an altar boy in white who swung a pot of incense as he walked. The saint was followed by a gaggle of school children, all dressed in white robes, and a line of townsfolk dressed in their Sunday best walked behind the children. Very sombre chanting floated up the natural amphitheatre from the procession, helped by the loudspeaker that the priest was enthusiastically chanting into.

There were balloon sellers with huge bunches of helium-filled balloons, food stalls and toy stands. Children played on the beach with their balloons tied to their wrists while parents chatted with friends. Groups of teenagers sat on the sand in circles, boxes of pizzas laid out between them. Everyone was now waiting for the evening finale, the fireworks display.

"Do you want to go down for the fireworks?" Wendy asked. She was perfectly happy to sit on the terrace and watch the display but admittedly also felt like she was missing out on the fun by not being down there.

"Nah," replied Amanda. "I'm fine here tonight. There will be other evenings like this. The one not to miss is Ferragosto in mid-August. They do the fireworks from a boat in the sea, and it's supposed to be amazing. We'll go down for that one, for sure!"

By the time the display started the girls were sleepy and almost ready to give up and go to bed. It was just as well they didn't though, as they would have been woken up by the noise. Surely nobody could sleep through such chaos! The explosions were deafening, reverberating and rolling around the mountainside like thunder. The fireworks were bright and colourful, reflecting patterns and hues onto the sea. It looked truly magical with the backdrop of the town clinging to the hillside and the sea below, the village down the coast glimmering with lights in the background. After a few minutes, the display got faster and louder, building up to a crescendo which ended with a resounding bang and then for a few seconds, silence. Somebody whooped and people started cheering and clapping, cars beeped from up on the road and Wendy could hear the sound of scooter engines starting up again and driving off. *They must have all pulled over on the road to watch the display*, she thought, yawning.

The girls blew out the candles and turned off the fairy lights, heading inside to check on Nerone who had squeezed himself under the bed, coaxing him out and giving him some fuss before calling it a night.

Francesco scooped up his son and settled him on his shoulders. He felt little chubby fingers fastening onto his hair and rolled his eyes in good-natured exasperation. Messy hair it was then! Elena was climbing out of the car, fussing about what she should take with them. It was hard to convince her to go out in the evenings, but she would always reluctantly agree to a walk around town when there was a Saint's Day Festival.

He had taken the car down, parking it in the car park in the centre of town and now waited patiently while she gathered together whatever she thought they would need for a simple stroll around the beach. As he waited, he watched the people walking down the road, wondering if he would see that girl again.

He had come across her twice in the last couple of weeks and was now sure that she was not just a passing tourist. But who was she and why was she here? Last week, she had crossed paths with him on the beach. He would have stopped her and asked if she was on holiday, but his son had taken that moment to charge into the sea, splashing her and he'd had to apologise and jump in after the toddler before he went under. By the time he had his son under control, she was long gone. He had watched her jump onto a boat and sail away with some friends, and he thought he had recognised a couple of locals. Maybe he would see her tonight at the festival. Elena slammed the car door and walked over, hefting her bulging hold-all over her shoulder.

"Come on then, let's go down." She smiled her shy smile and they set off.

Down on the beach, the marching band had gathered in the piazza by the lion steps and were playing a rousing version of the national anthem. Leonardo struggled to be put down and Francesco hefted him off his shoulders and set him free. They watched, laughing in amusement and the chunky little boy toddled up to the trombone player and bobbed up and down to the music.

They strolled the length of the beach, stopping to buy a balloon for Leonardo, *pannocchie*, corn on the cobs that had been boiled, then roasted and sprinkled with salt, and bottles of icy cold beer. They sat on the beach to eat, facing the church to watch the crowds pass by. Elena saw her cousin Carmen and waved her over to join them. Another friend drifted over from a group nearby and soon there was a gaggle of local women, all chatting as if they hadn't seen each other for years. Recipes were swapped, stories told, gossip exchanged and Elena seemed to be thoroughly enjoying herself. Leonardo was happily filling plastic buckets with stones, joined by another couple of toddlers and watched by the adoring eyes of all the women.

"Eli?" Francesco interrupted and pulled his wife away for a moment. "Are you okay if I go find Dom and have a chat with him? He must be on duty somewhere nearby."

"Of course, yes, meet me by the steps in an hour if we don't find each other sooner?" Elena gave him a small wave and turned back to her friends.

The light was fading, and the town lights were flickering on one by one. The procession was now making its way down the end of the beach, the way lit by twinkling candles. Everyone was out in their finest clothes, and the air was filled with a heady mix of church incense, candyfloss and roast corn. Francesco wandered through the crowds searching for Dom who he finally found on the jetty, standing tall in his uniform with a big smile on his face.

"*Amico mio*! How's it going? Where have you

left your lovely family this time?" Dom joked as he arrived.

"No fear, they're just over there with a gaggle of mothers and children; there was no place for me amongst them!" Francesco grinned, gesturing back to where he had left them.

Francesco and Dom went to the gym together three times a week. It wasn't really a proper gym with a load of equipment and machines – it was actually the middle school auditorium. There was a set of weights and a bench press, but other than that they had to make up their own exercises. A typical evening at the gym would involve ten minutes of warm-ups where everyone would follow the instructor, running around the room in a figure of eight, flapping their arms, skipping, jumping and kicking up their legs in a bizarre conga line. This was rather amusing to watch, especially when you knew that the other participants included a teacher, a very rich hotel owner, a bank manager and a local policeman.

The warm-up was followed by a few different activities. Dom, Francesco, and a couple of others would usually gravitate to the weights corner and take turns spotting for each other, and the others would concentrate on a mixture of mat work and aerobics for half an hour. After that, they would split into two teams and have a crazy game of volleyball or basketball before all slumping to the floor or on the blue crash mats for a good old gossip which would often end in a heated debate. On Friday evenings they would usually all go out for pizza afterwards. This last Friday, they had ended up at the newly decorated house of the hotel owner and now, on the jetty Francesco and Dom discussed the evening, the décor, and the cost of it all.

"I was just surprised there was so much peach colour! Not at all what I expected for a man like him …" Dom reflected, scanning the crowds, still alert for anything that might need his attention.

"Hmm, a bit too feminine in my opinion. Look, I'd better get back to Elena. See you tomorrow at the gym, yeah?"

"Sure, I'll be there – oh, and I heard that Dario and Astrid are back from Rome for the summer. They'll probably be having a small party next week sometime, you up for it?"

"Sounds great! Their evenings are always fun! Okay, see you tomorrow, Dom, *ciao!*"

He slowly made his way back to his family, scanning the crowds and saluting various acquaintances. He didn't see the girl with the red hair – maybe she had just been on a long holiday. All for the best, really; he had no idea why he kept thinking of her, he had no business to be doing so. He found Elena just saying goodbye to her cousins and they strolled over to the sun loungers together to sit and watch the fireworks in comfort.

Chapter 8

Positano, June 1986

"Hello, my dear, have you both settled in okay?" Lily, the old doctor's wife with the jangly bracelets found Amanda standing by the crates of fruit stacked outside the greengrocers, trying to juggle a bag of shopping, five yellow peaches, and Nerone, who was pulling on the lead trying to sniff something in the corner. She took a paper bag from a pile that Amanda hadn't noticed, hidden between the oranges and bananas, and gestured at the peaches.

"Oh, thank you!" Amanda dropped the peaches one by one into the bag and put the heavy shopping bag down on the floor.

"Nerone, sit! Why on earth don't they have shopping baskets here? Sorry! Yes, thank you, it's going pretty well. I'm still looking for a job actually ... well, I did have one, but it didn't really work out, so I'm looking again."

"Still looking, hmm? I might have something for you. How about your friend, I've heard on the grapevine she is working on the tour boats?"

"Yes, she's really enjoying it ... definitely got the best deal there, lucky thing!" Amanda was now juggling a bunch of carrots, complete with stems and leaves, lettuce, and a bunch of peppery rocket, something she had never seen in England but here was used as a garnish and in *panini* and salads and anywhere you wanted, it seemed.

Lily opened up another paper bag for the carrots and rocket. "Just put everything you want to buy in a pile somewhere. Look, the counter is free, put it all there." She took the lettuce and the bag of peaches and placed them on the tiny counter in front of the shopkeeper. The shop was so small that not more than three people could fit inside, including the shopkeeper. It was piled high with crates of vegetables and fruits and big plastic trays of mixed fresh breads in which one could rummage around to choose between baguettes, *focaccia, rosette,* and *pane cafone.*

While Amanda paid for her items, Lily chose a small piece of *pane cafone,* the local bread that was so soft on the inside and beautifully hard and crunchy on the outside. She carefully extracted a bunch of sweet cherry tomatoes, all still attached to the vine, and placed them gently in a bag and then chose six perfectly ripe apricots, blushed with pink, smooth and unblemished with a few leaves still attached.

Amanda waited while she paid, counting out a few small thousand lire notes and placing her purchases into a string bag.

"Come on, my dear, I'll walk down with you. I need to stop by the cobbler's anyway and I can tell you all about this job that I have in mind."

They walked down the road, past the little public garden that was so tiny it hardly qualified as a verge, let alone a public garden, and took the shortcut down a set of steps, past a black and white cat cleaning itself on a wall decorated with pieces of broken ceramic tiles like a patchwork blanket. The cat stiffened when it saw Nerone, but he couldn't have been less interested, and it relaxed again as he bumbled past.

As they walked, Lily told Amanda about Antonio. A flamboyant young clothes designer with a little shop on the beachfront who needed an assistant. He was extremely irresponsible, and prone to tantrums but great fun and made the most wonderful clothes. "He's an absolute darling but also a complete *primadonna*, although I'm sure you would have fun with him. Now, if you like I can have a word with him this afternoon and you could pass by to meet him this evening. He will be in the shop until late."

"If you don't mind, that would be wonderful. Thank you so much!" Amanda quite liked the idea of being the assistant of a flamboyant fashion designer. She promised Lily she would pop along to the shop that evening and left her outside the cobbler's, which was a house just opposite Rob and Ted's. Every morning from 9 am until lunchtime, an old man would sit outside the front door, pulling his table and chair out onto the postage stamp sized patio, where he would sit and mend shoes and boots brought to him by the townsfolk.

She let herself into the house and called out

to let Wendy know she was back, but there was no answer so she must have gone out. Nerone followed her downstairs and flopped onto his bed by the giant bread oven, one eye open while she put the shopping away. She made herself a cup of tea and sat there wondering what one wore for a job interview with a fashion designer?

The shop was in a narrow lane that ran under the shadow of the church and came out at the lion steps leading down to the beach. The alleyway was crammed with little clothes shops, the wares hanging so thickly on hooks outside that it was easy to snag yourself on a frilly bikini or a linen shirt and accidentally knock it all to the ground. The first thing she noticed as she walked into the shop was the big picture window at the far end with a fantastic sweeping view right over the beach. The second thing she noticed was the smell of marijuana. There didn't seem to be anybody there but then she noticed a puff of smoke drifting out from over a partition that led to the back of the store. The stereo was pumping out a song by a husky Italian singer who could have been male or female, drowning out any other sounds

"*Buonasera?*" She called out, hovering in the middle of the shop. Over the music she heard a toilet flush and a throat being cleared.

"*Chi é?* Who's there?" A young man walked out from behind the partition and looked enquiringly at Amanda. He was about the same height as her, slightly built and dressed in matching cornflower blue trousers and top, accessorised by a bright yellow belt and yellow wristbands. His hair was cut into a fashionable mullet, not too long at the back but fantastically bouffant on the top and his eyes were slightly red, presumably from the joint he had been smoking a moment ago.

"*Sei l'amica di Lily*? You are the friend of Lily, am I right? She told me you would come to meet me. Or am I wrong, and you are here to buy a fabulous dress from me?" He slapped his hands on his thighs and let out a laugh, then turned around and disappeared behind the partition again.

The volume suddenly lowered and he popped back out again, "Aah, now we can talk without shouting! Come sit." He led her over to a burnt orange sofa which sat under the big picture window and patted the seat next to him.

"Lily told me you need an assistant?" Amanda asked as she sat down, moving aside a big straw hat that was in her way.

"I need a whole tribe of assistants, that would be best! But *purtroppo*, unfortunately, I can only permit myself one, and dear Sabrina is very inconveniently having a baby and has left me to fend for myself. Do you think you can look after me?"

"Er … well, can you give me an idea of what I would have to do?"

He jumped up and ducked behind the partition again. From where she was sitting, she could see that there was a changing room, a little storage rail for clothes, the hi-fi system and on the back of the partition wall, a little shelf jutted out. Antonio picked up a few things from the shelf and came to sit down on the sofa again.

"Oh, you know. I need someone to organise my diary, to tell me what I am doing every day. Wake me up in the mornings …" He guffawed again, "No, don't worry, I am joking, my mother will do that." As he was speaking, he had taken two cigarette papers out and was sticking them together to make an extra-long one. "I need someone to be here in the mornings. I just cannot get up early so I want someone in the shop, which is also my office, from 9.30 to 3.30."

"So, basically, you want a shop assistant?" Amanda grinned, finding it funny the way he didn't want to use those words.

He had taken a bit of tobacco out of a pouch and was now mixing a hefty sprinkling of grass into the tobacco in a smooth polished coconut shell.

"*Ma no*, but no! Don't call it that, *cara mia*, it is so dull like that. Anyway, you will be doing other things for me, too. Now, let's smoke this and we can discuss the terms … *OH DIO*! You do smoke, don't you?"

This time Amanda laughed, took the joint out of his hand and lit it. She was pretty sure that this job was going to be much more interesting than the last.

Chapter 9

Positano, June 1986

As soon as she walked into the room, she saw him. The surfboard guy was sitting at the table having an animated conversation with the tall traffic warden who had been at the beach with him. *He's married*, she reminded herself, *he's out of bounds*. But another little voice in her head chirped up, *He is lovely to look at though, isn't he?* She ignored it and walked out of the room into the garden.

They had been invited to a dinner party in Praiano, the village down the coast that sparkled like a jewel set in the mountain at night-time. The house was at the top of the village, up a narrow road that zigzagged up, past a tiny church and eventually petered out into a dirt trail.

They arrived en masse by scooter, five bikes with ten passengers, the wind streaming through their hair and the warm air caressing their bare arms. Gianni and Claudia were leading the group. Simone, who had gone on the boat trip with them, had offered to take Wendy. Amanda was with Enzo, and there were another two boys following behind. Wendy had been surprised to see a fifth bike pull up just as they were leaving, with

Maria from work and Matteo, the fishmonger's son from the beach. Matteo had been at school with Gianni and Enzo, and apparently they were all good friends.

As they drove along the coast, the sun was setting and the sea looked magical, reflecting the pink of the sky. The air was thick with the scent of jasmine flowers and the cicadas were singing from the trees. *It's exhilarating travelling like this*, Wendy thought, smiling as Enzo passed by waving, with Amanda clinging on behind him. *Beats the stuffy London Underground, any day.*

The garden was shady and overgrown; rosebushes fought for space with giant birds of paradise plants and a yellow plum tree stood heavy with fruit in a corner. A string of lights was draped above the path and a couple of old gas lamps were lit and balanced on rocks amongst the flowerbeds. An old brick pathway led a curved path through the foliage to a small fountain, more of a bird bath, really. Wendy trailed her hand in the tinkling water and turned back to look at the house. It was hard to tell how big it was – like most houses here, it was partially built into the mountainside and who knows how far back it went. She could see that it was two floors high, painted a lemon yellow with bottle green shutters and doors. The door she had stepped out of led to the kitchen and was crowded with terracotta plant pots full of bright geraniums. There was a big fuchsia hydrangea bush growing by the wall and then another big sliding door that led to a sitting room.

"*Tutto bene qui fuori?*" A tiny lady appeared from the darkness behind the plum tree, a basket full of golden plums hooked over her arm. Her strawberry blonde hair was tied in a loose plait and draped over one shoulder. She was dressed in an Indian cotton kaftan, paisley swirls of purples and pinks with a touch of blue and two tassels with tiny bells on the ends that tinkled when she moved.

"Is everything okay out here?" she repeated in perfect English, tilting her head sideways.

"Oh yes," Wendy replied, smiling, "I was just admiring the garden. I haven't seen many gardens since I've been here." She suddenly realised that this was most likely the owner of the house and she, Wendy, was a complete stranger standing in her garden. "I'm sorry, I forgot to introduce myself. I'm Wendy Morris, I was invited by Claudia and Gianni."

The lady seemed completely unfazed to find a stranger in her garden and responded warmly. "Hello, my dear, I am Astrid, and it is my pleasure to have you here. Now, just make yourself at home, it's all very informal here as you will see. Plum?" She picked a yellow plum from the basket and gave it a quick rub on her sleeve before offering it to Wendy.

"Thank you!" She accepted the fruit and rolled it surreptitiously in her hand to check for wormholes before taking a bite. It was juicy and sweet, the skin slightly tart and juice dripped down her chin and onto her foot. "Mmmm, good!" She shoved the rest into her mouth to stop any more drips and then realised that she couldn't speak until she had discreetly spat the stone into her hand and swallowed the rest. Astrid took the basket over to the kitchen door and called for

Gianni to take it from her.

Maria and Matteo stepped outside. Matteo paused to pass the basket through the doorway, and Maria and Astrid exchanged kisses. "*Ciao*, Wendy," Maria briefly glanced over to acknowledge her, threading her arm through Matteo's and dragging him away into the garden.

Back inside, there was a flurry of activity. Huge pots were bubbling away on the stove being tended to by Enzo. Claudia was leaning over his shoulder, adding a sprinkling of salt, and the two boys that had driven with them were standing by the sink cleaning what looked like three big squids that had been supplied by Matteo from that morning's catch. The kitchen was dark and rustic; wooden beams traversed the ceilings, studded with hooks from which hung bunches of dried tomatoes, plaited onions and garlic, and a string of chilli peppers. A cassette player blasted out songs by The Cure and those standing were dancing while they worked. A big wooden kitchen table stood over by the window and Wendy noted that the surfboard guy was still sitting there, now talking to Simone and Astrid. He glanced up and looked straight at her, making her heart pound. Flustered, she broke her gaze with him, turning to find his friend the traffic warden handing out glasses of red wine with slices of peaches from a huge jug. He offered one to Wendy with a smile, "*Ciao!* Here, some sangria. I am Dom."

"Oh, thank you, Dom, I'm Wendy …" She didn't know what else to say but was saved by Amanda, who sidled up next to her.

"Can I get a glass of that too, please?"

"*Subito*! Immediately!" Dom handed her a glass. "You are Amanda, no? I remember you!"

"You do?" Amanda was stumped – where had she met him?

"What? You don't remember me?" Dom pretended to be offended. "Hmm, let me see. I remember a little blonde girl standing on a big rock at Laurito Beach, too scared to jump into the sea. She had a pink swimsuit with a little skirt on it like a ballerina and was very cute. So, I had to be her prince and hold her hand. She told me she would marry me one day … Have you changed your mind?" He winked at Wendy.

Amanda had gone bright red but pulled herself together, taking a gulp of wine and nonchalantly replying, "Well, we'll have to see about that," before turning, swishing her hair and stalking away.

Astrid called Dom over to help pull down a stack of plates from a high shelf and someone started clearing the table. Outside the door, a grill had been lit and the scent of grilled seafood was wafting through the kitchen. A couple of older men wandered in and were greeted enthusiastically by everyone.

Loaves of bread were being sliced, Enzo was grating a huge chunk of parmesan cheese, and Claudia was holding a giant sieve over the sink as Gianni tipped the big pot of pasta into it to drain the water. Wendy glanced again towards the table only to find the surfboard guy watching her again. He smiled at her. *Jesus*, she thought, *don't smile at me like that, you're a married man, it's not decent!* His smile was devastatingly sexy – why on earth did his wife let him loose in public like that, and where was the elusive woman, anyway?

"*La cena e pronta*, dinner is ready!" Enzo roared, nudging Wendy out of the way as he took a steaming bowl over to the table. More bowls and plates of food appeared, and everyone started to squeeze around and find places to sit. Another smaller table was brought in and a few more chairs were found. Maria and Matteo came in from the garden and sat at the smaller table, promptly followed by Gianni and Claudia who patted the seat next to her, looking questioningly at Wendy. She sat down quickly, relieved that she didn't have to sit opposite the surfboard guy and his dangerous smile.

Dinner was simple and delicious. *Tubetti e totani*, a much-loved local dish of short pasta tubes with pink squid cooked in a tomato sauce with a touch of chilli pepper. It was served in ladlefuls from the big steaming bowl and plates were passed over heads and past faces. Two of the boys took their plates outside and ate while manning the grill. When the pasta was finished, Gianni showed Wendy how to do *la scarpetta*, clean her plate for the next course by wiping it down with a piece of fresh crusty bread.

"See, like this!" He scooped up the remains of the pasta sauce onto his crust and popped it in his mouth. Wine flowed and soon they ran out. One of the elder men with a beard and a brown waistcoat was sitting next to Astrid who turned out to be her husband, Dario. He got up, grabbing a flashlight and an empty demijohn.

"Vado trovare il vino! I'm off to find wine!" He grabbed Amanda by the arm, "Come, I'll show you where Astrid hides it all!" Lewd comments and cheers flew around the room followed by hoots of laughter when Amanda grabbed Wendy as they passed by, dragging her along, too.

Outside it was cooler and the quietness was deafening. Dario comically tiptoed around the side of the house, holding his finger against his lips, shushing the girls.

"You have to be very, very quiet! Astrid's wine store is a big secret – you must not let anybody see you!"

He led them down a set of steps into a dark basement and clicked on the flashlight. Dom suddenly appeared quietly behind them, holding another demijohn and smiling. In the basement was a row of four big wooden barrels, each with a tap at the bottom. Dario stopped and scratched his head, "Hmm, which is the one?"

"The second one," Dom replied, "or if you want white, the next one."

Dario pulled a face at Dom and turned to the girls, "He know too much, that one!" He placed the demijohn under the tap of the second barrel and turned it on. A stream of red wine came out and Amanda gasped.

"These barrels are all full of wine? That's crazy! How much is there?" She could smell it now; the scent of fermented grapes rose from the barrel, mixing with the slight odour of mildew from the damp basement.

"We have grapevines up in the hills and make *il vino* every year. These barrels have five hundred litres each. It is good for all year! Also, good for parties, no?"

"Wonderful," murmured Wendy, trying to imagine having two thousand litres of wine stored under her house.

They filled the demijohns, laughing as Dario tried to drink out of the running tap and ended up with wine up his nose and in his beard. Shaking his head and sneezing, he closed up the cellar and they went back to the kitchen.

"*Finalmente, il vino!*" Someone shouted and glasses were refilled, and the food was passed around until it was finished. There were platters of grilled prawns and calamari, a bowl of octopus salad and plates of fried *alici*, anchovies which had been filleted and cut lengthways before being stuffed with mozzarella and rolled in breadcrumbs. It was loud and hectic, nobody sat still, everyone kept moving seats and conversations kept changing and were never really finished. Astrid suddenly stood up, which didn't make much difference as she was so short.

"I want some real music!" She reached behind her where a rather large tambourine was hanging off a nail on the wall, and taking it down, she shook it above her head. Everybody whooped and cheered and the man that had arrived with Dario pulled a dark box out from under the table. Somebody turned off the stereo and those sitting near Dario shuffled back to make room. Maria, who had ended up sitting at the big table, started to clear the plates away. The dark box contained an accordion, beautifully lacquered in red and black, and he started playing as soon as he lifted it gently out of the box. Astrid accompanied him with her tambourine and Enzo dashed off to another room, coming back with a smaller tambourine bedecked with ribbons and joined in, too. The songs were traditional Neapolitan folk music, obviously known and loved by all. Everyone joined in singing and spoons were drummed in time on the tabletop. The wine was flowing and someone had lit a joint; the smell of marijuana wafted around like a snake. Astrid was up dancing, swinging her tambourine around the room and Claudia was dancing with the two boys from the grill. Wendy watched in awe as the usually sullen Maria, straight-faced and calm, slipped off her shoes and climbed up onto the table, proceeding to dance the tarantella, stamping her foot and flinging her arms with abandon, cheered on by all the men.

It was getting hot and stuffy in the room and Wendy's head was beginning to spin from the wine and the smoke, so she stepped outside for a moment and took a few breaths of fresh air. Claudia and Gianni spun past her, dashing off into the darkness, giggling, and Simone appeared with a bag of rubbish that he propped up in a corner. She was about to walk back inside again but the surfboard guy suddenly stepped out of the door and smiled at her.

Simone looked from one to the other. "You two have met? No? Wendy, this is Francesco, Francesco, this is Wendy from England" And with that, he walked back inside.

They stood there under the glow of the lantern light by the rosebush and just looked at each other for a moment longer than necessary.

"Ciao Wendy, come stai?" Francesco said softly.

Wendy suddenly felt incredibly flustered and couldn't remember if she should have replied *bene* or *buono, grazie* and ended up switching to English.

"Oh, I'm good thanks, this is such a nice evening, it's so pretty in the garden, isn't it? Oh, I'm sorry, do you speak English at all? It's just that my Italian is not very good yet and I get embarrassed that I'll make terrible mistakes."

He laughed and nodded, "Yes, we can speak either, I don't mind. So, tell me how come you are here in Positano? I have seen you around a few times now."

"I'm here with my friend Amanda, the blonde one in there," she waved back towards the house and he nodded, "for the summer. We're dog-sitting for someone. I think I saw you at the bar the other day with a lot of lemons, is that right?" She swiftly directed the conversation back to him, hoping to find out more about who he was and whether he was really married or not.

A peal of laughter rang out from inside and someone darted past them brandishing an empty jug.

"Yes, I remember you there," he replied, the

corners of his eyes crinkling in delight. "I was just delivering lemons to the bar, I do this every day. My family, we have lemon groves above Positano and we sell to all the restaurants and hotels, and I do the deliveries."

"You have lemon groves?" She was delighted, "That is, like, the dream life, living on the Amalfi Coast with lemon groves all around you! Do you make limoncello, too?"

He laughed, "Of course we do! It is all part of the job."

"Amazing! So, do you live up there, by the groves?" Wendy watched his face for any change of expression, hoping to get some information about his family.

"Yes, we are very lucky. My father has a house near the road which is where I grew up and when I decided to marry, we built a small, how you say, cottage?" Wendy nodded. "A small cottage up in the groves which is where I live with Elena and our little boy, Leonardo, who you have seen on the beach, no?"

Wendy wasn't sure how she felt. He had admitted straight away that he was married. Her heart plunged a bit, but she was at the same time relieved that he was being honest.

"So how long have you been married for? You're quite young to be married aren't you?"

Francesco sighed and for a moment he looked

sad, but quickly altered his expression to hide it.

"I suppose so. We have been together since we were 16 and married since we were 24, so, yes, we were young." He could tell what she was going to ask next and preempted her. "I'm 32 now, so, yes, a long time. Okay, now tell me how old are you and is it true you are a fisherwoman? I have heard you are working on a fishing boat!"

Wendy laughed, although she was still processing the fact that he was seven years older than her. Her mother had always told her to find a man seven years older as it was the perfect match maturity-wise to a woman.

"I'm 24 and yes, I'm a fisher woman, but not really! Back in England I'm a beauty therapist , um, you say *estetista* in Italian, but here I'm working as a hostess on the big fishing boat that goes out at night-time. It's just for the summer – definitely different than what I usually do!" She took a deep breath and asked the question that she was most curious about.

"So, why is your wife not here tonight with you?"

Again, a moment of sadness flickered over his face. He gestured away from the house, "Let's walk around the garden and I tell you."

They strolled through the garden, ducking past the plum trees and rows of tomato vines, hidden amongst shafts of flickering light from the house.

"I love my wife very much; we have been together forever and maybe we are now more like friends than lovers, you know?. In the last few years she has changed. Since Leonardo was born, Elena is happy to stay at home."

Wendy looked at him questioningly, "But?"

He sighed, "I feel bad talking like this, but it is true. She is happy to stay at home – she does not want to go out anymore and this makes me sad. I want to be with someone who wants to participate in life with me, not just be waiting at home for me at the end of the day. She won't go to the beach anymore; I have to take Leo by myself. You saw that, no?" Wendy nodded in agreement.

"I like to go to the gym, to the beach, and sometimes to eat in a restaurant and I enjoyed doing all that with her but now, since Leo, she is not interested. I miss the company. I wanted her to come tonight, but she refused! My dream is to share my life with someone who enjoys doing the same things as me, not to tell them what I did at the end of the day. And here I am alone, but I am sorry, you did not need to hear all that"

"Oh, that's okay, it's my fault for asking you. I'm sorry."

They had arrived back at the house. Claudia and Gianni were stumbling tipsily back from a dark corner, saying that they really had to get back home, as it was getting late.

"We better go back inside, but it was lovely t⌐

talk with you." Wendy smiled at Francesco and then Claudia arrived, linking arms with Wendy, and they all went back inside.

More time had passed than Wendy had realised. Matteo and Maria had left already and so had Enzo and Amanda. *Hmmm, is something developing there?* she wondered. She kissed Astrid goodbye and thanked her for the evening, looking around for Simone but he seemed to be gone already. She stepped outside and went over to the gate to see if his scooter was there. It wasn't and now Gianni was driving away too, Claudia clinging onto him like a koala, drunkenly crooning in his ear.

Someone called her name and she turned to see Dom and Francesco (much nicer than Surfboard Guy) walking up behind her.

"Leaving already?" Francesco called to her, "Do you want a lift?" He gestured at a black car parked on the side of the road.

A lift with him? She hesitated. Was it acceptable to be seen in the car of a married man here? Would people talk, this being a small village? Was it safe, would he try anything? She decided to risk it as she had no other way of getting back to Positano and it was late, so there probably weren't too many people around. She relaxed slightly when she realised that Dom was coming in the car too.

Just be normal, she told herself. *Stupid girl, you've got a crush on a married man and there's no way anything will ever happen. Besides, he's far too good looking for you.*

He's just being kind, giving you a lift home.

"You sit in the front," Dom offered gallantly, "it's best so you don't get sick with his crazy driving!"

As they reached the outskirts of Positano, Francesco pulled over to let Dom out. She was now alone in a car with him and all she could think about was what it would be like to kiss him. It wasn't going to happen, *get a grip woman!* The atmosphere was tense, and she wondered if he could feel it too. He turned the volume up; Queen was chanting "Radio Ga Ga." She told him to drop her off at the Bar Internazionale, and he pulled over and got out of the car with her. The bar was closed, and the street was deserted. She walked over to the wall opposite the bar and looked at the view of the coast with Praiano glittering in the distance and the moon hanging high above, casting a trail of silver across the sea. She rummaged in her bag and pulled out her camera. She had hardly used it while she had been here but wanted to record this moment. She took a photo of the view, knowing that it would always remind her of this evening and turned to thank him for the lift, carefully avoiding getting too close to him. She said goodbye and walked away determinedly, hurrying down to the steps. She had never wanted to kiss someone so badly, and she had an idea that she wasn't the only one thinking that. The atmosphere in the car, even the way he looked at her! This was dangerous territory, and she had no intention of acting on her feelings. How could he be married? It felt so wrong. She unlocked the door and walked downstairs, through the kitchen and onto the balcony. Looking up towards the mountain, she could just see the headlights of a solitary car driving up to

Montepertuso. She watched until it vanished between the trees.

Cornwall
September 2016

"Mum, stop a minute." It was getting dark outside. Mia had sat patiently all afternoon listening to her mum reminisce about Italy but was still no nearer to learning anything about her father apart from the fact that he once carried a tray full of lemons into a bar and innocently gave her mother a lift home one evening.

"I know, love, you think I'm rambling, but I just want you to understand the whole story. It's not just about your father, there's more to it and I'm just telling you how it all happened."

"Yeah, okay, but first of all tell me, please, mum – is my dad the surfboard guy? And is he still alive?"

"Yes, love, and yes of course he is."

"So, basically, you had an affair with a married man, and I'm the result of that affair?"

"Well, yes, in a nutshell, but …"

"Mum! You do realise you could have told me all this years ago. I'm a sensible adult you know. You're not the first person to have slept with a married man!"

"Yes, I know that Mia, but other things

126

happened that summer. Just let me finish telling you what happened, it's time you knew the whole story."

At that moment, they heard the front door open. A couple of guests had returned, and Wendy jumped up to switch on the lights. The kitchen door opened, too, and Josh came barrelling in like a wet whirlwind, trying to get to the laundry room before his wetsuit dripped too much across the kitchen floor. They heard him dump it in the big ceramic sink and flip the water on to rinse it before he reappeared, pushing his hair out of his eyes.

"Mum! I'm hungry, what's for dinner?"

Wendy tried to grab him for a hug, but he wriggled out and headed for the biscuit tin.

"Love, we'll have to put the storytelling on hold. Can you give me a hand with the vegetables, please?"

Mia sighed, knowing that she was going to have to wait even longer to hear the story. This was going to take forever, but she had an idea.

Mia was much more spontaneous than her mother. She was known for seizing the day and just going with her feelings. Mum was more cautious – she always thought through her ideas and planned things out before going ahead with them. Like moving to Cornwall. She had sat everyone down and laid out a spreadsheet of her ideas, costs and possibilities, including property brochures of places that were suitable for her needs. Even though this was her lifelong dream, she hadn't gone ahead and done anything until she was sure that they were all on board.

Mia thought back to when she had followed Mum down to Cornwall. She had been happily living with her boyfriend Tom in a small flat in Clapham. Tom was a computer engineer or something – to be honest, Mia had never really understood what he did at work, apart from the fact that it paid well and was terribly boring. Mia had been working as a transmission controller. A job that hardly anyone knew about that at first had seemed extremely exciting, but in truth was also well-paid but terribly boring.

A transmission controller was the person who was responsible for putting television channels on air. She had fallen into the job as an assistant controller, straight out of university where she had studied Television and Broadcast and had been so excited to be earning a proper salary that she hadn't really thought about whether she was enjoying it or not.

She worked in a small dark room in the basement of the Broadcast House. There was an engineer and a tape librarian on shift with her and she had worked her way up from being the assistant to having an assistant. Mia was the youngest transmission controller that had ever worked there, and she had been so proud. She had the power to put a TV station on or off air, and direct microphone contact with the station presenters and newsreaders in the studios above. She sat in front of wall-to-wall monitors with a panel of buttons and levers in front of her that would not look out of place at NASA's Mission Control.

But to be honest, it was extremely boring. She

worked twelve-hour shifts, night and day, and rarely had contact with other people in the offices above. There were no windows in the basement; she never knew if it was sunny or raining, day or night, and the night shifts were the worst. She would get home, exhausted at ten in the morning and wouldn't know whether to eat breakfast or dinner. And waking up in the late afternoon, she would be so disorientated that sometimes she feared she had amnesia.

On one of the rare days off that had coincided with one of Tom's days off, they had driven away from the city and down to Windsor. Meeting up with a couple of Tom's friends that were newly married, they'd all had a lovely lunch by the river and a walk through the Great Park. On the way home, Tom had mentioned that maybe they should think about getting married and Mia had silently recoiled.

At that moment, without any further doubt, she knew that none of this was what she wanted. It took her a few more days to pluck up the courage to call it off with Tom. He was heartbroken and angry, but she knew he'd get over it and she had no regrets. She handed in her notice at work and worked out the rest of her time there happier than she had ever been because she knew it was ending soon.

She could have taken a year out and gone travelling, but she didn't want to be alone anymore. The job had been very lonely and she missed her family, and so she decided to go and spend some time with Mum and Josh and see what all the fuss was about in Cornwall. Of course, she loved it and never looked back. Tom had moved on and was now happily married to a girl that worked in his office, and their first baby was on the way. Mia had been gloriously single and loving it for the last few years.

Now, the morning after Mum had started telling her about how she came to be, although it seemed that part of the story was still a long way off, Mia sat down and, without thinking too much about the consequences, booked two air tickets to Naples for her and Mum, departing in five days' time.

She sat back and stared at the computer screen as the confirmation email pinged into her inbox. She then picked up her phone and dialled the long number that she had copied from her mother's old address book last night before she came back to the cottage.

It rang, two long foreign sounding tones before someone picked up and a female voice answered, *"Pronto?"*

"Yes, hello, is that Amanda or … Jess? I can't tell. It's Mia from England."

"Hi, Mia! It's Jess actually, but everyone always says they can't tell us apart on the phone. Did you want to talk to me or Mum?"

"Actually, I wanted a quick word with your mum if she's there?"

"Hang on, she's somewhere outside, I'll go get her. MUM, it's Mia in England!"

Across the phone lines, Mia could hear the

sound of Jess running into the garden; she could hear Italian birds in the trees and then she heard Amanda take the phone from her daughter and greet her.

"Mia, darling! Is everything all right?"

"Yes, don't worry, nothing bad has happened. Look, I need to ask you a favour. Mum got your letter and is in the process of telling me who my father is. She's taking bloody ages, so I still don't know much about it, but I've decided to hurry things along and I've just booked tickets to come and visit. She's going to kill me when I tell her, but can we stay at yours? Mum probably won't leave your house, so you'll have to put up with her all day long"

"Oh Mia, you are naughty! She is not going to be happy with you at all, is she? Well, of course, you can stay, you are both always welcome here but what if she refuses to come?"

"Then I'll just come on my own, of course!"

Mia had passed a sleepless night mulling over what her mother had already told her. She knew that with the distractions of Josh and the guests it could take ages to get the whole story out of her. Her father was alive and well and living in a town on the Amalfi Coast! Did she want to meet him? She wasn't sure, but she certainly wanted to see the town, get an idea of what it was like there and maybe see him from afar, to get an idea of what he was like. It probably meant that she had a load of blood relatives out there too.

She was probably making a terrible mistake in

booking the tickets, but she felt like it was the right thing to do. After all, if her mum was going to confess everything to her, she might as well show her the place where it all happened.

Oh God, Mum was going to kill her when she told her about the tickets!

Chapter 10

Positano, July 1986

"The oil has to be very, very hot. It has to melt the tomatoes, no wait, more hot. Put the chilli pepper in the oil first."

Enzo was giving the girls a cooking lesson, just a simple *spaghetti pomodoro* for now.

Amanda had come home from work full of tales about the flamboyant Antonio and how he had been bitten by a carriage horse in Sorrento. It wasn't a bad bite, just a bruise really, but he had decided that because of it he wouldn't be able to go to the beach for a few days. Instead, he was hanging out in the shop, smoking himself silly and dressing Amanda up in the clothes and instructing her to pose like a mannequin when clients walked in.

"Why would being bitten by a horse stop you from going to the beach?" Wendy wasn't concentrating. She had bumped into Francesco earlier at the bar and against her best intentions had ended up sitting and chatting with him for a while. He was so easy to talk to, and she was irresistibly drawn towards him and was consequently angry with herself for feeling this way.

She had gone in to get a coffee and found Francesco standing at the bar, chatting with an elderly man with trembling hands. His face had lit up when he saw her, and his eyes crinkled in delight.

"Wendy, what a pleasure! Can I get you a coffee? Come, sit here and I will join you!"

He pulled out a chair for her at a table in the corner and signalled the barman for another coffee. He slid into the bench seat opposite her, their eyes locked, and it felt like time stood still for a moment. He smiled and she broke eye contact, looking down at her hands, perturbed by the feelings a simple look could stir up in her.

"How have you been? I was hoping to see you the other day. I delivered some lemons to the fishermen for the night fishing but maybe it was too early for you."

"You were at the boat? Oh, what a shame, but I don't go down until about six mostly." She blushed – *he'd been hoping to see her!*

"I'll remember to come later next time then." He smiled that smile again and she couldn't help but smile back.

"How is your little boy," she asked pointedly, reminding them both that he had a family.

"Oh, he's fine, he's at the nursery this morning. Are you working later this evening?"

134

"No, not tonight. I'm having dinner with friends."

"Oh, but you must come up to the Festa tonight, get your friends to take you. It will be a lovely evening." His hand brushed against hers as he moved his empty coffee cup on the table, and she felt a jolt of connection. Her cheeks flushed and they gazed at each other for a moment before she moved her hand away.

He stood and pushed the chair under the table. "I have to get back to my deliveries but I hope to see you tonight, Wendy."

"Wendy!" Enzo shouted at her, waving a giant tomato in front of her face."

"Sorry! Yes, I'm listening!" She picked up a knife and saluted him with it. Enzo had brought a bag of *pomodori insalate*, bigger than beef tomatoes and had used one tomato per person, chopping them into cubes, swearing they would never again use tinned tomatoes if they learnt this recipe.

On the kitchen counter were a couple of cloves of garlic, squashed by slamming the olive oil bottle down on them, a bunch of fragrant basil leaves, a chunk of hard *Parmigiano Reggiano* cheese, and on the hob, a pot of spaghetti was already bubbling away.

"OK, it's hot enough now, put the garlic in the pan and then the tomatoes. You want to hear them hissing like angry cats!" Wendy obediently tipped the chopping board over the pan and the tomatoes hissed and spat hot drops of oil at her. She jumped back and landed on Amanda's foot. Amanda yelped and waved a potato masher at her threateningly.

"OK now, Amanda, use that to *schiacciare* the *pomodori*, squash the tomatoes, yes in the pan, just like that ..." Enzo nodded as Amanda attacked the tomatoes. The hot oil pretty much melted the tomatoes, but the masher helped reduce the size of the lumps, turning it into a sauce in a couple of minutes. Enzo added a liberal sprinkling of salt and wrestled the masher out of Amanda's hands.

"Ok, *basta*, enough. Now we let it cook for two minutes and we see."

"Are you coming up to the *festa* afterwards?" Amanda asked the others. There was a festival up in Montepertuso that evening, and the girls had been told they should go by various people around town. There would be a torchlit procession and a re-enactment of a local legend using fireworks to show how the Virgin Mary fought against the Devil and created the big hole in the mountain above the village.

"Er, yes, if you're going." That morning, Wendy had found out that Francesco, who lived up in Montepertuso, would be there too. She hadn't been up there yet and was now curious to see what the village was like.

Enzo shook his head, "I seen it many many times. I have things to do tonight. I have to meet a friend there but I will not stay." He turned back to the pan and gave the contents a stir.

"Now, it is good, see how it is already like a sauce? We put some grated cheese into it, no, I do it." Enzo brushed Wendy's hand away and grated the cheese directly into the pan, "You stir." She stirred as he grated and watched as the sauce lightened in colour and started to smell amazing.

"*Perfetto*, is done! Now we put the *basilico* ..." He took a few leaves from the bunch and tore them in two, scattering them into the sauce. "See girls, is very easy, you cannot make a mistake with this salsa. You can also make with the small tomatoes, it will be sweeter to taste."

They drained the spaghetti and mixed it into the sauce, grating some more parmesan cheese on top and carried it to the table outside to eat. It was a great recipe, Wendy thought as she ate hungrily, already imagining herself impressing her friends back home by whipping up this meal for them.

"I can't believe how much pasta people eat here though," Amanda said, twirling another forkful around on the plate. "Every day, pasta for lunch and sometimes even for dinner ... don't you get bored of it, Enzo?"

"Bored? Of pasta? Never!" He looked mildly offended and demonstrated his enthusiasm for pasta by air blowing a kiss and throwing it in the air with his hand. "Pasta comes in so many different forms and so many recipes, it is impossible to be bored with it!"

"But that's silly!" Wendy laughed, "Imagine if I gave you potatoes for lunch every day, you would get bored, no?"

"Potatoes ARE boring. Not like pasta," Enzo stated calmly.

"Yes, but one day I would mash them for you, the next day I could roast them, then a potato salad, then in jackets, then a potato gateau … it's the same thing. Pasta comes in different shapes but it's still pasta … doesn't change the taste of it."

Enzo stood up, "How dare you compare the potato to pasta, 'tis not at all the same thing. *La pasta* is by far superior!" And with that he took his plate and stalked off to the kitchen, mock offended. The girls fell about laughing, planning all the potato dishes they would feed him to make him understand.

Montepertuso was all dressed up for the *festa*. Rosettes made out of pink and blue ribbons had been tied to the railings all along the road that wound through the village. Strings of coloured fairy lights were tied to poles and draped across the piazza and up towards the church. The road had been closed to traffic, so the bus had dropped the girls off at the beginning of the town and they had walked into the little village, which was buzzing with life. Everybody was dressed up in their finest clothes, little girls in stiff party dresses, old ladies in black and most of the men in crisp white shirts. Along the street, market stores had been set up for the evening, catering almost exclusively for children: balloons, candy, toys, goldfish, and roasted cobs of corn on sticks. Amanda walked up for a closer look at a small stall that was covered with lemons and something white and unidentifiable.

138

"What on earth is that?" She peered close at the white thing that was on a pedestal surrounded by lemons.

"You want to try? Is *musso 'e puorco,* very good!" the vendor grinned at them. At that moment, Gloria from the fishing boat appeared and, laughing at the girls' confused faces, told them it was made from pigs' feet and cows' faces. Amanda recoiled from the stall in horror and Wendy's eyes bulged. Gloria jiggled with laughter and merrily led them away towards the church where there was a band playing. As they walked up the steps towards the church square, Gloria pointed out a ceramic painting embedded on a wall of the Virgin Mary, breastfeeding the baby Jesus.

"The statue is usually in the church, but it's out at the moment for the torchlit procession. Make sure you girls find a good place to watch from, it gets busy later."

The music was getting louder, and they had to all flatten themselves against the wall for a minute as the marching band passed by for another loop around the village. Children ran around the piazza in excitement, dancing and pulling on the balloons that their mothers had tied to their wrists. Two little boys had plastic swords with lights on them and swung them around in the air, and a small girl in a frilly dress held a little plastic bag full of water and tied in a knot. Inside the bag, a tiny goldfish swam around.

"I hope they have a fish tank at home!" Amanda said. "Poor fish."

Sandro the fisherman appeared and raised his arms, exclaiming in pleasure at finding two of his crew together. He was all dressed up for once, with combed hair and a clean white shirt, partly buttoned to show off a gold medallion nestled amongst the hairs on his chest.

"Come with me, I take you to where the wine is good and the music is better than this." He waved his hand dismissively towards the band then hooked his arm through Gloria's and led them back through the crowds down to the road. He turned left and slipped through a little gate which led to a house with a small courtyard. About fifteen people were milling around, listening to two men playing folk music, seated in a corner of the courtyard. One had a mandolin and the other a tambourine, known as a *tammorra*. Sandro and Gloria were greeted enthusiastically, and the girls were introduced; red wine sangria with floating pieces of peaches was ladled out of a huge bowl into plastic cups and handed out and they all found somewhere to sit.

The village was built around a gorge in with a rocky dry riverbed plunging through the centre. When it rained, the riverbed became a raging torrent that poured down the mountain towards the sea. The road curved around the end of the gorge and from the little courtyard they could see across to the other side of the village where they had arrived by bus. A firework suddenly went off, getting everyone's attention and making them look up towards the massive hole in the mountain that hung above the village.

"Look, girls," Sandro leaned towards them, pointing up, "now comes the torch-lit procession." The musicians finished playing and voices were reduced to whispers as everybody watched the procession slowly making its way down the zigzagging path towards the village. It took rather a long time and the noise level in the village slowly went back up again and more sangria with peaches was ladled out until the girls decided they'd had enough and decided to go out for another walk around.

They told Sandro and Gloria that they were going and started to weave their way through the people in the courtyard. More people had arrived, and it was rather crowded in there now. Just as they reached the exit, they noticed Simone standing in the shadow of the gate, talking to another man. Something was exchanged hand to hand and Simone patted the other guy on the shoulder and was about to walk away when he noticed the girls.

"Girls! You are having fun, no? Where you watch the fireworks from?"

Amanda shrugged, they hadn't given it any thought, but looking around she realised that people had started to sit down on walls and steps, and all the best places with a clear view of the hole in the mountain were taken.

"OK, I know the best place, I take you to it now, but then I must go!" He led them through the crowds on the steps up towards the church. A small elementary school was on the left just before the church square. The windows were decorated with cut-out flowers drawn by the children and coloured in with crayons. Simone led them around a narrow passageway to the back of

141

the school and looking up to the roof whistled loudly.

He whistled again and they heard a whistle in reply and a head popped over the side of the roof.

"*Fai salire le mie amiche!* Let my friends up!" Simone called up. A ladder was slowly lowered and the girls looked at each other in surprise; honestly, you never know what was going to happen next in this place!

"OK, girls, you go up and watch the fireworks from there. It is the perfect place!"

"But who's up there?" Wendy asked, giving the ladder a shake to see how sturdy it was.

"*Boh!*" He shrugged, giving the standard Italian exclamation that meant "no idea." "Just people, maybe someone from the other night, you will see. Now, go go!"

He held the ladder steady as first Wendy then Amanda climbed up and were gripped by an arm and helped over the edge onto the roof of the school. The ladder was hauled back up again and laid flat, and the girls looked around.

There were quite a few people up there, sitting in couples and groups on the flat whitewashed rooftop. They were sitting with their backs to the girls, facing the hole in the mountain, and as it was quite dark, they couldn't really see if they knew anybody. The procession was arriving; they could hear the priest chanting and people singing a chillingly solemn hymn

142

as they drew closer to the church. Amanda sat down close to the edge of the roof and carefully peered over the edge to watch as they passed by below. Wendy crouched down next to her.

The crowd below fell silent as the statue of the breastfeeding Virgin Mary was carried along on a pedestal by four men. The priest led the procession followed by an altar boy in robes who was swinging a chalice of incense. A lady dressed all in black was next, singing into a loudspeaker and followed by all the altar boys and other children, all in white robes and holding torches. As the procession arrived at the church, the girls repositioned themselves on the rooftop to get the best view of the fireworks. Amanda lay down to look up at the stars. Wendy flopped beside her. "I used to do this with my dad," she said dreamily. "When I was little, Dad used to take me into the garden at night and we would lie on the grass and stare up into the sky, looking for satellites."

"Satellites?" Amanda asked, "How do you know which is a satellite?"

"Oh, they look just like stars, but you can see them moving slowly across the sky, a bit like a plane."

Somebody was lowering the ladder behind them to let up some more people. Amanda sat up to watch and smiled when a head popped up and a voice exclaimed, "*Buonasera,* my future wife! Are you waiting for your prince to rescue you from this roof?" It was Dom, the local policeman. Wendy sat up quickly, her heart rate accelerating. Was Francesco with him?

143

But, no, it was just Dom, as he was helping to pull the ladder back up again. She was relieved and disappointed all at the same time.

Dom turned back to them, "Where are you sitting, here? No, it's too far back, come to the front with me. We have drinks there. I just had to go get this, we forgot ..." He waggled a bottle opener at them and led them around the dark huddles of people until they reached the front of the roof.

Francesco had been sitting there all along with some friends and his face lit up in a crinkly-eyed smile when he saw Wendy arrive, making room for her to sit next to him, Amanda and Dom were just squeezing in behind her when the fireworks started. They sat down quickly and there was no time to talk or exchange pleasantries as the display was deafening. Plastic glasses of local fizzy red wine were passed around, Wendy was hyper aware of Francesco's hand brushing against hers every time he handed over a glass to pass on behind her.

"Where is your wife?" Wendy asked during a lull in the explosions.

"Oh, she had to take Leo home, my son. He was so tired and fell asleep."

"Didn't she mind you staying out?"

"No, no! It's not a problem, she is always happy to be home. *Certo*, I like for her to come out too, but she always say no." He raised his hands in defeat and then gestured at the mountainside in front of them that was

144

briefly lit up by a flash of pink light. "You understand what is happening?"

"Er, not really … something to do with the Devil and the Madonna having a fight?"

The fireworks had stopped for now and recorded music was playing on loudspeakers with a voiceover telling the legend of the village, mixed in with the occasional loud explosions and bizarre growling noises. Francesco now gave Wendy and Amanda a brief rundown of what was happening.

Montepertuso literally translated means "pierced mountain." The legend told that it was here that the Devil challenged the Virgin Mary to a test of strength. He attempted in vain to make a hole in the mountainside using his hands, only to fail again and again. The growling and bangs that they were hearing were the sounds of the Devil trying to make a hole in the rock. The Madonna, pitying him, touched the mountainside with her finger and it immediately crumbled to dust, creating a giant hole.

"This is when the fireworks really go crazy! You will see soon."

The defeated Devil then fell from the cliff onto the rocks below where, still today, by the picnic area in the little pine forest, you can see the imprint of his tail and a footprint embedded in the stone.

"I would like to take you there to see," Francesco said quietly to Wendy so that the others didn't hear.

"Hmmm, I'm sure your wife wouldn't like that," she replied, looking at his beautiful face and raising her eyebrows.

"Yes, you are right." He looked dejectedly down at his hands. Why was he married? He could have actually been "the one." Surely that didn't happen to people? Finding the man of your dreams only to discover that he was already taken. Maybe it was all the wine she had drank but she suddenly felt tearful. She turned away from him, trying to concentrate on the display.

There was a flash of light and suddenly the hole above the village was lit by hundreds of fiery sparkles. It was fantastic and suddenly colours were exploding from through and around the hole, on the clifftop above and pouring down the mountainside, glittering and whirling. The bangs ricocheted around the valley so loudly that Wendy feared the mountains were falling down around them. It went on and on, building up to a crescendo and finishing with an almighty boom that reverberated for a while and finally faded away to a split second of silence before the crowd started cheering and clapping.

Below the rooftop, the crowds started moving towards the road. It was nearly one in the morning and most people had to get up early for work in a few hours. As they stood on the rooftop, waiting their turn to climb down the ladder Wendy knew deep down that something was happening between them. They hardly knew each other but she felt inexplicably drawn towards him. She had an idea that he felt the same way, by the way he looked at her. But he was married, he

146

wasn't available, and they were going to have to fight it. As Wendy followed Amanda down the ladder, Francesco had gripped her hand, using the excuse of helping her onto the rungs to have just a moment of contact. She squeezed his hand back and only let go when she had to step down, and at that moment, she knew this was going to end in heartache.

Chapter 11

Positano, July 1986

"I think Simone is dealing marijuana or something." Amanda was sweeping the kitchen floor and Wendy was following behind with a bucket and mop. Nerone sat and watched placidly from his bed by the giant oven.

"Really? Why do you think that?" She squeezed the excess water out of the mop and pushed it around the dog bed.

"Do you remember when we were on the boat, and he had to 'make a delivery' to that villa? He didn't have anything in his hands when he left the boat, so what was he delivering? And I just noticed a couple of other times, when we were at Astrid's in Praiano, he had a little exchange of something with her husband. It would also explain last night, why he couldn't come with just but was sort of there anyway, darting around furtively in dark corners." She emptied the dustpan into the bin and pulled the dog hair off the bristles of the broom, grimacing slightly.

"Well, let's ask him for some weed then!" Wendy grinned at her, "We've been smoking his and Enzo's all this time, it's probably about time we bought our own!"

Amanda laughed at this simple solution, "Now, why on earth didn't I think of that myself?"

"You like him, don't you? Enzo, I mean, not Simone." Wendy watched Amanda carefully, not sure if she was ready to admit it yet. When they were younger, Amanda would gush about all the stars she liked. Her bedroom walls were plastered with posters of John Travolta, Superman and Ryan O'Neal and she would kiss them and dream about them and compare them to the boys at school. But Wendy knew that when she really liked someone, she would go quiet and have to be nudged into talking about her feelings.

Amanda paused for a moment. "You can tell, huh?" She propped the broom up against the wall and emptied the dustpan into the bin.

"God, Wendy, I really do! I just can't tell if he likes me too and I don't want to do anything in case it ruins this little group of friends we've made." She looked at Wendy, "What do you think? Does he like me?"

"Probably!" Wendy laughed, "What's not to like? Just spend some more time with him, after all, he's an Italian man … aren't they honour-bound to try it on at some point?"

"I don't want him to try it on just because he feels obliged!"

150

"I know, I'm just joking. If it's meant to happen it will, right?" She felt a thrill run through her just thinking about that from her and Francesco's viewpoint, but then tried to dismiss that thought as soon as it had formed.

"I like someone too," she sighed, not sure how Amanda would react but needing to talk about it.

"You do? Who? Not Simone?"

"Oh please!" Wendy laughed. Simone was a bit creepy, they had both decided. They had caught him watching them a few times and he was far too thin and pale for either of their tastes.

"OK, so I know it's stupid and I shouldn't even be thinking about him, but it's Francesco." She stopped, waiting for Amanda's reaction.

Amanda had finished sweeping and was putting the dry plates away in the cupboards. She stopped and turned to Wendy in surprise.

"Francesco, Dom's friend? But he's married."

"I know." Wendy sighed again and sat down at the table, trying to balance the mop against the wall. It slowly, inevitably slid to the floor and upended, splashing water all over the tiles. "I can't help my feelings and I swear I've never felt like this before. I'm not going to do anything about it, of course."

"But you want to." Amanda sat down opposite Wendy. "Terrible idea, Wendy – we'll have to try and

151

find you somebody else as soon as possible. Nothing good will come out of starting up something with a married man. Especially here. He'll never leave his wife."

"Ok, stop! I know all this. I just wanted to talk to you about it, not get a lecture." She got up and flicked the kettle on before picking up the fallen mop. "Sorry, I just already feel crappy about having feelings for him. I know it's a stupid thing to let happen but ... I think he likes me, too."

Amanda didn't know what to say. They sat there in silence while the kettle boiled. Wendy made tea and passed her a mug, saying, "It's one of those weird situations where if you're on the outside, you just don't get it and disapprove automatically, but Amanda. Try and imagine if it was Enzo. Imagine that first night we saw them again with Rob and Ted. I could see that you were still interested in him. Could you have just switched off your feelings if he had said that he was now married to a girl from Sorrento?"

Amanda took a sip from her mug. "I don't know, Wend. I'm not going to disapprove, I just don't want you to get hurt, okay?"

Mauro the fisherman pushed the wheelbarrow, piled high with shrimp pots, down towards the jetty. He patiently steered his way through the tourists with their dripping ice creams and the throng of day-trippers loaded with shopping bags who had just disembarked off the ferry from Capri.

Sandro was on the pier waiting and together

152

they unloaded the pots, laying them in a line along the quayside, ignoring the occasional American who stopped to take photos. They could hear but chose to ignore the voices that called loudly to each other, "Honey, look! A real authentic fisherman, get a photo!"

The small bait bags had been prepared earlier, stuffed with rancid salty fish. Now, one by one, these little bags were tied by a cord inside the shrimp pots. As the fishermen worked in companionable silence, a small wooden boat with a big red fish sign stuck to the mast docked at the jetty nearby. A group of people, barefoot and salty from a day at the beach clambered off the boat and headed home.

The sun was setting behind the mountain, and the sea and clouds started taking on a pink hue like the inside of a shell. The water was calm and almost smooth, with small mauve ripples, like a silk sheet billowing in the breeze. Sandro walked over to the edge of the dock where a small plastic dinghy was tied to a metal ring in the wall. He lithely jumped in and, kneeling, rowed out to fetch his little orange fishing boat, moored in the bay.

Maria slammed the lemon onto the tiny workspace in the galley and stabbed it with a knife.

"I don't want them there!" She chopped the lemon into pieces and threw them in a large bowl, reaching for another from a crate on the table behind her. She had been arguing with Matteo about the wedding tables and was telling Wendy all about it.

Wendy wiped the tears from her eyes. She was

chopping the onions and trying to avoid making her mascara run by doing it with her sunglasses on, and consequently could hardly see a thing. She was also starting to feel a little bit seasick as the boat was rocking more than usual.

"Maria, let's take this out on the deck, I need some air."

They gathered up the rest of the onions and a chopping board and headed up to the front of the boat where they could sit and work without bothering the fishermen who were loading equipment onto the deck.

"They are gossips and are never nice to me so why should I have them on the main table?" Matteo wanted his two elder sisters sitting at the head table with them and the parents. Maria thought it should be just their parents and she didn't have any other family other than her mother, and besides, she didn't get on very well with his sisters. Yesterday, it seemed he had brought the subject up again after a bit too much to drink and they had ended up arguing fiercely and were now not talking to each other.

"And I tell him many times, they are not nice to me. I don't want them sitting with me but last night I became really angry and maybe I was a bit drunk, and I kicked him … *oh dio*, I am so stupid!" She looked beseechingly at Wendy and wailed dramatically, "What do I do now?"

Wendy was surprised that the usually cold-as-ice Maria had suddenly opened up to her and was sharing her problems. Over the last few weeks, they

154

had worked most evenings together but hadn't really become friends. Maria was a cold fish and gave off a superior air, making Wendy feel slightly inadequate. She would happily sneak up to the roof together for a sneaky glass of wine or a smoke together during work but had rejected Wendy's attempts to go out together or meet for a drink and had laughed meanly when Wendy put on the new sunglasses she had bought. Wendy felt sorry for her, despite the mixed signals she gave; she had come into work today looking a complete mess, had obviously been crying, and was still stabbing away at the lemons with gusto.

"Well, I think the first thing you need to do is apologise for kicking him. Will he be at home now? Can you phone him?" There was a row of public telephones in the archway just before the fishmonger's; it wasn't far away, and the boat wasn't due to leave for an hour yet.

"Look, there's plenty of time. I'll cover for you or say that you've gone to get ice. Go and telephone him and apologise. Tell him that you'd had too much to drink and would never mean to hurt him. Try to get him to agree to meet up with you tomorrow so that you can talk together. He's probably sitting at home waiting for your call, anyway."

Maria sniffed and looked over to see where Mauro, the grumpier fisherman was. He was on shore, wrestling with a pile of nets that should keep him distracted for a good while.

"Do you have any *gettone*? I will give you them back tomorrow." The public telephones took funny

155

ribbed coins called *gettone* that were the equivalent of 200 lire but for some reason were only usable in telephones or slot machines. Wendy usually had a few in her bag as she needed quite a pile of them for her Sunday evening call home to let her parents know that she was still alive. She handed three over to Maria, more than enough for a local call, and wished her good luck.

She watched Maria walk up towards the payphone and dabbed at the tears streaming down her face. The sunglasses didn't help much against the onions.

While Maria was gone, Wendy took the quartered onions and lemon back down to the galley and then filled Gloria in on the story while slicing the bread. Gloria loved to hear everyone's little stories and problems but was never a gossip. She didn't have a bad word to say about anyone and was a calming source of good advice. Wendy often enjoyed spending the late afternoon just sitting with Gloria on her stone bench on the jetty, before work, chatting about village life and watching the boats come and go.

"Don't be too hard on the poor girl," Gloria advised. "She's had a tough time of it, and I think she's very lonely. I know she's not the friendliest person around, but I really don't think she knows any other way to be."

"Gloria, *dove sei*? Where are you?" Mauro called out, interrupting the conversation. The night-fishing clients were starting to arrive and Gloria, as the hostess, had to meet and greet them and show them where to sit. Wendy jumped off the boat and unloaded the last of the supplies from the wheelbarrow. She placed them on the edge of the jetty and went to park the barrow in a corner, stretching her neck to see if Maria was still on the phone. It was no use – she couldn't see the arch from where she was standing, as there was a slight bend in the road that blocked her view.

A movement on the beach caught her eye and she realised it was Francesco. He was sitting up near the fisherman huts, watching her, while his little son kicked a ball around nearby. He raised a hand and waved at her, smiling the smile that made her heart pound. How long had he been there? She waved back, feeling as if she should go over to him, but knowing that she couldn't. She scanned the beach looking for signs of a wife, but he seemed to be alone again. Heading back to the boat, knowing he was watching, she scooped up the two bottles of oil she had left on the jetty and jauntily hopped aboard.

Ten minutes later Maria returned. She looked relatively calm and threw herself into the role of hostess, welcoming the arriving clients on board and getting them drinks. As the boat slowly headed out to sea in the fading light Wendy followed Maria down to the galley.

"So? How did it go with Matteo, is everything okay?"

Maria grabbed a box of salt from a shelf and pushed past Wendy, heading back out again. "I am sick of talking to people about my personal life."

157

Wendy stood there, mouth hanging open for a few seconds, wishing she'd never bothered giving the girl any advice at all. She should have left her to suffer on her own.

****

"Honestly, I spent over an hour listening to her sob story and trying to cheer her up and help her, and then she tells me she is sick of talking to people about her life … people! I hardly forced it out of her, ungrateful cow!"

It was the next morning. Wendy and Amanda had walked the dog and were heading over to the Bar Internazionale for a quick cappuccino and cornetto before Amanda had to go and open the shop.

"And then she basically ignored me for the rest of the evening … so that was my night." Wendy sighed and stopped, waiting for Nerone to finish sniffing a corner.

"Well, Claudia was telling me," Amanda said in a hushed tone, "a bit about Maria – it's quite sad, really. Her father died when she was young, had a bit of a drinking problem and crashed over the edge of the coast road on his way home one night. Her mother is elderly and can't really leave the house because she can't handle the steps much. Maria looks after her and does all the cooking and cleaning, so apparently, she feels guilty about leaving home to live her life with Matteo. She hates the idea of having kids, while obviously, Matteo wants a bus load of them, and to

158

make matters worse, she doesn't get on very well with his sisters. Claudia is helping to organise the wedding and apparently, the sisters want to be involved and are offended that Maria has turned to Claudia instead of them."

"OK I didn't know that about her parents ... But I'm certainly not going to bother asking her if she's okay ever again, if that's the way she thanks me! I'm supposed to be doing her wedding makeup, so she better be a bit nicer to me in future."

"OK, my turn!" Amanda had been waiting to tell her story, and it was way more interesting than talking about boring Maria. They had arrived at the bar and stood waiting while the barman made their cappuccinos.

"So, I was a bit hungover yesterday morning and as soon as I got to the shop, I kicked off my shoes and scraped my hair up in a bun. I basically looked like shit and was standing there with the bucket and mop, just to add to the glamour, and you'll never guess who walked in?"

Wendy dumped a spoonful of sugar in her coffee and gave it a good stir. "Um ... I dunno ... Domenico?"

"Who? No! Only flipping Rod Stewart!" Amanda squealed in excitement and carried on, having gotten Wendy's full attention. "It was so embarrassing, I looked like crap and was standing there with shaky hands, staring at a bucket, barefoot and holding a mop and he walked in with his girlfriend and a few others."

"Oh wow! Did you talk to him? Was he nice?"

"No! I don't know, I was so mortified that I slunk off behind the counter and pretended to be doing paperwork!"

"No autograph, nothing? You idiot! Did you tell Antonio?"

"No! Don't tell him either! He expects me to be perfectly turned out like the shop mannequins at all times and would be horrified if he knew I was barefoot with a mop in the presence of a rock star in his shop!" They were still laughing when Antonio walked in, dressed in mint green chinos that were rolled up at the ankles and a boldly patterned black and white shirt.

"Darlings, *ciao!*" He sauntered over to the girls, catching a glimpse of himself in the mirror behind them, and preened for a few seconds. "Amanda, my dear, I am going to be lunching at Laurito today with some very important friends from Rome, you know, I think I told you about the designer Giambà, no? We will be discussing the line I am creating, so we will have a beach meeting. It is more chic on the beach I think … I want you to be there to take notes. I know you are not a secretary, but you are my assistant, so you come and pretend, no? I'll feed you, too?"

"Er, what about the shop?"

"Oh, we close up, is not a problem. Just for lunchtime. You come, no? I will look more important with my assistant taking notes! Then we eat good food, we swim, and you can get the boat back and open the

160

shop again. Please?"

Amanda laughed, "No problem ... but I'll have to go back home and grab my bikini before I open, so I might get down a bit later than usual, is that okay?"

"Wonderful, darling, meet me at the jetty at one o'clock!" And he pranced out of the bar.

Wendy looked at Amanda with her eyebrows raised. "So you get to meet rockstars and fashion designers, sit on a beach, eat good food, swim, and go for a boat ride ... instead of sitting behind a shop counter...and he is asking you please? Hilarious!"

"Better than de-heading fishes!" Amanda said smugly, getting up to take the cups back to the bar.

The girls stepped out of the bar and started to cross the road. Over to their left was a noticeboard, mainly used for death announcements and any concerts that might be happening. The noticeboards were dotted around town, often near the bus stops or piazzas. Wendy was on a bus one day and had been fascinated to see the man who pasted the notifications onto the boards.

He was probably in his early thirties, skinny with floppy black hair, wearing a heavy metal t-shirt and black jeans. He had been driving his moped in front of the bus and Wendy had been standing right by the driver as there was nowhere to sit. As the bus drove past a noticeboard, she had watched the man drive his moped right up to it and in less than ten seconds he had whipped out a printed notice, slopped on some paste from a bucket balanced in the footwell, stuck it on the board and driven off again. The bus caught up with him and at the next stop she watched again as quick as a flash he pulled the notice from a roll under his arm, pasted and stuck and drove off again.

He was there now, at the noticeboard near the bar, but he had parked his moped on its stand and was taking his time. A full-sized poster was half stuck to the board. He was unrolling it and trying to paste the second half down, but it kept rolling back up again and he was cursing at it.

Wendy could just read the top of the poster. *"Venerdi 18 Luglio 1986, Grande Inaugurazione"*. She stopped and grabbed Amanda's arm, wanting to see what the big opening event was for. As the man rolled down the poster more words appeared: "Paradise Discoteca, Positano. Music by DJ Toni."

"18th July, that's in ten days' time! We've got to go!"

Chapter 12

Positano, July 1986

She slipped on the fins and, clutching the mask and snorkel in her hand, she let herself fall backwards into the emerald water. Hair slicked back, mask pulled on, she flipped over and dove down into the mysterious world below. Tiny silver fish and flecks of loose seaweed glinted in the blueness. Mossy rocks on the seabed hid baby octopi, and a sea bream poked its head out as she swam past its dark shelter. *Why on earth have I waited so long to do this*, she wondered as she came up to the undulating surface for air. There was a whole other world down there to explore!

As she broke through into the air above, the sounds of the beach hit her like a brick. Children shrieking and splashing, boat engines rumbling, stones being walked on and the buzz of hundreds of voices chattering away. She took a deep breath and dived down again; the sounds were muted instantly and all she could hear was water bubbling past her ears as she swam.

Up again for more air and Wendy trod water for a while, deciding where to go and explore next. She was just past Music on the Rocks, the disco in a cave at the end of the main beach. She kept on going, past La Scogliera, the rocky bathing platform where Enzo worked and where the cool kids liked to hang out. The fins on her feet made it so easy to cut through the water and soon she was past the beach and around a rocky outcrop where she found a tiny little beach that was completely empty. She swam over and, taking off the flippers, waded ashore and walked the length of the beach. Squeezing through two big rocks she was delighted to find a little inlet, a mini lagoon, surrounded by big rocks, with a clear shallow pool that was just begging to be swam in. She paddled into it and lay down, floating like a starfish, ears submerged and face tilted up to the blue sky. Minutes passed, and it was absolute bliss, so peaceful and relaxing, but the sun was starting to feel hot on her face so she eventually ducked under the water to cool off and waded back to the beach.

As she started to squeeze herself back through the rocks she saw movement, a flash of something white, and stopped. *Oh gosh,* she thought, *that's Francesco on his surfboard...did he follow me?* She froze and watched as he paddled to the beach and pulled the board part way out of the water. He couldn't have seen her – she'd been in the lagoon for at least ten minutes. What should she do? He looked up and noticed her at that moment; his face broke into a wide grin, and he reached out an arm towards her.

"Wendy! *Che piacere*! What a pleasure, you find my secret beach! Come, sit with me for a while." He patted the surfboard and she made to move towards him but a sharp pain in her foot as she put her weight on it made her yelp in surprise, pulling her leg back up. She lost her balance on the uneven pebbles and fell in an inelegant heap, letting out an "oomph" as she landed. Francesco was next to her in a flash, asking if she was all right.

"Yes, sorry, I trod on something sharp, I'm fine," she said, embarrassed as he helped her up. But as soon as she tried to put her foot down, she felt the stabbing pain again and cried out.

"Let me see your foot." Francesco sat her back down and kneeling in front of her took her foot in his hands, inspecting the sole.

"Did you go and walk in the little pool behind here?"

"Yes, ow! There, is it a thorn?" Wendy flinched as he ran his finger over the ball of her foot.

"Aah, you have stepped on a ... how you say in English, a *riccio di mare*?"

"A what?" He put her foot down and looked at the rocks nearby, then pointed at a dark spot, almost hidden in the shadow. Wendy shifted closer and peered at it.

"A sea urchin! Oh no!" She pulled her foot towards her and twisted it around and saw three black dots, three spikes firmly embedded in the ball of her foot.

"It is full of them over there, you have to walk very carefully. This is why no one comes here much."

165

He sat down next to her, and she noticed how his skin was the colour of caramel and how the droplets of water rolled off his arms as if he was water resistant.

"How are we going to get those out?" She tried squeezing but it hurt, and Francesco stopped her.

"No, don't do that, they will work their way in more. There is only one person I know that is good at removing *i ricci* – Sandro the fisherman. We have to go to him."

"Ugh, no! I was having such a nice time here." *And then you turned up and it could have been even nicer,* she thought to herself.

He smiled at her, that beautiful smile that made his eyes crinkle and made her heart melt. "I take you on my surfboard. Come, put your arm around me."

He helped her hobble into the sea and dragged the surfboard back in. "Climb on" he held the board steady as she scrambled up and sat cross-legged in the middle. He left her floating for a few seconds, darting back to the beach to collect her fins and mask, depositing them in her lap.

He carefully climbed onto the board behind her, getting her to shuffle forwards a bit so they were evenly balanced and pushed off from a rock with his paddle. Sandro lived near the fishmonger's, right over on the other side of the beach and it seemed that Francesco was in no hurry to get there.

"It doesn't hurt, does it?" He checked with her,

166

knowing that the embedded spines only hurt when weight was put on the foot.

"No, I'm fine. Thank you for helping me. I'm sorry I ruined your time at the beach. Wait, can I turn around?" Wendy felt uncomfortable talking to him without being able to see him so, very slowly, she started to shift around so that she was facing him. He stopped paddling and waited until the board stopped rocking.

"Okay, that is better; now I see your beautiful face!" He smiled at her, "I am stupid, why did I sit behind you?"

He was paddling in a wide arch, through the little boats that were moored in the bay, rather than straight along the seafront. Wendy realised that this was probably because he was a married man and to be seen on a surfboard with a woman that wasn't his wife was probably not a great idea.

"Am I going to get you in trouble if someone sees us?" She asked, trailing her hand in the water.

'Trouble? But I am rescuing a *signorina* from the dangers of the sea, I am doing nothing wrong! Was it better for me to leave you there, not able to walk? Please, don't worry, it is so nice to be with you, you have made my day!"

"Gee thanks!" She said, scooping up a handful of water and throwing it at him. "I'll try and hurt myself more often if it pleases you so much!" She laughed and he laughed too, but then stopped paddling and put his hand on her knee. "No, really I don't mean like that. I just enjoy talking with you."

He sighed and started paddling again. They were drawing closer to the other end of the beach

Any further conversation was put to an abrupt end by a small boat that pulled out from the jetty and passed by closer than necessary, causing the surfboard to rock alarmingly. They both gripped the edges and held on tight while the water around them subsided. The boy driving the boat raised a hand to acknowledge them and called out sorry before accelerating and speeding off.

Francesco paddled the last few metres to the beach and Wendy hopped off and sat down on the pebbles, pulling her foot up to have another look at the damage.

"Wait for me, I put the board away and take you to Sandro," Francesco called as he hefted the board onto his shoulder and carried it higher up the beach. Wendy sat and watched the little boats docking, people jumping on board to be taken to beaches along the coast, and tourists hopping off, ready for lunch at the beach or some shopping in town.

"Come, let's go find *Dottore* Sandro!" Francesco was back and reached out to pull Wendy to her feet. She couldn't put any weight on her foot as it would have driven the spikes in further, so she had to lean on him and hop with her arm around his shoulder. He wrapped his arm around her waist to support her.

"You're enjoying this aren't you?" Wendy asked. She could feel the heat of his body against her.

"*Molto!*" Francesco grinned and squeezed her tighter.

Sandro was sitting on a low wall just outside the fishmongers. In front of him was a big bucket of anchovies in a wheelbarrow – Wendy knew exactly what they looked like now from work – a box of coarse salt and a pile of big glass jars. The fisherman was packing the anchovies one by one, tightly together in the jars, and salting them before screwing the lids on tightly. The fish would last through the winter and be used in pasta sauces, on fresh brown bread with olive oil and pepper, and on bruschetta with fresh chopped tomatoes.

"Uh-oh, what have you done, my dear?" Sandro tilted his head at Wendy questioningly as he noticed them hobbling towards him. Francesco explained rapidly in Italian and Sandro got up, wiping his hands on a grubby cloth.

"I go wash my hands and get a needle." Wendy blanched at that, and Sandro patted her on the arm, "It will hurt you to get them out, but you must be brave, and after, you will be able to walk again. Francesco, find a chair!"

Wendy sat down on the low wall, next to the bucket of anchovies which didn't smell very nice. Francesco ducked into a small handmade sandal shop next to the fishmongers and came out with a battered wicker chair. He brought it over and placed it in front of Wendy and sat down. A couple of tanned kids ran past and ducked into a bar in the corner of the piazza; the door was open, and the electronic sound of video games being played drifted out.

"Are you okay?"

Wendy was not at all looking forward to being poked in the foot by a fisherman with a giant needle but didn't have much choice. She nodded tersely and said, "I'm fine, you don't have to wait, you know. You've done enough already, maybe you should go home."

Francesco looked offended, "No, I stay with you, it's not a problem."

Sandro came back, looking very studious with a pair of glasses balanced on his nose and turfed Francesco out of the chair. He had brought a bottle of vinegar, some cotton wool, and a sewing needle. He sat down on the chair and took Wendy's foot onto his lap, peering at the sole before dousing it with vinegar. He peered over his glasses at Wendy and then gestured with his head for Francesco to sit next to her.

"Maybe if we ask this handsome man to hold your hand and whisper sweet nothings, it will distract you?" He grinned at them both and gave them a big comic wink. "OK, now I start, and you tell me why you so stupid to go walking in the Bacino? Everybody knows it is full of *ricci* there."

"Well, I didn't know that, did I? I didn't even know the place existed until I found it this morning." Wendy huffed, vowing to never go back there.

170

He set to work, digging the spines out with the needle. Sea urchin spines are sharp, like thick needles but with rough sides, and they tend to work themselves further into the wound so can be tricky to dig out. It was very painful, nothing like digging out a splinter. Wendy tried to hold still and not flinch, distracting herself by deciding what to liken it to. Being impaled by pieces of spaghetti? Treading on a cactus? No, more like treading on a hedgehog or a porcupine, not that she had ever done that. Francesco moved closer and squeezed her hand. She was thankful that he had stayed. The sandal maker came out of his shop to watch, and after an extra loud squeak from Wendy, the fishmonger came out to have a look too. The two kids that had been playing video games came out of the bar and stopped to gawk for a moment until Sandro shooed them away.

"It is the most exciting thing that has happened today!" Sandro joked. "*Ecco*! One is out!" He held up the tiny spine; it was about half a centimetre long. The fishmonger and the sandal maker swapped stories about their experiences with sea urchins and Francesco quipped, "Tonight, you should eat dinner at Chez Blacks – they do a special spaghetti with sea urchin sauce!" Wendy laughed but was cut short by a sharp pain as Sandro retrieved the second spine. The audience grew as Gloria and Mauro turned up and stopped to see what had happened. Wendy didn't think she could take much more of the prodding and pain; it was excruciating, and by this point, she was gripping onto Francesco's hand for life. "Am I hurting you?" She asked him, loosening her grip.

"No, *cara*," he said softly, then speaking louder for everyone to hear, "it is a great excuse for me to hold

171

hands with a beautiful girl, no?"

"You hold her hand and I hold her foot … there is something wrong here!" Sandro quipped. "*Eccolo qua*! Here it is, the last one!" He triumphantly held up the last spine to a smattering of applause and cheers from the bystanders. Wendy slumped in relief and let go of Francesco's hand to inspect the damage to her foot.

Gloria bustled over to look and exclaimed, "We'll need some disinfectant and some sticking plaster on that." She turned to the fishmonger, "You must have a first aid kit in the shop, get it!" The small crowd dispersed, and Gloria took over, cleaning and bandaging Wendy's foot.

"Now, it'll hurt a bit if you have to walk on it today, but it should be fine by tomorrow. How are you going to get home – bus?"

Wendy stood up and tentatively put some weight on her foot. It was sore but not terrible. She could probably hobble up to the bus stop.

"I'll be fine, yes, I'll get the bus up."

"Bus?" Francesco came back from returning the sandal maker's chair, "No bus, I have my Vespa right here, on the service road to the beach. I take you home!"

Wendy started to protest but Gloria agreed with Francesco.

"Oh, that is much easier, Wendy, it will save the

walk up to the bus stop; go with him!"

Fate was definitely pushing them together today, Wendy thought as she sat behind Francesco, holding onto his waist as he sped her home. They passed the florist and he waved at the man who was watering the pots outside. He waved at the barman, sitting on the wall having a cigarette break outside the Bar Internazionale, as he pulled up in the alleyway between the hotel and the house and helped Wendy over to the door.

"I am sorry that you were hurt today. Remember to change the dressing later!" He smiled at her as he hopped back onto his Vespa.

"Thank you, Francesco, I appreciate your help. Sorry to keep you from whatever you should have been doing!"

"No problem, I enjoyed being your saviour!" He winked, "I see you soon, at the opening of the Paradise? You will be there, no?" He raised his voice over the rumble of the motor as he started manoeuvring back out of the alleyway.

"Yes, of course I'll be there, I wouldn't miss it for the world!" Wendy called back, waving as he sped off. She turned and limped into the house, patting Nerone as he came to greet her. Hobbling down into the kitchen she suddenly felt strangely alone without Francesco next to her.

Get a grip, girl, she told herself, *he is NOT available.*

173

Francesco drove home, feeling elated yet somewhat guilty. He had hoped to bump into Wendy down on the beach, of course, but he had never dreamed of being able to spend all that time with her on the surfboard and back on land. She was so different from Elena, who he loved dearly but who would never have gone snorkelling out at sea by herself. Wendy was fun and easy to talk to and he couldn't shake the feeling that they just somehow fit together.

He slowed down as he drove through the sleepy village, and then he parked his Vespa at the side of the road. He made his way up the steps that led to the lemon groves and the family home. He could hear his father telling his brother to prepare some bottles; he must be about to make a batch of limoncello. As the house came into sight, he whistled a signal, and within moments Elena's head popped up at a window and Leo came running out to meet him.

"Ciao Papá!"

"Ciao, little one! What have you been up to today?" He swept the little boy up in his arms and planted a kiss on the top of his silky head.

Leo struggled to be let down again, so he dropped him gently to the floor The little boy led his father into the kitchen where Elena was sitting at the table with his mother. They had been making pasta. The table was covered with piles of pasta shapes, *cavatelli* by the look of it, all dusted with flour. A big bunch of basil leaves sat on the counter, ready to be made into pesto at the last minute.

"How was your paddle?" Elena asked him, carefully sweeping the pasta off the table into a big bowl. His mother got up and lifted Leonardo in her chair, giving him a leftover piece of pastry to keep him occupied.

"Eh, it was going well, but I found a damsel in distress and had to save her."

Elena raised her eyebrows at him, waiting for the full explanation. There was no point in not mentioning what had happened. This was a small town and gossip ran rife. If he didn't tell Elena that he had helped Wendy, then somebody else would be soon filling in the details for her and, no doubt, elaborating on the story.

"There was an English girl that stepped on a sea urchin at the Bacino. She couldn't walk so I had to take her over to Sandro the fisherman. I dropped her home afterwards; it was probably quite painful."

"A tourist?" Elena asked whilst fishing out a large saucepan and filling it with water.

"No, there are two girls here for the summer, I think they are housesitting for that American couple. – what are their names, Bob and Ed?"

"Rob and Ted," Francesco's mother amended while cleaning the flour off the table with a damp cloth. She scrubbed an extra stubborn bit. "Those two are always off around the world. What adventures they must have!"

Elena reached up for a pile of plates to star'

175

laying the table.

"Well, there's work for you after lunch. There's a batch of limoncello to make and the spare bottles are all in boxes in the basement. You'll have to get them out and I'll sterilise them while you do the lemons."

"Have I got time for a shower before lunch?"

"A quick one, and rinse out your swimming trunks and put them on the line, don't just leave them in the bathroom!" Elena whipped a tea towel at his legs as he passed by and smiled at him. He traipsed off to the bathroom, thinking that she wouldn't be smiling if she knew what he was feeling towards the English girl. It would be so much easier if Wendy was just a tourist, then she would soon be gone, and he would no doubt forget about her.

Chapter 13

Naples, September 2016

Mia craned her neck to see further out of the plane's window as it flew precariously low over the hills of Naples. She saw beautiful old palazzos and villas surrounded by trees, streets full of tiny cars and big wide lakes. She turned to look across the other side of the plane and there was the sea, sparkling silver below the horizon. As the plane dropped lower, causing her stomach to lurch suddenly, she took her mother's hand and gave it a reassuring squeeze.

"You okay, Mum?" She asked, suddenly feeling guilty for putting her through this with hardly any warning.

Wendy had been furious at first when she had seen the tickets, but after a few hours of sulking and a long Skype call with Amanda, she had calmed down and decided that she would accompany Mia to Positano. They would be staying at Amanda and Enzo's in the little holiday apartment that they rented out in the summer months. If Wendy decided that she wasn't brave enough to go out and face the town, she would be comfortable just hanging out at Amanda's. They lived off to the side of the town and had a sprawling property with an olive grove and a vegetable garden to potter around. There were chickens and a couple of goats and plenty of things to do every day.

Mia knew that Mum had always longed to visit Amanda and Enzo at their home and up until now had never understood why they had never gone. Instead, the family had always come to visit them in England. Every other Christmas, Amanda would bring her flock to celebrate the holidays with family and friends back in the UK. Mia had always pleaded with her mum to have a holiday at Amanda's, but they had always ended up going to Greece or Spain or even Florida, but never Italy.

"I'll be fine, love. I'm actually looking forward to seeing it all again, in a strange way. Thanks for being so brave. I certainly wouldn't have done this without you pushing me!"

Amanda squealed loud enough to turn heads as they walked out into the arrivals hall. She flung herself at Wendy like a teenager and hugged her excitedly. Mia watched the Italian taxi drivers holding paper signs with names on them smile as they watched the two excited women.

They wheeled their bags out of the terminal, past two scary-looking soldiers standing at the entrance complete with rifles, over to a small car park. The sun was shining, and it was decidedly warmer than it had been earlier that morning when they had left Gatwick.

They chatted easily for a while, as they headed south along the motorway. There wasn't much to catch up on – Wendy and Amanda spoke to each other on Skype at least twice a week, so they gossiped easily about Ben and all the kids until they turned off at Castellamare and started the long winding road towards the Amalfi Coast.

"So, Mia, where have we got to so far in the story?" Amanda asked.

Positano
July 1986

She leaned over the bow of the boat in delight, watching as the sleek forms below ducked and dived, accompanying the boat out to sea.

"Maria! Quick, come see!" Maria had been keeping a lookout from the stern when the beautiful creatures suddenly appeared. It was early still, only just gone six in the evening, and the girls had been on the jetty preparing the crates to go on board for the evening's excursion when Mauro had mentioned that dolphins had been seen by the boats coming back from Capri. The girls had begged him to take them out to see if they could spot them, and he had grudgingly agreed to a quick sail around the bay before they started work.

As Maria carefully made her way across the boat to the bow, Wendy rummaged in her bag and pulled out her camera. She wasn't sure if she could get a clear picture of the dolphins, but she was going to try. They were so close, swimming right under the hull, that she was worried they might get hit by the boat.

"*Sono fantastici!*" Maria gasped as she leaned over to see. Wendy took a couple of shots and shoved her camera back in her bag, determined to not lose a moment of this magical experience. There were four of them; they were darker than she had imagined, a shiny gunmetal grey, and as they shimmied through the water, she could glimpse their lighter underbellies. The boat was about a mile out from the coast and the sea here was deep and dark blue. It was amazing how

180

the beautiful creatures were in tune with each other and their surroundings. They swam in a tight-knit pod, all noses pointing in the same direction and all calculating the exact speed they needed to cruise at to keep up with the boat above them.

After a few minutes, Mauro started turning slowly and the dolphins veered off towards the islands, spreading out and showing off with a few playful jumps, arching out of the water and diving back in again, before eventually disappearing from view.

Back on the wharf, Sandro had drawn a crowd around him. He had spent the afternoon out on his little fishing boat pulling up the lobster pots that he had left around the bay a couple of days before. He had just arrived back on shore and had offloaded a couple of buckets filled to the brim with pulsating sea life. A small crowd of people had gathered around, peering into the buckets as he held court and pointed at the various creatures. A woman shrieked and jumped back as an eel made a bid for escape, splashing its tail at her before sinking back below a wiggly octopus.

Wendy and Maria jumped off the big boat and went over to have a look.

"Aah, girls, there you are. I have a job for you," Sandro beckoned for them to come closer and turned to a wheelbarrow that he had parked next to the buckets. It was covered with an old sheet.

Theatrically he pulled the sheet off and the small crowd leaned forwards to see and gasped at the two big snapping lobsters that sat in a big tub of seawater.

181

Sandro reached into the tub and pulled out a lobster, holding it carefully from behind so that it couldn't pinch him. Completely deadpan he held it out to Wendy and said, "Do me a favour and take this up to the fish shop. Tell them it's from me."

Wendy hesitated, not sure whether she could hold a lobster without getting scared and dropping it, but Sandro, sensing her fear, turned his wrist around and guided her hand to where he was gripping it.

"Just hold it firmly here, don't worry, it won't be able to hurt you if you keep it like this. You got it? Okay, now go!" Wendy was suddenly alone, clutching a big snapping lobster dripping seawater down her arm. The crowd grinned in amusement as she started walking up towards the fishmongers as quickly as she could, her arm stretched out in front of her. She passed by the little restaurant, O'Caporale, and one of the waiters jumped out of her way, calling after her to bring it back, they could make spaghetti with it. The lobster had very long antennae which were waggling furiously; it was snapping away at the air with its big vicious claws and was starting to feel quite heavy.

She stumbled into the fishmongers, comically calling out for help.

"*Aiuto!*"

Matteo appeared from the back of the shop and grinned when he saw the look on Wendy's face.

"Wendy! Where did you find him?" He poked at one of the claws which snapped back at him, wavering

182

angrily.

"Just take the bloody thing before I drop it!" Wendy held it out to him and used her other hand to hold up her arm, which was starting to ache.

Matteo carefully took the lobster from her and dropped it into a slightly murky tank where a couple of smaller lobsters were already resigned to their fate, placidly sitting at the bottom.

Maria suddenly appeared panting, holding out the other lobster as far away from her body as possible. She marched straight over to the tank and dumped it in unceremoniously.

"*Ciao amore*, so kind to bring me lobsters but I prefer gelato next time, please!" Matteo joked and received a thump from Maria.

"They are from Sandro, stupid! Will you wait for me to finish tonight? Then maybe we go for gelato?" She tilted her head up to him for a kiss and Wendy stepped outside to give them some space.

"Maria, I'm going back to the boat, don't be too long!"

The sky was inky black as they slowly coasted back to town after a successful night fishing trip. Gloria and Maria were sitting in the galley, talking about the upcoming wedding plans, and Wendy was searching around on deck for the last few empty plates. It was incredible, she thought, fishing a plate with a crust of bread in it out of a coil of rope, where people would thoughtlessly leave their plates once they had finished eating.

Sandro was merrily entertaining the crowds, singing some Neapolitan love song while packing away the camping stove that he used to fry the night's catch on.

Maura was at the helm and catching Wendy's eye signalled for her to go over to him.

"It is soon August, a very busy time for us here in Positano," he told her, one hand resting on the helm, the other on his round stomach. "In the next few weeks, I will be doing some day trips to Capri with small groups of tourists, using the small boat. I need a hostess on board – you want to do it?"

"Um, sure, but what would I have to do?" Wendy still hadn't been to Capri, even though it was only a forty-minute boat ride away.

"Same as here, you talk to the clients, give drinks, tell them what they are seeing along the coast and then you'll tell them what to see and do on the island. We take them all around Capri by boat and show them the caves and the beaches, then they have free time to explore." He looked at her with eyebrows raised expectantly.

"Wow, it sounds amazing, but I haven't been to Capri myself. I don't know anything about the island."

"Is not a problem, you go tomorrow or next day, no? I tell you what to do and where to visit, then you

184

know!"

"OK, I can probably go tomorrow with Amanda, it's her day off. I'd love to do it, thank you!"

"*Bene,* good! We will pay you the same as the night trips, this is good, no?" Wendy agreed, it was good, yes. They paid her a set amount per boat trip; it wasn't much but it was enough to survive on for the summer. If she'd had to pay rent, she wouldn't have been able to make ends meet but seeing as the house was rent-free, she was managing just fine.

They were pulling slowly into the bay and the lights of the town seemed bright and orange after the darkness out at sea. The water was still, and the reflection of the town made the lights seem extra bright until the boat cut through the stillness and the ripples broke up the image. Coming into Positano at night by boat was always a magical experience. Wendy wondered if the old fishermen still appreciated the view of their commute home.

****

"Two returns to Capri, please." Wendy stood at the counter of the *tabacchaio* at the beach, swapped a pile of grubby Italian lire for four tickets that the shopkeeper had laboriously filled out by hand and turned to Amanda. "Do you think we should buy some more sunscreen?"

Amanda, who had been trying on straw hats struck a pose and shrugged, "Probably, but we can get some there if we need to." The little tobacconist shop sold an array of inflatable rings and rubber dinghies, sunscreen and snorkels as well as cigarettes, lottery tickets, and curious Italian sweets. Strangely it was also the place to go if you needed any stationary products, sellotape, biros and notepads. It was squeezed between a restaurant on the seafront and a small grocery store that would make giant sandwiches with fresh mozzarella, salad, and tuna fish, seasoned with local olive oil, salt and pepper, all wrapped up in brown paper.

As they walked out of the *tabacchaio*, they almost crashed into two small girls who were running past the restaurant. One of them had accidentally kicked off a flip-flop and they had both stopped to retrieve it, giggling and teasing each other in very English voices. They were about twelve years old and were dressed in identical Mickey Mouse beach shirts. They had obviously both been swimming already as their hair was dripping wet but what struck Wendy about them was the fact that one girl had the same deep auburn hair colour as her and the other had a short pudding bowl bob, but in the same shade of pale blonde as Amanda.

"Look!" She exclaimed, clutching Amanda's arm and laughing, "They look just like we did when we were little!"

The little blonde retrieved her flip-flop from under a table at the restaurant and slipped it back on. "Nicki, wait for meeee!" Not looking where she was going, she rushed ahead, knocking Amanda sideways.

"Celine, you're so stupid! Say sorry to the lady!" She rolled her eyes and shrugged dramatically

186

at Amanda, hands raised. Little Celine called out sorry over her shoulder and they grabbed each other, giggling, and disappeared into the grocery store.

"How funny! I think that could have been us in another life, a time slip perhaps! I quite like the name Celine. Come on Nicki, we'll miss the ferry!"

The hydrofoil to Capri was too big to dock at the tiny wharf, so they had to get on a smaller boat that taxied them out to the ship which was anchored out in the bay. Mauro had given Wendy a few sheets of paper with some handwritten notes of what to do once they got to the island.

"It is all the usual tourist things that you need to know, but you see for yourself, then is easier to explain to the tourists."

Now, reading through the notes to Amanda, Wendy was excited to finally visit the glamorous island.

"We have to get a funicular up to the town, apparently – what on earth is that?"

Amanda was staring out the window at the Galli Islands, which they were passing by. From Positano, it looked like one long island in the shape of a woman half submerged in the water, but now she could see that they were actually three separate islands.

"A funicular? It's like a small train that goes up hills." Amanda said, turning to read the notes too. "I want to go and see the blue grotto. Is that on the list?"

"Hmm, no it's not but I think that it's part of the boat trip, not what they see on the island itself. We should go anyway! I want to see it too." She had heard all about Capri's famous blue grotto from the American tourists that went on the night fishing trip. They all raved about it and one family had even said that the grotto was the main reason that they had come to Italy, which Wendy thought was a bit silly when you take into account all the fabulous things to see in Rome, Florence, and Pompeii.

"We have to go and see the Via Camarelle, that's where all the designer boutiques are. Your Antonio would love it there!"

"And there's a ski lift to the top of the island too! Wow, are we going to have time to do it all?" Amanda was excited too now. They could see the island out in front of them, getting larger by the minute, and soon the ferry was pulling into the lively harbour. Big white yachts were moored in rows and colourful little wooden boats bobbed around at anchor. The harbour was long and spread out with rows of pastel-coloured buildings facing out to sea. The girls walked ashore and were offered island boat tours and Capri taxi tours, but the prices were eye-watering. Following the instructions Mauro had given them, they walked along the road until they found the funicular station. It looked like a regular train station except the platform and tracks were tilting up on a steep slope. The train came down and they hopped on board the tiny carriage. There were a few other people, but it wasn't too busy. The carriage had only four seats but plenty of room to stand so they stood up against the window and watched as the train departed, magically taking them up the steep mountainside to the main town. They passed small, whitewashed houses with tiny gardens surrounded by lemon and oleander trees. The sea sparkled turquoise below them, and they could see a hydrofoil boat leaving the harbour. Within a few minutes, they had arrived and climbed the steps that led from the station into the centre of Capri town.

To the right was a railing overlooking the little port, now far below them. The sea seemed to be brighter shades of blue here and they could now see all the way across the Bay of Naples. Mount Vesuvius loomed on one side, a small circle of clouds floating around the top of the crater, and the city stretched lazily along the coastline, misty in the distance. Turning around, Wendy noticed the clock tower of Capri with its beautiful ceramic tiled clock face, and behind that the bustling Piazzetta with its cafes and bars and so many tables and chairs that it was hard to see where one bar ended and another one began.

"Mauro says we should walk through the piazza to the road on the right, which will take us to the main shopping street." They strolled through the tiny streets, admiring the lavish shop windows. The buildings were all whitewashed, and bougainvillaea grew in bright splashes of colour from terracotta pots and urns. Porters drove by on tiny little electric carts, piled high with luggage, and glamorous Italian ladies swanned past laden with shopping bags and hidden by dark sunglasses. They stopped at a little cart decorated with lemons and vines where a lady sold cups of lemon granita while she sang folk songs with a high clear voice. They stopped to listen for a while and Amanda bought two cups of granita. It was fresh and sharp but sweet too, and very refreshing.

The shops were very expensive with the most outlandish outfits displayed in the windows, and the shop assistants were impeccably dressed and incredibly snooty. After a while, Wendy consulted her notes and suggested that they head on up to Anacapri to take the chairlift to the top of the island.

The girls found their way back to the road and jumped on one of the smallest buses they had ever seen. As it weaved its way up the mountain to Anacapri, they understood why it was so small. The road was so narrow! There was hardly room for two vehicles to pass; every time they came across another vehicle, the bus either had to squeeze past with inches to spare or back up to a wider part of the road to let the other vehicle pass by. The road wound its way up higher and higher, clinging to the cliff and although the view was beautiful with the sea and the bay below, it was absolutely terrifying. The bus lurched and groaned and seemed about to topple over at any time. To distract herself Wendy tried to concentrate on the buildings they were passing by. Spectacular villas and hotels, all painted in various shades of pastel and white. The residents seemed to pride themselves on their flowers too, hydrangeas and alliums, various shades of bougainvillaea and hibiscus all decorating gardens and driveways.

Anacapri was quieter than the town below, and the girls could see the chairlift to Monte Solaro slowly clanking away behind a little square. They walked over and bought return tickets; apparently the hike back down was long and rugged, and it was far too hot to even contemplate attempting it. They were disappointed that they couldn't sit together and talk but the seats were single and nobody was waiting, so Wendy was quickly beckoned over by an operator who pulled her into position and pushed her into the chair before lowering the safety barrier, and off she went.

The chairlift swept her up into the air, swinging alarmingly at first but it soon settled down and she looked around. She was hanging above rugged mountainside, and below she could see grass and rocks and the occasional tree. Over to her right, the island dropped away to the sea far below. It was very quiet, away from the harbour and the roads, with no scooters or engines, no voices or clattering of plates. All she could hear was the hum of the chairlift and an occasional clank as it passed over a support column. She turned around to check that Amanda was in the seat behind her, who waved and kicked her legs up and down. She looked down again, they were passing over a few houses with neat little vegetable patches in the gardens, tomatoes and red peppers were splashes of red against all the greenery and there was another garden with a set of gnomes. No, it was Snow White and the seven dwarves set out amongst a pretty little rockery.

Monte Solaro felt like being on top of the world. From the chairlift they walked out into a wide-open paved area, dotted with deckchairs and a few umbrellas. There was a small cafe over to the left but most of the people were walking around by the railings admiring the view. The mountain sloped down below them with the town of Capri far below in a dip. The sea was spectacular from here, so much blue, translucent sapphire and cobalt, deepening to navy further out. It was so clear that they could see huge rocks and boulders laying on the seabed that must have tumbled off the cliffside centuries ago. Far away in the distance, the Sorrento Peninsular lay slightly obscured by mist, and the Galli Islands were tiny dots in the distance.

They walked around, drinking in the views from every direction before jumping back on the chairlift for the ride back down.

"Eccola qua! Here we go, *una magherita* for the lady on my left and *una capricciosa* for her lovely friend!" The rather good-looking waiter grinned at them and presented their lunch with a flourish. They had wandered around the village before sitting down at a table outside a small pizzeria for a lunch break. The young waiter had been very attentive to the two girls, asking them where they were from and telling them that he was working in his uncle's pizzeria for the summer, but he was studying law at the university in Naples.

"What are we doing next?" Amanda asked before taking a huge bite out of a slice of pizza that was threatening to flop under the weight of all the toppings.

"Um, well, we could either visit the Villa San Michele here or go back down to Capri town and see those gardens that Mauro put on the list."

"What about the Blue Grotto? I really want to go there!"

"Hmm, me too, but I'm not sure how we get

there from here. Let's ask the waiter." Wendy looked around and tried to catch his attention as he dashed between tables.

Eventually, he had a moment and came over with a menu tucked under his arm.

"Everything all right? You want to see the dessert menu?" He asked.

"No! Everything is fine, thank you. We just wanted to ask you how we can get to the Blue Grotto from here? Is it far?" Amanda smiled up at him.

"Aah, well, yes," he put the menu down on the table. "It is right at the bottom of the island and now, we are very much at the top of the island."

"Oh. Of course," Amanda flushed, slightly embarrassed. "Is there a bus that we can get?"

"*Certo!* Yes, you can take a bus but if you like, but I think it is closed today. You have never been inside?"

"No, what a shame!" Wendy exclaimed, slumping dejectedly back in her seat.

"Oh no," uttered Amanda simultaneously. "I really wanted to see inside."

"OK, girls, do not panic. Antonio will find a solution!" The waiter parted himself on the chest and made an exaggerated thinking gesture, eyes squinting upwards and miming stroking a beard.

"Let's see, I have an idea – do you have your swimsuits with you?"

Both girls nodded, looking slightly confused.

"*Perfetto*! So, you wait half an hour until I am finished work. I will take you in my car to the grotto and I will show you. We will swim inside, yes?"

The girls looked at each other with round eyes. "Swim inside? Are we allowed?"

"Is not a problem," Antonio declared, "I do it many times with friends, all the Caprese kids do this when it is closed to the public. You want to go? *Dai*, it is an unforgettable experience!" He looked at them with hands and eyebrows raised. It took about two seconds for the girls to agree to go with him.

"Sure!"

"Sounds amazing!" They looked at each other and smiled. Another little adventure was unfolding.

Half an hour later they were hurtling down an extremely narrow road with the most alarming hairpin bends in Antonio's powder-blue Fiat Panda. They had used the restaurant bathroom to change into their swimwear, slipping their clothes back over the top. Antonio was wearing swim shorts and a Best Company t-shirt, standard beach gear for all the locals, and drove barefoot with one arm hanging out of the window and the other alternating between changing gears and steering, while chatting away excitedly to his new friends.

He was explaining that the grotto was once the personal bathing pool of the Emperor Tiberius and how the entrance to the grotto was a small hole that couldn't be entered by boat if the sea was even slightly choppy, as there was the risk of bumping your head on the roof as you went through. It was apparently okay to swim in, if you knew how.

"There is a chain that you have to hold on to and pull yourself through, is easy, I show you – you have to go between the waves, so you don't bump your head!"

He parked at the end of the road – it didn't seem to go on any further – and they scrambled down the set of steps to the tiny jetty. The cave entrance was to the right of them, just a few metres away, and the sea in front of them was a deep blue and did look rather choppy. There was a tiny narrow wooden boat bobbing around nearby with an older man in it. He was nut brown and wrinkled from years of exposure to the sun, with a moustache reminiscent of a walrus. He was holding a fishing rod, although it looked like he was taking a nap as his eyes were closed.

Wendy swallowed, not sure whether she was brave enough to swim through that small hole, but Antonio was already flinging himself into the sea with a loud whoop and a splash. Popping back up out of the water, sleek as an otter, he waved at the boatman who had been startled out of his slumber and swam over towards the boat.

"*Ciao Ernesto, come va?*" They obviously knew each other, and the girls watched to see if they were going to be stopped from swimming in the cave. But

195

no, the boatman laughed and waved Antonio away, calling something out that the girls didn't hear. Antonio swam back over towards them.

"Come on girls, why you waiting? Ernesto is one of the grotto boatmen. He said he will wait to make sure we are safe. Is not a problem, he is the father of my friend."

"Come on Wendy, let's do it! Once in a lifetime!" Amanda shimmied out of her sundress and leapt into the sea with a shriek.

Wendy felt a frisson of excitement and fear but didn't give herself time to dwell on it. She kicked off her shorts and top, dumping them on a higher step and dived in.

It was cool and amazingly refreshing after a morning of exploring the island in the sun. They followed Antonio over to the entrance of the cave. It really was a small hole, Wendy thought, understanding why the boats couldn't go in unless it was calm. She watched a wave roll inside, but it was pitch dark and she couldn't see further than a metre.

As they trod water Antonio reached up and grabbed onto the chain that the boatmen used to pull the little row boats through the hole.

"OK, just do what I do, is easy so don't worry! See you inside!" He waited for a second and as soon as a wave passed, he pulled himself hand over hand through the hole with the chain.

Wendy followed him, scrambling through in a bit of a panic, but she passed through the narrow entrance with ease and found herself in a large dark sea cave. She couldn't see how far back it went but she could see Antonio's head in front of her.

Amanda popped up beside her, treading water and panting. "It's just a big cave, not so special," she said, disappointed in the darkness.

"You're looking the wrong way!" Antonio laughed at them. "Turn around and see the magic!" The girls turned, still treading water, and gasped in amazement. The whole left side of the cave was glowing an ethereal sapphire blue, radiating out from a gap in the wall under the surface. They swam backwards and the light spread, lighting up the whole cave. It was otherworldly and looking down into the water they saw that their submerged bodies were now an eerie pearly colour and covered in tiny silver bubbles. Antonio swept his arm across the water and the resulting splash was a thousand glittering droplets in cyan and electric blue.

"It's incredible!" Amanda shouted, gleefully splashing around in it.

Wendy ducked under the surface and opened her eyes – the colour was astounding, so bright!

They splashed around for a few minutes, enjoying the experience before a big wave suddenly rolled in, making a loud slapping sound as it hit the roof of the entrance.

"OK, it is time to go, before it gets too dangerous!" Antonio led them back out, one at a time, hauling themselves back through the hole with the chain until they blinked in the bright sunlight.

Ernesto, the boatman, was there waiting patiently. He rowed closer, letting them lean on the edge of the boat and rest for a few moments, chatting with Antonio before they swam back over to the small dock and climbed out of the water.

Antonio dried himself off with a towel that he had brought from the car and pulled his t-shirt over his head. "I have to go back up to the restaurant soon. What you want to do? If you need to go to the Marina Grande then Ernesto is going there and can take you, or you can come back up to Anacapri with me – but I think you have a ferry to catch, no?"

Amanda looked at her Swatch watch; it was almost four o'clock and the ferry was leaving at five. There wasn't enough time to do anything else.

"We'd better go with your friend," she told Antonio, "or we might miss the ferry back."

Antonio nodded and raised his hand, beckoning Ernesto to row over to the dock. The girls thanked Antonio for the fun afternoon and promised they would visit him again the next time they came to Capri. He stood and waved for a while as Ernesto rowed them away in the tiny little boat, before climbing back into his little car and driving back up the road.

The boat was very small and low. Wendy and

Amanda sat squashed together at one end while Ernesto faced them, rowing steadily. As Wendy leaned slightly over the side, squeezing seawater out of her hair, he started singing a classic Neapolitan love song.

"Vide 'o mare quanta bello, spira tanto sentimento. Look at the sea, how beautiful it is, inspiring so many emotions." To their left was a wild and rocky cliff face, with no buildings or beaches to be seen. Seagulls circled on the rocky shores, crying out as they swooped low over the little vessel.

Far away to the right, they could see a few boats traversing the Bay of Naples. It was quiet and peaceful out at sea, and Wendy felt her eyelids becoming heavy as she listened to the steady splash of the oars and the waves slapping at the boat. But soon they pulled into the Marina Grande and the sounds of boat engines throbbing, anchor chains rolling and the buzz of many people talking woke her out of her slumber.

Ernesto rowed right into the front of the harbour, stopping alongside a line of identical small wooden boats. He nodded at the girls, doffing his hat as they climbed out thanking him profusely for the ride.

"Grazie, Ernesto! See you soon!" They strolled along the road in front of the port towards the sign for the ferry, stopping off to buy mint chocolate gelato at a pretty little bar along the way.

As the ferry pulled away from the island, Wendy took Mauro's list from her bag and studied it briefly.

"We didn't do too badly; we missed the Gardens

of Augustus and the Villa San Michele but that just means that we can come back another time." She refolded the list and tucked it away.

"Lucky that we met Antonio," Amanda mused, staring out the window at the coastline. "That was brilliant fun, swimming in the grotto. I bet not many people get to do that!"

Chapter 14

Positano, July, 1986

There had been an undercurrent of excitement running through the village all day. Everyone knew that tonight was going to be one of the best nights of the summer. The hairdressers and barbershops had been flat out all day with townsfolk wanting to look their best. Outfits had been planned weeks in advance and were hung up, ironed and ready in bedrooms all around town. There was a village shortage of hairspray; it had sold out in every shop that Amanda had looked in. As the sun set, casting a pink glow across the town and the sea, the lights started blinking on and the anticipation grew.

It was just gone ten in the evening and the sky was the colour of homegrown aubergines, but a waxing gibbous moon had just started to rise from behind the mountainside in front of them and lightened the sky. It hung large and slightly lopsided, a big yellow glow that promised magical lighting across the sea later on in the evening. Wendy and Amanda were dancing around the main bedroom to "Spirit in the Sky" by Doctor and the Medics on one of their Top 40 mix tapes. Amanda had been dressed by Antonio and loved her outfit. It had been inspired by Madonna and consisted of a black net skirt – more of a mini tutu, really – that he had deftly stitched together in the shop one afternoon and a black bustier top. He had accessorised it for her with a dayglo pink belt and a wristful of matching rubber bracelets. A giant pink lace ribbon tied her scrunch-dried hair off her face.

Wendy was relieved to find out that Sandro and Mauro had made sure that there was no boat trip organised for the night of the opening. Mauro had grumbled and tutted and would probably stay at home and mend nets or something, but Sandro was secretly looking forward to going to the party and strutting his stuff.

Wendy wore a figure-hugging grey leopard print mini dress with bright yellow straps and a matching yellow belt and sandals. Her long auburn hair was loose and moussed, swept to one side with a yellow comb. She was considering painting her nails but wasn't sure they would dry in time.

"Don't bother!" Amanda whirled past, snatching the bottle of pink varnish from Wendy's hand. "Come on. Let's just go already!"

The Paradise was officially opening its doors at 10 pm, but they had decided to start their evening with drinks at the bar where they would meet up with the others and then head over to the new *discoteca*, hopefully when it was in full swing, avoiding the obligatory opening speech and ribbon cutting by the mayor.

The Bar Internazionale was pulsing with life.

The doors were all wide open and there was a crowd of people hanging around outside, beers in hand. A cluster of mopeds and scooters were parked haphazardly by the low wall opposite, and there was hardly a space left to sit. As the girls walked up the road and the buzz from the bar grew louder, they were amused to see the VEP, or the Saucepan Man, as Wendy now thought of him, standing on the corner of the crossroads, decked out in all his finest billboards. In addition to the red, white, and green painted sandwich board and the two signs on sticks, he now had a small sign stuck in the brim of his fisherman's cap and was ringing his bell. Together, the girls managed to translate one of the signs.

"Nature is our fountain of life and ecology must win."

They called out *Buonasera* to him as they passed by and he grinned at them, giving his bell a shake.

Crossing the road to enter the bar, they ignored a couple of catcalls and *Ciao Bellas* from a group of boys they had never seen before. Wendy was slightly relieved when Enzo walked out of the bar followed by his friend Simone, both clutching three glasses in their hands.

"*Ciao ragazze! Venite, siamo qui.* Hi girls, come, we're over here!" They followed him over to the wall where Claudia and Gianni sat talking to Maria and Matteo who were using the parked mopeds as handy chairs. Drinks were passed out and cheeks were kissed. Claudia was radiant in a short white lacy dress and brown leather sandals, her burnished skin glowing, and her mass of dark curls bounced and shone.

203

Maria was dressed up in a short black sleeveless dress with a ra-ra skirt topped with a lacy Day-Glo green crop top and matching belt. Her long black hair was swept back from her face with a black scarf tied in a jaunty bow. The girls complimented each others' outfits and spent a moment admiring Amanda's skirt and wondering if Antonio would make more.

"What do you want to drink, girls?" Enzo slung his arm casually around Amanda's shoulder. "We are having a very special drink called a power spritz. It gives you energy for the night ahead! Here, try it, you want?"

"Sure …" Amanda took a quick sip from his glass and passed it to Wendy. It was bright orange and stronger than a normal spritz. "What's in it?"

"It's like a normal spritz but with vodka for extra power. Wait, I get some for you!" Enzo bounded back across to the bar. Wendy looked around to see if she could spot Francesco anywhere but there was no sign of him or his friend Dom. Maybe they were already at the Paradise. A motorbike roared up the road, screeching to a halt next to them. Wendy recognised two of the boys from the dinner in Praiano; they greeted Gianni and Matteo enthusiastically, almost falling off the heavy bike as one of them leaned over to backslap Matteo good-heartedly. One of them hopped off the bike and headed into the bar while the other waited.

"*Che belle ragazze stasera,*" he gestured with both hands appreciatively at the four girls. Matteo and Gianni pulled their respective partners closer to them and grinned proudly.

Enzo reappeared with the drinks and passed them to the girls. They all sat there on the wall in front of the bar for about an hour, happily people-watching, chatting and joking around. Amanda noticed that Simone was very popular; quite a few people were coming to greet him and taking little walks with him down the road and back.

Amanda nudged Wendy and whispered, "Look, see! He's doing a roaring trade tonight." They watched carefully as Simone walked away again with a boy they had never seen before and, sure enough, saw a deft exchange of hands before the boy slipped his hand into his pocket. Wendy looked around to see if anyone else had been watching but nobody was interested. They were on their second power spritz and Wendy had just realised how strong they were. She already felt a little tipsy and while no one was watching, she tipped the rest of her drink over the wall where it trickled down to a rooftop far below.

People were starting to peel away from the bar now; it was almost midnight and time to head over to the Paradise nightclub.

"The procession is starting," Gianni called, clapping his hands. Amanda looked around, half expecting to see an actual procession like on the religious festivals and Claudia laughed.

"No, he means that it is time to go. I don't know why but everyone goes to the *discoteca* at the same time, never before midnight, so we call it the procession."

"Shall we join them?" Enzo was back and

gathering up the glasses to take back inside the bar.

"How exciting, *andiamo*! Let's go!" Amanda grabbed Wendy's glass off her and followed Enzo over to the bar.

"How are we going to get there?" Amanda wondered out loud, as Matteo and Maria climbed onto their scooter and Claudia hopped up behind Gianni. Enzo scratched his head and shrugged, "It's not far, we can all fit on my scooter, no?" He straddled his Vespa, kicked it off the stand and patted the seat behind him for Amanda to climb on.

"What about me?" Wendy wailed.

"Amanda, move closer to me, make room for Wendy!" Enzo pulled on Amanda's leg and she shifted forwards as much as possible, laughing and wrapping herself around Enzo like a koala.

"*Sìììì*! Like that is good!" Enzo laughed. "Come Wendy!"

"I can't fit there!" Wendy exclaimed, looking doubtfully at the sliver of saddle jutting out behind Amanda.

"You can! Try! We do this all the time, just hold on tightly to Amanda. I will go slowly, I promise!" Enzo revved the engine and Wendy had to inelegantly lift her leg over the saddle, flashing her underwear to Claudia and Gianni. Gianni let out a whoop and Claudia covered his eyes, laughing. Wendy blushed and tried to tug down her dress, but it was useless –

it had risen right up and was too tight to go past her thighs with Amanda in between them. Miniskirts and scooters did not go together.

"Hold on, we go!" Enzo yelled over the engine and accelerated. Amanda and Wendy squealed, and the three scooters sped off towards the edge of town.

The last time Wendy had been here with Enzo, it had been pitch dark and she'd had to feel her way down the steps. This time, there were two burning torches on each side of the entrance, which was now painted white with a wrought iron arch over the top. Two silver planters stood on each side of the gateway, each filled with white flowers, and there was a burly bouncer dressed all in black with a white tie. A few people were hanging around, waiting for friends to arrive and the roadside was thick with parked scooters.

As the club door opened below, the strains of "Walk Like an Egyptian" by the Bangles drifted up towards them.

"I love this song! Let's go dance, guys!" Claudia linked arms with Wendy and started dragging her down the steps. The others followed, and they ended up all running down towards the entrance. The pathway was lit with giant citronella candles placed at intervals and the bushes had been pruned back.

Another bouncer stood at the doorway and opened it for them as they arrived. Enzo and Gianni obviously knew him, and they stopped to exchange greetings.

The girls stepped into the Paradise and looked around. It was stunning! To the left was a long pale curving bar, studded with bar stools in front of it, snaking around a large spiral staircase that led down to another floor. Behind the bar, glass shelves were backlit, full of bottles and a hanging rack full of glasses mirrored from above the curve of the bar. It was hard to tell what colour the walls were exactly with all the coloured lights bouncing off them, but they were pale, cream or maybe beige. The bar undulated around the back of the huge room and tapered off beyond a column. To the right, those huge arched windows showcased the town below, sparkling among the dark sea and sky. At the far end, there was a mirrored seating area; curvy sofas, chairs and pouffes were set up against the mirrored far wall and the rest of the floor was for dancing. The girls pushed forwards through the throng of people towards the middle to find the dancefloor. The ceiling above it was covered with tiny dots of light, creating a starry sky effect. It was beautiful.

They danced out the next few songs, moving from one side of the dance floor to the other to get a good look around. More people were milling around exploring than people dancing, and it was hard to see over the crowds. Wendy thought she had spotted Dom and Francesco near the bar but was whirled around by Maria and didn't see them again.

There was a door just past the two arches that led to the small terrace where Wendy and Enzo had sat that night of the hair dye failure. The dance floor was packed. Wendy spotted Sandro the fisherman dancing with two very glamorous Italian-looking women and he saw her and winked.

"There's Antonio, oh my word, look what he's wearing! Come say hello!" Amanda dragged Wendy towards the bar where Antonio sat posing on one of the bar stools. He seemed to have been inspired by Prince and was wearing a pair of shiny purple drainpipe trousers with a matching purple waistcoat from underneath which peeked a frilly white shirt. His hair was slicked back at the sides and sprayed in a high quiff, almost a nod to Elvis, too.

"*Ciao* darlings! Isn't it wonderful? What are you drinking? I'm feeling generous tonight!" He stood to kiss them both hello and sat back down regally, summoning a barman.

"I'll have a vodka orange, please," Amanda shouted over the noise, "and a vodka lemon for Wendy!" She didn't need to ask. Maria and Claudia appeared from the dance floor and ordered drinks too.

"Where's the DJ?" Amanda asked, looking around. Antonio took her arms and turned her, pointing at a small booth that she hadn't noticed at the back of the room near the sitting area.

"I'll be right back!" She winked and strode over, no doubt to request a song.

A few minutes later, Antonio let out a very feminine shriek as "Let's Go Crazy" by Prince belted out of the speakers. Amanda winked at Wendy as he jumped up and pulled them all onto the dancefloor, where he whirled and wiggled, arms and legs flying, dancing with each of them in turn. The floor underneath was already sticky with spilt drinks; the crowd pulsed and throbbed as they bounded up and down, showered with flashing green lights and sparkles from the glitter ball high above. They danced for what seemed like ages, arms in the air, skirts flying. The boys appeared and they swirled and bumped and crashed into each other, laughing and singing. "The Edge of Heaven" by Wham came on, and Wendy and Amanda belted out the words they knew off by heart, dancing a routine they had made up years ago in their bedrooms, to the amusement of the others who surrounded them in a circle, whooping and cheering them on. As the song morphed into "Tainted Love" by Soft Cell, more and more people surged onto the dance floor and Wendy pushed her way out to leave her empty glass at the bar. Her head was spinning but she loved this song too and plunged back into the crowd – and suddenly came face to face with Francesco. She stopped in surprise for a second; he reached out to dance with her and, being a bit tipsy, she grabbed his hand, leaned back and twirled under his arm.

"*Now I know I've got to run away, I've got to get away ...*" She sang at him and spun away from him. He appeared in front of her again and she sang along, the words of the song doing the talking for her. "*Don't touch me please, I cannot stand the way you tease.*" She twirled away again but he followed her and as the song ended, she sang the words, "*Touch me baby tainted love, touch me baby tainted love ...*" And he grabbed her hands, not really caring if anyone was watching and spun around with her.

At that point, the music changed into "Crazy for You" by Madonna, the lights dimmed, and the dancers morphed from a heaving mass into separate couples

210

that swayed gently together. Wendy and Francesco froze for a moment, staring at each other, both wanting more than anything to wrap their arms around each other and dance this slow dance close together, but they reluctantly parted. Slow dancing with someone else's husband was definitely not possible.

"We can't. Ever." Wendy shouted in his ear, frustrated by how she felt and how impossible the situation was. She turned away and weaved her way through the dance floor over to the door that led to the terrace and stepped out into the cooler air. The door shut behind her and the noise from the club was muted. A couple was standing against the railings looking out across the town and another couple just leaving, walking back around to the front of the club.

She wandered over to the far end of the building. There was a giant terracotta vase with a prickly pear plant sprouting out of the top in the corner of the terrace and a narrow passageway between the side wall and the mountainside with an emergency exit sign on the wall. It was dark so she turned away and went to lean on the railing. Her head was spinning a bit from the dancing and the cocktails. The town was laid out below, shaped by the light from the houses and hotels. She could see the headlights of a car snaking around the dark unlit road, looping around the hairpin bends. Far below, she could see the little boats at anchor in the bay, all pointing west and bobbing gently. She heard a surge of music as the door opened and closed again; someone stepped up behind her and she knew that he had followed her outside. She felt him stand next to her, close enough that his shoulder was touching hers.

"I'm sorry," he sighed. "This is hard for me too. Wendy, I want to dance with you, I want to be with you, and you are here right by my side which makes me so happy, but of course, I can do nothing. I feel very confused right now."

She glanced sideways at him. "It's like I arrived too late. If I had come here and met you a few years ago, maybe you wouldn't have married, but now … it's too late. It's not fair!" She stepped back to see if they were being watched, but the other couple had gone back inside and there was nobody but them.

He stepped closer and sighed. "You know, that night in Montepertuso, after the fireworks, I couldn't sleep, my eyes were wide open and I was thinking of you. I feel like something new is happening to me … and yes, I know, I am married, and I love my wife and I swear I never, never have felt like this before. It is strange, but I think … maybe … you feel it too, no?"

Their eyes met and she felt a frisson of something fizzle through her. She could see the fear in his eyes but also tenderness as he looked back at her. The sensible part of her urged her to deny any feelings she had towards him, he was out of bounds for Christ's sake, what was the point in admitting she had feelings towards him?

But he'd just laid his feelings bare, and it didn't mean that they had to act on them.

"Yes," she said softly, "I feel something too. But you're married, Francesco! I have no intention of doing anything about it!"

"*Vieni*, come with me," Francesco pulled her gently over towards the emergency exit, into the narrow dark passageway. He spun her to face him and cupped her face in his hands, she thought he was going to kiss her, but he lowered his hands to her waist, leaned his forehead on hers and whispered, "I already know what is happening even if I don't want to admit it. I am sure of the symptoms. I can't sleep, my eyes stay wide open, and I think of you. When I gave you a lift from Praiano, I wanted to kiss you, but I knew it would be wrong. When I held you after you hurt your foot, it felt so natural to have you there by my side. How can this be wrong? I know myself well enough to understand when I am falling in love, Wendy."

She could smell his aftershave, lemony and peppery all around her. She could feel his arms wrapped around her and she heard the words he whispered – they made her shiver and melt at the same time. This was so wrong, but could they help it? How do you control who you fall in love with? Can you stop it from happening, and condition yourself to not feel the feelings? She lifted her face to his and perhaps because of the alcohol she had consumed, or maybe because of the words he had spoken, she decided to go with her heart rather than her brain and said the two words that changed everything.

"Kiss me." And so, he did.

As kisses go, it was pretty much perfect. There was no bumping of noses, no clashing of teeth, no stubble that scraped. He tasted of rum and coke and the peppery scent of his aftershave wrapped itself around her. It was everything Wendy had never known she'd

213

wanted so badly, a breathless dance between lips and tongues and hearts that seemed to have known each other a lifetime already. After a few seconds that felt much longer, they sprang apart, both slightly shocked that they had actually done it.

"I'm sorry ... Oh no, I just kissed a married man, I've made you unfaithful to your wife ... I'm so sorry..." Wendy started to say, but he shook his head and stopped her.

"Wendy, *tesoro*, do you feel the same as I feel?"

"Yes, but ..."

"No buts, no regrets. We just kissed, okay, it is not so bad. In fact, it was *bellissimo!*"

From the dark alleyway, they suddenly heard a blast of music as the door of the club opened and a couple stumbled out laughing. Wendy shrank further back into the passageway, reaching out for Francesco's hand to pull him into the dark. He stepped closer to her, and they watched as the couple kissed passionately against the railings.

"That's Amanda!" Wendy whispered in surprise, suddenly recognising her friend's distinctive hair and the tutu. Who on earth was she kissing? "Who is he, I can't see?" She whispered to Francesco. The couple turned slightly and they both recognised Enzo's profile as he raised his hand to push his hair back from his face.

"We should go before they see us, come."

Francesco led her along the side of the club in the dark. There was a staircase at the back of the passageway, and they felt their way up until they could see the light from the candles where it joined the main entranceway to the building.

"You go first, I'll wait a moment and then come back down."

Wendy slipped out of the darkness, guiltily looking around, but the staircase was empty. Everyone was inside the club or up on the road, so she made her way back down, heart pounding, relieved to have not been caught. She slipped back inside – where was the bathroom? Looking around, she saw the staircase spiralling down to the floor below. It must be down there. She ran down the stairs; there was a small corridor with four closed doors. Two were marked private and one had a picture of King Neptune on it; she chose the other door, which had a mermaid on it. Inside, there was a powder room with three sinks and a large mirror; three cubicles were at the back. Claudia was leaning over a sink towards the mirror, redoing her lipstick and Maria was washing her hands.

"*Ciao* Wendy! Where you go, hmm, we lost you?"

"Oh, I just popped outside for some fresh air … Er, have you seen Amanda?" Wendy shut herself in a cubicle to hide the blush that had surely crept up her neck.

"Not for some time," Claudia replied. "I last saw her sexy dancing with Enzo! I think he was enjoying it a lot!"

Wendy flushed the chain and stepped back out to wash her hands. Maria, silent until now, was now leaning against the side wall watching her.

"I saw Amanda and Enzo go outside on the terrace." A chill ran down her back. Had Maria seen her and Francesco, too?

"Oooh!" Claudia exclaimed, "They would be so sweet together! We must find them and ask!"

"Claudia! We can't ask them! I'm sure we'll find out soon enough." Wendy laughed, trying to act normal; it sounded fake to her ears, but she was panicking slightly as the reality of what she had just done kicked in.

"*Andiamo ragazze,* let's go." Maria pushed herself off the wall and swept over to open the door, pulling Claudia with her. Wendy followed silently behind.

As they walked back up the staircase, they bumped into the boys and Amanda, with a suspiciously red chin, who were just about to walk out the door.

"We're going for a smoke, you coming?" Matteo said, putting his arm around Maria and kissing her on the neck. Wendy looked around and spotted Francesco, standing at the edge of the bar with Dom. He saw her and gave her a secret wink, raising his arm to wave at them.

They all traipsed outside and up the steps to the

road. Amanda came up beside Wendy and whispered in her ear, "You'll never guess! I just snogged Enzo!" She squeaked and squeezed Wendy's arm in excitement.

"Wow! Really! How was it?" Wendy pretended to be surprised and squeezed Amanda's arm back. "It was brilliant, his stubble was a bit scratchy, but I really like him!"

They had reached the road and crossed over to the steps that lead up towards the path with a pond at the end.

"Enzo, no! Where are we going? I don't want to go hiking!" Wendy called out from the back of the group.

"No, no! We stop now and sit here, don't worry." They arranged themselves on the steps, just tucked out of sight from the road. Matteo and Enzo started skinning up.

"Guys, I was thinking it's not fair that we," Amanda gestured to herself and Wendy, "keep on smoking your weed. Can we buy some of our own?"

Enzo laughed, "But no! It's not a problem, we don't mind … but if you want some for yourselves, I can get you some." He rolled the spliff into a perfect cone and twisted off the end before lighting it.

Amanda shrugged, "Well, we don't really need any, we only smoke when we're out with you guys."

"Such bad influences … Amanda you should

217

have listened to your ex-boss!" Wendy teased. "Where's Simone? He was around earlier but I haven't seen him for a while?"

Enzo passed the joint to Amanda and exhaled before answering. "Oh, he's around somewhere, he wouldn't miss tonight."

"Is he dealing?" Amanda asked Enzo quietly. Claudia and Maria were sitting a few steps away, immersed in their own conversation. Matteo and Gianni were giggling about something or other and didn't hear the question. Enzo looked at Amanda then Wendy for a moment and nodded slowly. "Yes, he is, but please do not talk of it to anybody. Is only some weed, nothing more, but best to not talk about it."

"Sure, no problem," Amanda shrugged and turned to Wendy. "Told you!" she mouthed.

They sat there comparing their first impressions of the Paradise, all positive, before stumbling back down into the club for the last hour.

The music was fantastic, and the crowds had thinned out now; some people had work the next day and needed sleep. But this group were young and the night was magical. They danced and staggered and sang and drank. At one point, Amanda lost her balance and stumbled, pulling Wendy with her. They crashed into Enzo, who couldn't take the weight and in turn collapsed into Maria and Matteo, and the whole lot of them ended up in a heap on the dance floor, rolling around with laughter. They got up and dusted themselves off, carrying on unharmed. Francesco and

Dom joined them, and Wendy danced from one to the other feeling that special jolt of electricity every time she touched Francesco. Secret looks passed between them which no one else saw, and they both felt that this was somehow right, that they were supposed to be together.

All too soon it was three in the morning, and the music faded out and the lights faded on which made them leave faster, squinting in the brightness. Up at the road, there was a mass exodus of revving scooters and Vespas all departing together and heading back into town. Wendy saw Francesco and a few others split off from the group at the turning to Montepertuso, and she watched from the back of the scooter she was on as his rear light got smaller and higher and then vanished around a corner.

Back home, Amanda had lingered outside the front door with Enzo for a few minutes and Wendy had left them to it, going inside and leaving the door ajar. They met up in the kitchen for glasses of water to take to bed. Amanda was waxing lyrical about Enzo, but Wendy was quiet. She wasn't sure whether to tell Amanda what had happened. She was ashamed to admit that she had feelings for a married man and had kissed him. He would be in so much trouble if someone had seen them. *Probably best to not say anything*, she thought to herself, *it was surely just a one-off. It really can't happen again.*

She went to bed feeling elated and happy but also sad and confused until she dropped off into a restless sleep.

Chapter 15

Positano, August 1986

Wendy couldn't deny or ignore the massive attraction she felt towards Francesco, but she did not want to get involved with him and felt terribly guilty about the kiss. She even had the idea that they could just be friends and over time, the attraction they felt would wear off. The next time she saw him, a few days later at the beach, she told him that the kiss had been lovely, but it was a mistake and mustn't happen again.

"It was wrong, Francesco, and besides, everybody knows you here. I probably shouldn't even be talking to you. It'll get you in trouble."

She had been sunbathing at the front of the shore, the water lapping up her legs, when she had spotted him walking along the shoreline with Dom. They had both greeted her enthusiastically and flopped down beside her on the pebbles. Dom had soon sprung up again to chat with someone nearby and they'd had a moment to talk.

"I know, but really I do not care for the gossip. I can talk to whoever I want, there is nothing wrong with talking, no?"

Wendy sighed theatrically. "Fine then, talk to me. Why don't you tell me a bit about your wife? How did you meet, and how long have you been together?"

Francesco looked surprised. He picked up a handful of pebbles and shook them through his fingers. "Really? You want to know about me and Elena?"

Wendy secretly wanted to know everything about him, but she shrugged nonchalantly and nodded.

He leaned back and made himself comfortable on the beach, as if settling in for a long story.

"Well, I can't tell you when we met because she has always been there. This is a small town, you know, we are the same age, so of course we were at the school at the same time. I didn't notice her until I was sixteen though. My older brother was teaching me to drive his Vespa and we kept driving past this wall in Positano where there was a group of kids hanging out. Every night, my brother would make me drive up and down, up and down, with him sitting behind me, which made it very hard to balance. Then he would leave me and go to his girlfriend. I couldn't drive back up to Montepertuso alone, so one day I went to hang out with the group of kids to wait for him. Elena was there and she was friendlier than the others. We just started talking, you know, about films, music, people we knew in common. It wasn't like with you ..."

"With me?" Wendy asked, turning to look at him. She had been lying back on the sand, picturing the scene in her head, and sat up, jolted back to reality.

222

He lowered his voice, looking quickly around to check that no one was near enough to listen in.

"Yes, with you it feels like a lightning bolt has hit me. I know we have only shared one kiss and that I don't know you really, but I feel such an immediate attraction or connection with you. With Elena, it was not at all like that. I think we just gradually became used to being together and slowly fell in love." He sighed, "And then after a few years it felt right to get married. I didn't even propose properly."

"What? Why on earth not, you horrible man!" She threw a handful of tiny pebbles at him playfully. She had been feeling a bit sad, realising that they were childhood sweethearts still together, but on hearing that he hadn't proposed properly, she suddenly felt an inexplicable sense of … happiness? Relief? Hope?

"No," he continued, brushing off the pebbles. "I didn't. We just sort of talked about it and then decided to get married. Three years later, Leonardo arrived."

"And now you are three." They looked at each other.

"Hmm, and now four …" he said softly.

"Three," Wendy corrected. "Maybe I'm just your mid-life crisis." She felt a lump rising in her throat, a painful sadness of what could never be.

"I think you should go to Dom now; we shouldn't be talking like this in the middle of the beach. I need to go anyway, Amanda will be waiting." She scrambled to her feet and grabbed her beach bag, wrapping her sarong around her waist before trying to walk off, slowly and composed. She reached the beach bar and ducked into one of the toilet cubicles where she let out a single sob and then pulled herself together, splashing her face with cool water before making her way home.

He turned up at the house one afternoon when Amanda was at work and Wendy was alone. The doorbell rang and she opened it to find him standing there with a bag of lemons in one hand and a bottle of limoncello in the other.

"Special delivery!" He grinned at her. "You ordered lemons, no?" He winked at her and gestured his head sideways in case anyone was eavesdropping. She sighed and took him into the kitchen, firmly closing the bedroom door as they walked past.

"Why are you here?" She fiddled around with the kettle and teabags to keep herself busy, nervous to be alone with him.

"I just want to see you, to talk with you." He sat down at the table, dumping the bottle and lemons on the top, and made a fuss of the dog who had ambled up beside him. "Wendy, I can't stop thinking about you. I don't know what to do. I feel terrible for my wife, and I don't know if she can tell something is happening."

Wendy was flattered and horrified. She slammed a cup of tea in front of him and stood over him. "Francesco, no! We don't even know each other properly. There is nothing happening! It was just one drunken kiss! Yes, there is a feeling between us, I admit it, but we've spent no proper time together, and we can't! We can't get to know each other over dinner in a restaurant, we can't take a walk along the beach together or anything. I don't want to get involved with someone else's husband and sneak around hiding."

Suddenly she was crying, and he jumped up and pulled her towards him. She leaned into his arms and he just held her, enveloping her with that lemony peppery scent she was beginning to crave. He stroked her hair until she calmed down and then somehow her face tilted up towards his and they were kissing for the second time. A longer, deeper kiss that felt comforting and passionate and right, not wrong. It tasted of tea and tears and hope, not regret.

"Your eyes are beautiful when you cry. I'm sorry," he sighed, pulling away and caressing her cheek with his thumb. "I hate that it is me that makes you cry. Okay, let's talk about something else. Tell me about how you met Amanda."

Wendy sniffed and laughed, glad for the distraction. They sat down and she wiped her eyes with a paper napkin.

"Well, my parents sent me to summer camp when I was eleven years old and she was there too. We were put in a team together for a treasure hunt and that was it, we were friends. I remember her relentlessly chasing after this one boy. He actually jumped in the pool to escape her and she just went right in after him! I couldn't figure out at the time what was so interesting about a boy!"

"What year was this?"

"Oh, it must have been 1971." Wendy glanced at him, only to find him staring at her with a little smile. "What?"

"Oh, I was just imagining you in pigtails and how cute you must have been!"

She pulled a face and asked, "What were you doing back then?"

He pushed onto the back legs of his chair and stretched his arms over his head, revealing a strip of tanned midriff that she tried to ignore.

"Oh, I was doing my military service in '71. I was on a naval ship for 18 months, a total waste of time." He tipped forwards again just as the doorbell rang upstairs. Wendy froze like a rabbit caught in headlights. It was just gone four in the afternoon and Amanda had finished work half an hour ago. Her eyes travelled to the tabletop where Amanda's keys lay forgotten in a heap with a lipstick and a hair scrunch.

"Shit! Amanda's back, you have to hide!" Francesco looked around, not sure where to go but Wendy pulled him out of the kitchen and up the stairs, ducking into the little artist studio that they never went into.

"This is exactly what I didn't want to have to do, hiding and creeping around! Stay in here," she whispered. "I'll go let her in and when you hear us go downstairs, you can let yourself out." She was panicking and turned to go as the doorbell rang again. Francesco pulled her back and whispered, "It's going to be okay. I won't hurt you, Wendy, I promise." He kissed her quickly and she tore herself away, pulling the door closed behind her.

She opened the front door, heart pounding, convinced that they would suspect something was up, to find Amanda waiting impatiently with Enzo and Simone.

"Take your time why don't you," Amanda joked as they barrelled downstairs, passing the studio without a glance. Wendy followed them down and as she walked back into the kitchen, she heard the faint sound of the front door closing. *Phew*, she thought, *that was close*.

"There's a bag of lemons here, can we use these?" Amanda held out one of the lemons that Francesco had brought, and Enzo nodded.

"*Si, perfetto*! We make pasta with *limone* and tuna!" He took the lemon from Amanda, fished another two out of the bag and started to juggle with them, lurching around the kitchen.

"Wendy?" He called loudly, "Amanda? It is time for cooking lesson *numero due*!"

Wendy came in from the terrace where she had been gazing at the road to Montepertuso, glad of the distraction.

"Today we make a very simple dish that can be

eaten hot or cold! For this reason, it is good for summer or winter and can be taken in a box on *pica-nicas*."

"Pica-nicas?" Amanda howled with laughter and Wendy couldn't help laughing too. "Is that how Italians say picnic or are you just saying it wrong?"

Enzo put on a highly offended expression and stopped juggling.

"Do not." One lemon slammed onto the table.

"Make jokes." Another lemon slammed down.

"With the chef." He put the third lemon down more gently this time and picked up a knife, waggling it at the girls.

"Now, come here and take notes. Simone!" Simone jumped up from the bench and stood to attention. "You will be my sous-chef, now skin up and open some *vino*!" The girls laughed again, and Simone grinned, pulled a cigarette packet out of his pocket, and sat back down to complete his task.

"This is very easy and takes no time at all. Now watch." Enzo got to work and the girls paid attention as he put a pan of salted water on to boil for the pasta and placed a frying pan on the hob with a generous slug of olive oil. He finely chopped an onion and, turning the flame down low, scraped the onion into the pan.

"You want to let it cook on a medium flame. Too hot and it will burn, we want the onion to be brown at the edges." He stirred it and left it to cook. "Wendy, please find me some black olives. You have, yes?"

"Yes sir!" Wendy went over to the fridge and pulled out a jar.

"And tuna," he added. "Amanda, I need a – how you say – to make juice from the lemon?" He mimed twisting a lemon.

"A lemon juicer," Amanda managed to keep a straight face, pointedly not looking at Wendy because she knew she would laugh.

The ingredients were brought to him and he juiced a couple of lemons, chopped and de-stoned a large handful of olives and drained the excess oil from the tins of tuna.

"Simone! Where is the *vino*?"

"*Ecco*! Here!" Simone passed each of them a glass of wine and offered the joint to Enzo who stepped away from the cooker to take a couple of puffs before handing it over to Wendy.

"Pay attention *bimbi*! Now, all you have to do is put the juice and the tuna and olives into the pan with the onions." He mixed it all up with a wooden spoon and turning the flame down left it to simmer.

"When the pasta is ready, we mix it together and we eat! Simple, no?

Wendy took four plates down from the shelf and they decided to eat outside under the fairy lights. The pasta was delicious, lemony and fragrant with salty bites of olive and flecks of tuna.

"Should I get some parmesan cheese?" Wendy asked.

"*Parmeggiano*? No! Oh, you English girls know nothing! When the pasta is with the fish you never put the cheese on it!"

"Never!" Simone agreed, solemnly shaking his head.

In no time at all they had finished and were sitting back rubbing their stomachs.

"Where did those lemons come from?" Amanda asked Wendy, as she gathered up the plates.

"Um, I saw Francesco earlier, he gave them to me. I think he was delivering some to the bar."

"*Ah, sì*," nodded Simone, "his father has lemons. You saw him at the bar?"

Wendy hoped she wasn't blushing and nodded vaguely, getting up to help Amanda clear the table. In the kitchen, she grabbed four tiny espresso cups and the bottle of limoncello and turned to take them outside. Simone was standing right in front of her; she hadn't heard him come in and she jumped slightly.

"You scared me!" She laughed, but he didn't move out of the way. He stepped closer, towering over her.

"You are not interested in Francesco, I hope? He is a married man, you know this, yes?"

Wendy swallowed and tried to smile. "Of course I'm not interested in him! I hardly know him. Why do you ask?"

"Hmm, it would be a shame. I am not married, why don't we go out together, you and me? You like pizza? I can take you for pizza in a very romantic place." He suddenly lunged forwards and tried to kiss her. She stepped backwards and raised her arm to block him.

"Simone, no! I'm sorry but I don't want to go for pizza with you." He pushed her arm back down and could have been trying to lean in again for another attempt, but Enzo walked into the kitchen, and Simone stepped back, smoothly taking the limoncello bottle from her hand as if he had just come in to help her.

"Come on guys, let's open this bottle!" Enzo, none the wiser, shepherded them back outside.

"Ugh!" grimaced Enzo after taking a sip, "it is warm! You have to keep the bottle in the freezer." They drank it anyway, passing around another joint, relaxing in the evening warmth, batting away the odd mosquito. Amanda sat down and cuddled into Enzo who put an arm around her and kissed the side of her neck. They had been spending a lot of time together since they had kissed at the disco the other night and looked very happy together.

Eventually Wendy stood up and yawned, stretching her arms in the air.

"I'm going to bed, guys. I've got a long day tomorrow, a Capri trip and the night fishing too. Thanks for dinner Enzo, *Buona Notte tutti!*"

Simone quickly jumped up from the table too.

"You can't leave me with these two lovebirds. I come with you!"

They all laughed.

"Buona Notte Simone!" Wendy walked out and firmly shut the door behind her.

Chapter 16

Positano, September 2016

The sky was a delicate pink, reflected onto the flat surface of the sea. The air still had an early morning chill to it but would warm up as soon as the sun rose from behind the mountain. Mia walked barefoot along the quiet beach, trying to imagine her mum at 26 in a bikini, walking right here towards a young man with curly hair and a surfboard. It was not quite eight o'clock and there were a couple of boats starting to move towards the jetty on the far side of the beach. She hadn't been able to sleep much the night before and had snuck out of the house at first light to walk down the hundreds of steps to the road, which she had followed into town, and then made her way down to the beach. The narrow lanes were quiet except for a couple of early dog walkers, but a tantalising aroma of fresh coffee and baked pastries wafted out of windows and perfumed the air.

She made her way over to the jetty, curious to see the tile on the bench dedicated to the lady Gloria that her mum had told her about. She couldn't see any traditional wooden benches but there was a squat stone cube bench near the lower jetty. She walked up to it and immediately spotted the small, hand-painted ceramic tile. She crouched down and saw a fishing boat with a white-haired lady clearly sitting on the front, looking out to sea, watching the sunset.

"Hello, Gloria, Mum's been telling me all about you," she said softly, before hopping down over the wall onto the beach and walking slowly across to the other side.

At the end of the beach, there were a few steps leading up to a concrete bathing platform, bedecked with palm trees and luxury sun loungers with white umbrellas. This must be La Scogliera, Enzo's beach club, she was sure. She sat on a sun bed and stared at the incredible view. The grey beach with rows of blue sun loungers and closed umbrellas, waiting for the day to start and the town majestically rising to a point, way up high, houses and hotels all jumbled together. She squinted, trying to figure out where Rob and Ted's house might be, but it was impossible to tell.

"Scusa, signorina? Hello, Madam?" A voice startled her from behind; she had thought she was alone there. She turned to see a young man dressed in bathing shorts and a t-shirt with *"La Scogliera"* embroidered across the left side of the chest. He was barefoot and holding a pile of clean, folded towels.

"I am sorry," he continued in English, "you cannot sit here, this is a private beach club."

"Oh, sorry," Mia jumped up, "I thought it was closed still."

"Well, yes, but it is still not allowed." He smiled

at her in sympathy and placed a towel on each sun lounger.

"Would it make a difference," Mia said with a mischievous look in her eye, "if I told you that I am staying at Enzo Marisco's house? Your boss, I presume?"

"Oh!" He looked at her in surprise, "I am sorry, I didn't know, then, of course, it is all right for you to be here!"

"Well, actually I was going to go anyway. I've got a long walk up and it's getting warmer."

"Then you will need a coffee before you go, perhaps? Please, come, let me offer to you breakfast."

Mia followed him to a little bar that was built into the rocky cliff face. A few tables were scattered around nearby, and he gestured for her to take a seat.

"Espresso or cappuccino?" He asked.

"Ooh, cappuccino please!" He ducked inside the bar and came out a few minutes later with a tray bearing a foaming cappuccino, a small cup of espresso, and a plate with two giant croissants or *cornetti* as they were called here.

"So, here is your breakfast and by the way, my name is Andrea," he said, mock bowing to her as he placed the plate in front of her.

"Thank you, Andrea! Oh, I'm Mia, by the way!"

"Please to meet you, Mia. Is this your first time here?"

Mia nodded as she took a bite of the big flakey *cornetto*. It was delicious, crunchy on the outside and soft inside with a blob of apricot jam in the middle.

"Mmm, this is wonderful! Yes, I'm here with my mum, she's going to show me around. Well, actually, she's probably not, but I'm sure Jess will keep me busy."

"Jess? But of course, if you are staying at Enzo then you know Jess too! She is a friend of my sister, Anna, they were at school together. I am a bit older." He patted his chest proudly at that and Mia laughed.

"God, it's true that everyone knows everyone here then, isn't it?"

"Yes, it is a good thing and a bad thing!" He shook his head ruefully. "You are never lonely, but you can never hide either. Everyone knows everything about everyone!"

"I can imagine! It's pretty similar where I live now, too."

They chatted for a while until breakfast was finished and Andrea stood to clear away the plates. He was easy to talk to, his English was excellent, and he laughed, telling Mia that Amanda had taught him for years and it had helped to be friends with Jess and Rebecca as they often chatted in English when together.

"Thank you so much for breakfast! I'm sure I'll

see you again soon, bye Andrea!" Mia walked away smiling, feeling suddenly very energised and positive for her long walk back up the steps.

She arrived back at the house with trembling legs and threw herself in the shower. Mum and Amanda were wandering around the garden together, pointing out flowers and plants contentedly. Jess was in the kitchen, and she joined her, pulling out a chair at the table and helping herself to a glass of water.

"Where did you disappear to this morning?" Jess asked, reaching up to a high cupboard for a bag of flour.

"Oh, I took the steps down to the beach, I couldn't wait to see it and it was the perfect morning workout!

"Ha! You can say that again, we certainly save on gym fees living here!"

"I met a guy who says he knows you, Andrea, at the beach club?"

"You mean Andrea who works for Dad? Yes, he's lovely, is practically one of the family, he was always here for English lessons when we were small and then would always end up staying for dinner!" Jess started clearing everything off the table and Mia jumped up to help.

"Yes, he was nice, he offered me breakfast. What are you doing? Can I help?"

"Um, can you pass me that dishcloth, thanks? I just have to clean the table quickly so I can make some pasta. You can help with that!" She gave the clear surface a quick wipe over and took a clean tea towel to dry it.

"We'll be seeing Andrea tonight if you want to come with me. There's a group of us meeting for drinks after dinner."

"Thanks, that sounds fun, I'd love to come."

Jess weighed out half a kilo of flour and then upended the bowl onto the middle of the table. Making a well in the centre of the flour, she poured in some warm water and threw in half a teaspoon of salt and with her hands started kneading it, slowly adding more water.

Mia watched fascinated. "Don't tell me you always make your own pasta?"

"Not every time, no, but it tastes so much better than the dry pasta and if there are a few people around to help it's actually pretty quick to do. Once it's ready, we'll get Mum and your mum to sit and help us. I told them to go get the basil for the pesto, but they went into the garden about half an hour ago and never came back!" As she talked, she kneaded and pummelled the flour and water until it amalgamated into a smooth lump which she then dropped into a bowl, covered with cling film and put aside.

"So, Jess, I have to ask you," Mia decided to get straight to the point of why she and her mum were there. "Do you know who my father is?"

Jess looked at Mia with pity and sighed, "No, I have no idea who he is, I'm sorry. I know some of what happened that summer, it's local legend but I can't figure out who your father could be, there are way too many possibilities! What do you know exactly?"

Mia poked at the lump of pasta. "Not much yet. Mum is slowly telling me about it but there seems to be so much backstory that she never gets to the most important part. She started from when they arrived in Positano by bus and she's told me about all sorts of lovely things that they did, including an illicit meet up in the house they were in and, oh, yes, they went to the opening of a nightclub where they had their first kiss. I wanted to ask about that club – is it still there?"

Jess looked amused for a moment and, checking for lurking parents outside the window, dragged Mia outside and over to the front of the garden.

"First of all, I think our mothers have been liaising with each other. My mum has been slowly drip-feeding me the story too and has just told me about that opening night. Paradise, the club was called. It closed down years ago. Look I can show you from here."

Mia tried to follow where Jess was pointing. Right at the very top of the town, she followed the road out of Positano for a while and then spotted the building below the road. Two big arches showed where the picture windows were and where the terrace must have been where her parents first kissed.

"Can we go there? I'd love to see it."

"Sure," Jess shrugged, "it's not very interesting but we can go on the scooter sometime. Right, let's get these two in and we can start making pasta. They can tell us the next part of the story while we do it!"

Positano
July 1986

The Capri trips were really good fun to work on. Either Sandro or Mauro would take out small groups of tourists, transforming the little fishing boat by replacing the nets and lobster pots with wide flat cushions for the people to sit on the deck or sunbathe. Wendy would hand out drinks from a cool box and give the clients a little guided tour, telling them the history of the Galli Islands as they passed, pointing out the Green and White Grottos and the Capri lighthouse. Outside the Blue Grotto, she would help them climb from the boat into the small rowing boats that took them into the cave for a fee, always looking out for Ernesto and waving at him when she spotted him.

Once the clients had disembarked for four hours' free time on the island, she could do whatever she wanted. Sometimes she explored the island a bit, learning where the viewpoints were and visiting the ruins and villas away from the centre. Sometimes she would stay on board; the boat would anchor just outside the Marina and while Sandro or Mauro slept below deck, she would snorkel or sunbathe, reading and napping under the shade of the canopy.

One day, Amanda caught the ferry over to the island and was there waiting for her when they docked. They caught a bus straight up to Anacapri and explored the gardens of the beautiful Villa San Michele before stopping for lunch at Antonio's restaurant. He was delighted to see them again and told them about a scenic hike they must do one day that led down from the top of the chairlift to a centuries-old church on the edge of the cliff. He also suggested that they had lunch down at the Marina Piccola, the smaller harbour on the other side of the island.

"I know where that is," Wendy nodded, "we go past it on the boat, it looks quite busy."

"Yes,'" agreed Antonio, "but you will never see such a beautiful colour sea as there by the arch where the mermaids used to sing. You must go!"

"It sounds amazing," Amanda sighed. "Maybe we can do it next week on my day off?"

The sun had only just risen above the mountain, but it was already searingly hot as Wendy ran down the steps to the beach. She paused to appreciate the view at the top of the *Scalinatella*, the long staircase that looked out over the church square. Directly below, she saw Sandro trundling his wheelbarrow up to the fishmongers. He was dressed in baggy old jeans and wellies, his barrel chest bare except for his beloved gold medallion. A couple were walking a dog up towards the church and the tiny grocery store on the steps was just opening, boxes of fruit piled high ready to be placed on the shelves.

241

A man appeared from the steps behind the bell tower, walking across the church square. With an intake of breath, Wendy realised it was Francesco. As he arrived at the top of the steps he paused and looked up towards her. Could he see her? She waved quickly, looking around to see if anyone was watching but she was alone. She saw him realise it was her and he enthusiastically waved back, then jogged down the steps.

They met under the arch by the public telephones. He greeted her with the double cheek kiss that all Italians use, just lingering slightly too long and kissing her slightly too close to the side of her lips. She drew back and asked him, "What are you doing down here so early?"

"I have a ferry to catch. And you? Are you working today?"

"Yes, "she said, tilting her head questioningly. "Where are you going?"

"I have to meet a colleague in Capri this morning. Will you come and meet me for lunch afterwards? We could sit and talk with no worry about who sees us – if you have nothing else planned, of course?"

Wendy hesitated for a moment. Lunch with Francesco, on Capri? *Well, there's nothing wrong about meeting a friend for lunch, is there,* a little voice told her.

"Sure, I can meet you for lunch. Are you sure it will be okay?"

He smiled that heart-melting smile at her, delighted that she had agreed. "It is lunch, nothing else! Is not a problem, it is a dream come true!"

They started walking down toward the jetty and agreed to meet at lunchtime under the Capri clocktower as there were too many sailors from Positano in the Marina area. Wendy felt a wave of guilt and slightly sordid when he mentioned avoiding the sailors, but the thought of being able to spend a couple of precious hours talking with him outweighed the bad feelings. She casually raised her hand and walked over to Mauro's boat, calling *"Ciao"* over her shoulder and tried not to keep looking back as he waited for the ferry transfer boat to take him on board.

The clients on board were mostly American and easy to look after. There was a bit of confusion when they thought that the Galli Islands were Capri and got upset as the boat whizzed by, but Wendy soon calmed them down and told them the history of the islands.

"You all have heard the story of Odysseus and the Sirens, haven't you? He was on his way home from the Trojan War when his ship passed by these islands here which back then were inhabited by Sirens, creatures with human heads and the bodies of great birds. They were known for luring sailors to watery deaths, enchanting them with their music and singing. Odysseus made his men block their ears with beeswax as they drew closer to the islands and ordered them to bind him tightly to the mast, for he wanted to hear for himself the song of the Sirens. He told his men that they were to tie him tighter if he begged to be set free.

"As the ship drew close to the islands, he heard the magical song and felt the lure of the fantastical beasts. He struggled to be set free, longing to throw himself in the waves and swim towards the rocky shore, but his faithful crew tied him tighter and rowed away faster until he could no longer hear the music and came to his senses."

The tourists sat spellbound as they listened to Wendy. As she finished the story, they took out cameras to take photos of the islands. One of them asked Mauro if he had ever seen a Siren.

"They are long gone from here," he chuckled, shaking his head.

They slowly circled the island of Capri, Mauro steering the boat right up to the White Grotto and the Natural Arch which towered way above them on the cliffside. They drove through the hole in the Faraglioni, three iconic rocks that protruded from the sea. Legend says that couples that kiss as they pass through the rocks will stay together forever. Wendy always enjoyed telling this legend to the clients and then watching to see who kissed and who didn't.

They anchored for a while near another cave called the Green Grotto and the tourists jumped into the emerald waters for a swim. Wendy unfurled the shower hose, ready to rinse them off when they climbed back onboard.

They sailed on around the island, passing the lighthouse and stopping for a visit to the Blue Grotto. The clients laughed in delight when Ernesto rowed over and serenaded Wendy with his hand on his heart.

Finally, they docked in the Marina Grande. It was nearly midday and as she helped everyone climb onto land, she told them all to be back by four o'clock.

As they walked away, she turned to Mauro, "I'm going on land too today, do you want me back earlier or is four okay?"

"Four o'clock is good, *grazie*, Wendy. I will have a nice sleep now!" She threw him the rope which had been wrapped around a bollard to steady the boat and walked off towards the funicular station.

Her heart skipped a beat as she saw Francesco leaning up against the bell tower, waiting for her. He was wearing beige chino shorts and a white linen shirt that showed off his tan, sleeves rolled up and the top three buttons open. He grinned and came over to greet her before leading her off through an archway that led away from the piazza.

"Where are were going?" She asked, almost tripping over a tiny apricot poodle on a lead held by a tiny woman in a bright kaftan and a full face of makeup.

"*Scusa!*" she called after the woman who had tutted, pulling the dog out of the way.

"We go for a little walk to a beautiful cafe. Is near the natural arch, you have been, yes?"

"Actually, no. I've only seen it from the boat, I've been meaning to go there."

245

"Good, I am glad I can show you! So, we take a walk to the arch, there are some steps so it will make us hungry, and then we go for lunch." He casually slung his arm around her shoulder and gave her a gentle squeeze before letting go. They both noticed the jolt of electricity that passed between them.

"So, what were you doing here this morning?" Wendy asked curiously as they walked past a huge red bougainvillaea bush that was threatening to swallow a bench. A blonde lady sat there serenely, dressed all in white, just enjoying her surroundings. Wendy stopped for a moment, rummaged in her bag, and pulled out her camera to take a photo. Francesco waited patiently and as she tucked the camera away, and he told her about the meeting he had been to with the head gardener from the Luna Hotel. They had been discussing various types of lemon trees for the hotel garden and had gotten to talking about gardening. The gardener had told him how the acidity of the soil had changed the colour of the bougainvillaea that they had ordered for the gardens from Ischia, from an orange-red to a more purple hue that clashed with the other flowers and had gotten him into trouble with the owners.

Wendy listened, fascinated that the flower changed colour depending on where it was planted.

"That must be annoying buying a red flower and it suddenly turning purple!"

They chatted easily as they walked; it was as if they had always known each other. The pathway grew quieter, with only the occasional tourist passing by. Francesco took her hand and they walked hand in hand for a while. Wendy tried not to think of Elena.

Now the buildings had petered out and the pathway was surrounded by trees and dry scrub, and the sound of cicadas chirruped through the air. They passed by the cafe, which was quiet with only a couple of tables occupied. The sun filtered softly through branches of the tall pines, creating some welcome shade as they climbed the steps that led to the Natural Arch.

The arch was huge, looming above them. Wendy hadn't realised from the boat how big it actually was, and the rock was covered in other smaller holes. The cobalt sea glittered far below, and a family climbed the steep steps, bantering with each other and panting as they passed by. As they disappeared noisily around a corner, Wendy realised that they were completely alone.

"I wish I had met you years ago!" She sighed, stepping towards Francesco, unable to help herself. The sexual tension between them was excruciating. He took her in his arms and they kissed passionately, both wishing they were somewhere more secluded. She ran her fingers through his hair, and he slipped his hand under her shirt and around her waist, the feel of his hand on her bare skin turning her legs to jelly. The kiss intensified but they had to break apart, panting as they noticed a couple of hikers walking up the steps towards them.

"Voglio fare l'amore con te," he whispered in her ear. Her heart rate increased as she figured out what it meant, *he wanted to make love to her*! She looked at him longingly and nodded slowly.

"Me too, but no, Francesco, I don't want to be the other woman. Think about your wife and your son – it's not fair to them or me. I want it too, but we mustn't. "She stroked the side of his face and stared into his eyes, "I feel so bad," she said sadly.

"I feel terrible too, *cara*, but this feels so right as well. My brain is in turmoil."

They sat on the wall in front of the arch for about half an hour, kissing and talking quietly, savouring this moment, never sure if there would be another time like this together.

"Tell me about your first-ever kiss," Wendy asked, leaning back into his embrace.

"My first-ever kiss, eh? It was pretty normal for Positano. I was with a group of friends at the beach one night. It was dark and we were all sitting on the sun loungers, chatting and messing about. It was probably a town festa, but I can't remember which one. There was this girl from Napoli that I liked but I was too shy to ask her out. But somehow, we ended up talking and splitting off from the others. We sat together on a sun lounger, just a few metres behind the others, it was dark so they couldn't really see us. We didn't have much to say to each other, I hadn't got a clue what to talk about with her so I asked her if she wanted to kiss me and she shrugged and leaned in. We kissed, quickly, you know, tongues in and out like a lizard and then we got up and sheepishly went back to the group." He laughed and sweeping the hair back from his face, added, "I hope I don't still kiss like a lizard!"

Wendy waggled her tongue at him in a lizardly fashion, "Oh I don't know about that, maybe we should try again to assess the lizardness of your kisses."

She turned to him, and they kissed again before she pulled away, not wanting the situation to get too serious.

"Well, my first kiss was as awkward as they get. I was forced into it at a school Christmas disco. My darling friends, one of who you might know, knew that I had never been kissed before and arranged it all behind my back. We were happily dancing away when suddenly everyone had formed a circle around me and this boy from my class who vaguely looked like Rick Astley. They started cheering for a kiss and basically wouldn't let me out of the circle until I had kissed him! Terrible! It was very slobbery!"

"Slobbery?" Francesco asked, stumped at this strange English word.

"Yes, you know, wet and sloppy, here let me demonstrate!"

She tried but it turned out that not everyone can do slobbery kisses together, although they had fun trying for a while before heading back up to the cafe for some lunch.

Wendy found that she had no appetite and ordered an *insalata caprese*, simple slices of juicy mozzarella and Sorrento tomatoes decorated with fresh basil leaves drizzled in olive oil and oregano, which she picked at distractedly. Francesco ordered *tubetti e totani,* a pasta dish with the local pink squid cooked in a fiery tomato sauce. It smelt homely and nourishing and Wendy realised that she knew this smell well. It drifted out of kitchen windows all around Positano at lunchtime and she had never known what it was that they were cooking.

"Here, try some, is so good!" He held a forkful out towards her, and she tried it. The squid tasted surprisingly earthy and the chilli pepper was strong.

"Mmm, that's good! I should ask Enzo to teach me how to make this." She picked up her fork and stole another mouthful.

"Enzo is teaching you to cook?" Francesco laughed, pushing his plate nearer Wendy.

"Well, he's given us a couple of lessons, yes."

After they had finished the waiter brought them tiny glasses of ice-cold limoncello which they sipped slowly before getting up to leave. They strolled slowly back to town, comfortably arm in arm, and Wendy thought once again how easily they fit together and wondered what it would be like to make love to him. He was quiet too for once, lost in his thoughts until they reached the outskirts of the town and had to separate.

"You have to be back at four, no?" He asked her as they passed a marmalade cat sitting regally on a wall, the blue sea behind enhancing the orange fur. The cat watched them suspiciously, ready to spring away the moment they came too close. Wendy nodded and he suggested that they walk down to the Marina instead of taking the funicular. It would only take about fifteen minutes; they had enough time still. She agreed, glad for that extra time with him; they crossed the Piazzetta and ducked down into the stairwell.

The brick staircase that led down to the port was quiet and shady, walled in by whitewashed houses on both sides. As they walked underneath an open window, music filtered out. It was "Crazy for You" by Madonna, the song that had been playing in Paradise when Wendy ran outside and they first kissed. She sang along softly as they passed by, "I never wanted anyone like this, it's all brand new, you'll feel it in my kiss, I'm crazy for you." They stopped and kissed again for a few moments, gazing into each other's eyes, holding onto each other tightly, knowing that it was all so wrong, yet all so right.

"I think we have our very own song," Francesco said as they broke apart. "Wendy, you are *stupenda*! You make me so happy, and I think you are very important to me. I feel much guilt, doing this in secret, but I cannot imagine not knowing you."

Their eyes met and held for a moment until Wendy sort of deflated. She knew that nothing could be gained by these encounters with him. "I can't imagine not knowing you now, I've never felt so comfortable with someone and so drawn towards anyone. But, Francesco, I will not be the one to break up a marriage. That would probably destroy us, and you would feel guilty forever. I'll probably be going back to England at the end of the summer so whatever this is that we have, it can't go any further." But even knowing this, she couldn't stop herself and reached for him again, sinking into his kisses.

The song on the radio ended and an advert started blaring out, ruining the moment. They parted and carried on down towards the port, hand in hand. Just before the staircase ended, they said goodbye. Wendy left first, walking quickly over toward where the boat was waiting. Francesco waited a minute or so, kicked the wall in frustration a couple of times and then strolled out and made his way to the ferry port.

Chapter 17

Positano, August 1986

The humidity was so thick that it hung over the town in a dense mist. The top of the mountain wasn't even visible. It was scorching hot, surely in the mid-30s, and everything felt sticky and sweaty. She walked up the steep pathway that led to the villa and was conscious of the sweat dripping down her back and thighs. She had no choice but to plait her hair tightly off her face and there was hardly any point even thinking about putting makeup on. But she was on her way to do Maria's wedding makeup, so she was going to have to use all her tricks to get it to stay put today.

"Wendy! Quick, come here!"

Claudia saw Wendy as she walked through the gate of the Villa and beckoned to follow her. She took her into the office where the florist seemed to be packing flowers into a box rather than taking them out. Three or four people were milling around on the terrace, talking in hushed voices. Had something happened?

"Okay, so at the moment, the wedding is off," Claudia told Wendy quietly. "Yesterday evening Maria had a big, big argument with the sisters of Matteo and now they are not speaking. She has called off the wedding and was trying to go home, but we stop her and now she is in bed and won't get out."

"Oh, er, okay ..." Wendy stammered, "um, so what's going to happen?" She looked past Claudia to the kitchen where trays of food were wrapped in cling film and noticed the chef sitting at the table, dejectedly eating a sandwich, rather than frantically preparing for a party.

"Well, we have suggested that Maria and Matteo can maybe still do the ceremony and then go and have a private dinner just the two of them. The others could still have the party here. It is all paid for, and we cannot cancel anything at this time! It is a shame, no?" Claudia explained as Wendy nodded.

"But I think you have to go down and talk to Maria, see what she wants. Maybe she change her mind, maybe you help her? You also have to see if the sisters of Matteo and *la mamma* want to still be part of the wedding. *Mamma mia* ... they are the bridesmaids! Whoever heard of bridesmaids not talking to the bride? *Che casino!*"

The last thing Wendy wanted to do was to go and talk with Maria, but she had no choice. They had gotten together a couple of weeks ago for a trial run, and Maria had been delighted with the makeup Wendy had done for her. A soft wash of shaded bronze eyeshadow and a slick of black liner, a pop of orangey-red lipstick mixed with a shiny gloss and bronzed cheekbones complimenting Maria's green eyes and silky dark hair. Now she stepped out onto the terrace where Matteo and his mother were having an animated discussion in hushed voices. An elderly lady walked by, muttering that she would like to slap the bride.

"Vieni, Wendy, come, I take you to her." Reluctantly she followed Claudia down to the bedrooms. The villa was on the opposite side of town from the girls' house, but just as high up from the beach. It was set on three levels, each with a big terrace, dotted with lemon and olive trees and a view to die for. From this angle, she could see the whole beach below and the rocky jetty where all the boats came and went. The pyramid of haphazard buildings rose majestically to the side and she could see the house with their washing hanging out, and further up she could even see the distinctive two arched windows of the new nightclub.

Claudia led her down a corridor and knocked on a door before opening it without waiting.

She poked her head around the door, obviously with no intention of entering the room and announced, "Maria, Wendy is here," before stepping back to usher her through.

Maria was sitting in the bed, the sheets wrapped around her as if for protection. Her face was blotchy, and her eyes were teary and swollen from crying. She was shredding a tissue into pieces and Wendy could see that she had been picking off the nail varnish from her thumbnails. Her mother, a large, round woman, sat on a sturdy chair facing the bed, fanning herself with a magazine. Matteo walked into the room and took a seat at the foot of the bed.

"Okay", Wendy said, sounding far more confident than she felt. "Maria, Claudia's told me there's a problem and you're not sure if you want to go ahead with the wedding."

"*Bah*, look at my face!" Maria swung up from the pillows and looked in the mirror on the wall by the bed. "I cannot get married with a face all big and red like this, is obvious, no?"

"Well, you can actually. I have seen plenty of brides who cry before the ceremony, and it's my job to patch them up and make them shine. It's not difficult and we also have plenty of time. Now, I can go upstairs and get you some cold camomile teabags and some ice which you can use to put on your eyes to soothe them. Will you do that if I get them for you?"

Maria nodded, unconvinced, and Matteo patted her foot encouragingly.

"All right, I'll go get some in a minute. Now, have you thought about what you want to do? Don't just say you want to cancel everything. You still love Matteo, don't you?"

"Yes, of course! But how can I stand next to those two sisters that have said such horrible things to me? It is crazy! The whole family is now hating me, so how can I stand there in front of them all and pretend it is nothing?"

"They don't hate you, *cara*, it was just a disagreement – it will pass, I promise you." Matteo tried to soothe her, stroking her leg.

Maria was getting agitated again. Wendy could see the tears brewing in her eyes. "Okay, you have time, Maria. Please don't call it all off – it would be such a shame. Think about all the people that are coming and all the money that's been spent. It's all about you and Matteo today, and you two are fine!"

Maria's mother shifted in her seat and sighed, "Maria, *cara mia*, think! In the church, you will not even see the other people. You will be standing at the front with your back to them. Then, if you wish, you go, like Claudia said, and have a private dinner in one of the restaurants."

"But my face!" Maria wailed, pulling the covers back up and sinking back into the bed.

"Right, I'm going to get camomile and ice and you are going to calm down, please! Now, what do you want the sisters to do? Are they supposed to get hair and makeup done or not?"

"I don't care … they can do what they want." She shrugged and looked away. Wendy ducked back out of the room and made her way to the kitchen.

The hairdresser had arrived and was sitting at the table, happily making his way through a big plate of pasta. Claudia was sitting with him, eating a slice of focaccia, filling him in on the details.

"So?" She inquired, looking at Wendy and waggling her eyebrows.

"Well, she's very upset, but she didn't say that

257

she wouldn't get married. Let's give her a bit more time. Oh, and can you send down some camomile tea and some ice for her eyes?"

Matteo's mother walked over to them, followed by the two sisters. Anna and Sara were both in their late thirties, older than Matteo by about 10 years. He had been a late baby, a surprise and the much-wanted son to carry on the family fishmonger business. The sisters, both married with an array of five children between them were proper Italian housewives and had never been further than Naples. Their days were filled with cooking and cleaning, laundry and nappies, and they loved nothing better than a good old gossip and a cigarette while sitting on a bench in one of the village *piazzas* or standing at the school gate.

"It is against everything that I stand for," Anna said to Sara who looked as if she had also been crying.

"Oh, *Dio*, what are we to do? I just don't know how to *be*." Sara dabbed at her eyes with a tissue and looked around, hoping someone would have an answer.

"I'll get you some ice for your eyes," Wendy said and sloped off to the freezer, letting Claudia take charge.

"*Allora*, we have to decide what is best. IF the wedding goes ahead, are you going to participate?" Claudia looked from the sisters to the mother expectantly.

"Well, I have never been in such a position, but

258

I will do what I have to do for my son. It is his day and if he still wants to marry *her*, I will stand by his side." Matteo's mother did not look at all happy about this and the sisters did not agree.

"Mamma! But this is *ridicolo*! Are we supposed to wear the dresses she gave us? And stand next to her, smiling, after the things she said?" Anna wrung her hands in distress.

"Am I supposed to tell her she looks beautiful? After what she said to me? I think I cannot do such a thing, Mamma." Sara crossed her hands in front of her chest stubbornly.

Wendy sighed, knowing that she was going to have to take control of the situation. This was not the first time she had had to calm down an anxious bride or mother. She came back over with the ice and handing it to Sara said, "Look, maybe you should all get ready anyway. Maybe there will be a party and no ceremony. Or maybe you can all get pampered by me and the hairdresser and then take some nice photographs to keep. Or maybe you can all forget about the argument for a few hours and watch your brother marry the woman HE loves and stay quiet. What do you think?"

"It goes against everything that I believe in," Anna repeated, "but if I have to do it for Matteo, I suppose I can. Sara?"

"I don't know. I'm sorry, I cannot just forgive her. This is all just *wrong*."

Wendy patted Sara's arm, "You don't have to

forgive her or talk to her. You just have to be there for Matteo, okay? Why don't we get you ready anyway … look, it's all paid for already, so it would be a shame to waste it." Sara nodded reluctantly and the three of them slouched off to the mother's bedroom to start getting ready, followed by the hairdresser who was keeping out of the discussion.

It was the strangest wedding that Wendy had ever worked on. For most of the afternoon, she felt like a ping-pong ball bouncing between two different sides. Matteo's mother and sisters were still very angry and would have been happy to have been excluded from the wedding. Matteo was desperate for everything to go ahead as planned and was trying in vain to keep the peace. He knocked on his mother's door at one point, bringing in little gift bags from Maria to the bridesmaids that had been prepared before the argument. The sisters refused to open them and left them sitting on the bed. Matteo's mother ended up opening each bag and laying the gifts out in front of the sisters, forcing them to look at them.

Maria was still holed up in her room and with only a couple of hours to go before the ceremony was due to take place, she finally relented and decided that the wedding would go ahead.

Wendy left the sisters and went over to Maria's room on the other side of the villa. She was finally out of bed and had showered; her face was still blotchy, but it was nothing that a bit of makeup couldn't cover.

"Remember, not too much, I never wear much, you know." Maria sat down and tilted her face towards

Wendy. As she patted on extra strength concealer and blended it into the skin, Maria worried about how she should act when she saw Matteo's family.

"Bridesmaids! I cannot have them as my bridesmaids. The things they said to me … it is not possible. Mamma! Is it possible to cancel my bridesmaids?"

Wendy managed not to smile and suggested that they just pretend the sisters were normal wedding guests that happened to wear matching dresses. "Or," she said, thinking she had come up with a brilliant solution, "why don't they be groomsmaids instead of the bride's?"

Maria didn't think this was a solution at all. "Maybe they just sit at the back and stay there?"

As Wendy worked wonders with her brushes, the hairdresser was backcombing Maria's hair up and out, making liberal use of the hairspray and pins he had produced from his bag. Maria's mother had changed in the bathroom and was now dressed in a black sparkly top and mid-length skirt.

"Won't you be hot in black in this heat?" Wendy asked, trying to keep the conversation going. She had been wittering on inanely for a while now, asking Maria questions about how she met Matteo and where she would like to travel, just to keep her distracted a bit.

Maria's mother shrugged, "It is normal, for weddings we usually wear black or white."

There was a small debate about whether to pin fresh flowers in Maria's hair or just use the sparkly clips that she had bought. They tried both and eventually decided on the clip as the flowers would probably wilt in the heat. Soon, Maria was ready to get dressed.

Standing in front of the mirror, she looked at her reflection. Her hair had been sculpted into big shiny ringlets that fell past her shoulders and the sides had been pinned up with the diamanté clips. Her face was lightly done up with a hint of pink gloss on her lips, and Wendy had lined her eyes with a soft black pencil to hide the redness and smoked out the edges using a short-haired brush. There were no signs of blotchiness, and hopefully, the residual puffiness around the eyes would fade away in the next hour.

"Maria, you look lovely. Nobody will be able to tell that you were crying earlier. I'm going to go and check that everyone else is ready too. You'll be fine. I'm sure it will all go smoothly, and I'll see you at the church!"

Although Wendy hadn't been invited to the wedding party, she knew she could go along to the church and watch the ceremony. She had been amused to find out that in Italy anybody can walk into a church if there is a wedding on, and just take a pew and watch the event – no need to dress up or anything!

"Thank you, Wendy, you have been very kind. I'm sorry for all the trouble … but it was not my fault!"

Wendy left the room, slung her makeup bag onto her back and took a deep breath. What a nightmare!

She deserved a big glass of wine after that.

The church was very close to Antonio's shop, so Wendy made her way down along the bougainvillaea-clad alleyway with the sea to her left, across the road and down another steep set of steps surrounded by whitewashed houses and an avocado tree heavy with fruit, hanging over a garden wall. Some of them had dropped to the ground and smashed, which was a shame; no one seemed to be interested in picking them. She weaved her way through the tourists on the vine-covered cobbled street that led down to the church. A few artists had hung their paintings on the walls and were bartering with the visitors for a good price. Simone wasn't there with his jewellery – maybe he was invited to the wedding.

The huge church was built with a set of three marble steps leading down to a big wide piazza. There was already a crowd of people milling around, waiting for the bride to arrive. Local women stood with plates piled with heaps of confetti: a mix of uncooked rice, sugared almonds, and fresh petals which they would throw at the newlyweds as they left the church. The rice signified abundance and the sugared almonds hurt if they hit you in the wrong place, but this was the way it had always been done here. Men stood in little groups, catching up on the gossip, and a few early wedding guests preened and paced in their best clothes. Wendy noticed that the women were mostly dressed in black, as Maria's mother had said. She wondered how they dressed for funerals if they all wore black to weddings.

She passed the church and ducked down the dark narrow passageway that cut alongside the church foundations, festooned with clothes from the stores on each side, and into Antonio's shop. Amanda was standing by the clothes rail hanging up dresses that were draped over her arm.

"Hey, how did it go? Does she look amazing?"

"You have no idea … Oh Amanda, it was an absolute nightmare!" They sat down on the sofa and Wendy filled Amanda in on the morning's events.

"I don't believe it! What on earth was the argument about?" Amanda had listened rapt with attention, not sure whether to laugh or look sad.

"Do you know, I never actually figured that part out!" Wendy got up and went to stow her bag behind the partition. "Are you coming to see them in church? It's nearly time."

"I'll see if I can pop out for a few minutes, but I can't really just close up and leave here. Wait, let me try and call Antonio and ask." She walked over to the till and picked up the phone. As she was punching out Antonio's home number, Gianni appeared in the doorway, out of breath and very hot, all dressed up with a shirt and tie.

"Wendy! *Meno male*, thank God you're here," he panted, pulling a handkerchief out of a pocket and mopping his brow. "We have a problem, you must come!"

"Oh, for heaven's sake, what on earth has happened now?" Wendy didn't move from the sofa and Amanda put the phone back in its cradle to listen to Gianni.

He stepped into the shop and grabbed a flyer from the desk. It was advertising the opening of the new disco, but he used it to fan some air towards his face.

"The priest has sent a message that he will be late. The boy with the donkeys just came down by Vespa from Nocelle and the priest is doing the … how you say … the last blessing to a man that is dead. No, not dead yet, almost dead … how do you say? *Mamma Mia!* Everybody is waiting outside the church, but Matteo is gone around the back with Enzo for a spliff to stay calm …" At this, both of the girls exclaimed, but Gianni continued.

"No, this is not the problem. It is Maria. She is now in the hotel garden at the side of the church, so she is not seen but she has been crying again, and three times now she says she won't do it and changes her mind again. Can you come and fix her face?"

Amanda burst out laughing and commented dryly, "Maybe Maria should be smoking the spliff instead of Matteo!"

Gianni looked at Amanda and pointed a finger at her, "I think that is a very good idea! *Andiamo*, no? Let's go."

Amanda picked up the phone again, smiling. "I'm just going to call Antonio and tell him it's an emergency, I'll meet you in the garden!"

Wendy sighed, picked up her bag again and followed Gianni out of the shop and back up towards the church.

The church square was now busy with wedding guests, all looking very hot and bothered, talking in subdued tones, wondering what was going on. As Wendy followed Gianni past the bell tower and into the little private gardens of the Flavio Gioia Hotel, she thought it looked more like a funeral gathering with so many people dressed in black. No fascinators or hats either, she realised. Very different from the colourful British weddings that she was used to.

Maria was pacing back and forth in the little walled garden. Although they were right next door to the church they couldn't hear or see anything as the walls were high and the gate was closed. The hotel owner had been very understanding about the situation and said that the bride could sit there as long as necessary. Claudia was there too, trying to get Maria to sit still. Wendy thought the -nonsense approach might work best so she put her bag down on a table and turned to the bride.

"Right, come over here and let me have a look at you. Okay, come and sit down," she led Maria to the table and pushed her gently towards a chair. Gianni sat down next to her and whipped out a cigarette packet. He opened it and tipped out a little packet of cigarette papers and a small ball of hashish, wrapped in cling film. While he got to work skinning up, Wendy pulled out some cotton wool and a little bottle and started repairing the tear damage.

"You are very lucky that we used waterproof mascara, it's not bad at all. I'll have you patched up in no time at all."

"I don't know …" Maria started to say, but the gate opened and Amanda waltzed in, holding aloft a bottle of wine.

"So handy there's that little shop on the church steps! Now, who has a bottle opener?"

Everyone looked down at their laps as if they expected bottle openers to appear magically and looked back up at Amanda who shrugged and strode over to the hotel reception to ask there.

Within a couple of minutes, she was back out with an open bottle, followed by one of the hotel staff who carried out a tray of glasses.

Amanda poured the wine and thrust a glass into Maria's hand. "Drink it!"

Maria looked at Wendy and Claudia who both chorused, "Drink!" She took a gulp and sat back in the chair. Gianni lit the joint, took a couple of puffs and passed it to Maria.

"No, wait!" Amanda pushed Gianni's hand away from the dress. "We don't want to burn the dress, we need something …" She whipped a tablecloth off a nearby table and tucked it around Maria, covering the big lacy dress. "Okay," she declared. Taking the joint from Gianni, she passed it to the bride and instructed her to smoke.

Over the next forty minutes, Maria visibly relaxed, and so did everyone else. Two shared bottles of wine and a few spliffs did their part in banishing the tension. Everyone avoided talking about the evil sisters and instead they talked about the new nightclub, what it looked like inside, how often they would go and what sort of music the DJ would play. They became aware of a noise that was completely out of place with the area they were in. The church and the hotel next to it were in a pedestrianised part of town; there were no roads nearby, but they could hear the sound of an engine getting closer. Gianni went over to the gate and poked his head out.

"Guys? You have to see this!" He laughed, stepping out of the gate to see better. Wendy and Claudia rushed over to see while Maria hung back, still cautious.

The donkey boy from Nocelle was back, driving his Vespa down the cobbled pedestrian street with the priest balanced behind him, sitting side saddle with his long robes flapping around them. One arm was wrapped awkwardly around the waist of the donkey boy and the other clutched his purple and gold silk stole which, flapping in the wind had partly wrapped itself around the donkey boy's head, threatening to blind him.

The Vespa wobbled its way right down to the top of the church steps, in front of the hotel, Gianni quickly stepped forward to help the priest stand up. There was a small ripple of applause from the guests that were waiting outside the church, although most people had gone inside to escape the heat. The donkey boy, looking hugely relieved to have delivered his precious passenger safely, did a quick u-turn and motored off back up the hill. The priest patted his robes back into place, straightened his stole and looked around. He cleared his throat, noticing Maria who was peeking out from behind Wendy. "Sorry about that, couldn't be helped … *allora*, let's do this wedding!"

Gianni darted off to find Enzo and Matteo. Maria had to be kept in the garden until Matteo was waiting at the altar and all the guests were inside.

Maria had either forgotten about her argument with the sisters or was, by this point, too stoned to care. Claudia led her to the grand church door and beckoned for her mother who stepped out from the shade of the vestibule. The huge organ was playing softly and finally, everyone watched Maria walk slightly unsteadily down the aisle to stand side by side with Matteo.

Wendy and Amanda slipped into the last pew at the back of the church next to Claudia and Gianni to watch the ceremony. Matteo turned and watched Maria walking slowly down the aisle, gripping her mother's arm. She looked straight ahead, eyes fixed on him, studiously avoiding the possibility of searching the pews for Matteo's sisters.

Anna and Sara sat at the far end of the third pew, hair and makeup done, bridesmaid dresses on, expressions like thunder.

A few more people wandered into the church to watch the ceremony and a deacon appeared out of a side room, scanning the crowds. His eyes landed on Amanda, then he frowned and made a beeline for her. She looked behind her, thinking that there must be somebody there that he was looking at; surely he wasn't staring at her like that.

But he marched over, muttering at her in comic whispers, inexplicably patting his arms as if he was trying to warm himself up.

"Le spalle, le spalle! No, signorina! Fuori!" He shook his head, ushering her up and herding her towards the exit.

"What was that all about?" Wendy got up to follow.

"Oh, bloody hell," sighed Claudia, getting up too, and grabbing her bag. "You're not allowed in the church without sleeves to cover your arms," she whispered to Wendy as they walked out to rescue Amanda.

Claudia marched over to Amanda who was getting a telling-off from the irate deacon. She pulled a scarf out of her handbag and draped it over Amanda's shoulders.

"Tutto bene ora! All good now, we go back inside, yes?" The deacon backed off, still muttering and shaking his head.

"Actually, I really should get back to work. I'm sure I won't miss anything else … nothing else can possibly go wrong, I'm sure!" She gave the scarf back to Claudia and gave a jaunty wave to the deacon who was still guarding the doorway against bare shoulders, before skipping down the steps to the shop.

At home later that evening, the girls lay on Amanda's bed with the dog taking up most of the room between them. The balcony door was flung open to the night in the hope of a breeze and the sea sparkled darkly in the distance.

Wendy stretched her arms above her head and yawned.

"It was weird though, everyone just came out of the church and just *pretended*. The sisters pretended to be happy and had to kiss and congratulate the newlyweds, the two mothers were avoiding each other, and Maria was pretending to be nice to them, but you could practically see the daggers flying."

Amanda shoved Nerone off the bed and onto his rug with her foot. "I suppose they will sort it all out eventually … they're family now. It'll make for some interesting Christmas dinners, that's for sure."

"Oh God, can you imagine! Right, I'm off to bed, I'm flipping exhausted!" Wendy levered herself up and groaned with the effort, "Night, you two!" She patted Nerone on the head and dragged herself up to her room.

Chapter 18

Positano, August 1986

Sitting on her bed with Nerone looking on, Wendy popped open the back of the camera and pulled out the finished film roll. She took a new roll out of its little plastic container and threaded it into the back of the camera and wound it on with the little lever. She slipped the used film into the empty container and put it in her bag, ready to be dropped off at the photography shop to be developed.

She wandered downstairs, patting her thigh absently for Nerone to follow her and made herself a mug of tea which she took out onto the terrace.

Amanda was out with Enzo, and Francesco was no doubt at home with his family – she had no way of contacting him, which was probably a good thing, she thought morosely. She felt lonely and didn't know what to do with herself this afternoon. She had done a day trip along the Amalfi Coast with Sandro, and they had returned a bit earlier than usual, at four. She would normally enjoy a bit of downtime at home with no distractions. She had done all the necessary chores, swept the floors, and filled all the empty water bottles in case they turned the water supply off again. (They had come home the other evening to find that the water had been switched off and they had not been prepared. The next day, Enzo had pointed out the notices that they hadn't seen stuck on lamp posts all around town. All they had was a bottle of fizzy water, which they'd had to use to wash and clean their teeth with, forgoing much-needed showers.)

The bathroom now had six bottles standing ready in the shower and another four by the kitchen sink. She had tried reading and couldn't concentrate on her book at all. She couldn't stop thinking about him; she desperately wanted to see him and just talk to him, but of course, she couldn't, and she was angry with herself for letting her feelings get out of control.

She pulled a chair over to the railings and sat there, cradling her tea and watching the town. It was way better than watching Italian TV, which seemed to consist of dodgy old male presenters surrounded by scantily clad dancing girls and a myriad of people heavily made up and dramatically crooning love songs into their microphones.

The goings on of the town below her were much more interesting. She could see the tiny flower truck, a three-wheeled vehicle called an *ape*, trundling along the road, filled with flowers and plants wobbling precariously. She could see the beach still teeming with life, people swimming and strolling up and down the small promenade. She noticed one of the artists painting with an umbrella over his easel for a bit of shade; he had set up by the wooden steps of the first beach bar and a couple of people were standing by watching him paint.

She smiled as she saw the Saucepan Man, the VEP walking along another section of the road, carrying his signs and ringing his bell. There were a couple of stray dogs on the roadside too, walking along together, stopping to sniff things of interest as they went. The sun had gone, hidden by the hillside behind her and the light would soon fade. She heard a sound behind her and turned to see Amanda put her bag down on the kitchen table. For once, Enzo wasn't with her.

"Hi! I'm out here," she called. Amanda filled a glass with water from the tap and came out to join her.

"I've just been on a drug run," she said matter-of-factly, drawing up a chair and sitting next to Wendy.

"You what?" Wendy looked at her in surprise.

"Well, I think I have anyway. Simone and Enzo took me by car; it was somewhere near Naples, not a very nice area."

"A drug run?" repeated Wendy. "They took you to buy drugs? What drugs?"

"Oh, come on, you know what I mean! Basically, Simone was picking up some hash and Enzo wanted to take me to this town nearby, so we all went together. We didn't just do that – they took me to this town on the seafront that has water fountains with fizzy water! Amazing! Shall we go out for dinner instead of cooking?"

Wendy looked at her with eyebrows raised. "Yes, but you have to explain yourself better while we

275

eat. Drug runs and fizzy fountains? Sounds like you've been smoking a bit too much weed, my dear!"

They put Nerone on his lead and walked with him up to the Grottino Azzurro, a little vine-covered trattoria right next to the Bar Internazionale. A tiny, no-frills, family-run place where the father cooked, the mother sat at the till, and the two young sons waited tables. It was the sort of place that you would find filled with locals, rather than tourists, and the food was proper traditional home cooking, nothing fancy.

They sat down at a little table outside where there was space for Nerone to lie down on the floor by the big glass window. Amanda recognised the English lady, Lily, sitting with a group of friends and waved to her. The waiter brought them plates of cannelloni and a jug of fizzy white wine and Wendy listened as Amanda told her all about her day.

"So, we went to this place that he said was near Pompeii; it wasn't really a very nice area, lots of closed-up shops and tower blocks. Anyway," she paused to take a bite of pasta, "we parked outside this big block of flats that was basically in the middle of a wasteland and went up to a flat on the fourth floor. I thought it was going to be awful inside because the area around it looked so bad, but it was really weird. The floors were dark green marble with beige streaks running through them – isn't marble expensive?" She raised her eyebrows at Wendy but didn't wait for an answer. "The bathroom was huge and all made from marble too, with a huge gilt-framed mirror, and the flat seemed to be quite large. I don't think it was council property. Anyway, this guy was there with a pit bull dog and he pretty much ignored me. Simone went into another room and left me and Enzo waiting, so I don't really know what happened but," she lowered her voice and leaned forward across the table, "when we left, Enzo told me he'd bought some hash and if we were stopped by the police, we were to pretend that Simone was a guide taking us to the Pompeii ruins."

"Why on earth did he take you? What if you'd gotten caught?!" Wendy was angry with Enzo for risking taking her friend.

"But we didn't! He took me because afterwards, we went to this little seaside town, Castellamare. It was much nicer. It had an old-fashioned bandstand overlooking the sea and loads of mineral water fountains. There was one that he took me to – it was just a normal drinking fountain in the middle of the street. Enzo gave me an empty water bottle and told me to go and fill it up at the fountain for him and then made me try it. It was fizzy! Proper fizzy water coming straight out of a fountain! And then we had really good ice cream and walked along the seafront. He said that in the evenings there are loads of street food stalls; they set out lots of tables and chairs and everyone goes there to eat mussels and clams all night long. We should organise to go one night!"

"That sounds fun, and maybe we should go visit Pompeii beforehand, seeing as we're so close. It would be silly to go back to England without seeing it. But Amanda, no more drug runs please?" Wendy poured them another glass of wine from the jug and sat back, pushing her nearly empty plate away from her. "I can't eat anymore, I'm stuffed!" Nerone raised his head hopefully and she fed him the last bit of cannelloni, slipping it under the table where he gobbled it up happily.

The Grottino Azzuro didn't have a coffee machine so after dinner there most people would usually get up and go to the bar next door for a coffee or a *digestivo*. The girls decided to get icy glasses of *finocchietto*, similar to limoncello but made with fennel. Wendy hadn't been sure that she would like it as she wasn't a fan of liquorice, but it was actually really good, and she now preferred it to limoncello. They sat at the corner table of the bar and sipped them slowly. A couple of men nursed glasses of red wine and watched a football match on the TV above the bathroom, but other than that it was a quiet night for the bar.

As they walked home, they could talk more freely without worrying about being overheard.

"So, is Simone a big-time dealer or what, do you know?" Wendy asked as they passed by the steps, deciding to walk back along the road after the heavy pasta.

"Well, he said that he just buys for him and his friends, and then he delivers it to them and they pay him. So, yes, I suppose that is dealing but he's not admitting to being the town dealer or anything … he said he doesn't go out selling to strangers in the streets or clubs or anything. Well, that's what he said, anyway – who knows?"

They turned a hairpin bend in the road and crossed back over to the "sea side" of the road. They had learnt early on that here, if there was no pavement, you always walked on the sea side of the road, not the mountain side where traffic couldn't see you as it came around the bends.

"Oh, I nearly forgot," Amanda exclaimed. "Antonio is having a birthday party next week and we're both invited."

"Which day? I'll have to see if I'm working." Wendy held up her hand and crossed her fingers.

"On the thirteenth – it's next Wednesday. Can you come?"

"Perfect! Yeah, we're not night fishing on the thirteenth because they do some procession by boat thing on the fourteenth, and then on the fifteenth, it's Ferragosto so they take people out to see the fireworks. Where's the party?"

They were nearly home, and Amanda was fishing around in her bag for the keys. "It's on a beach. I can't remember the name of it, that little one just before Fornillo."

"The Marinella – that's perfect for a party! Knowing Antonio, it will be a fun night! I can't wait! I wonder who will be there?"

Amanda looked at Wendy and rolled her eyes. "You're not still mooning after that married man, are you?"

Wendy hesitated. She hadn't mentioned

279

Francesco again to Amanda, feeling too guilty to talk about what had happened, but maybe she should talk to her friend.

"Well, actually I need to tell you a few things, but let's wait until we get home."

Amanda gasped and her eyes were wide as Wendy filled her in on everything that had happened between her and Francesco. Finally, she shook her head, "Oh you silly, silly girl, you are going to get so hurt by him. You know he will never leave his wife, don't you? It's a classic… married Italian men are known for this!" She flopped back on the bed that they were sitting on and stared at the ceiling. Wendy flopped down next to her.

"I know he won't leave his wife, ever," she hesitated, "but he might … you never know." Amanda rolled her eyes, "Hmph, I'll believe that when I see it. What a rat!"

Wendy sat up. "He's not a rat! It's my fault too, and it's so hard to not see him. This town is so bloody small, I couldn't avoid him if I tried!"

Amanda got up, "Well, I'm not going to lecture you. You know what you're doing. Shit, Wendy, there are plenty of other men you could have chosen from. Simone for one!" She guffawed and ducked out of the room as Wendy launched a pillow at her. "I can't help who I fall for! I wish I could."

Simone had asked Enzo to bring both the English girls. They were much less likely to be pulled over by the police if there were two couples in the car, rather than just two men. It would have also given him another chance to try it on with Wendy. But Enzo had turned up with just the blonde one, so he had felt like a spare wheel all day. There were a couple of big evenings coming up in Positano – the gay guy's party and Ferragosto, the August national holiday – so he had to stock up. There would be plenty of business.

He had picked up another nine-bar of fresh, sticky, dark hashish and had decided to invest in ten grams of cocaine. He didn't have enough money for more, but he'd have plenty by the time he shifted it all in the next few days. They had driven back from Torre del Greco with no problem, brazenly stopping in Castellamare to show Amanda the drinking fountains and get ice cream. He smiled to himself, remembering the look on Amanda's face when she realised what had been going on at the boss's house in Torre.

He now sat in the bedroom he shared with his sister; she was out, thankfully. His mother wouldn't disturb him – she was ironing in the other room. He sat on his bed with the bedside table pulled up in front of him; a small set of scales with tiny weights lay ready, along with a lit candle, a roll of cling film, a pair of scissors and a couple of pages torn out of a magazine that his sister had left on her bed.

He unwrapped the oblong bar and inhaled deeply as the heady, earthy scent filled the room. The hash was partially covered in a transparent deep red plastic film, a trademark marking it out as Red Seal and he swore lightly under his breath. He had been hoping for Afghan Black, a superior quality to this, but at least

281

it wasn't the crappy soap stuff that he had been sold last time. He had the lit candle in front of him and a long knife that he had filched from the kitchen ages ago. His mother still harped on about the missing knife, but he couldn't put it back because of the burn marks on the blade, so he kept it on top of the wardrobe where no one would look.

Now he held the blade in the flame of a candle, turning it from side to side. The hash would be much easier to cut with a hot knife and he had a lot of cutting to do. Concentrated now, he cut the bar in half and cut each piece in half again and kept going. Hash was sold in eighths of an ounce, around three and a half grams, and each piece had to be precise because the first thing most people did once they bought, if it was convenient, was to check the weight and he had to keep his reputation as trustworthy to expand his client base. Each piece was then wrapped in cling film and soon he had a satisfying pile growing on the bed beside him.

Once that was done, he stored most of it away, hidden in a balled-up pair of socks at the back of his underwear drawer and put the rest in his bumbag, ready to sell later on that evening. Next, he started folding wraps for the cocaine that neither Amanda nor Enzo knew he had brought back with him. He was tempted to have a small line, just as a reward to himself for all the work he was putting in. He would squash a few of his mother's headache pills and mix the powder in with the coke to replace the missing weight, and nobody would know.

Francesco and Elena were holding a small dinner party. They had invited Elena's cousin and her family,

Dom, and a couple of nearby neighbours. The big trestle table had been set out under a canopy of lemon trees in the grove nearest to the back of the house and Francesco had rigged a string of lights up and over the table with a few old lanterns dotted around. The table was decorated simply with a much-washed flowery tablecloth, a big bowl of fresh figs and lemons, and a few citronella candles to ward off the mosquitoes.

Elena and Mamma had spent the afternoon cooking and preparing, and once everyone had arrived, they had brought out a succession of dishes, piling them on the table so that everyone could help themselves. There was a pile of garlicky bruschetta with fresh tomato and basil, dripping with olive oil. A platter of various salamis, Neapolitan, Milanese, spicy and homemade and thin slices of prosciutto to be eaten wrapped around balls of fresh mozzarella that floated in a bowl in their own juices. Mamma had made a pizza *rustica*, a thick crusty quiche filled with ricotta and spinach with a glossy crust, which sat next to an octopus salad made with black rice and cherry tomatoes. The neighbour, a busy man who spoke little, manned the grill and the scent of barbecued meats drifted tantalisingly through the village. A demijohn of homemade wine had appeared, probably brought over by the neighbour, and they had all sat contentedly discussing town politics and the latest scandals until the sky had gone dark and the kids had grown sleepy.

Now, Elena was putting Leo to bed and her cousin had taken the other children home. Mamma was clearing up the table and Papà had lit a pipe and was happily entertaining the neighbours. Francesco and Dom went for an evening stroll around the groves

283

to digest the meal.

"*Allora,*" said Francesco, turning towards his friend, "I don't know what to do, Dom, I cannot stop thinking about Wendy. I think I am falling in love … again."

"Again? How often does this happen, my friend?" Dom smiled, trying to make light of the situation.

"No, I mean again because I do love Elena, I am sure … but now I feel that I am falling in love again with Wendy and it feels different. Is that even possible? Can someone love two people at the same time, do you think?"

"I don't know, *amico,* but how about sharing some of that love? Two for you and none for me – that is not very fair now, is it?" Dom elbowed him in the side and Francesco nudged him back. They had walked up through a couple of groves, taking the steep stone steps that led from one terraced garden to the next, by torchlight. Now they arrived at the edge of a terrace where the view opened up in front of them. The sea sparked below in the moonlight and out in the distance they could see five fishing boats, the lanterns bright against the dark sea. The sky was a faded indigo, lit up by the moon, and the outline of the peninsula was clear to see, stretching southwest towards the island of Capri.

They sat down facing the sea. Francesco could see Orion's belt up above, something he looked for in the skies everywhere he went. He hadn't been to many places. Malta and Gibraltar were pretty much the extents of his travels, but he had recently been thinking it was time to visit England. Of course, he knew that this was purely because of his interest in Wendy, and he was already imagining visiting her once she had left, maybe later on this year or after Christmas.

But would he really? Was this just a passing desire or something deeper? Could he go so far as to destroy his family and everything he had worked towards up until now, to risk starting again with someone he hardly knew? And how would he know if it was the right thing to do or not unless he got to know her better? So often he had longed for something more and had often wondered if Elena was right for him. But she was so easy to be with, he had no reason to complain. Until now, with this huge new feeling inside of him.

They talked long enough to see the moon rise from behind the mountains to the left and float slowly upwards until its reflection could be seen in the sea. A cat crept past them and jumped up into a tree, vanishing in the darkness; an owl screeched nearby, and something rustled in the undergrowth.

"Here's an idea," Dom said quietly. "Come to Antonio's party with me at the Marinella on the 13th. She will surely be there and maybe you can spend some time alone with her, just to talk or whatever you want. Fornillo will be deserted, and you could just sit on the beach and talk or more. I'll cover for you, if necessary, but just think of it as your chance to get to know her better. Maybe some time alone together will help you decide what you want. Nobody else needs to know;

what do you think?"

Francesco looked out to sea and sighed.

"I don't know ... it just feels so bad. I'm not that type of guy. I'd hate for Wendy to think that I'm one of those guys that are always playing around, and what about poor Elena ..."

"Well, you have a few days to decide – let me know. Come on, it's late, I should go home."

They stood up, dusting twigs and leaves off their clothes. Francesco walked Dom back to the road and watched as he drove his Vespa back down to Positano. He lingered for a while, eyes unfocused on the empty road, thinking about two different ways his life could go.

As Domenico drove past the Bar Internazionale, he raised a hand in salute to Simone who was sitting on the wall opposite, watching for potential clients.

Chapter 19

Positano, September 2016

Mia sat in the Bar Internazionale letting the vibrant conversations in Italian wash right over her head. Andrea was sitting on the bench seat opposite her with a couple of male friends. She wasn't even trying to understand but was pretty sure it was just a heated discussion about football. Jess sat next to her, deep in conversation with a couple of girls at the next table. It was pretty obvious that everyone knew each other, and she curiously studied each new face that came in, always wondering if her father or even this half-brother that she now knew she had might be here in front of her.

Wendy and Amanda had continued telling their story while they had made and eaten the wonderful cavatelli earlier but frustratingly were refusing to tell the girls the name of the mysterious surfboard guy or his occupation.

"No, Mia, you will have to wait. If we tell you now, you would find him straight away. Just wait until you know everything that happened, please." Mum had pleaded and Mia had sighed and rolled her eyes in acceptance.

It had been funny though, Mum and Amanda reminiscing about the wedding of their friends, the priest on the Vespa and the stoned bride. Jess had hardly believed them.

"Mum, are you serious? You're talking about the lady that has that little old-fashioned clothes shop opposite the fishmonger's?"

"Yes, darling, I am, but you must never let her know that I told you this. We were never very close and I'm sure she would not be happy to find out the youth of the town know all about that disastrous day! She still doesn't speak to her sisters-in-law to this day!"

"Mia!" Andrea called again, and Mia blinked and turned to see what he wanted. "Jess says you want to see the old nightclub, yes? Come, I take you now! Jess, you want to come too?"

"I do, actually. I haven't been there before, but now that I've heard about the opening night, I'd love to see it for myself!"

Stepping outside the bar, Mia looked over to the wall where a line of scooters was parked. On their way from the airport the other day, they had driven past this spot and Wendy had gasped in surprise, saying that it hadn't changed a jot in all these years. Amanda had laughed and said that not much had changed at all in town apart from more tourists and fewer nightclubs.

She could almost see the ghosts of a group of friends hanging out right here, by this wall, dressed in 80s outfits, ready to go to the new disco. She could imagine the excitement and hype of that evening and decided right there and then that she would try and visit all the places her mum had mentioned in the story so far …

Jess had already climbed onto her scooter and was turning it around when Andrea grabbed her arm and gestured to a beautiful pistachio green Vespa. "Come with me! You have to ride a proper Vespa when in Italy!" She glanced over at Jess who gave her a thumbs up and sped off without waiting.

"Here, put this on," Andrea passed her a helmet and buckled it for her under her chin. "I hope the club will be unlocked. I went once last year and the door was open but maybe they have closed now, I don't know. We see. Ready?" He patted the small seat behind him and Mia climbed on, thankful that she had worn jeans.

"Andrea! *Dovè vai?*" One of Andrea's friends from the bar had followed them out and was asking where they were going. He was shorter than Andrea, with dark brown wavy hair and friendly eyes that crinkled when he smiled.

"Come with us! We're going to take a look at that old nightclub on the edge of town." Mia watched as the guy nodded and hopped onto another scooter to join them.

None of them noticed the older traffic warden, Dom, currently off duty, sitting on the wall watching them and looking as if he'd seen a ghost.

It only took a couple of minutes to arrive at the edge of town. Cars were parked all along the roadside but there were no people around. Andrea parked next to Jess and the four of them walked along the road a bit until they came to a small white gate, almost hidden behind a parked car. It hadn't been opened for a long time as weeds had grown all around it, almost hiding the steps that led down the other side. Andrea looked both ways along to road to make sure nobody was watching and easily hopped over the little gate, followed by his friend. Jess and Mia followed quickly and they ducked down the steps, feeling like trespassers and giggling like children.

They turned on the torches on their phones and peered around. The steps were overgrown with brambles and plants, and something dark was lying in the middle of them. Andrea went ahead, pushing branches out of the way and shone his torch onto the dark mass.

"Ugh, is a dead cat, be careful not to step on it, girls," he said softly. It had been there for a while, Mia thought as she carefully stepped around it. There wasn't much left except for fur and a partially mummified carcass.

"Wow, you would hardly know there was anything down here!" She commented, "How long has it been closed for?" She brushed a branch away from her face and ducked under it.

"Oh, ages, it was only open for a year or two," Jess explained. "It had been built illegally and the authorities closed it down in the end."

290

"My father used to come here when it was open," Andrea's friend said suddenly. "He said it held many memories, good and bad, and if it had never opened, his life may have been very different. I have no idea what he meant by that though."

"I heard that there were drug problems here." Jess shrugged, waving her torch around.

They had arrived at the entrance. A big broken vase lay in pieces in front of the door, and a few terracotta floor tiles were smashed with weeds growing up through the cracks.

"Let's go over here first, the terrace with the view." Andrea carefully stepped around to the side of the building. Mia followed, eager to see where her mother had first kissed the man that she was now thinking of as the Surfboard Guy.

Jess shone her torch around slowly and they gazed at the terrace. One of the big arched windows had a huge crack running through it. The glass was still intact but shattered into a million pieces, obliterating the view inside.

"Probably best to stay away from the edge," Jess warned as Mia stepped towards the railing. "Who knows how safe it is?" Mia took a step back. She tried to imagine her mother, standing right here, kissing a man that shouldn't have let her. Was it here? No, it had been down the side of the building. She turned and looked for the emergency exit. There were a couple of old broken plastic chairs crammed into the passageway at the side of the building and it was knee-deep in fallen leaves and weeds. It was too dark to explore it anymore, so she turned away. Andrea had walked back around to the entrance and the girls followed.

"It's still open! Come!" He stepped through the doorway and vanished.

"I can't believe they just left it open," Jess whispered. "It's so strange!"

They followed Andrea inside and stepped into the building.

It smelt mouldy and stale. The paint had flaked off the walls and ceilings, the floor was covered in a layer of crumbled paint, dirt and leaves that had blown in from the doorway. The once-white walls were streaked with green mould, running up and congregating in the corners near the ceiling. They shone their torches around the large room. To the left, a long curving bar stretched around the side of the room, empty of bottles and glasses, littered with flakes of paint. At the very end of the room, there were a few stacks of chairs and small tables. Jess wandered over and touched the back of one of the chairs.

"Just think, our parents probably sat on these chairs."

Andrea shone his torch up towards the ceiling. There was no sign of the lights and speakers that had once been there; everything had been stripped away.

"It's actually not too bad," Mia said, thoughtfully. "I mean, if someone was homeless, this would be a great place to come and shack up for the winter. You'd be warm and dry at least."

"Okay, Mia, you can stay if you want!" Jess laughed at her. "Come on, there's nothing else to see here – let's go."

"Yes, let's go and find our mums and get them to finish this story. I just want to know who this surfboard guy is and then figure out what the hell I'm going do about it."

Positano,
August 1986

"African drums!"

On the edge of the jetty, a pretty cliffside path linked the main beach to the beach of Fornillo. It was a ten-minute walk, passing by a circular ancient signal tower that was now a little house, a low stone seating area under the shade of an umbrella pine, and a shrine to the Madonna of Positano in which people left little gifts of seagrass and pebbles, ribbons and beads.

The sun had set and the sky was the colour of blackberry stains. Another ancient signal tower at the very end of Fornillo Beach was lit up with warm lights like something out of Fairyland, mysterious and ethereal, the waters below it glowing a ghostly green.

The girls were on their way to Antonio's party, which was being held at La Marinella, a tiny, secluded beach, encircled by cliffs in between the main beach and Fornillo, accessible by either a small tunnel in the rock or a very old and crumbly staircase that was safer to avoid. It was the perfect location for a party as no houses overlooked the beach and it faced directly out to sea, so they would have privacy and could be as noisy as they wanted.

"I can hear African drums," exclaimed Amanda again, "listen!"

She was right, Wendy could hear them too, a steady exciting beat that made her skin tingle and made her walk faster down the steps that led to Fornillo.

As they arrived at the bottom of the steps, the noise grew louder and the buzz of music and people having fun joined the beat of the drums. They stopped and peered over the wall. La Marinella lay below them as they had never seen it before. The tiny beach was crowded with revellers; lanterns and citronella candles were dotted all over the rocks creating a warm glow. On the left by the little tunnel stood three men playing different sized drums. They were dressed in colourful African clothing and were dancing and nodding their heads as they played. Near them was a drinks table, piled high with bottles and stacks of plastic cups.

"Wow!" Wendy exclaimed, patting her hair and tugging her skirt down. She was wearing a purple and black striped miniskirt that hugged her hips but annoyingly kept riding up, and a black batwing off-the-shoulder top. She had scrunch-dried her hair and used a side comb to pin it off her face on one side.

"This is going to be fun!" Amanda took Wendy's arm and pulled her down towards the little tunnel. They had to duck their heads to go through and they emerged right by the African drummers who nodded and smiled at them as they stumbled onto the rocky beach and looked around.

The newlyweds Maria and Matteo were the first people that they saw. Matteo was dipping a cup into a big plastic bin next to the drinks table. Maria waved and called them over.

"*Ciao!* Come, take a drink! There is very nice

sangria here, you try some." She passed the cup that Matteo had given her over to Wendy, who sipped it carefully.

"Mmm, it's good. Not very strong, is it?" It tasted of fruit and wine and something sweet; there were pieces of fruit floating in the barrel, peaches and melon and grapes.

Matteo handed another cup to Amanda who thanked him and tried it.

"Yum, this is lovely!"

"Be careful, it is probably stronger than it looks. I saw them add lots of alcohol to it earlier!" Maria confided, leading them over to a group of people sitting around one of a few small bonfires dotted around the beach.

Claudia and Gianni were sitting there with Simone and a few others who shuffled around to make room for the girls.

"Where's Antonio?" Amanda asked, looking around. People were dancing in the centre of the beach and a few brave souls were swimming, whooping and splashing in the inky black water.

"He's here somewhere. You can't miss him!" Simone sniggered and passed a joint to Gianni, who was stretched out on the pebbles with Claudia draped over him. She was wearing a very simple black tight minidress with a Bardot neckline; her brown feet were bare and a pair of tan locally-made sandals were sitting by her bag.

"Oh God, what's he wearing now?" Amanda sighed dramatically, causing everyone to laugh.

"You wait and see," Claudia said dryly, taking the joint out of Gianni's hand.

Over the music, Simone was telling them all about a thief who had tried to break into a house in town that morning, not realising that someone was in there. He had jumped out the window and started leaping across rooftops and terraces, being chased by a string of locals. Simone had been on the other side of town where they had been able to watch the whole scene unfold, yelling encouragement to the people chasing him and booing when he escaped to another rooftop. As he explained how the man had finally been caught when the gap between houses was too big to jump, Wendy looked around, distracted. She hadn't seen Francesco yet; she was sure he would be here, but was he with his wife or with his friends?

"Wendy!" Amanda nudged her. Claudia was holding out the spliff and she took it, turning back to the group and tuning back into the conversation.

"The *Polizia* were waiting on the road below and the men took him down to be arrested. As he was led off in handcuffs, everyone on the other side of town was clapping and cheering – it was fantastic!"

Suddenly Amanda let out a shriek as she was grabbed from behind. Antonio had arrived, sneaking up on her and enveloping her with the outrageous multi-colour sequinned cape that he had chosen to wear. Wendy turned to see Amanda's legs in the air and a confusing jumble of coloured sequins, blonde hair, and a hand clutching a bottle of champagne. She started when she realised Francesco was there too, standing behind Antonio with Dom, inexplicably carrying a tray of lemons.

"Ma che? Stai ancora lavorando? What, you're still working?" Gianni laughed, pointing at the lemons.

Antonio and Amanda were untangling themselves and Amanda's hair from the sequins and brushing off the sand.

"I finished the lemons for the red sangria, Francesco, he bring me more; he saves the evening!" Antonio shrugged. He made his way around the group, regally accepting birthday greetings and kisses from everyone.

"You like my musicians?" he asked, wiggling his eyebrows at the drummers. "They came to play for me especially from Naples. They are beautiful, no?" He turned to greet a new arrival, swishing his sparkly cape and taking a swig from his champagne bottle as he moved away. Francesco hefted the crate of lemons over to the drinks table where two girls were already chopping up more peaches.

"Does anyone want another drink?" Wendy got up, wanting to say hello to Francesco and using the drinks as an excuse. Five glasses were thrust at her, and she laughed, "They should have provided jugs!" She collected the cups and walked over to the table where

Francesco was unloading the lemons.

"Ciao," she said softly, brushing up against his arm as she reached a cup into the barrel.

"Ciao, Wendy, I've missed you" he replied, placing the last lemon on the table and bending down to store the tray underneath. Straightening back up again, he took the full cup from her and gestured to the barrel. "I help you carry them back; give me another two. But do it slowly so we have more time," he winked at her comically, noticing Maria coming over to help. He took the two full cups and turned, not giving Maria time to say anything at all. "Here. Take these to the others, we can't carry them all. Thanks, Maria!" She gave Wendy a look and stomped off again, having no choice.

"You think she suspects something?" Wendy asked worriedly, filling another cup and passing it to him. Their fingers touched and she felt the warmth of his touch as if it were fire.

"Maybe she thinks something, but we are doing nothing wrong, no? Okay, we go back now, maybe later we can talk more."

They carried the sangria back to the fire and passed them out. Francesco sat next to Simone and Dom, where he could watch Wendy over the small flames. The music and the drums were hypnotising, the sangria was strong as Maria had suggested, and Wendy could feel it coursing through her body. Embers from the fire shot up into the air and she tilted her head up to watch them. She felt soft around the edges, ready to melt away.

After a while, Enzo appeared from somewhere and pulled Amanda away with him towards the shore, kissing her on the neck, which made her squeal and skip away playfully. Claudia languidly unfurled herself from Gianni and pulled him towards the dancers in the middle of the beach. They danced barefoot and carefree, laughing and twirling together. Maria stood up and downed her sangria, tossing the cup on the floor and began to dance slowly around the fire. She was wearing a white lace-up bodice top and a long flowing black skirt with big red flowers printed on it. As she danced, her skirts swirled in a billowing circle, her hair whipped around her face and the men watched, spellbound.

The African drummers were on the move too, dancing around the beach in a line, followed by Antonio in his sparkly cape and a few others who were starting to tag along. They cut through the dancers who joined onto the end of the conga line that was forming, sweeping past the little bonfires and encouraging everyone to join in. Francesco and Dom were swept up, laughing and protesting. Antonio grabbed Enzo and Amanda as they passed by the shore and eventually nearly everyone was up and dancing, laughing and holding onto each other as the drummers drummed faster and they spun round and round under the light of the lanterns.

The line started breaking up, but the music was good and the revellers kept dancing. A few couples broke away, sinking into the shadows at the edges of the beach. Wendy found herself dancing with Dom and looked around for his friend.

Dom leaned forward so that nobody else could hear him. "He has gone for a little walk on Fornillo beach. If you want, you can go and find him, nobody will notice now." He smiled at her, "You can trust me, I won't say anything. And Wendy? You can trust him too – he has never done anything like this before."

"You know?" Wendy gasped, looking at him in shock. "We haven't done anything, just a kiss!"

"I know. He has told me how he feels about you. Now, you want to see him? Go under the tunnel." She looked around; the party was buzzing. Maria and Matteo were entwined on the dance floor, and she could see Amanda and Enzo, arms around each other, by the shore. She hesitated. "Nobody is going to miss you. I will say you went to find a bathroom if anyone asks." Dom raised his eyebrows at her, and she mumbled thanks and ducked through the tunnel.

Fornillo beach was dark and quiet. The sounds of the party were instantly muffled by the cliff that stood between the two beaches and she could hear the water lapping gently at the shoreline. Rows of sun loungers and closed umbrellas stretched across the length of the beach, and as she walked between them her footsteps on the stones sounded incredibly loud.

Where was he? It was hard to see anything in the darkness. As her eyes adjusted to the light, she saw a movement up ahead. He was sitting on a sun lounger in the second row, watching her as she walked towards him. He got up and met her, reaching out to hold her hand.

301

"*Ciao* again," he said softly as she drew closer, intoxicated by his perfume. She leaned her head on his chest for a moment and stepped back to look around.

"Can anybody see us?"

"It is completely dark, and even if they could, they cannot see who we are." For a moment they just stared into each other's eyes before succumbing to a passionate kiss that had Wendy shivering with desire.

"We can stay here," her whispered to her, "or we can go and watch the stars." He pointed to the tiny wooden jetty where she saw a small boat tied to the side.

"That's yours?" She asked in surprise.

"Is my cousins; we borrowed it to bring all the drinks and things here for the party. I have the keys so if you want, we can go out and watch the stars from the sea?"

Wendy knew she should say no and walk away but her heart yet again overruled her brain and she nodded, "Let's go watch the stars."

They slipped off their shoes and jumped in the boat. Silently, he untied the rope and drove them away from the beach, turning right, past the magical Tower of Fornillo and then straight out to sea. Wendy watched the town recede behind them, the lights from the party getting smaller and smaller. She hoped nobody had seen them leave.

When he turned off the engine, they were enveloped in silence. Wendy was sitting on a small, cushioned sundeck at the front and Francesco climbed over to it from the console, pushing aside a small crate of lemons and a bag of peaches, no doubt extras for the sangria. The crate teetered on the edge of the sundeck for a second before toppling over into the bottom of the boat. Lemons rolled everywhere and they laughed.

"Just leave them, it doesn't matter!" Francesco lay back, folding his hands behind his head, "Look at the stars Wendy – lie down and see!"

She lay down next to him and looked up. Out there in the middle of the warm undulating darkness, the stars were magical. Millions of pinpoints of light were scattered in clusters and patterns across the velvet sky which merged invisibly with the absolute blackness of the sea below. The starlight was bright but not strong enough to create light on the ocean below and the darkness cocooned them as they floated, just the two of them, alone in the middle of it all.

Wendy caught her breath as she saw a shooting star. She pointed but it was so fast that by the time her arm was raised it had vanished into nothing.

"*Le Stella cadente*, the shooting stars of San Lorenzo." Francesco said softly, turning to face Wendy and folding his arm under the side of his head. "Sunday was San Lorenzo, the famous night to see the falling stars and I think we are still in good time to see more tonight. You know you must make a wish when you see one, no?"

He caressed Wendy's face gently and her skin tingled where he touched her. She shifted closer to him, reaching out to run her fingers through his hair. Her mouth found his and her hands became brave in the starlit darkness that enveloped them, slipping under his white shirt and sweeping across his smooth skin. His lips crushed hers and their tongues caressed each other. She sucked his bottom lip and his hands slipped around her waist.

"I'm crazy for you, Wendy," he whispered, breaking away for a moment and looking into her eyes. "I want to feel your skin on mine."

She pulled back from him. This all felt more like a dream than reality. The sangria was making her head spin, or was it just the pent-up longing that she had felt for Francesco from the first moment she had seen him? She was falling in love and knew that he wasn't hers to love, but he felt the same and she knew it was right between them.

Tonight, she decided with her heart, was going to be her night. Out here, on this boat, real life didn't exist. It was just the two of them under the stars in a boat full of lemons.

Silently she reached out and started undoing the buttons on his shirt. She could feel the warmth of his skin radiating through the cotton. He sat up and slipped his arms out of the sleeves, discarding the shirt behind him. They were sitting facing each other on the small sundeck; the only sounds were the lapping of water against the hull of the boat and their breathing. She pulled her top over her head and threw it on top of his shirt. She stood for a moment, wobbling, and shimmied out of her skirt, turning to face him as he exhaled with desire and reached for her.

Their bodies came together, skin on skin for the first time and the passion that they had been holding back for weeks was unleashed. Hands roamed, stroked and caressed, lips collided and teeth clashed. His mouth tasted of sangria and salt, and his skin smelt of lemons and sweat.

He lay her down on the cushions and slowly stripped her naked, savouring the sight of her in the silver semi-darkness. He ran his hands up her body and bent over her, pushing his mouth onto her breast and she arched up towards him, running her hands down his silken back until she reached his shorts.

"Take them off," she urged him, and he obliged, wriggling out of them and leaving them to lie with the lemons on the floor of the boat. They lay together naked, exploring the parts of each other that they had only ever dreamed about. He slipped his hand between her legs and she parted them, catching her breath as he slipped a finger and then another inside of her. She reached across and cupped his balls before running her fingers up and down his length and enclosing it in her warm hand.

She couldn't believe this was happening. It was terrifying and it was erotic but also terrifyingly erotic and maybe they should stop before it was too late? He sensed her wavering and, pinning one of her arms to the deck, closed his lips around her nipple while sliding his fingers inside her, making her sigh with pleasure.

Whatever had kept them apart until now existed no longer. The past and the future and the people in it were inconsequential as their world narrowed to lips and fingers and limbs shiny with sweat.

His erection was pushing on her pubic bone, and she wriggled upwards until he shifted, and suddenly he was between her open legs. She could feel the tip of him gently pressing, waiting to be let in.

"Yes," she whispered, straining to get closer, wanting to feel him crush her with his weight. Slowly he slipped inside her and they both cried out wordlessly as she arched her pelvis towards him, wanting more. They moved as one, rocking, slippery and breathless under the starlight, and the spilt lemons rocked in harmony with them.

Afterwards, they lay in each other's arms, blissed out and satisfied, until their heartbeats returned to normal. A falling star streaked across the sky above them and Francesco murmured, "My wish came true; I cannot believe it."

"We'd better make some more wishes then," replied Wendy and they lay there waiting to wish upon another star, knowing that what they wished for was not impossible but would be extremely difficult. "Do you think we'll ever have a chance to be together?" She turned to him, then put her finger over his lips. "No, don't answer that, I'll just wish upon a star".

As they sailed back to shore and headed back to the party, Wendy was sure they would be caught or that somebody would have seen them. She slunk off first, feeling terribly guilty as she ducked back through the tunnel, but it seemed that nobody had missed her in the slightest. Amanda and Enzo were loved-up in their own little world, lying entwined together on a sun lounger in the shadows of the cliffside and the others were either still dancing or sitting around the fire. She sat down by the fire, opposite Gianni and Claudia, next to Simone who might have been watching her calculatingly. She tensed, but he smiled and just offered her a joint which she took a puff on before handing it back to him. Maybe she was just being paranoid.

She saw Francesco arrive back out of the corner of her eye; he grabbed a drink and mingled for a while before wandering over to them.

"Everything okay, guys?" He sat down on the other side of Simone and winked at Wendy. "You like our beach parties, Wendy?"

"Erm, yes! It's a shame you don't do them more often!" She smiled cheekily at him.

"We really should do this more often," added Claudia, dreamily, looking up in surprise as Francesco laughed out loud.

Wendy tuned out as the enormity of what they had done hit her. Shit! She had just had sex with a married man … No, she had just *made love* with a married man. A man that wasn't hers but a man that she was falling in love with. What had she been thinking? His poor wife, she would be distraught if she found out. Wendy could be responsible for breaking up a marriage, a family, if this leaked out! It mustn't happen

307

again, she decided. She sighed. She felt so comfortable with him, it was all so perfect except for the fact that he was not available.

"I think your friend maybe has drank too much sangria," Claudia said to Wendy, pointing to Amanda who was staggering towards them with her arm around Enzo's waist. He was supporting her the best he could, but as they watched she tripped on a rock and landed on the beach, laughing at herself.

"Oh dear," Wendy got up and went over to them. "Come on, up you get! You've had a bit too much to drink, haven't you?" She helped Enzo pull Amanda up and she wobbled between them.

"I think we have to take her home. If she falls asleep here, we can't get her back!" Enzo looked around at the others.

"Anyone else ready to go? It's going to take ages to walk her back to the main beach. I think we'll need help!"

Simone nodded, "I have to work in the morning, I should start going." There were nods all around; it was late, and time to call it a night anyway.

Francesco jumped up, "I have my cousin's boat at the jetty. We can take her in that, it will be much quicker. "

"That would be amazing!" Enzo thanked Francesco, "Can you bring it here to the shore?"

"*Sì, certo*! I'll be back soon!" He jumped up and went off, ducking his head through the tunnel.

Wendy looked around to say thank you to Antonio for the party, but he was nowhere to be seen. She shrugged and helped Enzo guide Amanda, who was hiccupping and singing softly to herself, down to the shore to wait for the boat.

As Francesco drove the boat around the mass of rock that divided the two beaches, Wendy was relieved to see that it was so dark she couldn't tell that it was him. So even if someone had seen them go out earlier, they would never have been able to tell who they were. He pulled right up onto the shore and they bundled Amanda onto the sundeck, Enzo climbing on and sitting next to her. Wendy, Gianni, Simone, and Claudia all squeezed in, balancing on the rubber sides of the boat.

"Why are there lemons all over the floor?" Gianni asked, picking one up that had rolled under his feet as they sped back to the main beach.

"Oh, I knocked them over earlier; they were for the sangria, but I brought too many," Francesco shrugged, catching Wendy's eye and trying not to smile.

It took quite a long time to get Amanda home. There was no chance of her staying balanced on the back of a scooter, so they thanked Francesco for the ride and said goodbye to the others. They walked up slowly, Enzo one side and Wendy the other, when the narrow stairwells permitted, ricocheting off the walls with Amanda hiccupping and singing most of the way. As they crossed the road up near the Bar di Martino, a police car drove by silently. Wendy felt the beady eye of the *carabinieri* inside the car watching them as they hauled Amanda across the road, but thankfully they didn't stop.

Outside the house, Wendy fumbled in the dark for her keys and thanked Enzo for helping and being so patient.

"Is not a problem! Amanda is now my girlfriend, so I look after her." Wendy opened the door and Enzo scooped Amanda into his arms and carried her downstairs to her bedroom.

"So, it's official then? This display of drunkenness hasn't put you off?" Wendy laughed.

"Not at all, it happens to all of us at some time! I'll come by in the morning and see how she is. I am sure she will be suffering!" He winced and waved goodbye, leaving Wendy to slip off her friend's shoes and tuck the covers around her.

Chapter 20

Positano, 15ᵗʰ August 1986

"Fantastico, darling, you are a very clever girl!" Antonio was in a good mood. He had just arrived at the shop to find out that Amanda had just sold the most expensive dress in the collection to a rich American tourist. He picked up a perfume dispenser and pointing it at her, squeezed the bulb and a cloud of Annick Goutal's Rose Absolute wafted over her. He breathed in the scent and nodding approvingly skipped around the shop for a minute spritzing the clothes and himself before coming to a rest behind the cash register.

"Cash?" He asked as he opened the till hopefully.

"Cheque," Amanda told him firmly as she got up and went to get her bag from the back. He had a habit of frittering away any cash that he found in the till which made doing the accounts a complete nightmare.

"Right, I'm off to meet Wendy. I'll probably see you at Paradise tonight – are you going?" She paused as she was walking out the door.

"Hmm? *Sì,* I'll be there, *ciao ciao!*" He waved distractedly, head in the till as he counted up his earnings.

Yesterday, Amanda had suffered the worst hangover of her life. She had woken sweating to find her tongue stuck to the roof of her mouth, her head throbbing nastily, and when she had dared to open her eyes, the bright sunlight had nearly finished her off. She had staggered into the shower and felt no better for it afterwards. Her knees were bruised and scratched and there was a huge tender bump on her thigh, and she had no recollection of how it got there. She had very carefully drunk a huge glass of water, only to have to run straight to the bathroom and throw up, before trying again. She hadn't managed to hold anything down until later that afternoon and had spent the most excruciating day at work wincing every time somebody walked into the shop. Antonio had arrived and taken pity on her, sending her home early, and she had gratefully gone back to bed with two paracetamol and woken up ravenous later that evening. After cooking herself an egg and prosciutto sandwich, in lieu of a traditional British fry-up as bacon and baked beans did not seem to exist in Italy, she felt much better.

Now she left Antonio counting his money and walked past the little newsagent shop next door, saying goodbye to Luigi, the owner, who was always lovely to chat to when there were no customers. She headed past La Cambusa restaurant and down the steps to the beach. She paused for a moment, looking out to sea and nodded as she spotted the distinctive mast of Sandro's boat heading back from Praiano. Walking briskly over to meet the boat, she waved at a waiter from Le Tre Sorelle that she recognised before looking around in surprise. The higher part of the beach had been transformed into a small marketplace. Stalls had been set up with strands of coloured lights draped between them. It was a similar set up to the festival she had been to in Montepertuso in July. The stalls sold an array of dried fruits, candied nuts and chewy *torrone*, which was like nougat. There were the usual plastic toy stalls and balloon sellers, and in the corner sat an elderly one-eyed basket-maker, surrounded by woven baskets of all different sizes.

She decided to come back and take another look later, as she wanted to meet Wendy on the dock as the boat came in.

Wendy saw her friend sitting with Gloria on the stone bench and waved as the boat pulled into the side of the wharf. She threw a rope over to one of the boys waiting and deftly jumped on land to help disembark the clients. They were a group of six Americans, probably in their fifties, all sunkissed and windswept and all a little bit tipsy. Sandro often would open a bottle of his potent limoncello and get Wendy to serve it to the guests in the afternoons until they were singing merrily away.

They clambered off the boat, thanking Sandro and Wendy profusely before weaving their way over to the bar at the Buca di Bacco to continue drinking.

"Hello dear, did you have a good day?" Gloria asked Wendy, patting the bench seat beside her. She loved chatting to the girls at the end of the day and they enjoyed swapping stories with her.

Wendy had a little story for Gloria so sat down

and started to recount her day.

"So, I'm pretty sure at least one of them had never been on a beach holiday before; you'll never guess what she did! At lunch, we all had spaghetti vongole and when the waiter came to take the plates away, one of the women stopped him and asked for a bag. She put all of the clam shells in the bag and said she was going to take all the beach shells home with her to decorate her living room!"

Gloria let out a peal of laughter and Amanda slapped her forehead with her hand.

"Clamshells? No come on!"

"Seriously! She rinsed them off in the sea before we got back on the boat and kept peeking at them all the way back. She was so proud of her shell collection!"

Gloria was still jiggling with laughter and chipped in, "You should have told her she could add to her collection from the trashcans in the alley behind any Italian restaurant in the US!"

"Somebody will surely tell her at some point!" Amanda shook her head and they moved on to discuss the evening's plans.

"We're going to go to Paradise tonight and watch the fireworks at midnight from there. But before that?" Wendy looked at Amanda questioningly.

"Let's have a walk around the stalls here before it gets too busy, then shall we get takeaway pizza for dinner? Gloria, do you want to join us?"

"It sounds lovely, girls, but I think I'm going to head home before the Ferragosto crowds pour in. I've seen enough fireworks over the years, and I'd rather be in bed, to be honest!" She hauled herself upright and they all walked back up, waving to Gloria as she passed under the arch with the phone boxes.

The girls wandered around the stalls, stopping to buy some candied peanuts in a cellophane bag and a thick chunk of creamy white nougat. They found a little stall where a man was making personalised bracelets, brown leather bands with any name branded into it, the letters painted in rainbow colours. They both decided to get one and were told to come back in half an hour.

It was getting busy, and they walked along the beach front watching the families gathering and claiming their spaces at the shoreline where they would spend the evening. Picnics, pizzas, and night swimming would be enjoyed before a warning firework signalled the start of the grand display at midnight.

A little boy ran past them, a string on his wrist leading up to an aeroplane balloon filled with helium.

"Look at his little outfit, so sweet!" Amanda pointed out. He was as brown as a berry and dressed in local linens, a tiny rumpled cream shirt and beige drawstring trousers with tiny turn-ups and bare feet. The girls watched as he determinedly ran along the pathway, followed by an exasperated mother dressed in similar colours. She looked up and gave an embarrassed smile, brushing her hair out of her face and flushing as she called out.

"Leonardo! Vieni qui!"

With a start, Wendy realised that this was Francesco's wife and son and looked around. Sure enough, Francesco was sitting on a sun lounger nearby. He was packing up an array of beach toys that lay strewn around him and looked up and spotted them, casually waving and calling out.

"Ciao ragazze! Buon Ferragosto! Hi girls, Happy Ferragosto!"

They waved back, as Wendy's heart pounded and her hands became sweaty. A wave of shame washed over her as she had a flashback from a couple of nights ago on the boat full of lemons. She was mortified that she had let her feelings take over like that; who on earth was she to come between this lovely couple?

But she wanted to stop and watch. She had a sick desire to see how he interacted with his family, what they were like together. She also had a moment where she wanted to run up to Elena and beg forgiveness. Luckily, Amanda grabbed her arm and started dragging her away.

"Ciao, Francesco!" Amanda called happily. Wendy smiled weakly in his direction, making sure to look at his wife and not him, then she reluctantly followed Amanda to the end of the beach. They sat for a while, watching the light fade and the town lights switch on. Amanda chatted away, but Wendy wasn't really listening as she sat and watched Francesco with

his family. He looked relaxed and happy as he played with his son and talked to his wife. She was quite tall for an Italian woman, with long, straight, light-brown hair. There didn't seem to be any disharmony between them, but they didn't kiss or touch each other either. She tried to concentrate on what Amanda was telling her, but her eyes kept straying back to where she had seen him, even after they had packed up the toys and left the beach. She sighed with frustration.

"Hungry?" Amanda queried and leapt up without waiting for an answer. "Come on, stop mooning over the married man, it's useless I tell you; he'll never leave his wife! Let's go order pizzas and collect those bracelets then we can eat and go get ready for tonight."

They ordered pizzas from Le Tre Sorelle and sat on the low wall outside until the waiter brought out the boxes and handed them over with a little bow. Thanking him, they went back to collect their leather name bracelets, which they loved and immediately strapped onto their wrists.

"I'm never taking this off," declared Amanda as Wendy admired her wrist. "Come on, let's get the bus home, I can't be bothered to walk all the way up!"

As they slowly walked up the church steps towards the road, Francesco appeared behind them, slightly out of breath.

"*Ciao*, Amanda, Wendy! Are you having a nice evening?" They made small talk for a few moments before he pulled an envelope out of his back pocket and handed it to Wendy.

"I am with my family tonight, but I wanted to give you this. You can read it later, it is nothing bad, I promise! I must go, but have a good evening. *Ciao ciao*!" He leaned forward to kiss her gently on the cheek, just grazing the side of her mouth and again on the other side, then turned and headed back down to the beach.

Wendy turned over the envelope. There was just the letter "W" on the front of it. Amanda looked at her with eyebrows raised. "Something you've forgotten to tell me, madam?"

"You were too hungover to concentrate yesterday. I have rather a lot to tell you and I don't think you're going to like it." She glanced at the letter and slipped it into her bag. She was not going to read it in the middle of the street; it would have to wait until later.

The bus was hot and crowded. Old ladies and children were given precedence when it came to the sparse seating, so Amanda and Wendy stood, side by side, gripping on for dear life to the handrail above as the bus lurched around the hairpin bends. Amanda had wedged the pizza boxes between her waist and her arm, which meant she was taking up more room than necessary and had received a few tuts and shoves from disgruntled locals. A child, sticky with ice cream and sand, stared at them unwaveringly from the comfort of his seat, grubby hand clutching the string of a balloon that bobbed too close to Amanda's face. She didn't have a free hand to bat it away so she stared back at the child in the hope that he would reign in the balloon.

He didn't and she sighed with relief when his mother finally took his hand and dragged him off the bus near the florist shop.

At home, they reheated the pizzas in the oven and ate them sitting on the terrace, watching the *festa* on the beach below. Wendy searched in vain for Francesco and his family, but the beach was too far away for her to be able to distinguish anybody. She filled Amanda in on the latest developments with him, flushing with guilt as she quickly mentioned the encounter in the boat.

Amanda was not so delicate. "My God, it's like you've been living a double life! So, you did the deed? He's married, Wendy! What the hell were you thinking?"

"Well, I wasn't really thinking at that moment," Wendy muttered, avoiding eye contact with her friend. "It was like a dream, Amanda. I don't think I have ever felt so, just so right with someone … it was perfect. But then as soon as we were going back to shore, I felt terrible. Really awful. And the worse thing is that if there was another opportunity to be with him, I would take it, without a doubt." She sighed and picked up a discarded pizza crust. She opened it out, exposing the soft inner layer before throwing it back down again.

"Maybe I should just go back to England before it all gets too complicated and try to forget about him."

"That would be a shame – we've got another month yet left. Why don't you read his letter. Maybe he just wanted a quick shag and now the deed is done

319

it's *sayonara* to you, babe!"

Wendy picked up the pizza crust again and threw it at her friend.

Sitting on the edge of the bed, she slipped a folded sheet of lined A4 paper out of the envelope and brought it to her nose. She had half expected it to smell of lemons and pepper, like him, but of course it only smelt like paper, dry and slightly musty as if it had been taken from a long-abandoned notebook left for years in a cupboard somewhere. He had filled one side of the paper with writing. It was long and rambling, all in capital letters, a few words scrubbed out and replaced. It was mostly written in black biro but near the bottom there were a few lines written in red.

In this moment I have a lot that I want to tell you, but it can all wait until I see you again. For now I will just write some of my thoughts, the most important ones.

Wendy, I wanted to tell you that everything we have done together has been very beautiful, meraviglioso, *wonderful. I am crazy with happiness when I am together with you and I want to continue being with you, talking, laughing, dancing, joking, arguing, annoying you and making you smile. I want to love you and I want to make you happy, and I want to do everything possible to be happy with you because I want to be with you.*

All this is difficult I know, there are many things that we cannot do. But when I think that I may not have know you and that we might not have had a chance to be together it makes me sad. Before I met you I was a happy man, but now I am twice as happy.

Since last night I have been thinking about what you said, whether we will ever have a chance to be together, to live our lives together...

I think that the chance is there, not because I want it, but because it is a possibility that can happen. Just think, many times I have already thought about leaving Elena one day. This is real, a problem that already existed for me before I met you. Am I bad to say this? Maybe. Is it wrong to think this? I don't know, but it is the truth that I have already thought about this. Of course there are many other things to consider, like how would I feel if I did leave her, what would I say to her, would I be able to live here afterwards and how would it affect my son? My mind is in turmoil at the moment but I do not regret anything that has happened between you and me.

I may have made mistakes but I am glad that I have done so because of how alive you make me feel. I want to ask you one more thing. Please don't be disgusted with me, with how I have behaved as a married man. Please stay close to me and trust me that I will never hurt you. I want you in my life, Wendy. Please give me the chance to get to know you more.

I lovissimo you xxxxxxx

She folded the letter away and slipped it into her underwear drawer, feeling a mixture of love, relief, hope and worry for what had been written and what was to come.

Amanda knocked on the door and came in before she had a chance to write a reply.

"All okay here? Come on, forget about him for tonight, it's time to partyyyyy!"

Paradise was quite busy, seeing as it was only eleven in the evening. There was a muddle of scooters parked out by the road and the burly bouncer was at the door and nodded to let them inside. A few people were dancing and at the bar they found Enzo and Simone, ordered rum and cokes, and headed over to the little seating area where they commandeered a table for the evening.

"*Perfetto*! Now we know where to find each other when it gets busy later!" Simone grinned and settled back in his chair to ogle a couple of American girls in short skirts on the dance floor. They were all quite content to sit there and people-watch rather than dance, saving their energy for later on that evening. Simone got up a couple of times, vanishing for a few minutes before sitting casually back down again. He was more jittery than usual, at one point dropping the contents of his bumbag as he delved for a lighter. He swore as he got down on his knees, searching under the table for his keys and various spilt objects. He cracked his head on the underside of the table as he tried to stand up again, causing the table to jolt and knocking over a half empty glass of gin and tonic which splashed onto his shirt, causing him to swear even louder and stomp off to the bar to get another.

"I think he's had too much already!" Enzo laughed, watching Simone stagger off.

At midnight, the DJ lowered the music as the warning firework was set off and everyone poured out onto the terrace to watch the display.

"Look at all the boats!" Wendy gasped as they leaned over the railings. Far down below, the sea looked like a constellation of stars. Hundreds of small boats had come from all the villages along the coast to watch the famous Positano Ferragosto display. The lights swayed with the movement of the sea and in the very middle of the boats was an empty circle.

"There," Enzo pointed at the circle, "that is the raft where the fireworks come from. The other boats have to stay away from him, or they will not start the display."

He pulled Amanda closer, and they stood with their arms around each other. The fireworks started with a whoosh and a crackle, and from above the illuminations looked like giant psychedelic flowers reaching up towards them, then falling away. The sea below was lit up with colours, changing from red to green to purple, and the explosions ricocheted around the bay. After ten hypnotising minutes the display finished with a resounding bang that echoed around the mountainside. There was a moment of silence and then to Wendy's delight all the boats in the bay started sounding their foghorns; the cars and Vespas along the roadsides joined in and the crowds way down on the beach clapped and cheered in appreciation. The sound from the boats was amazing – she had never heard anything like it, hundreds of foghorns of all different sizes and decibels sounding off together. After a while the noise died away and the DJ turned the music back up. Everybody drifted back inside the club, but Wendy hung back and watched as the little boats below started dispersing. It looked like a constellation was expanding slowly as they all moved away from the central raft and started returning to the nearby towns along the coast.

She was feeling depressed after seeing Francesco with his family earlier and she realised how silly she had been to dream of being with him. His letter had been lovely; he must have realised that she would be worrying. But realistically, she was sure that it was all too soon and far-fetched. He wouldn't risk leaving his wife; she lived on the lemon grove with his family. He couldn't just ask her to leave and install Wendy in her place – it would never work. What an idiot she had been. Tomorrow, she would have to look into getting a ticket back to England. It was surely the only solution.

She didn't feel much like dancing, and watching Amanda and Enzo being all loved up wasn't helping either. She took a gulp of her drink which was now warm and sighed, kicking the railing with frustration.

"You okay?" said a voice behind her. She turned to see Simone lurking in the shadows by the emergency exit. He finished rolling a joint and turned back towards the passageway to light it. "*Dai, vieni*, come share with me."

"Yeah … you know, just life." She muttered dejectedly as she walked over to the shadows and stood with him. He suddenly lunged at her and tried to kiss her sloppily before she pushed him away in disgust.

"Simone! Stop it, what the hell?!" She stepped backwards and crossed her arms defensively in front of her, frowning at him.

He shrugged and took a toke on the spliff, slowly blowing a stream of sweet-scented smoke up towards the narrow strip of sky above the passageway before replying.

"*Scusa*, I thought it would make you feel better." He shrugged again and continued. "You only have one life so you should make it the best you can because you don't get another chance. This is what Nonna always tells us. I see a beautiful girl look sad and think maybe a kiss make her feel happy, no?" His voice was slurring but he sort of made sense.

"Yeah, I know, but it's not always possible to follow your dreams. Please don't do that again." She took another sip of her drink.

"*Va bene*, I get it, I know I am not the man for you."

Before she had a chance to wonder what he meant, there was a blast of sound as the doors to the terrace opened and a couple stumbled out, laughing. Simone ducked back into the side passage, grabbing Wendy by the wrist and pulling her with him.

"*Vieni*, it's too busy here. I'm going to go sit on the steps above the road, you coming?"

Wendy shrugged half-heartedly and warily followed him through the emergency exit up to the road, where they darted across to the crumbly old steps that led up the mountain. Simone was drunker than she had realised; if he tried it again, she would slap him and walk away, but he seemed harmless enough and maybe someone should keep an eye on him. He was weaving slightly as he climbed the steps up away from the road, heading into the darkness. He brushed aside a few overhanging branches. A couple of small unripe olives pinged off and hit him in the face and he swore angrily under his breath. She was just about to suggest that they stopped and sat down when she heard a noise on the road behind them. Simone heard it too and turned around, reaching out to grab a branch to steady himself as they saw a fleet of cars pulling up outside the entrance to the disco. Silently, they watched as a group of men poured out of the cars and down the steps, a couple taking the exit he had just used himself.

"*Cazzo*," he whispered.

"What's happening? Who are they?" Wendy asked, confused.

"Shhh! *La Polizia*! It's a raid. Shut up or they will hear you!" He was carrying quite a few eighths of hash still, all in his bumbag, with a few grams of coke that he still hadn't sold. Too much to throw away – he would never make the money back. He was breathing rapidly and quickly decided the best thing to do was to go further up into the mountains, past the house with the pond and hide out for a while. The police surely wouldn't come up here, but they would be all over town like ants for sure. Wendy would have to come with him; she would give him away if he let her go back down now.

"We have to go. Quick," He grabbed her wrist again and pulled her further up the pathway, trying to be as quiet as he could.

Amanda and Enzo were sitting together at the table, heads bent towards each other. They both looked up as they heard shouting. Men were pouring into the club, fanning out in all directions. Amanda glanced at Enzo and saw his expression change from curiosity to wide-eyed surprise. She turned to see what was happening and all hell broke loose.

Someone shouted for the music to be turned off and the order was repeated. Enzo suddenly understood.

"*Cazzo*, it's the police, it's a raid." Most of the men were plain-clothed but some were in uniform, too. There were a couple of policewomen as well who stood and waited with stern faces. He wasn't the only one to realise what was happening and the crowd started murmuring, which built into a crescendo that suddenly stopped as the DJ turned off the record that was playing. A split second of silence and then chaos broke out as at same time he turned on the strobe light – whether on purpose or not, no-one knew. Amanda had no idea what was going on. The strobe made everything look like it was happening in slow motion.

Amanda was caught like a deer in headlights, not moving, sitting there watching the scene unfold. There was total confusion as people stumbled around in the strobe lighting. A voice declared that nobody must leave, everybody was to be searched and she suddenly realised that it was real and not a dream. They were surrounded by plain-clothed policemen who ordered them not to move until they had been searched.

She looked at Enzo in panic. There was a sheen of sweat on his forehead and his eyes were wide with fear. *Oh shit*, she thought, *has he actually got weed with him?* She took a step backwards and immediately felt a hand stop her and push her forwards again.

"*Non ti muovere!* Don't move," a voice warned her. She froze and waited. The police were lining people up and searching them, making everyone turn out pockets and bags, and take off shoes. They then searched the area around them with torches and lit matches. The strobe light was abruptly switched off and the coloured disco lights went on, bathing the room in a weird undulating swirl of colour that was oddly sinister without music accompanying it.

Slowly, the police made their way around the club, searching everybody and sending them over to the other side of the room when they were done. As a female officer searched Amanda, she tried half-heartedly to protest.

"Um, I'm a British Citizen, are you actually allowed to do this?" She asked, gulping with fear as she was made to empty her little bag. Her question was ignored, and the policewoman motioned for her to take off her sandals.

"*Zitto!*" which meant "shut up" was the answer that she got. She was sent to go and stand with the others that had already been searched, and then it was Enzo's turn. She watched, terrified, unsure whether he was clean or not. After a minute he was sent to stand with them, and she sighed with relief. The policemen moved on to the people from the next table. It was an Italian couple in their thirties, and they kicked up a fuss about being searched, the woman slapping away the policeman's hand as he went to take her bag and the man telling the policeman not to touch his wife. A couple of plain-clothes stepped forwards and one started searching the surrounding area with a torch.

"*Cazzo,*" muttered Enzo again under his breath, as a cry of delight went up from the policeman groping around on his knees. "Fucking Simone, dropped his stuff earlier." The officer stood triumphantly and took his findings over to the head of the police, a balding man in a suit and a pot belly who had called for the music to be stopped. He took the offering and barked out an order. More men dropped to their knees and hunted around on the floor with matches that they kept having to drop as they burnt their fingers. Three more little bundles and a couple of paper wraps were found, some under the seat where Amanda had been sitting and the others scattered nearby, by the Italian couple's table.

The policemen stood and discussed their findings for a few moments; they looked towards Enzo and Amanda a couple of times while everyone waited with bated breath. Then suddenly Enzo was being marched away, and a policewoman took Amanda's arm and led her roughly out of the disco, followed by the Italian couple who were shouting and struggling to be left alone. Another couple of boys were led outside too, and they were all taken up to the road without any explanation and pushed into a couple of cars.

"Simone?" Enzo looked around desperately "Where the fuck is Simone?" He ran his hand through his hair and looked down at his feet in despair.

"He left, I think," Amanda said quietly, absolutely terrified about what was happening. "Where's Wendy?"

"That bastard, I was clean!" He whispered, shaking his head as a policeman climbed into the driver's seat and started the engine.

"*Scusa!* It was nothing to do with me," Enzo tried to tell the driver, "it was some guy from Naples." The driver didn't acknowledge them at all.

She felt sick. She knew that she had nothing to worry about, really. She didn't have any drugs on her, and neither did Enzo. He had dropped a tiny bag of weed just before they had been searched; she had seen him kick it away, but there wasn't anything to prove that what the police had found belonged to them, so they would be checked and let go for sure. She glanced sideways at Enzo; he was silent with his head down. Well, they hadn't found anything on him, had they? It would be fine, surely …

The car pulled up outside the Town Hall. The police station was just down below it, and they were all led silently down the steps and buzzed into the building.

They were quite a way up from the road by now, and Wendy was hot and panting. She had to beg Simone to stop for a moment and he had eventually obliged, sitting down on a rock and agitatedly rolling another joint. As he fumbled around in his pockets for his lighter and cigarette papers, his wallet fell out unnoticed onto the pathway. He was hot, too, and undid his shirt, leaving it to flap open. Silvery moonlight shone through the trees, and he could only just see what he was doing. He mixed the tobacco and the weed together in the palm of his hand and sprinkled the mixture into a cigarette paper, rolling it, licking it, and twisting it into a cone. He got up again and pushed Wendy in front of him, gesturing for her to carry on walking.

"Hey, what the hell is the matter with you tonight? Calm down and stop pushing me around! You wanted to come up here – you can go first and show me the way." She stood hands on hips, giving him the side eye until he pushed past her. He stomped along smoking, unaware of his surroundings and the night noises around them. Wendy froze for a moment as a wild boar darted away from them, crashing through the undergrowth, sounding incredibly loud.

"Simone, shall we just go back now? This is stupid, it's dark and dangerous."

"Go back? Are you crazy? I have drugs on me, you idiot! If we go back I will be searched and arrested and so will you because you are with me. You want to go back or are you going to be quiet and come with me?"

Wendy felt a frisson of fear pass through her and turned back to look the way they had come. Should she attempt to go back through the woods by herself or stay with him?

Simone caught her arm and pulled her along with him, making up her mind for her. It was too scary to go back alone and what would she say if she was seen by the police? She wrestled her arm out of his grip and followed along quietly.

He was too caught up in his own world to notice the owls that hooted and the bats that swooped, or the fox that watched them pass by. He was fed up and not thinking straight anymore. His drink-addled brain had for now forgotten about the raid and the reason they were walking up the mountain path. He was more concerned about why Wendy had rejected his advances before. Everyone had a girl except him. Gianni had Claudia; Matteo, the idiot, had just married Maria, and Enzo had now paired up with that blonde English girl. This other English bitch was perfectly available so why had she pushed him away before?

There was a clearing in the woodland in front of them. Moonlight shone down, lighting up a small expanse of water. They had arrived at the old farmstead with the pond in front of it.

"Simone? Are we stopping here?"

If he had been thinking clearly, he would have stopped there for an hour or so, but it suddenly dawned on him that they could follow the pathway around the mountain, all the way to Montepertuso, and he could walk back home from there, avoiding the road. It didn't occur to him that it would usually take about two hours in the daylight and was a terrible idea to try and do it in the dark while drunk and stoned with no flashlight.

"No. We can go up to Montepertuso and walk home from there, is better. I don't want to camp out here. Come."

Wendy had no idea how far away Montepertuso was from their current location. She presumed it wasn't far and although she still could have turned back and made her way back down to the road, it was dark and a bit scary, and so she decided to stay with Simone, who surely knew his way around. On they walked.

Chapter 21

August, 1986

The mountain steps were seemingly never-ending. Up and up they climbed. Simone was drenched with sweat and stopped for a second to peel off his shirt, leaving it draped over a rock on the side of the path. He would pick it up on the way back, he thought. Wendy tried to talk to him every now and then, but it was hard. They were both out of breath from all the climbing and Simone was angry and muttering to himself, ignoring her questions.

"How long do you think until we get to the village?" She tried again, but he shrugged and stomped onwards.

The policemen had separated them. Enzo had been taken away with the Italian man, and the girls had been put in different rooms. Amanda could hear the faint murmur of voices, opening and closing of doors and the sound of a typewriter coming from somewhere down the corridor. Every now and then, the sound of footsteps going back and forth but other than that – nothing. She had no idea what was happening or what would happen to them.

Eventually, she was taken into a small office. A uniformed police officer sat importantly at a desk, behind a typewriter. There were boxes of files and piles of manila folders piled up haphazardly all around the room.

"*Carta d'identità!*" barked the man behind the desk, with his hand held out.

"Um, I'm English," she replied, "I don't have an identity card."

"Passport then!" He ordered.

"I'm sorry, I don't take my passport to nightclubs. I only carry it with me if I'm travelling. It's at home."

"You are required by law in Italy to carry official identification on you at all times!" He frowned and bashed something out on the typewriter. He proceeded to laboriously take down all her personal details, typing it all out with two fingers.

After all the personal details were taken, the questioning began. Amanda's head spun as he asked her where the drugs had come from, who had bought them and where, who was selling them, who was smoking them. She told him she knew nothing, that she was just an English girl on holiday for the summer. He questioned her about her friendship with Enzo, who was he to her, where did they meet, what did she know about him, who were her other friends. Did she do drugs, was she selling drugs for Enzo, how long had they been together. He wanted to know where she was staying, with two gay men? Ah ha! Did they do drugs, too? Of course they didn't! She denied everything and pleaded her innocence. He eventually finished typing up a document and pushed it in front of her, slamming a pen down on the table. "Sign this," he barked at her.

"What is it?" She tried to read it, but it was far too complicated and formal for her to understand. She pushed the pen aside. "I'm not signing that, I have no idea what it is, sorry." She shrugged and looked at the man who sighed theatrically and shook his head. He seemed to be completely devoid of humanity; she felt like she was playing the part in a film about the Gestapo.

Simone and Wendy were high up now; the pathway had zigzagged up through the woods and come out on a cliffside, winding around the edge of a deep ravine. If they turned left, it would take them up to Santa Maria di Castello, a tiny hilltop village where Simone would sometimes go for Sunday lunch with his family. Turning right would lead back around the big valley in which Positano was built and across to Montepertuso.

"Simone! Stop!" Wendy reached out and grabbed his arm. "Can we just stop for a moment please? I just need a break." She was panting and sat down on a boulder to show him that she wasn't going to move for a while. He hesitated stubbornly for a moment, not wanting to give in to her, but realised that he could probably do with a break, too. He sat down next to her, wiping the sweat away from his brow with his arm. She sat there, catching her breath, staring out at the blackness of the ravine in front of her, wondering why she kept making such stupid choices lately.

After being made to go in the bathroom and make a urine sample, Amanda was taken back to the small room she had been put in and was told to wait. It was a small featureless office with an empty oblong table and a couple of chairs. There was a window on one side, but the shutters were closed. The walls were painted a dull grey and unadorned. A strip light shone down garishly from the ceiling. Amanda paced for a while but eventually sat down, drawing the chair up to the table and laying her head on her folded arms, tried to get some rest.

"Why you push me away before?" Simone turned to Wendy, a devious look in his eye. "I'm not good enough for you?" Wendy swallowed uncomfortably. He really had to bring this up now, here, while they were alone in the middle of nowhere?

"I'm sorry, I …" she started saying, but he jumped up and, grabbing her arm, pulled her up with him.

"You what?" He sneered at her. "You like married men instead of single men, huh? Is that it?" Wendy reeled back in shock, but he gripped tighter, stopping her from moving away. "I saw you, getting off the boat with Francesco at the beach the other night. I know what you foreign girls are like." He shook her arm and she cried out in fright.

"Simone, no! It's not what you think, I …" He raised his hand suddenly, as if to hit her, roaring, "Shut up!" She flinched and ducked her head from him, twisting her arm to try and loosen his grip.

338

"You foreign girls come here to have fun with Italian men, no? You just want a bit of summer fun, I know this. Italian girls are not like this – they are for marrying and having babies with, but you foreigners? You just want sex. And then I see that you go and choose a man that is already taken when I am here and available. It is offensive, no? You think I am not good enough for you, huh?" He had been slowly getting closer to her as he spoke until she could feel his spittle hitting her face and smell the alcohol on his breath. She couldn't move backwards anymore; he had backed her into the boulder that they had been sitting on. His fingernails dug into the flesh of her underarm – she would have a bruise there tomorrow.

Her mind was working at double speed; what to do? Try to placate him, but how?

"Simone, no! It's not like that, I don't know what you saw but you misunderstood. We were only talking, I swear."

"You lie to me!" He gripped her arm tighter and shook her, then suddenly without any warning he raised his other hand and slapped her across the face. Wendy had never been hit or slapped before by anyone, and for a moment she literally didn't know what had hit her. Then the whole side of her face blossomed with pain and heat, and she brought her hand up to feel if there was any damage, staring at him in shock. He slapped her hand away and she cowered, expecting another slap, but he pushed her back onto the boulder so that she lost her balance and ended up lying awkwardly across the rock as he loomed over her. She quickly realised what a vulnerable position

339

she was in and struggled to get up, but he rolled her over onto her front, wrenching her arm up behind her back with one hand and started pushing up her dress. Wendy screamed and bucked; the only thing she could do was to wrap her foot around his leg to try and unbalance him, but he was already trying to pull down her underwear and it wasn't working.

Then for a moment he stopped to undo his belt and jeans and had to let go of her to use both hands, so she took her chance. Pushing herself up from that rock with an almighty roar, she barrelled backwards into him, causing him to lose his balance and fall. He grabbed her as he fell, and they landed on the edge of the path. His head lolled into the emptiness of the precipice before he tried to roll forwards and away from the cliff. He grabbed onto Wendy and they struggled, his movements clumsy and furious, but Wendy was like a cat in a bag. Arms and legs flying as she fought, kicking and scratching to get away from him and protect herself. They were too close to the edge, though, and it hadn't rained for weeks. The earth was dry and powdery and suddenly started to give way with the extra weight that it was holding. For a moment, he teetered on the edge before falling sideways into the emptiness of the steep drop off. As if in slow motion, Wendy saw his eyes widen in surprise before she felt an enormous tug on her arm, and she looked down to see that he was still holding on to her with a vice-like grip. As he fell backwards into the empty darkness, he dragged her with him and for a few moments they were chest to chest; she could feel the heat from his body on hers. Then they were falling, and screaming, and there was no-one around to hear them except the nearby owls that screeched in alarm and flapped up

340

into the air, the foxes and wild boars that crashed away from the terrifying noise. All the creatures of the valley awoke and screeched, squawked, darted and ran while Wendy and Simone and the dislodged dry, dusty, earthen stones tumbled, separately now, and bounced down the slope, catching on shrubs and bushes that were too small to save them. A few short seconds that felt like time had slowed down like thick treacle. But then she was caught by the branches of a robust myrtle bush and it held her, bouncing back and forth as hard unripened berries pinged around her. He came to a halt a few moments later, wrapped around a small oak tree, his body battered and broken, nothing moving except a trickle of blood that made its way slowly down his face and dripped onto the ground. The myrtle bush and the oak tree slowly grew still again, both holding on tightly to the two pummelled bodies.

Amanda dozed fitfully; dreams flashed by incoherently, policemen chasing her, trying to run but her feet sinking into ground that became like wet concrete. She tried to call out but her voice had gone, too. She awoke uncomfortably and sat up rubbing her neck. Shards of daylight filtered through the shutters, and she wondered what time it was. Was Wendy at home? Where had she been while the raid was happening?

Finally, she heard footsteps approaching and the door opened. She was led back into the office and told that they were being taken to Salerno. She fought back a rising panic as the man told her that seeing as no-one had admitted to owning the marijuana that had been found, they would be all detained in jail until the magistrate decided who was guilty. The drugs would be tested to determine their strength, which would also determine the sentence of those found guilty.

"But I haven't done anything wrong! I was just in the wrong place at the wrong time – you can't do this!" Tears sprung to her eyes, and she pleaded in vain. "I'm just here on holiday, this has nothing to do with me, I swear!"

The man paused and looked down at her.

"Now you take my advice, you tell the truth to the magistrate, and all will be good."

"But I have been telling the truth!"

"Well, someone tried to get rid of those drugs, so one of you is lying." With that, he pushed back his chair and escorted her out of the room.

They were piled into the back of a car and instructed not to talk, a tear-streaked Amanda and the glowering other woman who had been arrested. Enzo and the woman's partner were nowhere to be seen, probably escorted in a different car. The drive to Salerno took over an hour, along the narrow coastal road, passing by Amalfi and the bustling town of Maiori. As the car drove through the town along the seafront, she stared out at the happy holidaymakers and carefree children and wondered how it could have all gone so wrong so quickly. After a while, the car pulled away from the coast and onto a motorway, crowded with big lorries making their way to and from a bustling port that was laden with containers. She dozed on and off and felt quite carsick by the time they arrived at the prison. They pulled up outside a big red brick building, surrounded by tall metal fencing and backed by a low, undulating, shrub-covered mountain. As she stepped outside the car, she caught a whiff of boiled vegetables and overcooked pasta. They were led inside, and the heavy door clunked ominously behind them.

Simone's mother rapped hard on the bedroom door. The boy slept far too long – it was almost midday! She rapped again, calling his name, and opened it. He wasn't there. His bed was still made from the day before and there weren't any clothes lying on the floor. She had cleaned up yesterday, tutting at the laziness of her grown son who didn't look after himself.

A frisson of worry snaked down her spine but she shrugged it off, telling herself he had probably slept over at a friend's house and would surely be back for lunch. She ambled off to the kitchen where a tray of stuffed tomatoes was ready to be baked. Maybe she would make him some *mozzarella in carrozze* too; he would be hungry when he got back home.

Nerone whimpered hungrily in front of his bowl and then plodded back up to check the bedrooms, but neither of the girls were there. He walked up to the front door and sat there waiting patiently.

Of course, news of the raid on the Paradise spread around town like wildfire. When Claudia and Gianni realised that Enzo and Amanda had been arrested, they went straight over to the girls' house to see if Wendy was okay. They knocked on the door and waited; they could hear Nerone barking desperately on the other side of the door.

"Is she in? Maybe she went to work?" Gianni suggested.

"I don't think she would have just gone to work if she knew Amanda had been arrested. Where could she be? Do you know the phone number for the house, we could try and call?"

"No idea, but the hotel must have a phone book. Let's go ask."

They walked into the reception of the Villa Franca next door to Rob and Ted's and explained their predicament to the man behind the desk. He brought out a phone book and let they try to call the house but there was no answer.

"Can we try and phone Mauro or Sandro at the beach to see if they have seen Wendy?" suggested Claudia. Gianni ran his finger down the names until he found Mauro's home address. His wife answered and assured them that the fishermen were not going out until later that evening. "So, Wendy wouldn't be down with them, would she?" Gianni thanked her and hung up.

"If I may suggest," said the concierge, "we keep a spare door key for *I Signori* Rob and Ted in case of emergencies. If the housesitters are not there, then maybe you should take the key and go feed the poor dog? And maybe it would be prudent to inform the *Signori* about the current events, hmmm?" He rummaged in a drawer while he spoke and pulled out a key on a yellow fob, laying it on the counter and pushing it towards Gianni.

344

It was obvious as they opened the door that there was nobody there except Nerone. He was ecstatic to see them, and they immediately took him outside for a quick walk. Once he had relieved himself, they took him back home. While Gianni fed him and gave him some fuss, Claudia went to check the girls' rooms. There was no sign of Wendy having left and no signs of a breakfast having been consumed that morning in the kitchen. Her passport and her rucksack were there, as was her tote bag that she carried around in the day time. Her wallet was inside too.

"Gianni," she called, "it's strange about Wendy. All her stuff is here, even her wallet. Are you sure she wasn't arrested too? Can we phone and check? I don't understand where else she could be."

"Okay," Gianni said, raking his fingers through his hair, "let's go up to the police and check with them. We can get an update on the others while we're there."

The police were not very helpful. Wendy hadn't been arrested, they could confirm that, but they wouldn't consider her missing until at least 24 hours had passed by.

"She probably met a boy and went home with him," sneered one of the younger officers.

They decided to hold off from calling Rob and Ted another day, just in case Wendy reappeared, but by the next morning with no news at all, they headed back to the *Carabinieri* to report her as missing.

****

345

Walking into the police station, Gianni was surprised to see Simone's mother just about to leave, twisting a handkerchief in her hands.

"Signora, Buongiorno, tutto bene?"

"Oh, Gianni, have you seen my Simone at all?" She rushed over and placed her hand on his shoulder.

"Simone? Um, not since Ferragosto, *Signora*. We were at the discoteca, all of us, but Claudia and I left to watch the fireworks, um, somewhere more private." He reached back to hold Claudia's hand, drawing her closer. "Why, is he missing too?"

"Too?" Simone's mother shrilled, "Is someone else missing?"

"Yes!" Claudia joined in, "Our English friend Wendy has not been seen either since that night. Maybe they are together somewhere?" She looked hopefully at Gianni who looked more confused than ever.

"I wouldn't have thought they would go off together, but maybe ... I think we need to tell all this to the police, come on."

"My boy wouldn't just go off like that. He always comes home for his lunch, he does." Simone's mother followed Gianni back into the office. "Maybe now you take me seriously, there is another one missing!" She shook her hand at the weary-looking officer who perked up a bit at this new piece of information.

Once he had been filled in by Gianni, he puffed up importantly and picked up the phone. A few hours later, there were search parties out scouring the town and surrounding areas. A group of men abseiled down from the nightclub terrace, into the thick foliage that covered the mountainside, in case they had tried to hide from the police raid. Another crew started on the mountain pathway opposite the club but turned back once they had reached the pond.

Chapter 22

Positano, 1986

For the first time in weeks, Positano awoke to overcast skies. It was warm and muggy, but the sun was hidden behind a blanket of pale grey that would probably burn off later in the morning. The town had woken to the droning hum of a helicopter. It swooped and hovered low over the valleys and crevices, searching from above. The noise of the rotor blades resounded throughout the village, making it hard to think about anything else. Everyone was anxiously waiting for news, wanting to know what had happened.

Simone and Wendy had been missing for three nights. At first, with all the chaos that had ensued after the police raid on the discotheque, nobody had been aware that they had vanished at all.

Simone's parents had presumed that he had stayed at a friend's house the first night. Then, on hearing about what had happened at the nightclub, they had gone to the police, expecting to be told that he was being held with the rest of them. Except he wasn't and there was another girl missing too, a foreigner. No-one had seen either of them since before the Ferragosto fireworks when they had definitely been seen on the terrace at Paradise with the kids who had been arrested.

The radio crackled to life. The pilot listened, one hand pressing his earphone closer to his head. A shirt and wallet had both been found, seemingly discarded on a mountain pathway high above the town. The pilot flew towards the Paradise discotheque, balanced on the hillside at the top of the town. The pathway started just behind it. He flew higher until he could see the search party below, orange ropes keeping them secure as they scrambled over a dry stream bed, checking in the shade of boulders and narrow gorges. He flew higher still, ahead of the searchers, following the pathway where they could see it and scanning the areas below the sharp drop-offs. Was that something blue down there, under a tree that clung to the steep slope? He hovered closer, nodded, and picked up the radio.

Two policemen were dispatched to inform the boy's parents and from the moment Simone's mother's wail of grief was heard by the neighbours, the news spread around town like wildfire.

The boy had been found lifeless, wrapped around a small tree 22 metres down a steep gorge. He had been carrying six grams of hashish and one and a half grams of cocaine in his pockets and had subsequently been taken to Naples for an autopsy. The girl was still alive, but in a coma, and had been airlifted to a hospital in Naples.

****

Amanda had arrived at the jail in Salerno with the other woman who had been arrested at the Paradise. They hadn't been allowed to talk on the journey and she only found out her name as they stood in the prison reception area and had their names called out and ticked off a list held by a thin, pale warden.

"Ricci, Giovanna?"

The woman stepped forwards and was handed a pile of what looked like clothes and bed sheets.

"Hobbs, Amanda?"

She swallowed and stepped forwards to receive her new belongings and they were led through to a corridor. The warden talked them through some brief rules as they walked; lights were out at 10pm, no food in the cells.

First, they stopped in a drab, bare room with a couple of tables and chairs and, surprisingly, were given a meal. They hadn't slept and had been given no breakfast that morning, and it must have been coming up to lunchtime, so they were both hungry and sat down to eat the simple *pasta al pomodoro* that was brought in on two moulded food trays with plastic cutlery. The trays were compartmentalised and there was also a slice of bread each and a small, wilted salad which consisted of lettuce and shredded carrot, heavily doused in oil and salt. Amanda ate it anyway.

The warden stood watching them eat and as soon as they were finishing instructed them to take off their day clothes and change into the clothes that had been provided. Rifling through the pile of provisions that had been handed to her on arrival, Amanda found a pair of loose trousers, two plain t-shirts, a pair of pale blue pyjamas, and a pair of slip-on plimsolls.

"You will receive your clothes and any belongings back when you leave here." The warden crossed her arms over her chest and waited, pole faced as the girls shimmied out of their club wear and into the trousers and top. As Amanda tucked the shirt into her waistband, she was buoyed by the fact that the warden had mentioned "when they get out of here" rather than "if." She clung onto that phrase as she handed over her dress and sandals and followed the warden to the cells.

They turned onto a long corridor, exactly what one would imagine a prison to look like. White barred cells ran along both sides of the corridor, and the paintwork was peeling and dilapidated. The warden stopped at the fourth cell on the left and opened the door, gesturing for Amanda to step inside. The walls were painted a yellowish green up to shoulder height and white above that. There was a small sink attached to the back wall and a single bed with a thin mattress, a small fold-down desk and a chair at the wall adjacent to the bed, and no window. The bed was bare, with a pile of folded bedsheets, a pillow, and a brown blanket waiting to be made up. The door was left open as the warden led Giovanna to another cell nearly opposite Amanda's.

Fighting a rising sense of panic, Amanda sat down on the unmade bed. She looked at the provisions she had been given in reception. There was a rough bath towel and a bar of soap, a plastic bowl, a mug and a set of plastic cutlery. There was another larger bowl which had a fitted lid. She had no idea what that was for. A tear ran down her face and plopped onto the bedsheets. She was about to curl up for a good cry when the warden appeared at the door again.

"Make your bed properly. One sheet over the mattress, one folded on top, neat corners please and the blanket if you need it folded down over the top sheet. Dinner will be at seven."

"What if I need the toilet?" Amanda asked, looking wildly around the tiny room. Was she supposed to use the sink?

"You have a pot." The woman gestured to the provisions that Amanda had been given and had dumped on the bed. She looked to see what the woman was referring to. The warden stepped in and pointed to the pot with the lid on.

"You use this; in the morning, you will empty it and wash it. Now, make your bed." She stepped out and the door shut with a clunk.

Amanda woke up stiff and uncomfortable. It couldn't really be called a bed; the mattress was lumpy and narrow, and the pillow was rock hard and far too thick. She had a crick in her neck from trying to sleep on it. She sat up and rubbed her neck, a wave of worry passing over her again. She was getting used to this feeling of fear, panic, and worry that threatened to envelop her and smother her at all times of the day and night. At first, it didn't seem real. How could this possibly be happening to her? She was sure she would wake up any time soon and find herself back in Positano with Nerone at the base of the bed. But three nights had passed by, and she was now accepting the fact that she was in prison and was probably going to have to let her parents know – if they didn't already.

One of the wardens was coming along the corridor, opening the cell doors, shouting for them to get up and slop out. 33 females were being held in the prison; five of them were foreigners and none of them spoke English. Amanda was having a crash course in Italian whether she liked it or not.

As her cell door opened with a clunk, she staggered out of the room, blinking at the harsh strip lighting in the corridor. She followed the other inmates to the far end of the corridor to empty and wash their slop pots, trying not to breathe too deeply. The smell of unwashed bodies and urine was unbearable first thing in the morning.

Her first morning here, she had not known what to do and had walked out of her cell empty-handed, not sure where they were all going. The other inmates had glanced at her and sniggered until one took pity on her and whispered in Italian, "Where's your pot? You not going to wash it, you dirty foreigner?" She had realised that they were all carrying the slop pots to a big sink at the end of the corridor where the contents were tipped away and the pots were scrubbed clean. She had turned around, trying to get back to her cell and was pushed and bumped by the inmates behind her.

"What the fuck are you doing?" one hissed at

her. She ducked back into her cell and carefully picked up the pot of wee. She'd had to go twice in the night, squatting over it on the floor, dying of shame as the woman in the cell opposite watched her blankly.

She had backed out into the corridor and joined the queue at the end where she eventually tipped the contents down the stinking drain and used the brush on a string to scrape the pot in cold water before taking it back to her cell.

Now, three days later, she already felt like a pro. She washed the pot and slipped back into her cell where she washed her face and armpits the best she could at the tiny sink before dressing for the day.

She now knew that the bed was to be made a specific way, to army standards, and they were not allowed to get under the covers in the daytime. They were permitted to lay on top of the bed, but no blankets until bed-time.

Twenty minutes later, they were all taken down to breakfast, clutching their mugs and cutlery. The first day, finding somewhere to sit had been a bit of a minefield. She had hesitantly tried to sit at the end of one table but an elder woman with a craggy face had sprung up and roared, "Who the hell said you could sit here?" Amanda quickly got up again and, backing away with her tray, was grateful when Giovanna called out for her to sit next to her.

After they had eaten, they would line up to wash their mugs and cutlery before being led back to their cells. The highlight of the day was the hour outside where they were encouraged to walk around the barren courtyard to get some exercise. Other than that, it was eat, cell, sleep, repeat, mind-numbingly boring interspersed with panic attacks and tears.

All she knew was that she would be held in prison, guilty until proven innocent, until her appointment at the Tribunale was set up. Then she would be taken in front of the judge and allowed to declare herself innocent. She had no idea if Enzo would be there too, whether Wendy would be allowed to visit her in the meantime, or if her family had been informed. Had anyone tried contacting the British Consulate to get her out? She had been told it could take up to ten days before she went to court. Another week here, please God, no! It was strange that Wendy hadn't been already to see her; maybe she wasn't allowed visitors yet …

****

Of course, once the authorities realised that it was Simone who had been selling the drugs, Enzo and Amanda and the other couple were released on day five after all the necessary paperwork had been completed. The two other boys were kept in as they had both been clients of Simone earlier that night and had both been found with a small amount of hash on them during the raid.

Amanda had been so angry that Wendy had not been to visit her in prison those first three days.

With no outside contact, she'd had no idea what had happened to her friend. Nobody had informed her of the events in Positano since she had been arrested.

When they were allowed to leave, she was handed back her own clothes, the black net skirt that Antonio had made and the lacey bustier, wildly inappropriate now. She had blushed with shame when Enzo's father had met them outside the prison, tight-lipped and awkward. He drove them slowly back to Positano in a battered, old, red Fiat, asking Enzo to tell him his version of events and listening without interrupting as his son explained what had happened.

He drove slowly, along the coast road, passing Maiori where happy tanned Italians strolled along the promenade with children and ice creams and large beach bags slung from their shoulders. As they drove through Amalfi, Amanda, in the backseat, stared at a policeman in his silly helmet, importantly directing traffic around the roundabout. She wondered if he had been there that night and she looked away disdainfully. Before they reached Praiano, Enzo's father pulled over in a sun-scorched lay-by and told them the news while they stood by the railings looking out to sea. Simone had been found lifeless with drugs in his pockets, and Wendy, found unconscious nearby, was now in a hospital in Naples. Her parents had flown out the day before and were there by her bedside. Enzo staggered and clutched his middle as if he had been shot. Tears streamed down his face, and he let out huge, unchecked sobs. Amanda distractedly thought that an English man would never have reacted in such a passionate way before she ran to the side of the lay-by and vomited on the ground in front of her. She sank to her knees afterwards, depleted from all the trauma, but she didn't cry at all. Simone dead and Wendy in a coma? It couldn't be real; her brain refused to accept it. She felt numb and watched as Enzo cried and his father stood over him, also wiping away a tear for the boy that he had watched grow up with his son.

As they finally drove into Positano, Amanda realised why Enzo's dad had stopped and told them the news before they had arrived. Death announcements for Simone were plastered over every billboard in town, pasted on top of the opening night posters for the Paradise. He had been forced to tell them in advance before they read it for themselves.

Claudia and Gianni were waiting with Nerone at the house. They had taken over dog duties and had moved in for the last few nights and were now going to stay and keep Amanda company, so that she wasn't alone.

Claudia had hugged her and led her downstairs into the kitchen. Nerone wagged his tail gleefully and nuzzled her hand, happy that she had returned.

"Can we phone the hospital, now? I need to know how Wendy is, has she woken up yet, and when can I go see her?"

Gianni patted the chair beside him at the kitchen table and Claudia poured lemony iced water out of a jug, passing a glass to Amanda so that she would sit down.

"I already speak with the hospital, one hour

ago. Wendy is still not awake but they say she is *stabile*, er, how you say …"

"Stable?" Amanda asked in a small voice.

"Yes, she is stable, so please we must just hope and pray for her."

He pushed a piece of paper towards her. "This is the address and the hours that you can visit, but for now only family are allowed in. Her parents are both there and here is the hotel they are staying at in Napoli."

Claudia chipped in, "If you want to go tomorrow, there is a hydrofoil that leaves at eleven. I will come with you."

Amanda took a shower. A very long, hot, soapy shower, and scrubbed away the feel and the smell of prison. She washed her hair and left the conditioner in while she finally shaved her stubbly legs and dried herself on what felt like the softest towels in the world. She pulled on the most comforting clothes she could find, a pair of colourful, wide, harem pants and a white vest top. The outfit that she had been wearing on Ferragosto and to come back home in went straight into the bin. She would never be able to wear that again.

Later, she phoned her parents, using Rob and Ted's house phone and asked them to call her back, yes, she knew it was expensive, but it was important and she would pay them back the money. She didn't tell them about her stint in Salerno – that could wait until another time, preferably face to face … if ever – but she told them about Wendy's accident, glossing over why Wendy had been up a mountain in the middle of the night. She reassured them that she was fine, that Wendy's parents were in Naples and she would see them tomorrow. Yes, she would keep in touch, yes, she would let them know when Wendy gained consciousness, yes, she loved them both too. She sighed with relief as she put the phone down, feeling slightly guilty for not telling them the whole truth. But, she was an adult. She didn't need to go running to tell her parents everything that happened to her. Some things were best left unsaid.

Chapter 23

Naples, 1986

Wendy woke up slowly to the sound of her mother's voice complaining about the lack of tea.

"What sort of place doesn't offer a simple cup of tea? Absolutely shocking it is."

She lay there for a while, slowly realising that she hardly had the strength to open her eyes, let alone wonder why her mother was complaining about the lack of tea facilities. She drifted off again before anyone noticed she had been awake.

She awoke again a few hours later. This time, she opened her eyes and slowly the world around her came into focus. Her mother's face appeared above her and gasped as she saw Wendy's eyes were open.

"Oh darling, there you are! Nurse! Doctor! Somebody, come quick! She's awake!" Two more faces appeared above her and her mother was pushed out of sight. What was going on? Was she in hospital? Her head felt muddled and for a moment she couldn't remember anything. What day was it? She tried to sit up and a hand gently held her down.

"Stay still, Wendy, let us just check you over. I am Dottore Somma, you had an accident. Do you remember?"

An accident? Wendy could only remember hearing her mother complaining about the tea facilities or something. She drifted away again.

Finally, she woke up for good. Her father was sitting by the bedside this time and calmly whispered, "Hello my love, stay with us now, there's a good girl." There was a suspiciously wet glint in his eyes and his hand squeezed hers reassuringly.

"Hi Dad," she replied, her voice rusty from not being used. "What's happened?"

"You took a bit of a tumble, love. Were you out hiking or something?"

For a moment her mind was blank, and then it all came rushing back. Positano, the Paradise club, the police and Simone and then that awful feeling of helplessness, tumbling down that steep slope in the darkness and then nothing.

"It was … we were … he grabbed me and fell, oh Dad!" She tried to move and felt a jarring pain in her chest and a heaviness in her leg. She looked down at her body, hidden under the bed sheets.

"What's wrong with me?"

"It's okay, don't panic love. Just a few broken bones; you were very, very lucky. Now, I'm just going to call the doctor to have a look at you, don't you go anywhere now."

Dottore Somma came into the room and re-introduced himself to Wendy before carrying out a few tests. Patiently, he explained that she had cracked two ribs and had fractured her tibia and fibula, requiring surgery to pin the bones back together. The surgery had gone well and in a couple of days they would be putting a plaster cast on her leg. She had been in a coma for seven days, but after running a few routine tests and questions it had been established that she had suffered no permanent damage or memory loss.

"A week? ... But where am I?" Wendy murmured, once the medical explanations had finished.

"Oh, of course, I'm sorry," the doctor replied. He looked at Wendy's father and something passed between them before he cleared his throat and replied, "You were picked up by the rescue helicopter and brought to the International Hospital in Naples. Maybe in a couple of days we will get you up and into a wheelchair. There is a *bellissima* view across the bay of Napoli from the balcony." He gestured to a door by the window, but from Wendy's position in the bed all she could see was the sun-bleached sky.

"And Simone? Is he here too? Can I have some water" Wendy asked, trying to swallow, and realising how dry her mouth was.

The doctor stepped around to the other side of the bed and poured some water into a small glass from a jug on the bedside table, and her dad came forward.

He patted her hand," All in good time; a lot has happened, but we need to concentrate on you getting better first. Drink slowly." He shot a look at the doctor who stood with his hands together and uncomfortably cleared his throat. "The police will want to talk to her about what happened—"

"But that can wait!" Her father cut in firmly. "My daughter has just woken up after a seven-day coma. The police can wait. She hasn't even seen her mother yet."

"Mum's here too? Something about tea flickered through her mind but was gone before she could hold onto it.

"Of course she is, we flew out as soon as we got the call. She should be back soon. She went out to the bar down the road – it's the only place she can get a cup of tea. They only have coffee in the hospital canteen."

Francesco was up in the lemon terrace furthest away from the house. Bees buzzed around him, and he swatted them away as he filled crates with the big, sweet fruits. The lemon-picking season was almost over. Soon it would be time to start pruning the trees back, systematically working from the top terrace down towards the road. A trickle of sweat landed in his eye, causing him to swear and he stopped to wipe it away with his t-shirt which he had taken off and partly stuffed in his pocket. Now, he took it out and folded it from corner to shoulder before winding it around his forehead like a bandana and tucking in the edges, effectively stopping the sweat from dripping down his face.

He had spent the last week in secret turmoil. First of all, he had heard about the raid on the nightclub and thought that Wendy had been arrested, but that had turned out to be her friend and nobody knew where Wendy was. She had vanished.

Then finally she had been found, and with the body of that shifty guy, Simone. The whole town had been reeling in shock at the loss of a young life and the revelations that came with it. The foreign girl in a coma had almost been forgotten about. Most people had presumed that she was an accomplice or Simone's girlfriend, and it hurt to hear the things that people were saying about her around town. What had she been doing with Simone halfway up a mountain? He couldn't figure it out and there was no one he could ask.

He was shocked and distressed by what had happened to Wendy, but of course had had to carry on as normal in front of his wife, acting as if it hadn't bothered him when all he wanted to do was to jump in the car and drive to Naples to see her.

Dom had been fantastic, had met him outside the bar or even come to hang out in the groves a couple of times and kept Francesco up to date with news of Wendy via Gianni and had kept him sane, letting him vent and worry his thoughts out loud.

Filling the crate to the brim, he hefted it onto his shoulder and started making his way back through the grove, down the uneven steps to the next terrace and back towards the deposit. He heard a distinctive whistle coming from somewhere below him. *That must be Dom again*, he thought and whistled back. Dom met him just behind the house. He was in his uniform, without a jacket and hat, and was panting from taking the steps up from the road too fast.

"I have good news for you!" He came closer, speaking quietly just in case anyone else was nearby. "She's awake again! Here, let me get that."

Francesco nearly let go of the crate in surprise. "*Oh Grazie Dio!*" he smiled as Dom helped him lower the heavy box to the ground. "Is she okay? Has she spoken? Who told you? Hang on, let's go into the shade and you can tell me."

They walked over to the lemon storage shed, a ramshackle building patched with overlapping sheets of rusty corrugated iron. A few colourful empty crates were piled up to one side of the door. Inside, it was cooler and quiet; stacks of bottles and demijohns full of limoncello lined the shelves. A corner was taken up with a huge pile of black netting, tied up in a bundle with twine and straining to escape its restraints. There was an old white sink fitted along one side and Francesco filled up a couple of Nutella jars, decorated with pictures of Smurfs, with tap water and offered one to Dom, who took it gladly and gulped it thirstily.

"I saw Claudia and Amanda this morning – they were walking the dog. I asked them how she was, and Amanda told me that yesterday Wendy had woken up and spoken to her father. She's going to be okay by the sound of it and I reckon that we can probably go visit her in a few days, if that's what you want to do?"

Of course he wanted to visit her; he would jump in the car and go right now if he could. He suddenly felt, for the first time, a flicker of annoyance towards his wife. If it wasn't for her, he could go right now, but instead he would have to find a way to go without her knowing … No! What was he thinking? The best thing to do was to tell her that he was going with Dom and maybe the others all together to visit her.

"Hey, *tutto bene?* All okay?" Elena appeared at the door, tea towel in her hand with Leonardo trailing behind her.

"*Certo!* Everything is fine, Dom just stopped by with the latest town news," Francesco jumped up and rinsed the jam jars out at the sink.

"Do tell!" Elena looked at Dom curiously, wondering what could have happened now after such an unusual week.

"Well, the good news is," Dom smiled at her, slowly standing up and stretching, "the English girl who was in a coma has woken up again and is going to be okay, which is wonderful! I met her and her friend when we were little you know, they both have been coming here for years. I'd seen them a few times this summer, and was actually hoping to get together with the other one, but Enzo got there first!"

"Oh, it was perfectly clear she was going to choose Enzo over you, anybody could see!" Francesco laughed at his friend, winking at Elena when Dom jokingly clutched his heart in offence.

367

"Well, I am glad that the girl is going to be okay," Elena said, scooping up Leonardo who was about to grab a glass bottle. "Anyway, I popped by to say that lunch is nearly ready – there's enough for you too, Dom, if you want to join us."

Dom thanked her for the offer, declining as he had to be back at the office by 2 pm. Elena asked him where he had eaten and when he replied that he hadn't had time yet, she rushed off to pack up some food in an old ice cream container for him to take back to work.

"You've got a good one there, friend. Are you sure you know what you are doing?" Dom watched Elena carrying the little boy back into the house and turned to his friend.

Francesco sighed deeply. "To be honest, I haven't got a clue what I'm doing … I just don't know."

They told her about Simone the next day. She was devastated, of course, but also slightly relieved that he would never touch her again. He was the first person that Wendy had known who had died from something other than old age, and of course, she thought she was partly to blame. She had survivor's guilt and kept going over and over the evening in her head as if she could somehow change the facts: If she hadn't stopped to talk to him out on the nightclub terrace, or if she had simply gone back inside instead of following him, then he wouldn't have taken her with him and tried to rape her. They would both have been better off going back inside and being arrested … at least he would still be alive.

Once the doctors said she could have visitors, a stream of people arrived at her bedside. Amanda, of course, was the first, turning up with Enzo who was almost hidden behind an enormous bunch of flowers. His eyes were swollen, and he was subdued and quiet. Amanda rushed to her bedside and leaned over to hug her gently.

"I'm so sorry about what happened. I was so upset with you for not visiting me, I had no idea that you had even gone missing. They told me nothing in there! How do you feel?"

"Battered," Wendy joked, gesturing to her leg, now heavy and immobile in a thick white cast. "Just don't make me laugh, my ribs kill me if I even think about laughing. I've never been so terrified of sneezing in my life."

"Oh, poor you!" Amanda sat gently on the side of the bed. Enzo was still standing near the door clutching the bunch of flowers.

"Why don't you go and find a vase for them," Amanda told him, gesturing at the bouquet. "Here, leave them on the bed and go ask a nurse."

Once he was gone, glad to have something to do, Amanda asked about her parents.

"Mum and Dad have been great; they've been with me most of the time. As we knew you were coming this morning, I made them take a day off, so they've gone to visit Pompeii."

"That's nice, good." Amanda stood up and walked to the window, not looking out at the bay and the volcano, but leaning on the sill with her back to the view.

"Can I ask you what happened? I don't want to upset you, but what on earth were you doing with Simone halfway up a mountain?"

"Yeah, sure, let's wait until Enzo comes back, though, because he should hear it, too. Um, have you seen Francesco by any chance?"

"Not at all, but I think he has been getting Dom to give him news about you. Dom has been asking for updates pretty much every day. But Wendy, you really can't—"

The door opened and Enzo walked back into the room with a white ceramic vase. "*Allora*, where do you want these?" He picked up the flowers, checking that they fit the vase and looked around the room.

"Put them on the table there, by the window," Amanda instructed. "Wendy wants to tell us what happened."

Wendy quietly told them what had happened when they had left the nightclub. Amanda reached for her hand as tears ran down her face while she told of the struggle with Simone and what he had tried to do. She also told them about the other times Simone had lunged at her, in the kitchen one evening and out on the terrace of Paradise.

Enzo sighed, running his hands through his hair and not even trying to hide the tears that streamed down his face.

"I am so sorry Wendy. If I had known, I would not have brought him with me. This was not the first time he has gotten carried away. There was a problem with a girl last year that he became obsessed with. She had to report him to the police to stop him from coming near her."

They sat in silence for a while contemplating this information before Wendy changed the subject and asked them to tell her about life in prison.

Gloria arrived with a very smart-looking Sandro. He had dressed up for the occasion and was wearing clean jeans and a white shirt, with his hair combed neatly, and he was holding a small tray of pastries from the bar. Gloria fussed around Wendy, plumping up her pillow and rearranging the light sheet over her cast until her mum came back in. "Mum, this is Gloria, who has been living here for years. And this is Sandro, one of the fishermen who I was working for. Where's Mauro, by the way?"

Sandro took Wendy's mum's hand in his and gave it an elaborate kiss, causing her to blush deeply.

"He doesn't leave the village except by boat, so he stayed behind to mend the nets, but sends his regards to you!" Gloria patted her hand and sent Sandro off to find a couple of extra chairs so that they could all sit down and enjoy the pastries.

371

Two policemen turned up one day, serious and business-like, notebook in hand, ready to take Wendy's statement. One of them spoke very good English; he had probably been assigned to this case on purpose and he listened carefully as Wendy told them exactly what had happened from the moment the fireworks had gone off until they slipped off the mountain pathway. She didn't cry this time – she had done that when she had told her parents and Amanda and Enzo. She hoped it didn't make the policemen think that she was cold-hearted or uncaring. She hoped they believed her.

She was in a ward with three other beds but two of them were empty. There had been a lady in one for the first couple of nights who had broken an arm in a scooter accident, but she had been discharged. Now, there was just one elderly lady in the far bed who moaned occasionally and spoke in such a thick Neapolitan dialect that Wendy didn't understand anything that she said. They had given up trying to communicate and just waved to each other in the mornings. Wendy wasn't even sure what she was in the hospital for.

So, she had plenty of time alone, to think and mull over the events of the last few months. She learned to steer her thoughts away from the what-ifs and started thinking about the what-nows.

She had been reckless and selfish, putting her own feelings above the lives of other people. She had acted on feelings for a man who was not available to her and had put his whole family at risk. A man had died, and she had been, if not part of the cause, then at least a factor in the events causing the death. She could not be responsible for causing any more destruction in Positano. She knew that she would have to go back to England soon, anyway. Her parents would be taking her home as soon as she was discharged. There was no way she could even go back to Positano, let alone stay there with all those steps and a broken leg. Whatever had started between her and Francesco was finished, there was no other option.

When Francesco turned up one afternoon with Dom, Wendy was sitting in a wheelchair for the first time, her leg raised in front of her. Her mother was reading her an article from an English magazine she had brought with her but when the boys walked in, she asked her mum if she could leave them alone for a while.

"I need to talk to them alone, Mum, please."

"Ok love, I'll pop back to the hotel then. Do you need anything from the shops? They had some lovely looking peaches in the market near the square yesterday."

"No, Mum, I'm good, thanks. I'll see you later."

Dom conveniently disappeared to get some drinks and left them alone to talk. Francesco wheeled her out onto the huge, long terrace which was in front of the room. It was a beautiful day, the sun sparkled and glinted off the sea in the bay and they could see Mount Vesuvius, all hazy in the distance. The light seemed to have changed from a hot summer harshness to a softer, more golden glow, signalling that the summer would be ending soon.

She had already decided what she was going to say. Enough bad things had happened, and she just couldn't take responsibility for anything else. Amanda had warned her that, unfortunately, rumours about Simone's attack on her had spread like wildfire around the village, and many people were questioning whether Wendy had encouraged him or not. They were wondering why the English girl had followed him up the mountain path in the first place. There had been comments about the fact that she had been wearing a short skirt and that she had been seen around town with various men over the last few months. Her time in Positano was raked over and dissected by the gossips with a fine-tooth comb. She had been seen on a scooter with her arms around Enzo. She had been seen on a surfboard with Francesco, and she had been seen talking to Dom and Simone on more than one occasion.

She made Francesco pull up a chair and sit down next to her wheelchair. She held his hand, stroked it for a moment and swallowed before she began.

"Francesco, I've had a lot of time to think, and I know that I am forever going to be remembered in Positano as the girl that fell off the mountain with the drug dealer that died. Nobody is going to forget that and there will always be suspicion and talk about whether it was my fault or his and what actually happened. I don't want to be that person, the one that nobody fully trusts and the one that has a story to her name. You know that's what it will be like if I stay, don't you?"

"Well, yes, for sure it will be like that for a

while, but it will pass. When the next big item of gossip happens, it will be forgotten about, I'm sure." Wendy stopped him, laying a hand on his arm.

"But it's not just about that," she said softly. "I don't think I can be that person and also the person that breaks up a family and destroys a marriage. It's not just about the two of us, Francesco. There are Elena and Lorenzo to consider as well. I love you, I have never felt like this before and I know that you and I could be so wonderful together, but I just can't do it. I can't!"

"Oh, Wendy! I do understand what you are saying, but I think we could get through all this together. We could move somewhere else, we could …"

"No, Francesco, listen to me! It won't work, too much has happened and we might not even survive the fallout. I want you to stay here with your lovely little family, bring up a happy son and a contented wife and forget about me if you can or just remember me with fondness."

"Wendy, I could never forget about you, you know that. How could I?" They both had tears in their eyes and were clinging to each other's hands.

"One day it will all be forgotten, Wendy, the next time there is some other scandal, this will all be old news."

But Wendy had made up her mind. She couldn't break up his family and live with the guilt.

"We can write to each other. Maybe I can come and visit you in England, no?" But she refused that, too. "No, my darling, it's not worth the risk; the postman might say something, or Elena might come across a letter. We have to have a clean break and just remember what we had and how beautiful it was." A tear trickled out of her left eye and he reached to wipe it away tenderly.

Head bowed, Francesco agreed that Wendy was right. He knew deep down that there was no solution without creating so much upheaval in his life and the life of those around him.

Eventually, he gave her his address anyway, just in case, and she folded the slip of paper, tucking it into the book she was reading.

They had spent one fantastic night together. Was that better than nothing or worse because they now knew what they were missing out on? He had tears in his eyes and she cried, but she had been crying for days on and off by that point anyway, so that was nothing new, but by God, how it hurt to finish things with him like this. When he finally walked away, Wendy felt like her heart was breaking into a million pieces. She was letting him walk away! But she knew she had no choice and she let him go.

Chapter 24

Positano, September 2016

Wendy shifted on the sofa and wiped a tear from her eye. Mia and Jess sat silently, not sure what to say, but she hadn't quite finished. Amanda took her hand and squeezed it in encouragement.

"I flew back to England with your grandparents a couple of days later. I had to move back into their house to recuperate from my injuries and a few weeks later, I realised I was pregnant. I was overjoyed with happiness that I would forever have a part of Francesco with me, but at the same time, I was wracked with guilt that I was going to hide this huge thing from him. But, of course, if I told him, it would tear apart his family and have huge consequences. Surely his wife would never accept that he had another child, younger than his son, with another woman, and a woman with a such a terrible reputation, too? I was sure that I was doing the right thing by keeping you a secret. Can you understand now why I never told you?"

"Wow, Mum … I had no idea. I thought he knew about me and didn't want anything to do with me. So, you're saying that he still doesn't actually know I exist?

"No, love, he has no idea. And I have no idea how we should go about telling him."

"Budge up, Mum, let me hug you. You poor thing. I can't believe all that happened to you, and you've never mentioned anything." Mia squeezed herself in-between Amanda and Wendy and hugged her mum tightly. "I'm not angry with you, I promise, but I do wish you had told me before. The one thing I don't get is why now?"

Amanda extracted herself from the sofa, leaving space for Mia and Wendy. "I wrote to your mum a couple of weeks ago, remember? I told her that his wife had passed away a couple of months ago and maybe it was now time that the two of you had a chance to meet."

Jess was muttering to herself, putting two and two together, and suddenly jumped to her feet. "I think I've got it!" She exclaimed triumphantly! It must be that man with the lemon groves, Leo Limone's dad! Right, Mum? His mum died not long ago, I can't think of anyone else, and the ages match."

"Leo Limone? Leo Lemon?" Mia looked at Jess and then turned her head quickly to see Wendy and Amanda's reaction. They had both frozen in surprise but then Amanda sighed and nodded.

"Yes, Jess it's Francesco, Leo's father." She rolled her eyes and shrugged at Wendy. "Well, that's that then, no more secrets ... the problem with living in a small town is everyone knows everyone, and you can't hide much."

Jess was hopping around in glee, "Oh my God, Mia! You are Leo Limone's sister! I can't believe it!"

Mia looked at Jess, shaking her head, "Wait, who on earth is Leo Lemon and please don't tell me that is his actual name?" At that, Jess and Amanda both burst out laughing.

"What?" Mia and Wendy both yelled at them, half laughing too.

Jess was almost doubled over in mirth. "Oh, that's so funny, Mia! If that was his real name, then your real name would be Mia Limone, which translates to My Lemon ... which sort of fits perfectly, considering who your father is!" She howled with laughter again until she realised that maybe it wasn't so funny for Mia, who still had no idea who she was talking about.

"I'm sorry, Mia," she said, wiping tears from her eyes, "I forgot. Leo is the guy that came to see the nightclub with us yesterday! You've already met your brother – you just didn't know it at the time!"

Wendy sat up straight upon hearing this and Amanda looked surprised too.

"You met Leo already?"

Mia shrugged and replied, "Well, we weren't actually introduced. Nobody ever said his name and I didn't speak to him, but he seemed nice. What did he say, Jess, when we were in that old club?

Jess was still in a high state of excitement and

nearly squealed as she remembered. "Oh my god, yes! He said that his dad had said that his life may have been very different if it wasn't for that nightclub! Wow, Wendy, this is soooo romantic!"

Wendy looked shellshocked and Amanda decided it was time to crack out the strong stuff.

"I think we all need a drink. Jess, go get the bottle of grappa ... or ..." she looked slyly at Wendy, "darling, would you prefer some local limoncello made by someone you might have once known from Montepertuso?"

At that point, Mia snapped.

"Guys! Sorry, but for fuck's sake! I am still here, you know, and I am still in the absolute dark. You all seem to have forgotten that this is all about ME and who my father is, and you still haven't told me! I want a name and an explanation NOW, PLEASE! Who the hell is my father?"

There was a moment of silence and then a flurry of activity. Jess clinked bottles and glassed and poured drinks for them all, apologising for laughing and forgetting. Amanda, too, was apologising to Mia and Wendy was trying to get them both to shut up by flapping her arms at them which wasn't working.

"Mia, darling, your father is a lovely man called Francesco Marchesi. He has a lemon grove," Wendy looked over to Amanda, who nodded for confirmation, "in Montepertuso and is the producer of one of the best limoncellos around. His son, Leo, is about four years older than you. His wife was called Elena and she was a lovely, quiet woman who loved her family very much. Amanda, did they ever have more children?"

Amanda shook her head, "No, it was just Leonardo."

"Thank you," Mia said stiffly. She picked up her glass, then swiped the limoncello bottle and started to head towards the door. Hesitating for a moment she turned back. Holding up the bottle she asked, "This is his limoncello, right?

"Yes," both Amanda and Jess replied.

"Good. Then it's mine, too," Mia declared and stomped outside.

The Piazza was buzzing. Cars and scooters weaved around the bus that was off-loading passengers while a throng of people pushed to get on board. Colourful clothes hung outside shops and wafted in the light breeze. A waiter with a tray full of drinks darted from the bar across the road to a covered terrace dotted with tables, and a big, shaggy dog lay in the middle of the square, one eye open, watching as people walked around him.

"I was just sitting on the wall, minding my own business, and this group of kids came out of the bar, and I did a double take. It looked just like you and Wendy with Amanda and Enzo at first. I swear I thought I had gone back in time – it was like seeing a bunch of ghosts." Dom claimed, distractedly waving on the traffic that was slowing down as it passed the

Piazza Dei Mulini. Francesco had stopped off to chat with his old friend on his way to the bank and was amused by Dom's story.

"So, how much had you had to drink?" Francesco joked, stepping aside as a trail of tourists walked past, obediently following a tour guide who was holding up a stick with a plastic sunflower stuck on the top of it.

"Not much, really. Of course, I then realised that one of the girls was Amanda's daughter and the one that looked like you was Leo, of course. But the other girl looked just like Wendy except with darker hair … Well, she looked like what I remember Wendy looked like, anyway." He blew his whistle at a scooter that was loitering at the bus stop, motioning for him to drive away, and turned back to grin at his friend.

"Wouldn't it be weird if it turns out that Leo has met a girl that looks just like your one-that-got-away?"

"Oh please, no! That really wouldn't be fair on me!" Francesco laughed and patted Dom on the shoulder. "I must go pay these bills, see you later, *ciao!*"

He walked up the road, away from the busy Piazza and towards the bank. It had been a tough couple of years for him, what with Elena being diagnosed and the trips back and forth to the hospital until it was clear that nothing was working. Her illness had dragged on slowly and by the time she died, it had felt like a release. And although he had been extremely sad and missed her terribly, it had also been a relief that her suffering was finally over.

He was suddenly alone for the first time ever, and, of course, it had stirred up all sorts of thoughts over the last couple of months. He had never forgotten meeting Wendy and the feelings he'd had for her. When she had gone back to England, he had quietly gone on with his life, cherishing the memories of the short time they had spent together and hoping that maybe the next year she would come back. But she had never returned to Positano, even though her friend Amanda had stayed and married Enzo.

A could of times in those early years, Francesco had tried to ask Amanda about Wendy, begging for some information on how she was or an address he could write to her at. Amanda had been tight-lipped, though, telling him that Wendy was absolutely fine and was getting on with her life. She refused to pass on any letters, knowing that it would just cause more sadness. The only concession she had made was to give Francesco a photo.

One Kodak print photo, slightly grainy, of Wendy, looking happy and relaxed, smiling and salty-haired, on Sandro's boat. He kept it in the bottom of a desk drawer in the lemon grove office, in an old cigar box with a few other random photos from the 80s, just in case anybody asked. He had looked at it often the first few years, but gradually pulled it out less and less as time passed by.

Should he contact Wendy? Maybe just to see how she was? He had mulled over this idea for a couple of weeks and eventually decided that it was best to leave things as they were. No doubt she had forgotten all about him over the years and was hopefully living a happy life in England. Who was he to upset the balance and disturb her or upset her again? Best let sleeping dogs lie.

He must remember to ask Leo who he'd been out with the other night, though. It would be interesting to see whether Dom's recollection of Wendy matched his. He pushed the bank door open and walked inside, just as a scooter whizzed by.

"And that's the bank, just in case you need the cash machine," Jess indicated as they sped by the yellow building. A man was just stepping inside, and Mia watched the door close behind him. She noted the cash machine in the wall by the door and pushed her helmet back up off her eyes; it was a bit too big for her and kept slipping down.

Jess was driving her around town, pointing out various places of interest. They had driven back over to the abandoned nightclub and walked a few hundred metres of the pathway up to the mountains opposite the gate. Mia had seen the house that Rob and Ted used to own, where their mothers had stayed that summer. Someone else was living there now but there were two ceramic tiles on the wall outside dedicated to the two men, rather like the one for Gloria down on the jetty. She had asked if the town did that for everyone that died but Jess had said no, actually it was just those three people.

Jess had pointed out the house where the VEP, Wendy's Saucepan Man, had once lived. He was long gone and there were none of his hand-painted signs left; it was just a whitewashed domed building now.

The local traffic warden had been standing in the Piazza Dei Mulini and Jess slowed down just before they arrived.

"Look! That's the guy that was always with your father, his traffic warden friend!" She sped off before he saw the scooter and told them to move on.

They were both secretly hoping to bump into Leo Lemon again or even better, his father, so that Mia could see what he looked like. They hadn't really come up with a plan yet of how to break the news to him that he had a fully grown daughter. It was a tricky one.

Jess slowed down again once they passed the bank. They were driving up a long straight road, past Le Sirenuse Hotel and a row of shops on the left, and Jess stopped for a few seconds to point up at a hotel.

"That's where they filmed part of *Under the Tuscan Sun*, the part where he's on the balcony and she's below, talking up to him. It's now the most requested room in the hotel!"

"Mum always refused to watch that film. Now I know why," Mia replied.

Jess drove on slowly. "Look at the view behind you, to the right!"

Mia turned and looked. There was the most breathtaking panorama of the pyramid of houses with the whole beach laid out in front of it. They passed a small bar, tiny tables crammed onto the narrow pavement. Two women were sitting drinking coffee.

385

One of them watched as they drove slowly past and suddenly grabbed the wrist of the other lady and pointed toward them. They both looked surprised to see Mia and Jess driving past.

Claudia and Maria met up every now and then for a mid-morning coffee and a chat. They had noticed a few years ago how Amanda and Enzo's elder daughter looked just like Amanda when she was younger. Now they stared in surprise as they watched her driving past with a passenger that looked just like Amanda's old friend Wendy.

"How funny!" Claudia remarked, "That was just like a Deja vù. Young Amanda and Wendy back to haunt us!"

"Maybe it was," Maria shrugged, turning away. "Maybe she has a daughter; it would make sense. I have not thought about her for years!"

"She did your wedding makeup, didn't she … your first wedding, that is?"

"Ha! And what a waste of time that was. There were enough things that went wrong on the wedding day that I should have known it was destined to fail."

"Hmm, well, at least you have actually been a bride, twice, too! I've given up all hope. Honestly, thirty-three years together, two kids, three dogs, and I'm still waiting for Gianni to pop the question!"

Within minutes they had forgotten about the two girls on the scooter and spent the rest of their time together light-heartedly slating their husbands.

Jess pulled over outside the Bar Internazionale and turned off the engine. "There's one more place I can show you if you want." She twisted to try and see Mia behind her. Mia leant forward a bit.

"Where?"

"The lemon groves, of course! Do you want a sneak peek?"

"Shit, yes! Of course I do! Why on earth didn't I think to ask? Let's go now!"

"Wendy, this is ridiculous! You can't just hide out at my house the whole time you're here!" Amanda took the last of the clean pillowcases off the washing line and folded it neatly.

Wendy was hanging out a second wash load and sighed.

"I know, but I just have no idea what to say if I see Francesco. How the hell do I tell him about Mia?"

"You have just got to get it over and done with. There's no easy way to do it, so just say it gently … if you see him. Honestly, you probably won't bump into him, anyway; I hardly ever see him around. We'll have to arrange to meet him somewhere where you can talk in private."

Amanda continued, "Actually, the lemon groves sound pretty private to me. Let's call him!"

"Wait!" Wendy hesitated, "Okay, no, do it, before I can think and back out."

Amanda quickly googled the website for the lemon groves and called the number. It was a landline and rang and rang.

"There's no answer. He's probably either out around town or working on his land. What do you want to do?"

"Can we go there? Will you take me up, please? I've never been before so I don't know where it is."

"Really? You're sure?" Amanda was surprised Wendy was suddenly facing up to it.

"Yes! But now, before I have time to change my mind. I just want this feeling of dread about telling him to be finished. I can't stand it anymore. Yes, he might hate me and never forgive me, but do you know what? That's OK as long as he knows about Mia, and I don't have to feel this guilt anymore. Let's just get it over and done with."

Amanda looked slightly astonished but grabbed the car keys and her bag.

"Okay, I'm ready!"

Wendy walked over to the bathroom and checked her hair. She raised a finger and spun towards Amanda playfully. "But first, lipstick!" She winked comically and delved into her bag. A few minutes later they were walking down to the road to where the car was parked.

Francesco left the bank and pulled his phone out of his pocket to call Leo.

"Where are you?"

"Just finishing up here, Pa, I'll be on my way in a minute."

Good, I'm just walking up from the bank. Come and pick me up at La Sponda." Leo was making a limoncello delivery at a hotel near Praiano; the timing was perfect to pick Francesco up on the way back home.

He walked up the road, calling out to a couple of shopkeepers along the way, past the new cocktail bar where the American tourists queued up in the afternoon to drink overpriced drinks and take photos for Instagram. He shook his head in amusement as he walked past. He waved to Clementina, the owner of Bruno's Bar, and she came out to ask how he was doing after losing Elena. He chatted politely with her and made his excuses and carried on. He saw Claudia and Maria sitting at a table a bit further up and waved to them, not planning on stopping. But they called him over and he spent a few minutes chatting with them until he saw Leo pull up in the *ape*, the little lemon truck, at the crossroads ahead.

Mia could feel the air becoming cooler as Jess drove the scooter up the winding road towards Montepertuso. It was leafy and green and much quieter than in the busy town below. She craned her neck upwards as the huge hole in the cliff face appeared above them, and as they passed through the village she looked eagerly, trying to spot the school where her mum (and her father too) had watched fireworks from the roof.

They passed through the peaceful village and followed the road upwards. Mia spotted a peacock in a garden by a tiny waterfall, and a balcony proudly displaying figurines of Snow White and the Seven Dwarves, which so many Italian gardens seemed to have. Jess pulled over on a relatively straight part of the road and pointed upwards.

"Here we are! This is your inheritance!" She joked, receiving a shove from Mia.

"Oh please! The man probably won't want anything to do with me and I am certainly not looking for anything from him. I just want to meet him. Out of curiosity, that's all."

"I know, sorry, that was a crap joke. Hold on, let me turn the scooter round and park."

Jess drove on a few metres and started to turn in the road, but at that moment a cat shot out in front of them, and she jerked the handlebars back the other way as she was in mid-turn. Jess yelped as she realised they were keeling sideways, the cat froze in front of them, the scooter wobbled for a moment and Mia, not having a clue how scooters worked, tried to lean against the wobble which just helped the scooter fall sideways even faster.

The cat darted away as they landed in a heap on

the ground.

"Oh my God, are you okay, Mia?" Jess cried. She had managed to push herself away from the seat and landed clear of the heavy Honda. Mia was lying on her side, but it looked like the scooter was pinning down her leg.

"I'm fine, I think, but I can't get my leg out. Can you lift it?"

Jess scrambled onto her feet and noticed that her palm was bleeding where it had scraped on the ground as she landed. She winced as she grabbed the handlebars and tried to lift the scooter up, but it was impossible, she knew that. Scooters often blew over where they were parked in strong winds, and she had always had to call for help to lift hers back up again. She knew she couldn't lift one by herself – it was too heavy.

"I can't lift it! Does it hurt? Oh shit, what do I do?" She was starting to panic and looked around wildly. Mia lay there, trying to figure out if anything was broken. She didn't think so.

"Jess, calm down, I'm not dying. Look, just lean against the bike, no, push it up a bit first, like that, yes, there! That at least takes the pressure off my shin."

"But we can't stay like this!" Jess was frantic and Mia nearly laughed.

"We're in the middle of the only road in the village, someone is bound to come along soon and help, don't you think?"

At that moment, they heard the sound of an *ape* puttering up the hill. It stopped right in front of them, and two men scrambled out to help.

"Oh shit," Jess muttered. "Of all the people in town ..."

"What's that?" Francesco said, squinting at the road ahead of them.

"Someone's had an accident!" Leo replied, slamming on the brakes. They jumped out and ran over to the bike.

"Jess! Are you okay?" Leo recognised his friend and ran towards her. There was another girl on the ground with her helmet still on, but her leg was trapped. Francesco ran round behind Mia and crouched down, ready to pull her away as soon as the bike was lifted.

"*Ma che e successo? Hai fatto male?*" Francesco asked Mia as he looped his hands under her armpits, ready to shift her.

"Um, I'm English," Mia said, wincing as Leo and Jess lifted the scooter.

None of them noticed Amanda's car pull up next to the *ape* until Amanda and Wendy came running round. Wendy only saw Mia and the scooter, lying in the middle of the road, and let out a shriek, and dashed towards her daughter. "Mia! What happened? Are you hurt?"

All of a sudden, Mia's leg was released, and Francesco pulled her backwards into his arms as Wendy knelt down in front of them.

Mia wiggled her leg experimentally. Nothing seemed to be broken, although her shin was stinging and there was some blood seeping through her jeans. "I'm okay, Mum, really … Mum?"

Wendy was not looking at Mia anymore. She was staring at Francesco, right there in front of her, holding her dau— no, *their* daughter in his arms. He was staring right back at her, shocked into silence for a moment.

"Wendy?" he queried, tipping his head sideways.

"Er, hi, Francesco," she replied, drinking in the sight of him. He hadn't changed much over the years. His hair had some grey in it, he was a bit heavier and the smile lines around his eyes were stronger, but it was still him and her heart pounded.

"Mum!" Mia was struggling to unclip the chin strap of her helmet. "Give me a hand with this thing, will you!"

Wendy snapped back to the moment. "Sorry love, here, let me do that." She forgot about Francesco as she slipped Mia's helmet off and checked her all over for signs of damage.

"We need to get your jeans off and check your leg."

Francesco was staring at Mia now, realising that this was the girl that Dom had mentioned. "This is your daughter?" He looked at Wendy questioningly. "I have a first aid kit in the office." Wendy nodded and was about to say something, but Jess interrupted, stepping in front of Francesco. "You alright, Mia? I'm so sorry, that stupid cat made me lose my balance. Should I call an ambulance?"

"No! I'm fine, really." Mia reached out for Jess to pull her up. She carefully put some weight on her foot as everyone watched her.

"Look, I'm fine, just a bit squashed, that's all." She looked at the people standing around her. Her mum was looking at Francesco again, entranced. He was glancing from her to her mum and back again. Jess and Amanda were watching Francesco, and Leo was busily checking the bike for damage now he knew that no-one was hurt.

Mia finally had a moment to really look at Francesco. He was good-looking, very different from Ben, but seemed easygoing and friendly. She glanced at his hands; they were just like hers – shorter fingers than Mum's, different shaped nails. She had always wondered if she had her father's hands. She raised her eyes and caught him looking at her.

"Well, hi there … Dad?"

There was a collective intake of breath from everyone watching; Mia noted the look of horror pass over her mother's face and saw Amanda slap her hand over her mouth in shock.

"Wait. Didn't you just all arrive together? Had you not told him yet, Mum?"

"No," Wendy said faintly.

"What did she just call me? Wendy?" Francesco had visibly paled and continued to look from Wendy to Mia as if they were playing ping pong. Wendy looked at him and nodded.

Suddenly, there was a loud angry beep and they realised that they were all still in the middle of the road, and there now was a small line of cars waiting to pass. Amanda and Leo ran to move their vehicles and Jess turned towards her bike. Francesco and Wendy both helped Mia limp towards the entrance to the lemon groves, where she sat down on a step.

"Sorry," she said looking warily at Francesco, "I didn't mean to spring it on you like that. I thought you had already talked to Mum, as you arrived together.

"We did not arrive together! I 'have not seen Wendy for 30 years. Why you call me Dad? I'm sorry but how many years do you have?"

"I'm twenty-nine." Mia suddenly felt quite sick; she'd really messed things up now. What if he refused to believe she was his daughter?

Francesco looked at Wendy and did a classic Italian gesture with his hand, shaking his fist in front of his face, fingers and thumb facing up and clenched together.

"Wendy?" He growled.

"Francesco, I'm so sorry … this is Mia, she's, er – she's your daughter. I didn't want you to find out this way. I was coming to find you to tell you about her, I swear." She sat down next to Mia and protectively put her arm around her.

"My daughter? But how is it possible. We only had one night together."

"Well, that's obviously all it took," Mia quipped, trying to lighten the atmosphere. "If it makes you feel better, I only found out the truth about *you* yesterday. My creation has been the biggest kept secret ever."

"Wendy? Is this true? You had a baby from that night, and you didn't tell me? Okay – this is crazy. We need to talk properly. Let's go inside the house; we cannot do this here."

Wendy nodded mutely, tears in her eyes as they all trooped up the path to the little house.

Francesco sat back and sighed. "So, I have a daughter. I always wanted a daughter." Wendy had explained to him her reasons for not telling him about Mia, and he had grudgingly accepted that it would have created huge upheavals in his family and life.

Mia had made it clear to him that she thought of Ben as her actual father and didn't want to hurt his feelings but was happy to get to know him as a friend or maybe an uncle.

"I suppose if I really like you, I can think of you as my other father!" she quipped, causing a few weak smiles.

And, of course, she couldn't wait to get to know Leo, her half-brother, if he came round to the idea. When Leo had realised that his father had had a thing going with Wendy when he was three years old, he had quietly left the group and stomped off into the groves. Francesco had gotten up to follow him, but Wendy had stopped him, laying a hand on his arm and gently telling him to let Leo have some time to come to terms with the news.

There was an awkward silence as the conversation ran out and everyone sat contemplating what had just happened. Wendy stood up and stepped away from the farmhouse table where they had all gathered.

"I think it's time to go," she looked at Mia and then Amanda. "We could maybe organise a dinner all together in a day or two? Give Francesco and poor Leo some time to talk and then all meet up for any questions … or whatever? I'm sorry, I don't really know how this sort of thing should be done."

"Yes, that is fine, I need to talk with my son, and of course, then I would like to spend some time with the daughter I didn't know I had… er, can I call you that?" He looked at Mia questioningly.

"Sure," she shrugged, "tell Leo I am sorry but that I'd love to get to know him." She stood up, wincing as she felt her leg throb. Jess helped Mia hobble back down to the car and Amanda followed, leaving Wendy and Francesco a moment to talk together.

"I'm so sorry," she told him again, "I never meant to hurt you. Do you think you can forgive me?"

Francesco stepped towards her and took her hands in his. "You have denied me her whole childhood, but you did it to save my marriage and my reputation. I do understand this, and I wish things could have been different. There is nothing to forgive, Wendy, *cara mia*; you have given me the greatest gift, albeit late in life, but hopefully we will have many years to all get to know each other again. Go now, and I look forward to seeing you both soon." He leaned forward and kissed her gently on the forehead before stepping back and letting her go.

Wendy walked away from the house. For the first time in weeks, she felt light and worry-free. A huge weight had been lifted from her shoulders, one that she had carried with her for nearly thirty years. She took a deep breath and sighed, and it felt like her lungs had taken in more air than ever before. She smiled as she walked, the feeling of Francesco's kiss still tingling on her forehead.

"Well, that went fairly well, considering …" Amanda said as she drove them back down to town. Nobody replied, each lost in their own thoughts, so she stayed quiet for the rest of the journey home.

Amanda insisted on stopping off quickly at the Red Cross to check Mia's leg, but in the end, there was nobody there, so they went home, and Mia was administered an icepack and some arnica cream for the bruising.

"I'm really okay, guys, my foot was just a bit squashed for a while. Please stop fussing!"

Francesco phoned the next morning. Amanda passed the phone to Wendy who took it outside, shutting the door firmly behind her so she could have some privacy.

"I am very confused at the moment, Wendy. I am angry with you, sometimes so angry that you hide this thing from me for all these years. But also, I do understand your decision and I respect it. But I am angry about it … Of course, I am also so happy to find I have a daughter, but I have lost so much of her life. And Leo," he sighed. "Leo is furious with me. He has learned that I betrayed his mother and is not talking to me right now. Can we meet up to talk, just you and me? We have a lot to talk about, I think."

"Yes, of course, that's a good idea. I'm so sorry Francesco for not telling you. I don't know what I can say to make things better, but thank you for giving me the chance."

"I will pick you up at 11 o'clock, be ready." He hung up and Wendy wiped a tear from her eye before going back inside.

They spent the day walking around Sorrento, stopping at a pizzeria for lunch and later at a gelateria that had over forty different flavours of gelato and a wall covered with photos of the long-haired owner standing next to various celebrities. They talked as they walked and when they sat and stopped for cappuccinos. There was so much to say and so many years to cover, but mostly they talked about Mia. Francesco wanted to know everything, from the birth to the first words to how she had been with her other father. They walked along the Main Street, looping down the side alleys, past grocery stores with piles of colourful fruits in baskets outside. Leather goods stores jostled with lemon stores, glowing a fluorescent limoncello colour from the many shaped bottles that lined the walls.

They walked to the very end of the Corso, past the old hospital and onwards along the coast road. Wendy spoke of her doubts and guilt over the years, of the letters left unwritten and the silent conversations she'd had with Francesco in her head. They walked on past a row of grand old hotels with the sea sparkling on the right below them, and Francesco told Wendy about his life with Elena and how hard it had been to lose her and how he had also felt guilty about feeling relieved when she had died.

They stopped opposite the Bristol Hotel and leaned over the railings. Below them was a picturesque small harbour with rows of gently bobbing boats and pastel-painted houses. *Quite similar to Cornwall,* Wendy thought, *but so much more colourful.*

"Do you think you would have left Elena if I had told you I was pregnant?" Wendy asked as they watched a fishing boat putter out of the harbour below.

Francesco sighed. "Honestly, I have no idea what I would have done. What we had, you and I, was so strong, so passionate that I like to think we would have conquered the world together. But to leave Elena and Leo and probably the house and the groves … After all that had happened after you and Simone in the mountains, I think I would have had to leave everything I knew and go to England with you. Wendy, I don't know if I would have been brave enough to do all that back then."

Wendy put her hand on top of his which was gripping the cold railing. "Then," she said softly, "you mustn't be angry with me anymore … please Francesco? I did what I thought was best for us all."

He turned his hand upwards, and his fingers wrapped around hers, squeezing slightly.

"Yes, I do understand, and I do forgive you, Wendy, but you must allow me to be angry or frustrated sometimes for what I have lost."

They strolled slowly back along the cobbled side street that ran parallel to the main shopping street, pausing to look at a church fresco and turning down an alleyway crammed with cafes and waiters that tried to entice them to sit down to eat.

As they drove back to Positano, Wendy mused on how much lighter she felt. This secret which had weighed on her for nearly thirty years, causing guilt, sadness, and worry had suddenly dissipated into nothing and it felt amazing. If she could bottle this feeling, she would be a millionaire.

It was getting dark as Francesco pulled up

outside Amanda's house and turned off the engine.

"I'd like to spend some time with Mia, to get to know her more. But I need to talk with Leo, too. I think I have to tread carefully. I will call you soon, okay?" He gave her hand a squeeze and before there was a chance for any awkwardness, she opened the car door and stepped out.

"Thank you for today, Francesco. Thank you for understanding and for listening to me."

She closed the door and walked towards the house. There was definitely something between them still, but whatever it was had to take second place until the kids were sorted out. It was complicated enough already, and they both seemed to recognise that whatever their relationship was to be had to wait until later on.

Chapter 25

Positano, September 2016

Andrea had called and asked Mia if she would like to go to Naples with him. She wasn't sure if it was a date or just a friendly outing but was curious to see the city and happily agreed. Andrea arrived in a beat-up, white Fiat Uno – not the most impressive car, but typical for the area. She had noticed that the driving was rather wild and unpredictable and reasoned that it was not worth investing in new cars, as they'd only get battered and scratched.

"I thought you might need a break from all the family drama," he stated simply as they drove out of town. "So, today I will be your tour guide of Napoli and you can just enjoy yourself. Of course, if you feel like talking about things with me, that is fine, but I think maybe we can just enjoy a nice day out, no?"

He took her first to Resina first, a large second-hand market that backed onto the ruined city of Herculaneum. The area was poor and dirty, graffiti covered the buildings, windows were broken or boarded up. But clothes hung off every available space. Old wedding dresses hung off scaffolding, jostling for space with leather and fur jackets from the '70s. Racks of white nightgowns stood in front of doorways and tables piled high with colourful shirts and jeans. The market stalls were full of bric-a-brac, clothes, and friendly sellers gossiping while smoking cigarettes and drinking coffee. The pavements were lined with second-hand boots and high heels, sparkly platform sandals and old Converse. Andrea bought a few t-shirts and a pair of jeans; he held them up for Mia to admire, "These would have cost three times the price in Sorrento!"

They climbed back into the car and bumped along the uneven cobbled streets, Vespas whizzing past, scarily close. The city was throbbing with life, cars and bikes, horns honking, people shouting and calling, musicians playing for coins on the streets. It was dusty, dirty and unseasonably hot, but what an atmosphere! They parked the car in a little, dark, cobbled piazza, buildings looming over from four sides, small alleyways letting in shafts of light. A small man appeared with his hand held out and Andrea gave him a few coins. "He is an unofficial car park attendant," he explained to Mia. "He will make sure the car is not stolen if you give him coins. But if you give him nothing, you might come back to no car or no radio inside."

He led her through the streets, past fish markets, churches, clothes shops and cafes. They wandered through via San Gregorio Armeno, the street that sold Christmas decorations and nativity scenes all year round from every shop along the way. They walked through SpaccaNapoli, a long narrow street that cut right through the heart of the city, dark with buildings looming up from each side but so straight that you could see all the way from one end of town to the other. They stopped for pizza and jostled for a table among crowds of tourists in a small, crowded pizzeria where Bill Clinton had once eaten. His photo was proudly displayed on the wall. The pizza was like nothing Mia had ever eaten before. Thin and light, brushed with fragrant tomato and puddles of melted mozzarella on top. The crusts were crispy from the wood-fired pizza oven and tasted almost better than the pizza itself. Usually Mia left the crusts, but this time she ate them all. Andrea ordered a Coke and a Peroni, and when they arrived, he mixed them together, pouring a bit from each bottle into two plastic cups. He laughed when Mia turned her nose up and winked at her when she tried it and liked it.

After lunch, he led her through the beautiful, elegant cloisters of the monastery of Santa Chiara. "Take off your shoes, come on!" Andrea urged her as they stood in a corner near the entrance.

"Why on earth would I do that?" Mia asked, laughing at him as he kicked his shoes off and wiggled his toes.

"Just think of all the history we will be walking around on, come on!" She followed his example and together they padded around barefoot on the cool tiles, peering closely at the old paintings and trying to reach the oranges growing above them. They ducked around a corner and hid, like two naughty school kids as a couple of monks passed by.

He led her past piazzas and churches, along a busy shopping street and then through the Spanish quarters – tiny, narrow, dark passageways where the sunlight hardly entered and families of 10 lived in one room, so small that the sofas were often outside on the street. "You really should not come here alone; it may not be safe," he warned as a child of about nine years old drove past on a scooter. A woman yelled from a dark window and somebody down the street yelled back at her. Mia could feel the atmosphere had changed in this part of town and she shivered slightly.

Later as the sun was setting, they wandered along a street of shops selling musical instruments and arrived at Piazza Bellini. They sat down outside the Arab cafe, where men crouched on their haunches, smoking hookah pipes, and Andrea ordered strong Arabic coffee which arrived with a plate of tiny pastries, made with honey and almonds. As it grew dark, strands of fairy lights, hanging in the trees lining the piazza, were switched on. The scent of marijuana permeated the air, and the piazza was buzzing with students.

"So, you like Napoli?" Andrea asked, leaning back into the colourful cushions.

"Oh, it's amazing!" Mia replied. "Honestly, it's nothing like what I thought it would be. You hear such bad things about it on TV, I almost didn't want to come with you! But I love it, really – I think this could be my new favourite city!"

Andrea smiled and reached for another pastry.

"And today we have hardly seen anything. There is so much more to show you, that is if you would like?"

"Yes, Andrea, I would like!" And she reached

over and kissed him so suddenly that he dropped his pastry in surprise.

As they headed back to the car via the port, the sky was violet with a bright orange line fading into the horizon. The volcano stood proud in the distance, and across the bay they could just make out the shimmering lights of the Sorrento peninsula. They strolled arm in arm, happily chatting about the many other things to do and see in the city. They paused for a kiss every now and then, looking into each other's eyes, surprised and eager to explore this new possibility of them that had happened so suddenly.

Epilogue

December in Positano is mild and understated. The sun often shines throughout the day, balmy enough to sit outside and soak in the warm rays. The town is quiet and slumbering with few visitors and tourists disturbing the peace. Shops are mostly closed, although they will dress up the window displays for Christmas. Simple Christmas lights hang off lamp posts and festive poinsettia flowers are dotted around town. One large Christmas tree stands in the Piazza Dei Mulini and the hole in the mountain is decorated with a giant lit shooting star that hangs above it.

The evening was cool, but the sky was lit with stars and the lemon grove sparkled with strings of fairy lights. The old long table was covered in chequered tablecloths and groaned under the weight of so much food. Two tall gas heaters stood each end of the table, casting a warmth down towards the people milling around the food.

Amanda's daughters, Jess and Rebecca appeared from the nearby house, carrying steaming platters of pasta, closely followed by Wendy's son Josh carrying a basket of fresh bread. Rebecca and Josh had flown over a couple of days ago; it was Josh's third time in Positano as he and Rebecca had been together for a couple of years now. But he was curious to meet Francesco and see for himself how things lay.

Amanda and Claudia frantically tried to clear room on the table for more food while Enzo, Dom and

Gianni loitered under a nearby lemon tree, swigging from brown Peroni bottles and chatting easily together.

Mia and Andrea were sitting at the end of the table, heads close together as they laughed and whispered secrets to each other. They had become inseparable over the last couple of months. After Mia and Wendy had flown back to England in September, Andrea had held out for only nine days before buying himself a flight and turning up in Cornwall. Mia had been delighted. It was still early days, but everyone was pretty sure they were made for each other.

Wendy, sitting the other end of the table, looked around at everyone, counting them off in her head. Only Francesco was missing. Leo was now talking with Josh, smiling and gesticulating through the language barrier. He had been slow to accept what had happened with his father and Wendy, staying loyal to the memory of his mother. He had so far avoided talking to Wendy, nodding briefly whenever she appeared but moving away and avoiding conversation. Strangely he had accepted Mia with open arms. He had longed for siblings when he was younger and to suddenly find out he had a sister was pretty cool. She hadn't asked for any of this, so he had no reason to resent her. They had hung out a few times back in September and although they didn't have much in common, they got on well together.

In September, Wendy and Mia had flown back to Cornwall after ten days. Mia and Francesco had met up a couple of times, getting to know each other and slowly feeling their way around this new relationship. The three of them had gone out for dinner too, a strange evening for Wendy as she couldn't help but think that this could have been her family and her life – and Ben, Josh, and Cornwall might never have happened.

Francesco came out of the kitchen now, with a bottle of champagne and a corkscrew. He joined her at the head of the table and put the bottle down, picking up a spoon and banging it against a glass.

"Come and sit down, everyone, before the pasta gets cold!"

Chairs were shuffled and plates were passed, wine was poured and seconds were dished out. They ate and they talked, conversations branching off into different groups and joining back together. They helped themselves to platefuls of mozzarella, marinated anchovies and salmon, orange and fennel salad and a pizza rusticate that was like a big vegetable pie, stuffed with red peppers and olives. The cannelloni, piping hot and filled with ricotta, mozzarella, and minced beef were devoured and to follow there was a giant roasted fish.

Seats were eventually pushed back, trouser buttons were discreetly undone, and a few groans were heard. Francesco stood up and called for a toast.

"Dear friends and family. Words cannot express how happy I am to have you all gathered here tonight. This last year has been one of many changes, good and bad. I lost my wonderful wife Elena, and my son lost his mother, someone who we loved dearly and who can never be replaced. We miss her every day and hope that she is now in a better place. A few months later, to my surprise, I gained a daughter and Leo gained a sister, a completely unexpected event that admittedly at first brought anger and confusion but was quickly replaced with wonder and happiness.

"Today is Christmas Day, and I have invited you all here today because, for me, you are all family. You have all played important parts in my life, whether you are related to me by blood or friendship, and I am grateful to know you all and have you all in my life. Who knows what life has in store for us in the coming year? As this past year has shown me, life can be full of surprises. But losing Elena has also taught me that life is short, and you only get one chance to live it well. So, I urge you all to grab life by its horns and live it the best way you know how.

Cheers and Merry Christmas to you all!"

As everyone stood and cheered and whooped, Francesco opened the champagne bottle. Glasses were held out and passed around. As everyone broke up into smaller groups, Wendy walked up to Francesco and waited until he had finished pouring. "Come with me a moment," she whispered, linking her arm through his and pulling him over to the trees. They stood in the starlight, under a canopy of lemons, and their eyes locked. The surroundings faded away and she leaned forwards and kissed him. His arms wrapped around her, and they melted back into each other as if no time had passed at all. But she pulled away.

"I've waited thirty years for that kiss. You're right, Francesco. I want to grab life by its horns and live it the best way I know how, but the only way I know how to do that is with you by my side."

He sighed and pulled her towards him again. "I think that sounds like a good life plan. Now kiss me again, just to be sure!"

As he wrapped his arms around her, she caught the scent of lemons and pepper and hope. There was still time for a future together; it was never too late to start again. Francesco had been right in the end: the stories of the past had faded into history and now they could be together for the rest of their years.

We will leave Wendy and Francesco together under the lemon trees, as the party carries on in the nearby grove. Thank you for reading my story. It is not at all what I had planned to write about, but it was obviously there inside me waiting to be let out.

Some parts are true and some parts are not. A few things really happened and some characters really exist or existed. But not all the events are based on reality and not all of the places exist. I won't tell you what is fact or what is fiction, but if one day you visit Positano I am sure you could have fun trying to find the locations and, who knows, some of the characters too!

Acknowledgements

First of all thank you to Carlo for sitting patiently in the pool and listening while I batted around ideas, and for feeding it through google translate bit by bit and being so impressed that I could actually write!

Of course thank you to Celine and her parents Ivor and Sandra for taking me with them to Positano in 1986 for the first time.

Thank you to my parents for letting me go with Celine's family and funding that first holiday to Positano, and Dad, thank you for being you and being there for me, always.

Thank you to my English teachers at school for encouraging me to write from an early age. Thank you to Jesse Smart for being such a lovely Editor.

Thank you to Martin for telling me about prison life and to Saverio for telling me about police raids.

And thank you to all my wonderful followers on Instagram who just kept on egging me on to write a book. It may not be what you expected, but it is not what I expected I would write either!

It probably won't win any awards but who cares because you know what? I did it, I wrote a book!

You can keep up with our adventures in Positano either on Youtube @The Positano Diaries or follow me on Instagram @nickipositano

Note from Author

No, this is not an autobiography! I know that's what you are wondering, but no, I am not Wendy or Mia or Amanda. Well not much anyway, there is probably a bit of me in each of them.

To be fair a lot of the events in this story did happen in real life, in some way, but a lot of them didn't. Most of the characters are made up, although a few of them are or were real people:

Gloria was a wonderful friend of mine, exactly as described here, there was even a memorial tile dedicated to her on the jetty but last winter it got swept away by rough seas.

Many years ago I did spend a week house/dog-sitting for an American couple, Bob and Ed. The house was as described and they had a big black dog that terrified me when it climbed into bed with me at night.

The VEP, Wendy's saucepan man, was a real environmentalist who would march around towns, covered in signs and ringing his bell.

Lily, who the girls met in the bar and at the grocery store is a character from another book based in Positano , Stones of the Madonna by Jan Mazzoni. In Jans story Lily is the young wife of the local Doctor, just before the Second World War. I thought it would be fun to meet up with her again, with Jan's permission, a few decades later.

Made in the USA
Las Vegas, NV
30 June 2023